"The best novel I've read in a long time—compelling, inspiring, a delight to read—*The Giuliana Legacy* also accurately describes many psychic abilities and puts into words what we feel during a psychic or spiritual opening. With enchanting, graceful prose, Alexis Masters both invites and ignites the reader's own latent psychic and spiritual gifts to unfold as Julia, the Giardani Heiress, claims her birthright and reawakens to deep soul-memories of the ancient Goddess and Her Mysteries of Love."

—**Beth Hedva, Ph.D.**
transpersonal therapist and clinical parapsychologist
author of *Journey from Betrayal to Trust*

"Julia is a beautiful priestess of love's mysteries. *The Giuliana Legacy* will open doors for many into new interior, spiritual realms, bringing healing and the reconciliation of opposites. A wonderful blessing!"

—**Mara Lynn Keller, Ph.D.**
director, women's spirituality, philosophy and religion
California Institute of Integral Studies

"*The Giuliana Legacy* is a moving invocation of Aphrodite in all her ancient, transforming power. Here she is the Goddess not only of erotic love but of love itself—caritas, agape—love, the great healer that lives in each of us. Giuliana's legacy is our legacy, too. In her evocative, loving novel, Alexis Masters inspires us to claim it."

—**Elizabeth Cunningham**
author of *The Return of the Goddess, A Divine Comedy* and
Daughter of the Shining Isles, volume I of *The Magdalen Trilogy*

THE
GIULIANA
LEGACY

A Novel by
ALEXIS MASTERS

Health Communications, Inc.
Deerfield Beach, Florida

www.hci-online.com
www.giulianalegacy.com
www.visionaryfiction.com

We gratefully acknowledge The Regents of the University of California for granting us permission to reprint material from *Sappho: A New Translation*, by Mary Barnard, copyright ©1958 The Regents of the University of California; © renewed 1986 Mary Barnard.

We gratefully acknowledge Art Images for College Teaching (AICT) and Mr. Allan T. Kohl of the Minneapolis College of Art and Design in Minneapolis, Minnesota, for granting permission to use the cover photo of the Ludovisi Throne.

Library of Congress Cataloging-in-Publication Data

Masters, Alexis, date.
    The Giuliana legacy : a novel / by Alexis Masters.
    p.   cm.
    ISBN 1-55874-785-0 (trade paper)
    1. Women—Religious life—Fiction. 2. Goddess Religion—Fiction.
3. Spiritual life—Fiction. I. Title.
PS3563.A8146 G58 2000
813'.6—dc21

                                   00-028118

Publisher: Health Communications, Inc.
           3201 S.W. 15th Street
           Deerfield Beach, FL 33442-8190

Cover design by Andrea Perrine Brower
Inside book design by Lawna Patterson Oldfield

IN LOVING MEMORY OF MY MOTHER

Phyllis Theresa Masters

SEPTEMBER 23, 1917–JANUARY 27, 2000

And Circe bore in love to steadfast Odysseus
Agrios and Latinos, faultless and strong, and Telegonus
by the will of golden Aphrodite and
these far away in the bays of the Isles of the Blest
lead all the famous Tyrsenoi . . .

—Hesiod, *Theogony* (L. 1101–1016)
Eighth Century B.C.E.

*This, by one of the most ancient Greek poets, is the earliest literary refer-
ence to the Tyrsenoi, called Tyrrhenoi by later Greek authors, Tusci or
Etrusci by the Romans, and by us Etruscans. . . .*

The name Turan (the Etruscans' Aphrodite) *is particularly interesting
linguistically; it is very likely related to the non-Greek (probably Lydian)
word* turannos, *"lord" . . . Turan, then, is the lady . . . the Great goddess,
and the very name Tyrsenoi may mean "the People of the Great goddess."*

—Emaline Richardson
The Etruscans: Their Art and Civilization, 1964

PROLOGUE

WEST-CENTRAL ITALY
SPRING EQUINOX, 465 B.C.E.

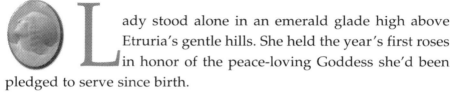 Lady stood alone in an emerald glade high above Etruria's gentle hills. She held the year's first roses in honor of the peace-loving Goddess she'd been pledged to serve since birth.

Invaders were close. Already across the valley, long lines of warriors now snaked up the slopes of her own Sacred Mountain. Her younger brother hid near the edge of the woods, his mind calling out—*Wanassa . . .*

Wanassa, the age-old ritual title from which Lady's name derived. She lifted her face above the fragile cloud of roses, turned toward the call, prickly stems biting her short, sturdy arms. The breeze whipped loose strands of coppery curls against her cheeks as she scanned the woods, searching, then meeting the boy's gaze, asking her silent question—*The Sacred Kestos?*

The boy's response—*Buried. Safe. But the people . . . scared.*

She frowned, bit down hard on her chapped lower lip. *Lead them far from here. Hurry! Don't return to the Gardens until the warriors tire of pillaging, until the mountain is peaceful again.*

The boy's resignation came like a moan—*Lady, we love you.* She watched him disappear into the woods, worry for her people gnawing at her mind.

A messenger brought the warrior king's proclamations at dawn. The clan's *Wanassa* would preside at Sacred Mountain no more. The king would be priest. The people must submit to his will. If their priestess surrendered herself, those she loved would suffer less, the women and girls would not be raped. Lady was here to enjoin the king's pledge.

Her clan had known desperate times before, when they'd sailed to this land from their island home far to the east. The people here welcomed the clan, gave honor to the Goddess they served, even took part in Her most sacred celebration each May Eve. This was the clan's home now, this sanctuary almost as hallowed as the one they'd been forced to leave before coming here and the one before that on the vast alluvial plain where their first *Wanassa* was born so long ago. Lady's mother had told her all this and more, as had her mother's mother and hers, as well. Only once had the chain of transmission been broken, only once after this would it be broken again.

The virgin forest above the glade was dense, but below farmers had thinned the trees, and Lady could see clearly. The soldiers climbed two abreast now. Closer, only minutes away. Their march bruised fields freshly plowed but not yet sown. They hauled a battering ram they wouldn't need. Lady's mountain had no fortress at its crown, only a small outdoor shrine, a simple, holy place consecrated to the Lover of Mortals.

Of the shrine's hidden altar Lady dared not even think with the warriors so near. Its hallowed outer *temenos* she'd secured only an hour before. She'd sealed off the vortex above the raised ritual dais and pushed the waiting mound of stones, the shrine's sole planned defense, from the rocky cliff above. They smashed down and covered the dais, tumbled over into the sacred spring, crushing ferns and moss, the lilies that seemed always to dance in the basin below.

The heart of the mountain had seemed to quake. Lady's own heart felt dashed by each stone. The memory made her reel, yet to leave the *temenos* intact to be defiled by strangers was unthinkable, a calamity no *Wanassa* would ever allow. And these warriors would have defiled it. She sensed their rage, their determination already. She took a deep breath, locked her knees against their trembling, braced herself for the worst.

The daughter in her womb would die with her, but the long-treasured Sacred Kestos was safe, its powers undiluted. Her brother, the only male child in a dozen generations, could not carry the legacy forward, but his seed would bear the gifts of the Goddess until Lady, reborn, could reestablish the sacred lineage. With the legacy suspended, the people would know less beauty, less grace for a time— a generation, two at the most—but the Mysteries would be restored here again, for they were eternal.

The battering ram rumbled and creaked as it lurched over the crest of the hill. It lumbered into the glade, warriors swarming around it. Their cries were gruff, their language guttural and harsh. They pointed at her. Their faces were fierce, contemptuous, but their bravado could not mask their terror of her and the Goddess they knew she served.

The warriors formed a circle and stomped rhythmically, exorcising their fear. Their sweat reeked of terror. One thick-browed warrior ripped boldly at Lady's gown, his frothy spit marking her bared shoulder. Another, wild-eyed, tore the roses from her arms. Pale petals splashed the grass, pearly surrogates for tears Lady wouldn't let herself shed.

Bonding her unborn child's consciousness with her own, she turned her attention inward, beyond this too-brief life and far from *Hieron Oros*, her beloved Sacred Mountain. Silently, she prayed. *Mother, receive us swiftly!*

BOOK ONE

RETURNING

I will sing of stately Aphrodite,

beautiful and gold-crowned

whose dominion is the walled cities

of all sea-set Cyprus.

—HOMERIC HYMNS, VI (L. 1–5)
SEVENTH CENTURY B.C.E.

ONE

Julia Giardani reached the Berkeley Rose Garden at dusk. She always loved the walk from her hillside condo to her father's house, especially loved the view from here, even tonight, with worry driving her every step. She paused at the top of the steep, terraced park and juggled her armful of books. A scattering of smoking chimneys across the hills gave a peppery bite to the air. Fanning out beyond the Garden and bordered by the slate-blue mirror of the Bay and the distant purple hills of Marin was Berkeley's north side, crowded, yet charming as ever. Too much so for her taste these days, but her father still loved it.

Her father. He always seemed to know just when she'd arrive. There he was now at the edge of the trees, ambling up the ramp in her direction. He showed no sign of the haunted look that lately had caused her such concern. Still handsome and energetic in his late seventies, he seemed especially chipper this evening. When he reached up and waved, she could tell he was smiling, already turning on the charm to get back in her good graces.

The rascal. His word, but it fit him to a tee, especially lately.

3

He'd shocked her silly two days ago with sudden revelations of old family skeletons. Secret religious traditions—ancient, Pagan ones. And some kind of legacy—her rightful inheritance, he'd called it.

Then he'd clammed up, refused to say another word or answer even one of her questions since. He hadn't returned her calls either, he'd finally explained this morning, because he was still trying to organize his thoughts. Well, she planned to help him. Tonight. Thus the books, which his silence had forced her to buy at a local book-shop other than his, a Bay Area fixture for over thirty years. She wrinkled her nose at the books, an odd assortment of Jungian psy-chology and early Greek religion—everything she'd found on ancient Goddesses.

"Such a face," her father teased, coming up beside her. "You look as if you're holding a nest of vipers." He reached for the books, raised a bushy eyebrow at the trendy store's bookmark sticking out of the largest. He tapped the only hardcover with his knuckles. "At these prices, it's a good thing you nabbed at least one decent title. The rest are useless."

"You could have told me what to read yourself."

He gave her a tired grin, tucked the books under one arm and started down toward his house. "I truly wish I could have. I already told you that, Lady."

Bristling at the old nickname, trying to ignore the distress in his voice, she fell in behind him and hurried to catch up. "Darnit, Dad, you promised to stop calling me that years ago, but lately—"

"Look, you might as well face it. You will always be Lady to me." Meaning he'd always consider her his little girl, too, she supposed. His deep-set, green eyes sparkled as they hadn't in days. He reached out and ruffled her hair as if she were twelve instead of twenty-eight.

"Better watch out. There are worse things I could call you."

"Sure, like witch!"

Arriving at his backyard gate, he gave her the exasperated parent look she'd rarely seen since she'd grown up. "There's nothing shameful about being called a witch." He rested his hand on the gate, above which dangled an old brass plate inscribed with their family name in a flowery script. "Especially when it's true."

"True for Julian 'Tony' Giardani." Scowling, she put her hands on her hips. "You've called yourself a witch for as long as I can remember, you've taught me to respect your Goddess, but you've never tried to push your witch stuff onto me before."

Until recently, he'd never been one for mood swings either, had always seemed steady as a rock. Except for the first year or two after her mother's death, long ago, Julia had rarely seen him down—let alone anxious and vulnerable like this.

His eyes looked troubled again, his normally robust complexion much too pale. "I knew the witch element of the family's story would hit you like a bomb." The lines in his face seemed deeper than they had only moments before. "I've wanted to tell you what I've managed to learn about this for years, but couldn't, and I'm not sure what will help you most right now."

She'd never seen him indecisive before, either. It chilled her to the bone. "Is this so-called legacy material, Dad, or just some quaint family customs?"

"The legacy's important, Julia, there's nothing quaint about it. It's genetic, apparently lays dormant until triggered from within." He stared at her in that intense, assessing way he'd developed only lately, then opened the gate and walked under the rose arbor. "As the last female in the Giardani line, the family gifts and their age-old responsibility have finally passed to you."

Frowning, Julia followed him. "Earlier you said you've noticed some change in me. Is that why you were finally able to tell me about this?"

"Yep. Until I noticed that change, I was sworn to silence." His backyard was large for this part of Berkeley, the landscaping old-fashioned and lush, the craggy stone wall built by his own hands. He hesitated on the patio, stared at the bench he'd later added in one corner. "These last few weeks have been great, Lady, with you put-tering around here like old times."

There it was again, that new telltale catch in his voice. It had opened the well of her anxiety, forced her to face the fact he wouldn't live forever. She'd curbed her independent streak, spent more time with him, even asked his advice a few times. "I enjoyed myself, too." Beneath the bench, the violets Julia planted the month before had bloomed.

He glanced down at the tiny purple flowers. "It's not the garden I've loved watching blossom," he said gruffly. "It's you. I always knew you would."

"Thanks." The breeze blew a lock of his hair across his cheek. She tucked it behind his ear. "I think."

"Trust me." Still tense but clearly happy again, he led her indoors.

Delicious aromas hit her the instant she entered the kitchen. Her stomach growled.

He chuckled. "We'd best have dinner before we talk."

"Not on your life."

"I have a few presents for you, first."

"You've got to be joking."

"Honestly, Kiddo." He gave her a look her Italian-born grand-mother used to say reminded her of *folleti*, those cute little sprites from Tuscan fairy tales. He put on his glasses, raised an eyebrow as he gave her outfit a penetrating gaze. "You *really* need those presents."

She glanced down at her soft, faded jeans, tugged at the hem of her baggy and equally faded gold flannel shirt, an old favorite she'd pulled on over a newer beige turtleneck. Her usual style. He knew she worked with homeless kids and their struggling parents. Dressing like a fashion plate was out of the question.

"You've never cared how I dressed before."

"I never said anything before. There's a difference. Besides, you're gonna need a new look. For your new life."

"New what?" Her stomach tightened, and she all but choked.

"You heard me."

"I don't want a new life." She'd never fit in with her fast-track generation. Building something that worked for her had not been easy.

"That's what you say now, but believe me, a Giardani Heiress can't run around Tuscany looking like a scruffy tomboy."

Heiress, with a capital *H*. There was no mistaking that, or the challenge in his eyes. Nudging his glasses down his nose, he glared at her over their rim. There was no mistaking the Tuscany bit, either. She stared into his eyes, her alarm changing to astonishment. "Dream on, Dad. I can't drop everything here—the shelter, my work with the kids—and head for Tuscany. I just can't do it."

"Maybe you can't today, Lady Bug, but soon you must."

Lady Bug? Another silly childhood nickname. He seemed to be dredging them up from some fathomless pit of parental memory. He caught her gaze and held it by the sheer power of his unabashed hopefulness.

How could anyone so thoroughly lovable be so exasperating? She clamped her mouth shut, bit down hard on her lower lip.

"I promise you, Julia, your legacy will become your greatest passion. It's immensely valuable—for your life and for the world. You'll understand later, but for now, just imagine a power passed down through the women of our family for three thousand years—think how special that is."

"If it's so special, why haven't I known or felt something before?"

"I know it doesn't make sense. All I can say is, my mother dropped the ball, and now, as the Giardani Heiress, retrieving the legacy and saving it for future generations falls on you."

The Giardani Heiress. Beneath her resistance, Julia was fascinated, had been since his first hints of this. "I'm ready to learn more, but it all sounds so foreign—so bizarre—I'll need your help to sort it out."

He looked away. "I'm afraid I might not be around to help."

Her stomach took a dive. "Why on earth would you say that?" She grabbed his arm, searched his eyes. He seemed at war with himself, wouldn't answer her, but the look on his face sent icy chills down her spine. Squeezing his cold hand in both of her own, she had the distinct impression he was withholding things to protect her, that he knew men who would kill for what he knew. Power-hungry, evil men. "Listen, Dad, if you're in some kind of danger, you can forget about sending me away—to Tuscany or anywhere else."

"Fine. Be stubborn, like the Taurus you are." Seeming undaunted, he pulled his hand away and headed for the living room. "Stubborn runs in the family and will serve you well. . . ." At the doorway, he turned back and beamed her his most enigmatic smile, his eyes dancing with mirth and mystery. "Just as long as you change your mind by May Eve."

MARCH 24

Tony Giardani was as good as dead. He glanced around the office of his bookshop, so weakened by Danilenko's interrogation he could no longer move. There would be no escape for him, no promised last dinner with Julia, no final disclosures about the Giuliana legacy, either. For weeks, Tony had sensed a dark menace closing in on him, hungry for the ancient sacred artifact at the heart of the legacy, but he'd totally miscalculated how much time he had left, how close Gregor Danilenko was, how insatiable the man's greed, his lust for power.

This afternoon, Danilenko swept into Tony's shop like a vulture honing in on a fresh roadkill. Only Danilenko wasn't just any vulture—he was the Arch Vulture. The worst of them all, had been since Paris, World War II, when Madame Racine booted Danilenko off the Allied Task Force that had brought together a bunch of young psychics from all over the world to ply their talents for the Allied cause.

Intuiting what Hitler's astrologers were advising. Telepathically sending false information to Berlin. Tracing Axis spy movements. They did good work, back then—honorable work, Danilenko's last.

Now, Danilenko and a young, rough-looking American punk were up in the front of the shop, arguing over when and how to wrap up their hours-long interrogation. If Danilenko had his way, he'd keep grinding away with his psychokinetic torture—a unique and deadly PK—until he learned where Tony had hidden the ancient artifact. Tony prayed the young tough's rashness would prevent that, for his daughter's sake.

His daughter. Tony swallowed hard.

He'd never see Julia reach her full potential, never see her finish her transformation from the impish, impetuous, extraordinarily loving soul she'd been since birth to the embodiment of Divine Love she was destined to become. Her quest would be hard, especially so without the final disclosures he had saved for their dinner tonight.

The existence of her sacred heirloom was one thing he was truly glad he'd kept from her, now. He knew she'd find the artifact eventually, but hopefully only after she learned to be comfortable and much more proficient with her nascent psychic talents. In the meantime, she couldn't lead Danilenko to the artifact before she was strong enough to withstand the lethal PK Danilenko had abused all his life and which now, clearly, controlled him.

Tony heard footsteps approach, glanced toward the darkened door frame. He fought the urge to cringe from Danilenko's shadow. A real Orson Welles look-alike back in the war years, Danilenko had always been stocky. Now he looked gross, his face pasty, his leaden eyes malicious. Searching Danilenko's features for any sign of the good-looking, part-Gypsy Russian cub he'd known in wartime Paris, Tony saw only the spiritual abomination the man had become. He looked away.

"It is senseless to resist any longer, Tony," Danilenko growled in his old Slavic accent, the latest sign of the stress he clearly felt. "My assistant grows impatient."

Tony caught a whiff of musty smoke, that aroma peculiar to old books burning. "Too impatient, it seems, General." The accomplice— young fool—had set a fire at the front of the shop.

Tony grinned as the fire registered on Danilenko's face. The big man turned and trudged back into the shop, cursing the young American for the incompetent idiot he surely was.

The fire provided just the diversion Tony needed. Danilenko would have to get clear of here now or get caught. Tony had to contact the Alliance's inner circle and fast. Formed from the Allied Task Force and expanded over the years, the inner circle today were men and women of goodwill the world over, some more psychically talented than others, a few not overtly psychic at all, but each unerringly driven by a shared vision of global renewal. He'd handpicked most and loved every last one of them.

Although psychic communication normally was far from dependable, after half a century of frequent contact, Tony's telepathic channel with the Alliance was relatively easy to activate. He sent the ethereal handshake that announced his need to connect. Thank heaven, they responded.

Julia's future hinged on their willingness to bend the hands-off rule that kept them from intervening in worldly events. Directly or indirectly, the inner circle had to help protect Julia in his absence, even if she wasn't in a position to seek their help herself.

Near suffocation, Tony felt himself slide to the floor.

∞

In the midst of the shelter's evening meal, smoke suddenly burned Julia's eyes. Chalky ash coated her mouth. An image of her father engulfed by fire swam in tears that blurred her vision. She heard the roar of flames, saw them—not in the fireplace across the room, but in her mind.

Fighting nausea, confusion, she jumped up from her chair, grabbed her warm, Nepalese woolen jacket from its peg beside the shelter's back door, bolted out the door and into the parking lot.

Irrational, she scolded herself, heading for the bookshop in a panic. Unnecessary, this need to tell her father she loved him. Respected him. Thanked him for everything he'd ever done for her. He knew all that. She'd never held anything back from him. Nothing that really mattered.

She reached her VW in the next breath. Pain like she hadn't experienced since her mother's death welled up inside. She felt wracked by a sense of loss.

"Dad," she whispered. The chilly twilight air around her erupted into flames, another wild illusion. "No!" Stamping her foot, she pulled on her jacket and squeezed her eyes closed. "Wait for me. Wait!"

Fear made it difficult to breathe, let alone drive a car. Good thing there wasn't much traffic. Sheer dread pushed her pedal to the floor. She sped through a long open stretch, slowed near her father's shop. She gripped the wheel, leaned forward, not wanting to believe what she saw.

Her father's small, single-story building was completely ablaze. Flames leaped from its roof. Her stomach flipped. She hated fire. It terrified her. The shop's plate-glass window burst. She stifled a scream, ducked as a cloud of smoke and debris billowed into the street, prayed the bystanders all safely reached cover.

Following an unnerving but unmistakable hunch, Julia pulled the VW into the alley that led to the shop's back door. Of all the impressions she was receiving, the strongest of her father came from there. The strobing lights of an arriving fire engine reflected in the window of the building next door as she sprang from the car. She raced toward the shop, blocked out the sirens and squealing tires of other emergency vehicles skidding into the intersection out front, focused on the impressions, fainter with every second.

"Dad!" Her shout sounded loud, but was it loud enough?

Get away, Julia! Stay safe!

She stopped short. If that was her father's telepathic message, she was grateful. It meant he was still alive, and she would find him. She reached for the doorknob then realized it might be too hot.

Ripping off her jacket, she shoved it deep into the bucket of rainwater beside her father's window-box garden, hoisted it, unwrung, over her head. She used a heavy, dripping sleeve to clutch and turn the doorknob.

"Hey! Are you nuts?" someone shouted.

She glanced over her shoulder. A firefighter had entered the alley a block away.

"Stay where you are! You're under arrest!" he boomed, more desperate than angry.

No time to spare, she hunkered down as far as she could, braced her shoulder against the office door, pushed it open. The fire was closer to the door than she'd suspected, the smoke so thick she couldn't see a thing.

"Dad?" She coughed and batted at ashes and smoke.

Flames roared in answer. She took a deep breath, slid onto her belly and held herself still. *Dad! Where are you?*

A moan. The faintest of coughs. Just beyond her reach.

A rafter over the shop's blazing doorway twenty feet away split and crashed to the floor. Cinders spewed everywhere. Sparks singed her nose, sputtered and popped on her dripping jacket. The thick wall of smoke belched apart. She squinted, coughing and flailing at the smoke, saw something pale.

Her father's hand? She lunged forward, grabbed it—yes!

Soot cut her eyes. She tugged her father with both hands, pushed up onto her knees, tried again. Better. Her father's limp body slid closer. One of his feet brushed a waist-high pyre that had been a stack of books. The stack teetered but didn't fall over. His briefcase, leaning against it, was now barely more than a handle above a flaming frame.

She tried to stand. Fumes seared her lungs, drove her back down. Heat scorched her head, pounded at her neck and shoulders through the now-steaming wool jacket.

Men's voices barked from the alley.

"Whaddya mean, couldn't stop her?"

"Crazy, Captain . . . yelling for her father . . ."

The door crashed open. "Where is she?"

A flashlight peered through the spark-shot murk.

"Here!" Julia rasped, choking on bits of ash.

"She's alive!"

"My father, too," she yelled through her pain. "I've got him." She braced herself and dragged her father a good four feet toward the sooty light.

Her sneaker connected with a huge rubber boot. Strong, gloved hands wrapped around hers and pulled. Three steady heaves were all it took for them all to be free of the smoke and flames.

A firefighter grabbed Julia around the waist and helped her stand up straight. Another slapped oxygen masks over her father's face and her own. Gratefully she gulped. Soothing cool slid down her throat.

Someone—a paramedic—lifted her father onto a gurney. She clutched its edge and held on, unable to keep from staring at her father's face through his mask, praying for him to wake up.

She felt her sense of time—of everything—blur. Probably shock. She gripped the gurney more tightly, fought to stay alert. Beyond the alley, organized bedlam reigned. She stared up the block through strobe-lit smoke. Emergency crews scrambled back and forth. Hoses and efficient-sounding orders flew through the air. It seemed the fire would soon be contained, apparently hadn't spread to neighboring buildings. Small comfort.

Her father was extremely weak, his pulse so faint the two paramedics now laboring intently over his gurney looked gravely concerned. She didn't want them to tell her to move any more than she wanted them to spell out why they let her stay.

Her father hadn't been burned, but his face was highly flushed. Soot blotched his skin. It smeared when she wiped her fingers across his brow, touched the smile lines in his cheek. She studied his features and, beneath the soot, the wispy curls that years ago had been as copper as hers. She wished she could see his eyes.

He was still. Too still.

The paramedics exchanged a glance. They never stopped swiftly preparing their patient for the ambulance ride, but their expressions conveyed how alert they were to every nuance of his obviously worsening condition.

Julia bent closer to her father's cheek, yanked off her mask. Reaching down, she cradled her father's hand between her own, lifted it, held it against her cheek. "Hey! Tell you what," she whispered. "You stay here with me, and I'll let you call me any silly nickname you like—even Lady Bug."

Her father's hand twitched. So did a muscle near his mouth. He was trying to communicate.

Come on, Dad. Come back!

TWO

Julia needed to quiet the voice in her head, which was all but screaming the fire was murder. She needed to calm the pounding of her heart, concentrate on what her father was trying to get across.

He coughed. "Racing . . . help . . ." His voice was barely recognizable.

"Right, I came racing to help."

"No." A slight jerk of his head. "Not racing . . ." A pause. "Ray seen." Julia felt rather than heard his next few words. *For help. Ask!*

"I don't get it." Julia's ears were ringing. Her father was dying, and she couldn't understand. Her chest tightened. "Ask what?"

His hand twitched again then relaxed. She felt a sucking sensation in the middle of her ribcage. He was slipping away.

"Oh, God." She squeezed his hand tightly, willing him to live.

He opened his eyes—their deep, rich green was entirely shot through with red. "Not God . . ." *Goddess. Remember your legacy.*

Shaking her head, she choked on a sob, wiped her tears with the back of his hand. "Too late now."

"Not . . ." *For a true Giardani.* He seemed to stare past Julia's shoulder. His eyes flickered in the light from the street lamp and closed.

"Let's move it!" the female paramedic shouted as if from some parallel dimension.

She nudged Julia aside and deftly administered CPR while her partner slammed the gurney toward the open rear door of the ambulance. Julia climbed into the front seat, clipped on the seat belt, tugged out enough slack to turn around and lean toward the gurney, her arms hugging the back of the seat. The ambulance started rolling, its siren a high-pitched wail that mimicked her heartbreak.

During the one brief lull in the storm of frantic CPR, her father somehow reached her again. A sense of his urgency pressed on her mind but barely registered through the shock that had fallen like a shroud over every level of her awareness.

The legacy, Lady. Only your love can save it.

AVENUE KLÉBER, PARIS

Pressing her fingertips together, Madame Racine pulled out of the inner circle's telepathic link. She was sick at heart, on the verge of exhaustion, every muscle quivering from strain.

She glanced across her library at Tony's photograph and slumped back in her chair. He hadn't even made it to the hospital. James waited patiently by the door. Not only her butler but her closest and most accomplished colleague, Racine had never appreciated him more than she did now.

James had been every bit as fond of Tony Giardani as she. Sadness bowed his normally buoyant posture. "He's gone."

"*C'est fini.*" Racine placed a hand over her solar plexus. "I can't imagine anyone in the inner circle could have missed Tony's parting message, but we must send the entire Alliance our official statement of loss."

James nodded, his eyes misty. "I presume I'm to remind everyone that direct intervention is forbidden?"

Tony's request—that the Alliance take active measures to help or at least protect his daughter—was highly irregular. Unreasonable, really. Racine would deal with its implications, but after careful deliberation, not in the emotional turmoil of this moment.

"Oui, mon ami." She looked down at her hands. "For now, our role must be to inspire and nurture only, no matter how desperate the situation."

She need not elaborate. As a founding member of the inner circle, James knew how much was at stake. Sensitive as always to her needs, he slipped silently from the library. Racine covered her cheeks with both hands, gave her head a small shake. Tears stung her eyelids, swelled in her throat, but she forced them back. If she gave in to tears now, they would overwhelm her. She stood, wrung her hands, then clasped them behind her back and paced slowly, deliberately avoiding another glance at Tony's photo.

More timeworn memories were what she needed now. Her dear friend's death required a grander context, one only deep recollection could illuminate. She closed her eyes and stood very still, letting her all-too-vague remembrances wash like veiled watercolors through her mind. Her association with the Giardani had not begun with Tony. It was much longer, spanned generations.

Lifetimes.

It started long ago, in an age the patriarchs struggled for centuries to banish from memory. An age of unparalleled grace, when the rhythms of Nature's wheel turned year into peaceful year, unbroken by civilized man's uncivil attempts at domination. Such memories eased even the worst griefs.

Racine walked over to her Etruscan archaeological references. Wonderfully diverse, gracious and accepting, those earliest people of west-central Italy allowed the migrant clan that came to be known as the Giardani to settle in and continue the harmonious lifestyle they had always lived. Many even adopted the Giardani's Goddess and

Her annual rites of community renewal, which came to be known in those parts as the Mysteries of Love.

She rubbed her fingers over a few well-worn bindings. Returning to her chair, she pulled the pins from the heavy chignon she wore for formal occasions and combed her fingers through her hair, resting her gaze again on the embers in the hearth. *Tragique,* that today's world so misperceived those ancient ways.

To see Mysteries like those of the Giardani restored on every continent of the globe was the very core of the great plan Racine and her Alliance served. Obscured by time, decimated by the rationality of the twentieth century, all but lost, the Giardani's was still the most retrievable of the old Mysteries traditions. It was the first and best hope of the Alliance in fulfilling the plan for the new millennium. Aiding Julia now might be worth the gravest consequences—even the sacrifice of Racine's hard-won inner circle—if it meant keeping the likes of Gregor Danilenko from seizing the ancient treasure Julia was born to protect.

Tony should not have gone to his death worried about Julia's ignorance of her legacy. He'd done the right thing. *Absolument!* The less Julia knew now, the less vulnerable she would be to Danilenko's treachery. At least until her gifts fully awakened. After that, he'd be no match for her.

Thanks to Tony's final transmission, Racine knew the legacy was within Julia's grasp. The golden-rose color that signaled the Giardani lineage now tinted the young woman's aura. Tony's daughter would be every bit as dazzling as the earlier adepts of her line—if she lived long enough.

The Alliance would have to intervene, at the very least to augment Julia's own budding powers. The task at hand was simply to find a way to accomplish Tony's request without breaching the cohesion of the inner circle.

There had to be a way.

BERKELEY, CALIFORNIA
MARCH 27

Gregor Danilenko paused on the front porch of Tony Giardani's house and glanced quickly left then right to assure himself the street was still empty. The house sat well back off a quiet street barely wider than an alley, its front door masked by a dense privet hedge.

Danilenko edged toward the door, frowned and concentrated on the brass lock securing the front door. With Giardani's daughter, friends and neighbors attending his memorial service, this was the time to search the place undetected.

Focusing intently, Danilenko shot a steady stream of PK at the lock. He heard a distinct click. A gentle push against the heavy oak door and he was inside. He mopped the sweat from his brow with his coat sleeve, waited for his vision to adjust in the dim central hall, then stepped into the sitting room. A shame he couldn't open the draperies for a better look.

Traversing the length of the hall, Danilenko came upon the kitchen. He walked to the sink, glanced out the window. The sight of the garden sickened him with memories. He recognized Tony's artistry in every detail. The stone wall and bench nestled into its corner. The mosaic Medusa on the base of the bird bath that stood in the center of the patio.

Tony's plantings were meticulous. Enchanting, of course, even this early in the year. During the war, Danilenko had proclaimed Tony's the greenest thumb west of the Volga. The Allied Task Force was stationed at Madame Racine's Paris townhouse, which had only the smallest of gardens. Once Tony arrived, though, it became a marvel of abundance, a vibrant haven in which Task Force members could unwind and recover from the rigors of their psychic endeavors. Danilenko and his sweet first love, the little Gypsy Magda, met there from time to time, before things went so irredeemably wrong between them.

Paris. His first tastes of friendship. A time of loving, of knowing he was loved. The memories always brought to mind Katchaturian's *Masquerade Suite,* that ultimate Soviet waltz. Magda in his arms on a moonless night. Racine encouraging his talents. Tony calling him Dani, not General.

Danilenko turned away from the window, leaned back against the kitchen counter. Those days were past. Long gone. There was only one thing to focus on from that segment of his life: the heirloom Tony smuggled out of Italy just after Hitler's forces dug in there in 1943. Danilenko had always sensed the heirloom had great occult power, enough that Tony apparently believed it threatened by the Nazis' well-documented obsession with such things.

Danilenko never learned what the relic was. Indeed, the group's circumspection about that entire foray behind enemy lines had been his first indication his Task Force comrades had begun to mistrust him. Then came his humiliating expulsion from the group, only days after his friends' return to Racine's townhouse. With no explanation, no chance to justify himself, Danilenko was abruptly transferred to a new unit. He hadn't grieved over the expulsion for long. That very transfer began his ascent up the ranks of the fledgling organization that became the mighty KGB. Hadn't *consciously* grieved for long, he corrected himself. The incident had never ceased to grieve him at a deeper level, eating away at his soul—or what remained of a soul in him.

When, precisely, did he realize making good on the Task Force had been his last chance for salvation? While he was still in Paris? As he marched into ravaged Berlin with the victorious Soviet Army?

No. Danilenko lifted his hands and stared at his palms. It was when he first handled the German Führer's occult library that he relinquished all hope of redemption—that loss affirmed when he secreted and transported the library, including Hitler's stolen hoard of highly charged artifacts, from Berlin to Moscow.

He had always possessed plenty of psychokinetic ability, but

touching those artifacts had greatly enhanced and magnified his own
PK. Especially the authentic spear that pierced the side of Christ, a
thousand times more potent than the fake in the Hofburg. Danilenko
smiled. He'd become a glutton for power. There was no denying it.

Since the demise of the Soviet Union, as the Nazi hoard passed once
again through his possession, he'd become even greedier. Today, there
were only a few items left whose powers he had not bled off for himself or one of those fanatical, fundamentalist-inclined would-be
occultists who called themselves the Guardsmen—his associates of
late, but not for much longer.

He'd been a busy boy, as Tony used to say. The last shipment of
Hitler's trinkets would slip, unnoticed, from Sevastopol through the
Middle East and on to Western Europe in a matter of weeks.
Danilenko would then need other sources to sustain his youthful
prowess, his voracious psychic faculties.

After fifty years, he'd finally determined to go for the Giardani
heirloom, become committed to seizing it, intent enough to confront
Tony and let him be killed, as it turned out. The idea of keeping the
heirloom exclusively for himself had grown more attractive recently,
was substantiated by the prophetic dream he'd had the night of
Tony's death.

Once Danilenko had the heirloom, he would have immortality
itself—and be strong enough to leave his old life behind for good.
That life was hard enough when his sacrifices were for his country.
When the U.S.S.R. died, so had something in him. A practiced nationalism. A love for the communist vision, misplaced though it might
have been. Disillusioned, caught up in the unrestricted free-market
mentality, he'd assumed money could buy him another chance, a
fresh start, but he'd since learned otherwise.

Only the Giardani heirloom would bring him a truly fresh start.
Once he had it, there would be no more covert actions. No more
obscene demands from the insatiable dilettante wizards who comprised the Guardsmen's rank and file. He'd even be free of the

organization's dark heart, the all-but-invisible movers and shakers who instigated and thrived on the insidious, the disastrous, the corrupt. He cracked his jaw left and right, pushed away from the kitchen counter.

Whatever the heirloom turned out to be, no matter where it was hidden, he would find it. He had to find it. He had no choice left, just as he'd been left no choice about Tony's death.

Twenty minutes later, Danilenko still had not the slightest sense of where the artifact might be hidden. He'd tried every trick in the book. He'd even used the fine ruby divining pendulum he pilfered from Hitler's collection on his last trip to Moscow. After dancing a few times over some worthless books carelessly piled about the house, the pendulum had failed him, gone dead in his hand before he'd found even a trace of what he sought. He was at a loss about how to proceed with his search, imagined Giardani taunting him. Bile rose up and almost gagged him.

He wasn't wrong, and he knew it. His memory was clear. His dream had been adamant. Giardani *did* smuggle something special out of Italy. It simply was not on these premises anymore, if it ever had been. Revisiting the study, he noticed a cardboard box stashed in the closet, some packing tape, a wad of bubble wrap and a few parcel post labels stuffed inside. It gave him pause, but only for a moment. Tony would never have entrusted a priceless family heirloom to the U.S. mail.

Again mopping sweat from his brow, Danilenko scanned the bookshelves, his frustration mounting and rattling the windows in the study. His PK. Best to leave quickly, before he lost any more control. He made a final round of the house, stopping for a last glance around the dining room. His gaze traveled slowly over the books stacked haphazardly on the sideboard, then came to rest on a family portrait taken, judging from Tony's age at the time, about twenty years ago.

The daughter could not have been older than ten. A lovely child. Lovelier as a woman.

Danilenko smiled, recalling his impressions of Julia Giardani from afar earlier today, greeting guests arriving for her father's memorial service. Graceful as a fawn. Obviously generous of spirit, smiling, if rather sadly. Beautiful in the same innocent, irresistible way little Magda had been beautiful. He could fall for Tony's daughter as completely as he'd fallen only that once before. The thought shocked him. Pleasantly. Whatever else Tony might have lied about before he died, he hadn't lied about the daughter. She truly was as ignorant about the heirloom as he'd insisted she was. Danilenko had realized that as soon as he'd seen her today and, even before he sensed she wouldn't remain ignorant for long, he'd devised a way of keying his ruby pendulum to her energy field.

He walked over to the bay window and exchanged the ruby pendulum for the crystal pull on the lamp hanging between the wicker chairs. Sooner or later, Tony's daughter would be certain to touch it, imbue it with enough of her energy to make tracking her movements easier for a time. Danilenko needed to keep a close eye on Julia Giardani. Undoubtedly, she would lead him to his goal.

MARCH 29

Julia couldn't understand why being in her father's house now made her feel apprehensive and uncomfortable, half sick to her stomach. Was it grief that made her like this? Edgy. Paralyzed by her memories. Avoiding even the happiest ones, because they all caused her so much pain.

Maybe she needed therapy. Or maybe it was her avoidance of the legacy that was sapping her energy. Her father had implied as much in his last phone call to her, only hours before the fire. She gnawed the soft flesh inside her lower lip. Wrestling with fate, he'd called it, an exhausting process.

Another terrible storm raged outside the rain-streaked window, spilling gloom into the kitchen and giving its usually sunny yellow walls a clammy pall. She paced from the sink to the round oak table in the breakfast nook, but she couldn't make herself sit down. Pivoting on her heel, she walked quickly to the dining room.

She didn't know what else might be wrong with her but, beyond a doubt, she was troubled about this house. She'd grown up here. The house contained everything material that remained to her of family. Of stability.

She should feel good here, but she didn't. She should want the place for herself, yet she couldn't wait to sell it. On the advice of her Realtor, Julia had decided to redecorate the house quickly to speed its sale. Between her responsibilities at the shelter and the heavy midwife case-load she'd taken on in January and couldn't bring herself to cut back, she would depersonalize the cozy old home, turn each room into a page from *House Beautiful,* a look her father would have hated.

She sighed and walked around the dining room, which would be the hardest to transform. She'd decided to replace her father's beloved cluster of watercolor originals and family photos with impersonal prints from a local import shop. She would empty the sideboard and put her mother's silverware, china and crystal into an insured storage locker across town, along with her Giardani grand-mother's tapestry table runner.

Too bad her plans couldn't lift the heavy weight she'd carried since the fire. Across the hall, she clasped her hands behind her back and peeked into the study. She'd need to store most of her father's library. His metaphysical titles had caused the Realtor such concern, they'd simply have to go. The remaining shelves of books held innocuous volumes on gardening, old roses and history.

She'd earlier looked for her father's tarot card collection and his books on witchcraft. Oddly, none of them came to light. She hoped they hadn't been in the briefcase she'd seen burnt to a crisp in the fire. The thought made her heart ache.

There were indications her father recently had done some packing, perhaps mailed a few things from the looks of the study the day after the fire. Could be he'd mailed the missing items, but if so, she'd never found any clue as to where he'd sent them or to whom.

In the living room, she peeked out the front window, but rain was coming down in sheets too dense to tell the Realtor's cranberry Lexus from any other midsize car. She frowned and pulled her flannel shirt closed, paced over to her father's brown leather recliner. If only she could relax into it, close her eyes and daydream a while. She turned her back on the chair. Even the idea of sitting down suddenly gave her goose bumps. She hated that. She rubbed her arm, gave it a pinch through her sleeve, wondered who was living in her skin these days.

She spotted the books she brought the other night on the bottom shelf of the entry hall table. On top of the stack sat the hardcover her father had considered the only good title in the bunch, a rather scholarly tome on ancient Greek religion. She walked over, grabbed it and headed back to the dining room. Settling into one of the armchairs in the bay window, she reached up and tugged at the ruby-colored pull of the overhead lamp, but suddenly felt too nauseous to read.

She tried to resist reliving the fire, tried to resist the excruciating pain she'd felt during the last minutes of her father's life, but it was no use. Tears pooled in her eyes. Every cell in her body ached with grief. She forced her mind from that memory only to be swamped by recollections of how excited her father had gotten about the book on her lap. She glanced down at it, smoothed her index finger over the curling edge of its red dust cover.

She'd gone all but numb on the subject of her legacy since the fire, had avoided anything that reminded her of her father's impossible expectations. It was too late to do anything about the legacy now. Surely, her father couldn't have believed she could carry on the family tradition without him, that she'd take off to find it, whatever it was, with only the few bits of information he'd shared before the fire. She had nothing even remotely substantial to go on, didn't even know where to begin, so she'd avoided the subject entirely.

Closing her eyes, she felt a tear course down her cheek. Avoidance had never been her style, and she hated to think she'd indulged in it, even unconsciously.

Outside, the rain intensified, ricocheting off the porch and splattering hard against the panes of the window. A clap of thunder made her jump. The book toppled off her lap. Out spewed three paper rectangles that bounced off the rug, skimmed across the polished hardwood floor and out into the hallway. She rushed after them, flicked on the light, bent and scooped them up.

The rectangles were postcards, addressed to her as Julia G. in her father's hand, all stamped but never mailed. She choked back a fresh flood of tears. Aside from the few things he'd conveyed right before he died, these cards were his final messages to her.

They were brief. No signatures. No good-byes. They were cryptic, as if he'd been afraid to disclose something someone other than she might readily understand. They had obviously been penned in haste, as if he'd known he hadn't long to live. He'd used the private code they'd developed during her college years, a tiny Roman numeral at the top of each card that implied order in their meaning or importance. She tried to calm down, but it was no use.

She studied the card marked Roman numeral one. On its face was a glossy photo of a beach lit by a rosy sunset. PETRA TOU ROMIOU, CYPRUS, it was labeled. On its back, the message read: "Julia—IT all started here." She stared at the note, her stomach churning. Given her father's preoccupation when he'd written the message, IT had to be the legacy.

The second card's image was a cartoonish tourist map with illustrations depicting Etruscan tombs, museums, hilltowns and such inserted here and there. Labeled LA CALDEROLA, the map apparently represented a region of Tuscany. Her father had inked an X near its center. A corresponding "X marks the spot!" scribbled on the reverse transformed the whimsical postcard into a treasure map. She slid it behind the others.

She'd seen the image on the third postcard often in her art history textbooks. It was a photo of the Ludovisi Throne, an ancient sculpture of Aphrodite ascending from Her bath, maiden attendants holding a graceful drape across her belly. The muted photo would have lent appropriate dignity to the Goddess image were it not for the garish V-shaped smudge just above the folds of the drape. The golden V and her father's penned words, THE GIULIANA LEGACY, made her heart skip a beat.

Puzzled, she flipped the card over. A fragment of Sappho's poetry was imprinted on the back. She read it aloud. "Leave Crete and come to us, waiting where the grove is pleasantest, by precincts sacred to you. . . ." Beneath the Sappho was another message, jotted quickly it seemed, barely legible. "Find the place and take a seat there. Thoughts of your ancestors, waiting to receive the keys you need, will bring their bequest back to light your world."

"You rascal, Dad," she whispered with a smile. Her father knew full well she'd never been any good at waiting. Not for anything. Moreover, she didn't have enough *keys* to understand what these messages meant, let alone to enlighten her world.

Provided she still wanted to search for the legacy at all. For the first time since the fire, she imagined searching for it. Just the thought made her feel all tingly, more alive than she'd felt for days.

Maybe it wasn't too late.

Maybe these cards weren't much to go on, but she could probably come up with a few wild guesses to go with them. She tapped the cards against her cheek, felt a thrill akin to the old exuberance her father used to call her natural joy. She definitely hadn't experienced much of that since she'd started resisting her passion for the legacy. She smiled and felt the joy expand, felt a rush of gratitude for her father's tenacity.

A calm certainty descended on her, freeing her from the anxiety that had hounded her for weeks. What her inheritance might have to do with a distant island was hard to imagine, but if she learned anything about the Giuliana legacy there, a jaunt halfway around the globe would be worth the effort and expense.

Then Tuscany . . . she closed her eyes and whispered, "*La Calderola.*" The name rolled pleasantly across her tongue in the lilting Italian she learned as a child on her grandmother's knee.

And Crete, too? Or was there something else her father meant to convey with this particular poem of Sappho's?

Never mind. She'd figure that out later.

IT began on Cyprus. So would she.

THREE

Greek bouzouki Muzak rattled over the plane's PA system. Julia sat up in her seat and rubbed her eyes then fingered the corners of her father's postcards, tucked inside her cardigan pocket. She checked her watch. Almost midnight, Cyprus time.

She felt dazed from the twenty-six-hour journey from San Francisco but excited. During the transatlantic leg of her trip, she'd listed in a notebook everything she could remember ever hearing about her family, their Italian roots, their psychic talents. She'd reviewed the list on the shorter hop from London to Cyprus. The project had engrossed her and helped the hours speed by. She was almost at her destination.

The plane tilted downward, lost altitude and leveled off. Below her window, a few dim lights speckled the dark Mediterranean Sea. The pilot's voice crackled over the Muzak. Cyprus Airways Flight 505 would circle a few times before landing on time at Paphos Airport. There was some turbulence aloft, but the weather below would be *polí oraío*, very beautiful, typical for early April, when temperatures sometimes ranged into the high seventies.

29

Applause rippled through the plane's cabin. Julia smiled and drummed her fingers on the armrests. Not waiting for the next announcement, she clipped her seat belt closed and moved her seat to its upright position.

Suddenly, an electric chill grazed the back of her neck. She shifted in her seat and glanced over her shoulder, spotting a man she'd first noticed at Heathrow Airport. He was big, in every sense of the word, with once-handsome features set off by the way he trimmed his black-and-silver beard. His dark eyes seemed lonely, poignant in contrast to his rakish smile. He must have been quite dashing in his day, still wanted to be, judging from his black Armani suit and his silver-streaked stubby black ponytail.

Back in London, he'd pressed close to her as she stood in line to check her luggage—all but the nylon carry-on bag stashed under her seat—through to Florence. She'd extended him the benefit of the doubt then, even granted him a polite smile, but now he was crowding her again. He stood in the aisle just behind her row of seats, leaning toward her. Although it seemed absurd, she was glad she hadn't taken the postcards from her pocket. Julia liked all kinds of people, but not this man. She averted her gaze.

The plane chose that moment to lurch. The man grabbed at seat backs along the aisle. The senior flight attendant, a bleached-blond fortress of Greek propriety, bustled toward him. Her steely eyes flashing, she scolded him loudly for not returning sooner to his seat then shooed him back up the aisle.

A prosperous-looking businessman seated across from Julia grunted and tipped his head in a respectful nod. "I have been watching that antiquated Casanova mooning over you," he said with a smile. "Like a bear with an empty honey pot. He is not from Paphos. With luck, your path won't cross his again." Before Julia could respond, the plane's engines howled. The wheels clunked down. Her neighbor sucked in his breath. "We land."

The runway seemed minuscule. The plane bounced twice and

skidded to a stop. Cypriots seated all around her burst into cheers. Young men jumped into the aisles. Smiling fathers hoisted sleepy-eyed youngsters onto their hips, while young mothers deftly balanced squirming babies and diaper bags.

A wizened old woman clutched Julia's seat. She carried a battered suitcase and a shopping bag so stuffed it threatened to split. Julia gave her an encouraging smile, slipped the strap of her carry-on bag over one shoulder and stood. Taking hold of the shopping bag, Julia offered the woman her other arm then reached for the woman's suitcase. Her gentlemanly neighbor grabbed it first and lined up behind them. She smiled at him and tucked the old woman's arm snugly through her own.

The commotion all around her was astounding, the crush in the aisle almost suffocating, but Julia didn't mind. The Cypriots were ecstatic to be home. She'd just be glad to get off the plane as quickly as possible. She avoided looking back up the aisle, but she felt Casanova's stare boring into her back. Though the fire had been decreed an accident by Berkeley's crack arson team, Julia still suspected her father was murdered. As a result, she'd been feeling anxious and pretty exposed, and something about Casanova made both feelings worse. She rolled her shoulders and squared them, pushed up her sleeves and inched her elderly charge toward the plane's exit.

APRIL 3

Of all the villages he'd seen on Cyprus, Andrei Anatolin loved Yeroskipou best. Its people had taken him to their hearts when he'd first arrived from Moscow over two months ago, made every attempt to draw him out of his exile's shell. They were surprisingly successful. It would be much more difficult to say good-bye than he ever would have anticipated.

Yeroskipou was not much different from other Cypriot villages. It was small, a hodgepodge of architectural styles aligned in hapless Greek fashion along a handful of heavily rutted thoroughfares. Every day here seemed to replicate the day before. Mostly whitewashed stone structures gleamed in the pale sunlight. Bright geraniums, ubiquitous, tumbled over the rims of their tubs, and tendrils of budding morning glory clambered up any untended wall. Village women swept and scrubbed their courtyards, banishing every particle of dust and grime before settling on their steps to sew. Children scampered around the weathered fountain in the central square, their playful shrieks contrasting with the somber mood of the old men who sat outside the sagging *cafenion*, sipping coffee with an aura of timeless ease Anatolin had hoped to cultivate in himself.

He'd failed, of course. Abysmally, but he supposed he couldn't be blamed for that. The villagers' ease derived, no doubt, from the fact that this island was their home. It would never be his, no matter how much he might love it.

Russia was no longer his home either—might never have been in the true sense of the word. Exile had taught him that and much more. The years of isolation had broken his nationalism but not his individuality. By gifting him with clairsentience, it had amply demonstrated Siberia was not the barren wasteland the uninitiated assumed it to be. Best of all, the vast, silent taiga stretching down toward his shore of Lake Baikal had weaned him from all dependence on Mother Russia.

He'd been reborn there, becoming son and servant to a Greater Mother. Until he learned how he was meant to serve Her, he would gladly remain homeless, searching, enduring his apprenticeship—however long—as he'd endured his incarceration. Not surprising that the first task of this apprenticeship would begin here on Cyprus.

Not surprising, either, that it involved former KGB General Gregor Danilenko, the man responsible for Anatolin's exile.

Information had started coming to him weeks ago, one piece at a time. Telepathically, mostly, though at times clairaudiently, his ears ringing with snippets of talk similar to what one hears over a spotty telephone connection. In time, the bulk of Danilenko's scheme came together in Anatolin's mind. Using the same Crimea–Cyprus–Marseilles–to points unknown itinerary his renegade unit once used for transporting illicit Soviet armaments, Danilenko had earlier today smuggled more priceless—and more dangerous—contraband out of the island's main port, hidden in a convoy carrying cheap crude oil and even cheaper Soviet-era industrial equipment.

The artifacts comprising the contraband were the last vile remnants of Hitler's notorious occult library, transported clandestinely from vanquished Germany to the U.S.S.R. under Danilenko's direction, with Anatolin's mother, Ilina Mikhailovna Anatolina, called away from her Task Force work in Paris and ordered to assist with the transfer. A primary reason the Soviets resolved to reach Berlin before the Americans in 1945, the library had lain forgotten in sealed vaults practically ever since, its dangers incomprehensible to governments anywhere, its very existence largely denied. Anatolin knew better than to think he could hand over the matter to the usual authorities. Nor could he hope to intercept the contraband alone.

Only his next step vis-à-vis the artifacts was clear. He'd received an invitation to visit his mother's friend, Madame Racine, in Paris. On the way there, he'd see the shipment arrive in Marseilles. He'd figure out how to track the artifacts from France when the time came. One step at a time, that was how he'd been taking life since his release, how he'd gotten to Cyprus in the first place. Back in Siberia, he'd planned never to participate in another parapsychological investigation, but the notable research institute in Paris that had invited him here to assess a well-known Cypriot healer had saved him years of scraping together funds to start his new life.

He lifted his face to the sunshine. "Yeroskipou," he whispered.

The name was a modern corruption of the ancient Hieroskepos, the Sacred Gardens of Aphrodite, a fact that never failed to bring a smile to his lips, given the main things that bloomed here these days were rickety stands heaped with locally produced Turkish Delight. Nonetheless, Anatolin appreciated the sanctity of the ground beneath his feet, a sanctity driven deep by centuries of forgetfulness, to be sure, but still present. Strolling here once, he'd squatted down, placed his palms on the soil. He'd hoped impressions of long ago would rise up and take shape in his mind, but, though he'd become more psychic than ever, he could not claim psychometry—the ability to perceive impressions from the past through touch—as one of his gifts.

"Good morning, Doctor!"

Anatolin recognized the gregarious widow, Demetra Kalligá. "Good morning, Kyria Kalligá." The linguist in him relished how much his Greek accent had improved during his weeks on Cyprus.

"Your eyes have a dreamy look." The woman shook her head, feigning displeasure. "You have visited that old fraud Takis Hadjitakis, again."

Anatolin chuckled. He would never understand why the villagers spoke of their neighbor in such deprecating terms. "It was time to thank the Magus for his help these past weeks. Time to say good-bye."

"*Po-po-po!*" The old woman looked surprised. "So it is true, what they say. You really shall leave our island."

"It is true, I must leave."

"You handsome devil! You have broken our daughters' hearts and now you go!"

He could think of no response to the kind woman's compliment.

She raised her hands, palms up, in an eloquent gesture that implied surrender to a cruel fate. "*Ti na kánoume?*" What are we to do? It was a question directed to God, not Anatolin, one he'd heard the women of Cyprus pose repeatedly. "Well," she continued, "if we

couldn't get you married off, at least tell me we persuaded you not
to become a monk."

Anatolin grew self-conscious under her protracted gaze. Despite
his precautions, his off-hours canvassing of the island's monasteries
apparently had become known.

Clasping his hands behind him, he rocked back on his heels. "Let's
just say I'm persuaded not to become a Greek Orthodox monk."

She clicked her tongue and busied herself with tightening the
black shawl wrapped around her shoulders, but her fussing couldn't
disguise her sadness. Or her pout of disapproval. "Takis Hadjitakis is
not the only seer on this island, Doctor." She met his gaze, seemed to
be peering right through him, scrutinizing his soul. Her eyes
glittered. "I predict you will never make it into a monastery. Not in
this lifetime, anyway. Come here," she ordered, reaching out and tilt-
ing her cheek in Anatolin's direction.

"Thank you, Kyria Kalligá," he said as he brushed a polite kiss
over each of her withered cheeks. "I won't forget you."

"You are a good man." She smiled slowly, took a step backward,
and waved good-bye. "*Sto kalo.*" Keep well.

"I will. You, too." Anatolin turned and walked away.

At the corner, he cut off the main street to avoid other poignant
encounters. This breather on Cyprus had been wonderful, but it was
well past time to put his life as a parapsychologist behind him, the
investigation of the Magus absolutely his last. Although Anatolin
had earned his excellent reputation, he would never again accept
work in his profession, either in a laboratory or out in the field.
Parapsychology. The pursuit of it seemed useless now. The Soviets
had employed his training in dubious, sometimes disgusting ways.
That aside, what true benefit could the objective study, classification
and analysis of paranormal phenomena afford the world?

In the depths of his exile, he had decided to do some good with the
rest of his life. Find some meaningful way to serve the Great Mother
he'd come to know during the years in Siberia. While Danilenko's

convoy crawled toward Marseilles, Anatolin would have a few days to explore monastic communities in southern France, perhaps find the right place to rededicate himself to the contemplative life to which he felt called.

He walked quickly past the alluring scents issuing from a crumbling taverna on the village outskirts, quickened his stride. If he didn't get on with it, the day would slip away from him. Watching Danilenko board the lead tanker and set off with the convoy had earlier cost Anatolin a precious hour, but he still had ample time to travel across the Troödos Mountains to Khrysokhou Bay, where he'd spend his last night on Cyprus with friends. Their hospitality would fortify him for Marseilles.

First, though, one last visit to Petra Tou Romiou.

∞

Julia tried to curb her impatience with the huge Mercedes taxi rambling slowly along a narrow coastal highway gouged through chalky dunes. To her left sprawled gentle, mostly deforested mountains beneath a bank of cumulus clouds. To her right, motley gulls cruised above the shore. Farther out, the convoy led by the rusty oil tanker she'd noticed earlier skulked single file toward the horizon.

The taxi decelerated again, barely limping along. She leaned forward, peeked at the speedometer and rolled her eyes. The driver caught her in the rearview mirror and offered another of his sleepy smiles. "*Si-gà, si-gà.*"

Julia had heard that particular phrase all too often today. It meant something like "settle down," or maybe "take it easy."

"Slowly, slowly," the driver translated in his lazy drawl. "It has turned into an exceptional day."

"Yes. Just great." She smiled at the driver, who had no way of knowing why she felt impatient. She'd awakened early and, disappointed by the heavily overcast sky, had waited for the chilly morning to warm, passing the time in a bookshop close to her hotel. There she'd realized why her father directed her to Cyprus. Browsing through a guidebook, she'd come across another photo of the beach called Petra Tou Romiou, this one labeled "The Rock of Aphrodite, Birthplace of the Goddess of Love."

Something clicked in her brain. She remembered learning about Cyprus being Aphrodite's birthplace during her college years, but she hadn't connected modern Cyprus with the Goddess her family had apparently worshipped since deep antiquity. Stunned by her memory lapse, she scanned everything about Aphrodite on the shelves but didn't find anything that looked more informative than the scholarly tome her father had admired, now somewhere in the luggage she'd sent on to Florence. After the bookstore, she went to the tiny Paphos Museum for a glimpse of the few relevant artifacts housed there.

On the advice of the museum guard, she took it *si-gà, si-gà* and saved Aphrodite's beach for after the sun broke through the clouds. It hadn't been easy to restrain her curiosity. She pulled her father's first postcard from her pocket and stared at its glossy image of the beach until her eyes began to smart.

The taxi driver shifted down to take another steep grade. "We Cypriots don't go to the beach so early in the year."

She slipped the card back into her dress pocket, smiled again. "Really?" It had warmed up quickly once the sun was shining. "It's perfect weather for a walk by the sea."

The driver grunted in answer, clearly not convinced. He eased to a stop at the side of the highway. "It may be some time before another taxi comes this way. Are you sure you want me to leave you here all by yourself?"

"I'm sure."

She knew the man thought she was peculiar, but her need to visit this place alone was strong. She felt like she was on a pilgrimage, though she'd never say that to a stranger. Tugging her carry-on bag and sweater behind her, she climbed out of the cab.

The driver shrugged, lit a cigarette, and ground the car into gear again. *"Americana!"* he muttered, but his grin was friendly and untroubled.

Julia held out two large Cypriot bills. The driver took them and rolled back onto the highway. Smiling, he leaned out the window. "I'll radio the other drivers to look for you."

"Thanks!" She watched him pull away then stepped onto the wide sloping path leading down to the beach. A small bench off to the right was the perfect spot for her bag. She folded her sweater on top, turned, and scanned the sun-drenched vista.

From the horizon, billowing clouds scudded toward the shoreline, dappling the cerulean sky. The small cove below glowed all pink and buff. Beneath the cove's low cliffs, a pebble beach cradled a calm aquamarine sea gilded by the sun's platinum reflection. The beach was empty. She'd have it all to herself.

Halfway down the path, the breeze turned salty and moist. It misted Julia's cheeks, lifted the hair off her brow. At the foot of the path, she turned and contemplated the Rock of Aphrodite. The pictures she'd seen hadn't prepared her for the rock's magnitude, its primordial beauty. It towered over the farthest point of the bay. Gnarled silver-green tufts of sage rooted in its crags looked stunted but rugged. Etched by the elements, its gold-streaked surface glinted in the sun.

It seemed majestic. Enduring.

Indestructible.

Julia walked on. Up close, the rock loomed even more massive, dwarfing her, making her more aware with each step of her human frailty. She reached the rock and brushed her fingers across its coarse surface.

How different this immutable mass from the ethereal images of the mythic Aphrodite. The rock's ancient Cypriot namers surely knew a thing or two about their Goddess later Greek poets never bothered to record. Julia's father had certainly disagreed with the poets. He'd insisted Aphrodite's contemporary symbolism was seriously distorted, that Her worship in ancient times had little to do with how She was regarded today.

The rock drew Julia like a magnet, until she found herself leaning into it, resting her forehead, almost reverently, into a shallow niche. For a moment, she listened to the surf rasping against the rock's seaward face, then her forehead started to tingle and burn.

She sensed strange images, foreign yet eerily familiar, taking shape in her mind's eye. Maybe she shouldn't resist, but it felt too odd. She pulled back, shook off the sensations, and started east, along the shore.

The soles of the rubber beach sandals she bought earlier in the hotel gift shop crunched over multicolored pebbles. She bent and plucked a pink heart-shaped stone from the beach and slid it into her pocket. The play of the surf on the glistening pebbles lured her over to watch it. She sat and tucked her skirt beneath her, bent her legs and rested her chin on her knees.

The postcard crackled under her elbow. She didn't need to read it again now. Its message was etched in her mind.

∞

From a rocky ledge above Petra Tou Romiou, Anatolin watched Danilenko's convoy vanish, one ship at a time, into the haze at the western horizon. He wouldn't waste time now wondering what would happen when he caught up with the old spy's contraband. Better to concentrate on the young woman who had arrived on the beach sometime in the past few minutes. He'd felt startled by how lovely she was.

Except for a rainbow-hued scarf tied around her slender waist, she wore all white, like an initiate in some ancient holy rite. She'd walked along the shore for a while in a confident gait that made him think she might be American. Each footfall was sure, despite the inconstant landscape of the rock-strewn cove, familiar to him only after several weeks. Now she sat at the water's edge, her pale skin glistening in the sunlight, her hair floating on the breeze like curling wisps of silk.

How long it had been since he'd stared at a woman. He felt shocked that he couldn't seem to stop. Perhaps it was the way she held herself, taut yet graceful. She was the most beguiling female he'd ever seen. Different. Even from this distance, he could tell that. She seemed dynamic, a bundle of unlimited, unlimitable potentiality.

"Extraordinary," he said, his chest so tight his voice was just a whisper.

FOUR

Julia dug her toes into the pebbles and leaned back on her arms. The air was warmer down close to the beach, made her feel like lingering a while. The sun's warmth penetrated her hair, her scalp, put her half into a daze.

Here at Aphrodite's supposed birthplace, she wished she'd had time to study the book her father had so admired. She'd never forget him pouring over its pages, his finger tracing a hasty line down over its text. He'd first gone to the table of contents, then to the middle, where he'd browsed through a chapter entitled Ritual and Sanctuary and another entitled The Gods, slowing at the section on Aphrodite.

Julia tried to get him to say what he was looking for, to share with her what he knew and how he'd come to know it. He'd remained stone-faced until she remarked on Aphrodite's tarnished reputation.

"Sorry, Dad," she'd said quite seriously. "I just can't identify with the sexpot of Olympus." She had all the natural erotic impulses of any normal woman her age, but her one serious venture into Aphrodite's realm was such a disappointment she was in no hurry to go there again. "Besides, I hardly fit the bill."

"You can't believe that." He'd seemed incredulous, had just stared at her a moment before he continued. "Don't worry, you won't be required to model your behavior after hers. Anyway, you're thinking too narrowly, buying into the good old boys' carefully prevaricated perversions."

41

"Well, wasn't Aphrodite the Goddess of love and desire?"

"Sure, but of a greater, vaster Love, more powerful than mere erotic desire. Any of her old meanings will take you closer to the Goddess your ancestors knew than what is conveyed by popular mythology. Think of Aphrodite as the Divine Creatrix. The Golden One who transforms even basest matter into spirit. The ever-near Lover of Mortals who draws us unrelentingly toward the path of harmony and beauty, toward union—both procreative and mystical."

"Big difference." Julia had been both confused and oddly relieved.

"Huge, but genuine, nonetheless."

"Is this an exclusive Giardani interpretation, or are there others who think this way?" She'd felt a bit suspicious, she had to admit.

"Don't beat it to death, Lady. You'll catch on."

His mischievous grin was so clear in Julia's memory it was hard to believe he was gone. "Don't beat it to death," she whispered. She'd catch on. She stood and looked across the calm waters of the cove, rested her gaze on the huge Rock. "And you'll help me, won't you?" she added more loudly.

Her voice seemed to echo around the cove, the air was suddenly so still. What if her father had spoken a *literal* truth when he said if a Giardani called upon Aphrodite, the Goddess would answer?

There was no way to find out without trying. She squared her shoulders, stretched as tall as she could and, lifting her skirt, stepped into the waves. The water chilled her ankles, her calves. She thought she'd be too cold to stay long, but she wasn't. Hiking up her skirt, she waded in until the waves lapped her thighs. Lovely, the way the currents danced warm and cool around her, the way the water swirled blue then green.

Shifting her skirt over one arm, she dropped her other palm to touch the crest of a passing wave. The wave tickled her palm, and she laughed. She leaned back, let her body sway in the tide. Gradually, the knot she'd carried between her shoulder blades began to dissolve. In its place came more tingling of the sort she'd felt back at the Rock.

She refused to worry or resist it this time. Relaxing felt too good. She breathed a deep sigh and closed her eyes.

Stone and sand, whispering in the placid tide, stirred muted echoes in her mind, formed from its depths an ageless invocation. "Come to me now, Immortal Cyprian . . . fulfill my heart's desire— forever be my ally."

The words played through her with amazing force and clarity. She opened her eyes, and her stomach lurched. She felt disoriented.

Gold.

The entire bay was limned with gold. The very air seemed tinged with gold, the water itself, golden. She could no longer tell where the water stopped and the air began, felt like she was drowning in golden light.

She made herself take a calming breath. The air pulsed suddenly with rose-colored light. She blinked. Something about the rosy hue reassured her. Fiery tingling heated her palms, the soles of her feet, scorched up her arms and thighs. She couldn't stop it, didn't really want to. Deep within, she felt a shift, a movement like sand giving way beneath her feet. She clutched at the air then made her fists relax. The rosy light expanded, became a cloud of vibrant mist that softly cloaked the bay.

Her awareness shifted again. She felt dizzy, adrift in currents she couldn't control. The misty cloud intensified around her, enfolded her in a luminous veil, delicate and yielding. Strange sensations energized her body. Arousing. Compelling. As the sensations spread, euphoria swept through her. Closing her eyes, she sought some meaning for this experience. Symbols swirled in her mind but made no sense: spirals of golden rose; iridescent triangles meeting and merging; figure eights like fluorescent bands twisting on their sides; patterns coursing in a wild dance.

All a jumble, but never mind. What mattered was the aliveness surging through her. No longer disoriented, she loved the delicious tingling charging through her body, heightening her awareness.

The air turned softer, suffused with the scent of violets, of roses. It played over her skin like the touch of velvet gloves. Tantalizing.

A melting heat deepened in her belly, mild at first then increasingly intense. Surprised, she resisted the deepening, but it was no use. A sound like the tinkling of golden bells disarmed her.

Laughter?

A chill bolted up her spine. She fought a rush of panic.

The enchanting sound wafted all around her. Her brow tickled, then burned. She started to tremble as an image filled her inner vision. A female image, robed and belted in dazzling gold, like nothing Julia had ever seen, yet inexplicably familiar. Smiling. Beautiful.

Honeyed words, indistinct like a muffled song, sang through Julia's mind. She held her breath, listened, but couldn't decipher the melodious strains.

The vision shimmered brightly, laughed even more sweetly, and disappeared. Vanished. Though Julia still felt very odd, her pulse slowed almost to normal. She supposed she should be relieved, but she felt bereft.

∞

Julia scanned the cove. How long had she been here? Impossible to judge, she'd been so caught up in the vision. And what a vision! She smiled, chuckled a bit hoarsely.

Shivering, she realized how cold she'd become and waded quickly toward the shore, dropping her skirt as she reached shallow water. She stepped out onto dry rocks and paused. Spreading her arms wide, wishing she could embrace the entire cove, she spun round and round, barely able to contain her joy. Nothing in her experience had prepared her for what had happened in the water. The euphoria. The power of that luminous energy.

She turned and ran back across the beach to the path, carefully watching for larger rocks, didn't see the man coming down until she crashed into him. He grasped her gently by the shoulders, steadied her as she regained her balance, then let her go.

She glanced up and smiled to cover her embarrassment. His eyes, deep blue, seemed kind, his expression a bit dismayed, as if he, too, had just experienced something extraordinary.

"Oh! Excuse me." She stepped to one side of the path.

"No problem," he said with an accent she couldn't identify. "Excuse *me*." He smiled, a charming lopsided smile, gave her a slight, almost courtly nod, then stepped around her and continued on his way.

Still in a daze, she walked on up the path as fast as she could. She was shaking uncontrollably from standing too long in the chilly waves. Or maybe from shock.

Why didn't matter. Her imagination, which had felt flat since before her father's death, had reawakened with a vengeance. This vision had been no simple daydream. This had been something else entirely.

She turned back toward the beach and focused her gaze on the jagged crown of the Rock of Aphrodite. Recalling the Rock's grit against her brow, its sturdy mass against her torso, she felt suddenly certain her father had known that coming here not only would start her so-called new life with a bang but also would empower her for whatever lay ahead.

The message on his postcard rang true. Julia would always feel that for her, as for her ancestors, "IT all started here." The only thing she had to figure out now was exactly what IT might comprise.

"Excuse me, Miss."

Julia jumped, then realized the man she'd crashed into hadn't gone all the way down to the beach after all. He stood beside her, holding her bag and smiling his lopsided smile.

"Whoops!" She crossed her arms and gave them a rub. "My bag."

A blush warmed her neck and cheeks. "I forgot all about that thing. Thanks."

"My pleasure. It's easy to become preoccupied on Aphrodite's beach."

The man's accent had a decidedly British edge, but Julia could tell he wasn't British. He reached over and placed the bag beside her, then held up her cardigan stretched between his hands in a sweet, old-fashioned gesture. She slipped her arms into the sweater and stepped back. "Thanks, again."

Smiling, he cocked his head to one side. "It's a very special spot, this beach."

"Yes, magical." She felt surprised, a bit annoyed with herself at the breathless sound of her voice. While she wasn't particularly interested in meeting any man right now, this one was gorgeous. His resonant baritone was wreaking havoc with her senses. She was in no rush to have him leave.

"You were brave to go into the sea this early in the season," he said, a hint of concern conveyed by the forward tilt of his head.

She smiled. "I leave Cyprus tomorrow. This was my only chance."

"The beach is said to be Aphrodite's birthplace, but I don't agree."

"Why is that?"

"There's another spot that comes to mind when I think of her origins, a grotto on the Akamas peninsula."

Julia closed her eyes. Surprising, but she almost *saw* a dark, tiny grotto. The man paused a moment, as if to assure himself of her interest. She stopped musing and gave him her full attention.

"Local folklore associates the grotto with Aphrodite's mythic baths, but it's much more than that. It's a primeval place, alive with elemental power."

Again, she saw an image of a grotto. It grew in her mind, becoming solid, distinct. "I love it!" she blurted out, unable to stop herself. She rubbed her forehead with both hands and gave her head a quick shake. "Sorry, I don't understand what's going on with me today, but I have to know how to get there."

He chuckled. "This is also the end of my visit to Cyprus." He looked at her a bit shyly. "I'm making a farewell pilgrimage there, myself. Friends of mine have rooms to let in their home, not far from the grotto. I'm sure they could accommodate you, also, this time of year."

Oddly compelled by the grotto's image, she had again closed her eyes. The man hesitated. She smiled in apology. "Excuse me, you were saying?"

"If you'd like to come along but not stay over on the Akamas, I'm sure you could hire a taxi back to Paphos this evening." His seemingly innate understanding was irresistible, his manner of speaking charming.

He was so proper. Normally, Julia would never consider accepting such an offer from a stranger, let alone in a distant country, but he'd called the trip a pilgrimage, which made him seem a kindred spirit. His was an invitation, not a proposition. "That would be lovely. I accept. Thank you."

"Lovely, indeed." He paused, still smiling. "I'd planned to take the scenic route, up through the mountains, but you might prefer to go directly to the Akamas."

"No! I mean—I wouldn't want you altering your plans on my account."

"I'm fairly certain you'd enjoy the itinerary I had in mind." He held up her bag. "Everything you will need is inside this?"

"My trip was so short, I decided to travel extra light."

"Unusual for an American, or do I presume?"

Julia laughed. "Does it show?"

He laughed, too, a mellow, harmonious sound that rumbled up from deep inside. "I have a sixth sense about these things." Still smiling, he raised one eyebrow and nodded to the blue compact parked at the edge of the highway. "I've been here for weeks, and this is the first time I've leased a vehicle. I'm glad someone besides myself will benefit from the freedom it provides."

Walking toward the car, Julia stopped suddenly, glanced up. "We should at least introduce ourselves. My name is Julia."

"I am Anatolin." He gave her another almost imperceptible bow. "Andrei Ivanovich Anatolin."

"Russian?"

"Yes."

Julia felt puzzled. "But your accent—"

He laughed. "My childhood tutor was British. A linguist. He raised me on Byron, Descartes and Homer. We had no translations. According to my mother, that tutor was a Western defector, a British double agent pensioned off by the KGB near our summer dacha in the Crimea."

"I guess you were pretty lucky."

"Indeed I was. The old spy wasn't, though. Pining for the languages of the glamorous West, I shadowed the poor fellow every summer of my childhood. Finally, he agreed to instruct me. It was a bizarre education, learning several languages at such an early age, but it has proven useful."

"Sounds like you were relentless."

"I suppose I still am when I want something." He stared at her, a moment too long for his comfort, it seemed. He cleared his throat, smiled politely. Then, falling silent, he started the car and headed onto the road.

"I know how that is. I'm so stubborn I almost refused to leave home."

"Really? From afar, you seemed so adventurous, and quite naturally at one with Aphrodite's beach."

Julia turned her gaze out the window. A great deal changed when she went to that beach. The vision, the symbols and sensations, those haunting, indecipherable words. They all meant something, she just didn't know what. And then there were her latent psychic talents, which clearly weren't so latent anymore, just as her father had predicted during their last dinner together.

According to him, the Giardani gene pool carried a considerable array of psychic abilities that manifested in unpredictable combinations and to different degrees with each generation. His strongest talent had been mental telepathy, the ability to transmit and receive thoughts, messages and emotions at will. His mother's was some kind of healing based on telepathy, but he hadn't been certain which kind. Apparently, there were numerous forms of healing, all of which the family had been known to perform at one time or another, along with clairvoyance, clairaudience, precognition, geomancy, psychometry and psychokinesis—PK he'd called it—in its supposedly numerous manifestations.

Julia sighed. At least he hadn't claimed their ancestors could levitate. She'd always been half aware he was once a spiritual teacher of some renown, even that he was a rather famous—or infamous—psychic, but what that might actually *mean* had never registered until that night, when she'd caught him reading her mind several times. Had she ever had any privacy, at all?

Enjoying the Cypriot countryside changing as the car gained altitude, Julia realized the question of her privacy didn't bother her as much as it had before the fire. The only thing that really bothered her these days was how closemouthed her father had been about the very things she needed to know.

He'd been in true form that last evening at his house. Pinning him down on what her gifts might turn out to be had been impossible. All she'd wrung out of him were offhand remarks about seeing indicators of psychokinetic healing energies in her aura, speculations about her being unusually receptive to past-life information, whatever that meant. He'd cut off further questions with a glib, "Let it come to you, Lady. Trust it."

One of the most frustrating conversations of her life, yet she'd give anything if she could bring him back and live it all over again. The big sadness in her chest since the fire sometimes grew especially heavy, but not today, not here on Cyprus, where her father sent her. She wouldn't let it.

She fought back another sigh, sat up straighter. She hadn't known what she should search for here, but she'd been hoping to find something tangible. All the mystical stuff was a puzzle, and she had a feeling the beach experience was just the beginning.

∞

Anatolin's objectivity and the hard-won detachment upon which he'd always depended had never let him down before but they were fast slipping away. To compose himself, he drove with excessive care. He had witnessed something marvelous back there on the beach—a phenomenal energy that turned Julia's aura into some kind of conduit then inundated the entire bay. Caught up in observing the exquisite event, he had become mesmerized, was mesmerized still. The supernatural force she'd catalyzed when she stepped into the sea was still evident in her aura. Golden. Rose-hued. More powerful than anything he'd observed in his entire career.

Former career. He had to remember that. He hated the ambivalence most strangers experienced when he announced his profession. Inevitably, they confused his work with the possession of occult powers. The fact that he did possess uncommon talents had been a real hindrance. Professionally, he'd had to be especially diligent, adhering to the most rigorous methodology, never allowing his extrasensory perception to influence his findings. In personal relationships, he'd learned it was essential to establish a solid rapport first, introduce his work and his talents later.

Julia reached up, tucked a curl behind her ear, and caught him looking at her. Her eyes, light amber intensely flecked with gold, seemed lit from within. Candid, almost childlike in their clarity.

Childlike. Yes. A blissfully young woman.

Perhaps in her late twenties, she was more than a decade Anatolin's junior and, he assumed, unscathed by the more arduous twists through which Fate had spun him. How best could he aid her in the few brief hours they would spend together?

It was still early. Reluctantly, he broke the lovely silence they shared. "We have time for a couple of brief stops. Since you're obviously interested in Aphrodite, you might enjoy seeing how her influence has survived in the least likely of places."

"I would." Julia's voice had a honeyed quality not unlike music. "Are you some kind of historian? A classics scholar? You sound like an expert."

Anatolin felt his cheeks burning. "You don't like experts."

"Oh, yes, I do! Experts are handy to have around." She laughed, reached over, and gave his arm a slight squeeze. "I'm sorry. You don't have to tell me what you do when you're not touring harebrained Americans around little-known islands."

He rolled his head back over the sudden aggregation of tension at the top of his shoulders. "It's hard to spend more than a week here and not become something of an expert on Aphrodite. Everywhere one turns there are associations with her mythology or her worship, which apparently lasted centuries longer here than elsewhere. The Cypriots make the most of it."

"I've read there are numerous temple ruins, but I planned to visit only the one at Old Paphos."

"An excellent choice. Temples aren't the only remains of the Goddess here, though. In their attachment to their ancestral ways, the Cypriots have managed to preserve a sense of continuity lost to the modern world."

"Hmmm—" Julia smiled dreamily then gazed back out the window.

"I'm boring you." Anatolin was usually far more circumspect than he'd been this afternoon, was often accused of being curt. Could he be trying to impress this girl? "Please forgive me."

"Don't you dare apologize!" For perhaps the tenth time in as many minutes, she patted her pocket, which seemed to contain something she valued. "It feels great to sit back and listen to someone who knows what he's talking about. Believe me, I'm enjoying myself. Relaxing." She leaned toward her window and stretched like a sleepy kitten.

The car rattled over a pothole in the narrow road. Anatolin realized he'd been staring at her again. Self-discipline was another quality that had never failed him. This was no time for it to lapse.

Focusing on the winding incline, he spent much of the next ninety minutes sharing what he knew about the island. His intention was not to monopolize the conversation but rather to help his young companion recover from her psychic episode. Her electromagnetic field was still vacillating wildly. She was not yet entirely composed.

He was glad he'd cast off the shackles of his training. If he were still a clinician, he'd probably feel obliged to start documenting her case at once, start probing her psychic talents, prying into her past, digging for any memories she might have of similar experiences. Instead, he continued to dwell on quaint island anecdotes he'd heard—Christian churches built over Pagan ruins—the plethora of names for the *Panayia,* the Greek Orthodox Holy Virgin, whose powers closely mirrored Aphrodite's and whose Cypriot titles derived from her epithets, especially *Krysse* or *Chrysse,* Golden. In two months, he'd come across nearly a hundred such names. For some reason, it seemed urgent Julia learn about them.

FIVE

Long shadows stretching across the mountain road made it seem much later than two-thirty in the afternoon. Julia looked over at her escort. His name was as striking as he was. Andrei Anatolin. She liked the way it sounded in her mind.

Andrei *Ivanovich* Anatolin.

She smiled. He was certainly a very nice man, as kind as anyone she'd ever met. There seemed no need to shield herself like she sometimes did when she met a strange man. Not that he wasn't attractive. He just wasn't *trying* to be. Maybe it was his maturity. Whatever, she found him refreshing.

She draped her arm across the seat. Her fingers brushed the steely-blue leather of Andrei's jacket, almost the color of his eyes. She withdrew her hand quickly, resisting an urge to touch his hair, black, with waves that curled handsomely just above the jacket collar. Folding her hands in her lap, she sat straight and considered Andrei's profile. "You smile a lot. I like that!"

Andrei chuckled. "I am anticipating your enjoyment of our first stop, which is up here around the next bend." He cut the car sharply to the right and drove down a narrow lane.

Julia was stunned by the loveliness of the view beyond the turnoff. Pine forest covered the chalky mountainside, all but embracing a large structure surrounded by neatly planted terraces. Andrei pulled alongside it and turned off the car.

"What is this place?" She stared up at the building's steep gables.

"A monastery. It's called Trooditissa, but its old name was *Panayia Aphroditissa*."

"One of those you were talking about earlier."

Julia opened the car door, stood and stretched. When Andrei joined her, an old monk resting on the porch of what looked like a chapel suddenly sat up and seemed to take notice of their arrival. Gnome-like beneath his ecclesiastical beard, he beamed a smile and greeted Andrei the way one would an old friend.

Andrei turned to her. "Julia, this is Brother Stellios."

The old monk nodded and bowed. Pompoms on his bright red hand-knit slippers peeked from below the hem of his somber robe. Julia swallowed back an irreverent chuckle.

The monk led Julia and Andrei through a door into the shadowy, slightly musty church. Muttering, he pointed out the beat-up offering boxes hung strategically about and headed for the tall, ornately carved screen dividing the front of the building from the rest. He shuffled out through a faded red satin curtain strung across a passageway in the screen's center.

Julia stared around the room, gave a short whistle. "Pretty fancy."

Andrei grinned. "The screen is called an iconostasis."

"I'm impressed, though I can't say why." She'd read that the painted icons and garish metal plaques hanging all around were prayer offerings. "I don't have much experience with places like this. My parents weren't religious."

"My mother wasn't, either, in the orthodox sense. There was no religion in the old U.S.S.R."

"Right. Of course."

She gazed up over her head at a double row of silver lamps and egg-shaped orbs hanging from carved wooden beams. Handmade lace, draped here and there, shimmered in the light created by dozens of blazing, multitiered candle stands. "You've been here before, though. The monk seems to know you."

"Yes." Andrei clasped his hands behind his back and turned abruptly away. Clearly, he didn't want to elaborate.

Julia walked toward the screen. One of the icons hanging from it was sheathed in silver. She leaned closer to examine the detail.

"A famous icon, very ancient," Andrei said. "It's considered too sacred for mere mortals to view, so they covered it in silver."

"Is this what you brought me here to see?"

"Not exactly." Andrei smiled.

A bit mischievously, Julia thought. From the corner of her eye, she caught a flash of red against the stone floor. Looking down through the screen's carved base, she saw little pompoms bobbing closer. Rapidly. She smiled at Andrei, raised her eyebrows. "What—?"

Breaking into a chant, the monk swirled around the edge of the screen, his robe swishing wildly. He held a heavy medallion-studded belt that swayed pendulously between his hands, its brass hook-and-eye clasps polished to a bright glint. In a flash, he slipped behind Julia, encircled her hips with the belt, and hooked it around her waist with a triumphant shout.

Quite heavy, the belt slipped down low on her hips. Julia had felt like laughing but, suddenly befuddled, instead made a steeple with her fingers and pressed them close to her lips.

She glanced at Andrei. "This is a joke, right?"

His eyes danced with amusement. "Not really."

The monk flourished his cap in one hand and bowed. Standing up again, he solemnly traced a cross in the vicinity of Julia's forehead.

"Is he *blessing* me?"

Andrei smiled, nodding slightly.

"How sweet!" Julia bowed her head and lowered her hand to touch one of the polished silver medallions attached to the belt.

"Oh!" She felt something odd, jerked her hand back.

It was not a sensation like hot or cold, but something more subtle that pulled strangely on her emotions. Words, whispered buzzing like bees through the depths of her mind. *Holy Mother, I beseech you!* She touched the medallion again, then its neighbor. *Panayia, a son! A daughter to care for me when I'm old!*

Tears stung her eyes. "Prayers," she said.

Dropping to her knees, she bent her head down to examine the belt. Though oiled to a lustrous sheen, the belt's dark brown leather was so old it was cracked, even splitting and curled here and there, but she could tell it had once borne a pretty carved pattern.

Gripping the belt with both hands, she traced her index fingers round the spiral engravings at the center of each medallion. "Hundreds of women's loving prayers," she whispered. She held out her hands, palms up, stared then quickly dropped them.

"Julia, Brother Stellios seems quite moved by your reaction to the Holy Belt," Andrei said softly.

She looked up, glanced at the monk then at Andrei, gave her head a shake. "Sorry?"

"He says he's sure the *Panayia* will bless you with many children."

"Gracious!" She stood up. "This thing supposedly increases fertility?"

"According to tradition, but only if the woman's prayers are strong enough to reach the *Panayia*'s heart."

Julia smiled. The prayers she'd sensed had been plenty strong. Remembering a story her father once told her about his mother's and grandmother's childbearing difficulties, she added a little prayer of her own then removed the belt and gave it back to the monk. "Thank you, Brother Stellios."

"*Oraío*," he answered, bowing his head. "*Polí oraío*."

Beautiful? Greeks seemed to use that expression for a lot of things. She looked at Andrei. "I've been told the women of my family have always had trouble conceiving children. Would it be appropriate to tell him I especially appreciate his *Panayia*'s blessing?"

"Absolutely."

The monk listened seriously as Andrei translated then pointed to a pair of silver earrings dangling from the screen above the icon and spoke excitedly.

"Stellios is offering you a truly rare blessing, now," Andrei said with a wink. "Perhaps you'd like to pray wearing the Lady's earrings? Supposedly, they give special blessings for women who need to conceive sons—"

Goose bumps raised on Julia's arms. "What did you say?"

"The Holy Belt grants fertility, but those earrings—"

"No, Andrei, before that. *Whose* earrings?"

"The *Panayia's*." Andrei looked slightly concerned. "*Panayia* strictly translated is 'All Holy,' but its usage is similar to 'Lady' in English."

Lady.

"Right." Julia's ears started ringing again, and she felt muddled. Her voice sounded odd. "Of course." For a moment she thought she heard soft, bell-like laughter again.

"Julia, is there some problem?"

"No." There was no point in whining about her dilemma to Andrei or anyone else. She just had to get a handle on what was happening to her, and why. "Except . . ." she added, grinning at Andrei, widening her smile to include the monk. "I suppose it would be much too rude to tell Brother Stellios, but I'm pretty sure my ancestors would roll over in their graves if I ever prayed to conceive a son."

∞

Anatolin was happy Julia would have the memory of the view from the taverna beside the last monastery on their route. It was something few tourists ever saw. He took a sip from his wineglass, gazed out, and scanned the gentle twilight that spread below the taverna's terrace, their final stop before heading down to the Akamas peninsula. Sunsets here had always taken Anatolin's breath away, but he suspected a different cause for his near breathlessness now.

Until a moment ago, he'd been quite comfortable. Then his arm brushed against Julia's, his fingers almost touching hers, and he'd started to sense her thoughts. She was thinking about how much she enjoyed his company, how good it felt to stand beside him, how natural it would seem if he entwined his fingers with hers.

She was right—it did feel good—would seem perfectly natural.

It wasn't going to happen. Over a decade had passed since he'd felt genuine physical attraction. Glad though he was that the attraction was clearly mutual, he also realized it was time to make his intentions clear. "I hope you weren't too put off by my friend Stellios and his little performance."

"Heavens no, I loved it!" She glanced up at him and smiled.

"Did you?" He had to swallow hard before continuing. He turned to face her, put his glass down on the nearest table, crossed his arms over his chest. "I came very close to entering the community at Trooditissa Monastery, but somehow I couldn't quite picture myself ensnaring unsuspecting female tourists with the Holy Belt." He forced a chuckle.

Silence.

Julia took a slow sip of wine, turned away from him, and stared into the lowering darkness. Anatolin cleared his throat.

"I almost joined this monastery, also." He picked up his glass again but suddenly didn't feel much like drinking. He swished the wine then set it down. "It's certainly the most serene of those I've looked into thus far." He paused, wishing Julia would look at him, but she stood very still, her gaze straight ahead. "I can see myself serving somewhere like this. Growing things." He swayed slightly toward her, forcefully willed himself back.

The lights flickered on over the taverna's door, seeming to startle Julia. She shivered and drew her sweater closed at her neck.

"Right," she said in that determined tone he'd heard her use earlier. "I can see you growing things, too. Nurturing new life." She raised her chin and gave him a quick half smile. "But definitely not here." Before he could say another word, she plunked her unfinished wine down beside his and took two steps away. "Don't you think we should get moving again?"

Not waiting for him to answer, she turned and started for the car. Anatolin followed, struck again by the indomitable spirit expressed by her gait. His gaze traveled from her staunch shoulders to the gentle swell of her hips, lingered a moment before he got hold of himself.

She glanced over her shoulder and smiled. "Thanks for the lovely respite, Andrei, but the sunset definitely is beginning to fade, and though I hate to admit it, so am I."

Anatolin cleared his throat. "Straight down to the peninsula, then, and dinner." He caught up with her, opened the car door, and saw her securely belted for the last hour's drive.

∞

Julia breathed deeply, savoring the rich scents of garlic, oregano and thyme. No wonder this taverna was supposedly the most popular one on the entire peninsula. It was filling up quickly, as Andrei predicted it would before he went off to speak with the owner about what he'd called a special feast in honor of her visit. Too bad she hardly felt up to it.

She leaned her elbows on the table, propped her chin on her fists, and concentrated on the taverna. Musicians on the small corner stage were warming up with a set of lively Greek tunes, the lusty bouzouki strumming over the guitar, the violin, and the sometimes strident clarinet. The only waiter, the son of the couple who'd rented Julia and Andrei rooms for the night, sped between the tables, balancing heavy trays high above his head, joking with the musicians, shouting robust greetings to arriving diners, a smattering of tourists and large Cypriot families.

Settling back in her chair, Julia crossed her arms then her legs, shifted. She reached up and propped her chin on one hand, covering her frown with her fist. Why was she so antsy? Glum, really. She had no logical reason to feel as she did. That Andrei planned to become a monk shouldn't concern her at all. Who was she to decide his vocational choice was entirely the wrong one for him?

It wasn't as if she couldn't identify with the need to follow a spiritual urge, regardless of the outcome. She was doing the same thing, in a way. She liked him. She needed to try harder to respect his calling, stop considering it a tragic waste.

"Julia, are you all right?"

She jumped slightly, looked up at Andrei, who had reappeared beside her. She dropped her fist to her lap, smiled. "Jet lag." Sitting up straight, she reached over, and patted his chair. "But never mind. I want to hear all about how you decided to enter a monastery."

"Oh, no," Andrei groaned playfully. "That's too long a story for someone with jet lag to sit through."

She peered at him through narrowed eyes. "I imagine it will take a while to consume the feast you ordered. Should be long enough for you to get a start on the short version."

Andrei chuckled and took the chair beside her. "I'll bore you."

"Try me!"

"Exile is boring, Julia. Siberia is boring. On that subject, I am indeed an expert."

Julia searched his face for signs he might be joking, but clearly he was speaking in absolute earnest. He really had been exiled to Siberia. She leaned forward, covered his hand with her own. "What happened?"

"I was once a scientist." He hesitated, probably because the musicians had stopped, then he smiled wryly and continued. "I participated in an unauthorized information exchange with Western colleagues. I didn't act alone, but the others in the exchange transmitted their classified material quietly, without repercussions. I called a press conference."

"Heavens!" She leaned toward him.

He shrugged, but his gaze stayed focused tightly on hers. "Nothing I sent was too highly classified. Nor could any of it have been used to harm the U.S.S.R. I was prosecuted, anyway. As an example to others, they said."

"Why did you feel some kind of statement was necessary?"

"Think back to 1986. Springtime."

When she didn't respond, he continued.

"Chernobyl, that's why I went public. When the Russian people finally learned the facts about the massive nuclear disaster made worse by state secrecy, continued secrecy of any kind seemed too steep a price to pay."

Julia felt stunned. "You were a hero."

Andrei laughed. "I was a fool. Like many of my hot-headed young compatriots, by then, I was finished being a pawn. The army had requisitioned me years before, forced me to participate in experiments to determine if there were potential military applications for my particular science. There was nothing I could do about it. After that, I was assigned to the KGB, even worse."

She gasped. Andrei paused but seemed not to hear her.

He stared off across the room. "From the first TOP SECRET stamped across a report I wrote, I searched for a way out of my predicament to no avail. The KGB pushed me to the breaking point. Chernobyl pushed me past it."

"Sounds awful."

He waved his hand dismissively. "They detained me in Lubyanka prison during the prosecution, then in Siberia, where I served my sentence. Nine years." He paused thoughtfully. "Actually more because, I believe, someone deliberately misplaced my paperwork."

She shivered. "You must have felt terribly isolated there."

"There's the joke, Julia, and the reason I'm sharing all this with you." He tilted his head, his blue eyes shining. "I was entirely isolated, totally cut off from news, restricted from all forms of communication, even with my keepers, and most of the time I loved it." He stared across the taverna. "I could spend whole weeks in contemplation and meditation."

"All those years." Given her own need to balance her quiet times with great bursts of activity, Julia would have gone nuts in Andrei's shoes. "That's a whole lot of meditation."

"It seems I needed it. Though I now recognize I've always had spiritual leanings, I had been brainwashed to believe they were misguided, even dangerous. In Siberia, I had a rare opportunity to develop an inner life." His gaze seemed far away, suddenly passionate, intense. "Thrown back on myself, I learned about myself for the first time in my life—what I value—what it might mean to serve a greater good—those issues one seldom takes pause to examine. I eventually had to acknowledge how deep was my need to know the Divine. You might call it a compulsion."

"For God."

He winced, as if embarrassed. "Or Goddess." His eyes softened, and he leaned toward her. "Regardless of the label, Julia, the Divine became my sole companion up there in my solitary cabin above Lake Baikal, and I need that companionship to continue."

"But it must feel good to be free again."

He smiled, a bit sadly, Julia thought. "The meager conditions of my exile notwithstanding, I almost regretted my release when it finally came. Entering a monastic community now seems the only way for me to resume a relationship I came to desire above all else."

"So, that's what you intend to do."

"What I believe I must do."

"Well, then—" Julia started to wish him well but was interrupted by the approach of the waiter, who immediately started unloading his tray.

"Your *mezedhes*." Flashing his flirty smile, the young man covered every inch of table space with small plates heaped with appetizers. "*Kali oréxi!* Good appetite," he said before zipping away.

Julia stared down as Andrei identified the dishes—a salad of pureed eggplant and garlic, another of ground chickpeas and sesame butter, an assortment of herbed pilafs, and a plate of thick sliced *haloumi*, a white sheep's-milk cheese apparently unique to Cyprus. Her mouth started to water. "Looks fabulous."

She hadn't realized how hungry she was. She reached for the plate of *haloumi* then, near the taverna's entrance, she caught a glimpse of a man who reminded her of her unwanted admirer from the plane. She dropped her hand, closed her eyes, fought off a sudden chill.

"Julia?"

She stared across the room and studied faces, then decided she really had to be mistaken. There was no one over there who even remotely resembled that man. She shivered a bit and relaxed with a sigh.

"You really must have jet lag," Andrei said.

"Hmmm?" Julia turned to him and smiled.

"Your attention is wandering, despite our magnificent feast."

"I thought I saw someone I recognized, but it was a hallucination."

"Starvation induced, no doubt." Andrei's lopsided smile took the edge off her chill.

She laughed. "Probably." Amazing, how much she enjoyed this man's company, how totally comfortable, even comforted, she felt beside him. A real shame they'd be going separate ways very soon.

∞

Above the taverna, on a narrow tract leading up the hill toward the nearest village, Gregor Danilenko waited. He had propped himself up against the darkened doorway of an abandoned house, shielded from the flickering yellow street lamp in the intersection below. Danilenko truly hated Cyprus. Its lazy, carefree ambience rankled him more than ever, harkened up fonder memories of the efficient postwar Stalin era back in the old U.S.S.R.

Come to think of it, his life hadn't really begun until then. Earlier times had brought a mixed bag. Some pleasure and a measure of renown. Mostly pain. Under Stalin, Danilenko had soared, had even been privileged to help establish the Soviets' Paranormal Intelligence Directorate, his own branch of which he'd steered through the KGB years. His preeminence in covert psi activities was still unrivaled, but he no longer led his former apparatus in Russia's new S.S.V.R. Instead, he'd taken the entrepreneurial route to even greater success.

His contract firm, a direct offshoot of his extracurricular KGB operations, today catered to the unsavory ambitions of degenerate multinationals and certain factions of their governments. In return for his services, Danilenko often tapped the vast intelligence and financial resources of the Western occultist group called the Guardsmen, an exceptionally sorry specimen of which had bungled his interrogation of Tony Giardani and probably cost him months in his quest for the Giardani heirloom. He tensed and relaxed his shoulders, shoved his gloved hands deep into the pockets of his gray, mink-collared overcoat.

He was a patient man. His immediate objective now was to catch another glimpse of the woman lucky Andrei Ivanovich Anatolin met on the beach near Paphos earlier today—Tony Giardani's daughter, Julia. Watching from the tourist pavilion high above the beach where his helicopter dropped him earlier, he'd imagined holding her, imagined her pliant, responsive to the touch of his lips on her tender neck. But then the beach had flooded with the most spectacular energy, obscuring the woman from his view. Though the blazing force had disconcerted him, it had also served to remind him how powerful the Giardani Heiress might be, how crucial it was for him to keep his distance.

He was usually clever enough to stay unobserved when he needed to. He'd once been a world-class predator. It was time to dust off his skills. Neither of the young people would have recognized anyone as far away as the tourist pavilion, but an hour ago he'd almost given away his return to the island when, overcome by curiosity, he'd briefly ducked inside the taverna. Fortunately, Andrei Ivanovich had not caught sight of him. That could have spelled disaster for his plans. Andrei Ivanovich might well have recognized him, cost him the considerable edge his anonymity afforded him.

He must not make any more mistakes. He'd made mistakes enough in his pursuit of the Giardani heirloom. Accepting the so-called aid of the Guardsmen's Palm Springs faction, allowing their minion, a certifiable pyromaniac, to assist with Tony's interrogation. Terrible blunders with grievous consequences.

The breeze had further chilled the air. He lifted his collar up around his neck. The door of the taverna opened, and muted bouzouki chords drifted out onto the air. He peered through the mist, then slumped back into the doorway. The woman he sought was not among the laughing group that spilled, arm in arm, onto the road headed east toward Polis. Maybe he should be glad for that, after all.

Seeing the offspring of his once-cherished Task Force comrades together today had wrenched his mind back again to those years when he'd loved life. He was still suffering from painful recollections. He might as well face the inevitable reality that the young people's meeting was engineered not by some fickle Fate, as one might assume, but by the inexhaustible Madame Racine. Daunting, the prospect of those three aligned against him, too hauntingly reminiscent of his youthful folly to be contemplated at this late hour.

Somewhere nearby, a dog barked. The damp, salty breeze rousing the tide of Khrysokhou Bay chilled Danilenko's nose. His legs felt tired. He hated the additional twenty kilos he'd put on over the last ten years. But so what if his legs ached and his back gave him misery? So what if his whole body was going to hell? Hitler's artifacts would provide him a temporary infusion of youthful vigor, and once he obtained the Giardani heirloom, he would never feel old again.

Fortunately, the sensitive ruby pendulum he'd planted at Tony's house after the fire, keyed now to Julia Giardani's energy field, would make it a breeze to keep tabs on her. He buttoned his coat collar, turned, and started back down toward the shadows closer to the taverna. The heels of his boots resounded hollowly as he picked his steps across the pockmarked asphalt. The dog barked again, its plaintive cry echoing Danilenko's misery in the cold Cypriot darkness.

SIX

Julia clapped as the taverna's musicians finished another set. She leaned back in her chair and glanced at the young woman who had just taken the chair beside her. Eleni was the latest of Andrei's acquaintances to stop at their table to tell him good-bye.

"So, what do you think of our island?" Eleni asked.

Julia smiled. "I've loved everything I've seen so far. Especially Petra Tou Romiou."

The sensations she'd experienced at the beach had started up again, clustered now into bands of energy skittering through her body. Unsettling. She shifted in her chair, crossed her legs, but the sensations didn't stop.

Eleni looked wistful. Her elbow rested on the table, her chin in her palm. "You would love that spot. You're such an Aphrodite woman!"

Julia tried to ignore the chill that crept up and settled at the back of her neck. "What do you mean by that?"

"You look like Aphrodite." Eleni's English was excellent, peppered with Greek inflections. "She was golden, you know. She was beautiful and graceful, just as you are."

"Ridiculous!" Julia burst into laughter, gave her head a brisk shake.

"I'm serious!" Eleni looked at Andrei. "I think Julia resembles Aphrodite, has Aphrodite's charisma, don't you, Doctor Anatolin?"

"Charisma, yes indeed." Andrei's smile seemed relaxed enough, but Julia could tell he was uncomfortable.

"She seems not, however, to share Aphrodite's penchant for seduction." Eleni gave Andrei an appraising look then chuckled. "Too bad. I think you could use a good dose of seduction."

Julia blushed, hoped Andrei didn't notice. She had never been one to indulge in casual seduction, hadn't even wanted to flirt with a man for the last several years, though she might have been tempted to try this afternoon, before she'd learned of his plans.

The music started again. Eleni's face lit up. "A *syrtaki!*" She pointed at Andrei. "I don't think I've ever seen you dance!" She frowned, wagged a finger under his nose. "*Po-po-po!* But you shall tonight. There is a saying, 'No visitor can leave Cyprus without dancing at least one *syrtaki.*'"

Andrei's smile had a brittle edge. "Incredible though it may seem, I've never heard that one before."

"Come, Doctor!" Eleni glowered imperiously, gave Andrei's arm a tug, and hauled him to his feet. "This is your last night here. It's now or never."

Two little girls scurried over and urged Julia to join the dance. She laughed and stood up between them. She and the girls linked arms and squeezed into the circle across from Andrei and Eleni. Without missing a beat, the dancers made room for them, crashing up against them as the *syrtaki* swung back in their direction. Before long, everyone in the place was dancing, even a pair of sinewy German students in holey jeans and bulky sweaters and a sedate Japanese tourist and his petite wife.

Instinctively, Julia gave herself to the rhythm. Across the circle, Andrei glided beside his Cypriot friend. He was an excellent dancer. Elegant, even. He seemed so familiar to her, like she'd known him all her life. She stumbled. Frowning, she looked down, watched the steps of the other dancers, and slipped back into rhythm. The tempo of the music picked up, growing faster, it seemed, with every beat.

Glancing across the room, she watched dancers skim through a tight spot between two carelessly abandoned chairs and surge into the crowded center of the room. Andrei had apparently left the chain. Eleni was following the sprightly boy who now led the dance. Julia squeezed her small neighbors' shoulders, swung her head from side to side, and dipped down with them, concentrating hard on the complex pattern of steps.

Eleni snatched a thick cotton napkin from a nearby table, swirled it wide high above her head, and cried out a rousing "Ó-o-op-pa!"

Startled by a firm touch on her wrist, Julia swung to her left. Andrei squeezed in beside her.

He was smiling, wearing the same almost-dazed expression she noticed when she bumped into him on the path. "Julia." He nodded politely, but his gaze and his tone of voice felt intensely intimate.

"Looks like I'm fated to bump into you again," she tried to joke, aware of his arm intertwined with hers, of the gentle grip of his hand on her shoulder as they sidestepped with the other dancers, of his index finger resting high along her neck.

"Fate had nothing to do with it." His voice was soft, barely audible above the clarinet's sudden blast. He shook his head gently, as if perplexed, then spoke more normally. "I wanted to dance beside you just once."

Julia didn't trust herself to answer him. Didn't trust herself even to look at him. The tingling sensations coursing through her torso had become almost unbearable. The way she felt, one glance into his blue eyes and her legs would surely give way.

The music rose to a deafening pitch, grew more frenzied, yet strangely easier to follow. The snaking dancers tugged Julia swiftly across the floor. She tossed her head back and tried to call up the relative composure she'd felt before Andrei crowded in beside her. It was no use. She was acutely aware of Andrei's closeness, of her desire for him. She could give in to it in an instant, and that made her uncomfortable.

Worse was the certainty his desire equaled hers, maybe even sur-passed hers. That wouldn't do. However right or beautiful it might seem in the heat of this moment, the last thing she needed was a fling with a man who had determined to be celibate.

The music's volume dropped. Julia took advantage of the lull.

"I've had all the carousing I can handle," she shouted, pulling back from the chain. Andrei came with her. Bracing herself, she squeezed her eyes closed for a second then turned toward him and gave him her most virginal smile. "Think we could call it a night?"

Andrei's hand trailed down the bare inside of her arm, taking hold of hers. Bending slightly at the waist, he brushed her fingers across his lips. She saw his jaw tighten with the effort to control himself. "As you wish, my Lady."

"My dad used to call me Lady," Julia said, relief warring with regret. "Nobody else ever has, but I like how it sounded when you did."

"It seems to suit you." His easy smile was back. He'd obviously steadied himself, his seemingly innate courtesy prevailing over his desire.

She walked back to their table and whisked her sweater off of her chair. Taking his arm, she steered him toward the door.

"It's wonderful to make a new friend halfway round the world, don't you think?"

"I have the distinct impression you make friends wherever you go."

Julia smothered a yawn and chuckled. "That sixth sense of yours, again, I suppose?"

Andrei raised an eyebrow, seemed to hesitate. "We'll talk about that some other time." He took her elbow and led her toward the exit.

"Why not now?"

"Because you have jet lag and another big day ahead of you tomorrow." He gave her a congenial wink. "You shall simply have to wait."

AVENUE KLÉBER, PARIS

Madame Racine paced her library, her high heels clicking on the parquet floor as she stepped off the Persian carpet at the far end of the room. She paused, patted her chignon, adjusted the rhinestone buttons on her purple Givenchy suit.

The library's opulence usually helped steady the most flighty soul. Its elegant serenity usually induced the most agitated subconscious to relax. She'd designed the room years ago, and it had served the Alliance well, had been an agent for many unexpected and thoroughly unexplainable shifts of diplomatic policy. It certainly wasn't helping to calm Racine tonight. Not in the least. Her contact in Cyprus had just confirmed that Julia Giardani had encountered Andrei Anatolin on Cyprus. The die was cast, as the old saying went. Both young people were now in gravest danger, but such was the price for taking up Tony's plea, for overriding the restriction against intervening in worldly events. The inner circle were still incensed that Tony asked the Alliance to protect his Julia. They reasoned that as a founding member, Tony had known the rules as well as the rest of them.

Disappointing—even if they were correct that, during the War, the Alliance had permitted the Task Force to intervene in human affairs only because the directives from on high clearly condoned intervention—that in this present crisis, the guidelines had been far more ambiguous. Racine's only alternative to the inner circle's assistance had been to bring Julia and Andrei together. Now, the old wound that bound them to Danilenko's evil would have to be purged.

AKAMAS PENINSULA, CYPRUS
APRIL 4

Julia awoke before dawn. Four o'clock, according to her glow-in-the-dark watch. She sat up straight in the narrow bed and stared at the chalky, thin partition that divided her room from Andrei's. Listening hard, she heard gentle snoring coming from the other side.

She rubbed her eyes and climbed out of bed. The room was cold, the linoleum beneath her feet like clammy slate. It would likely be even colder in a damp, sunless grotto. She'd packed only her father's fancy gifts. They would just have to do. She grabbed her leggings, pulled them on, covered the silk T-shirt she'd slept in with a white turtleneck sweater dress and its matching cardigan, then added an apricot tunic length sweater vest, the last of the warm things she'd brought to Cyprus. No warm socks, but two pairs of cotton knee-highs probably would do the job.

Pushing the fingers of both hands through her hair, she gave it a few quick fluffs and turned toward the door. The palm-sized flashlight she always traveled with stashed safely into her vest pocket, her boots tucked under her arm to put on outside, where she wouldn't disturb the others sleeping in the house, she was ready to go.

Tiptoeing out of her room before dawn felt odd, but she just couldn't wait for Andrei, or anyone else, to wake up. Since the moment she'd heard of Aphrodite's Bath, known locally as Loutra Tis Aphrodite, she'd felt the grotto calling her. She was determined to answer that call as soon as she could.

After the dancing last night, Andrei had walked her up the asphalt road to a sign that pointed to the grotto. With a clearly marked path and her flashlight in hand, it shouldn't be hard to find. What she'd do when she got there she couldn't imagine. She didn't even know if there would be a dry seat in the place, but if there was, she'd probably stay for a while. Daydreaming, she hoped. She felt ready to try, at least, a real change from the way she'd felt the last few days.

Her heartbeat sped as she carefully closed the door of the house behind her and stepped off the porch. Balancing on one foot and hopping a bit, she pulled on one boot, shifted feet and pulled on the other. She braced her palms against her thighs and gave a quick bounce to assess the weight and bulk of her odd getup, grinned. If her father could see her now, he'd probably laugh at the way she'd transformed his elegant gifts into her usual moppet's attire.

"I have good feelings about this place, Dad," she whispered. "Sure wish you were here to share it with me."

She stood and started up the road, turned left and continued silently up the ever-narrowing pathway toward a dense clump of trees hugging the shadowy headland of the bay. The air was damp and cool, tasted fresh and slightly tinged with salt. She heard waves lapping against the shoreline below, a soothing sound, soft and low. It was still very early, dark, despite the waxing moon riding high in the sky.

The darkness deepened when she reached the clump of trees, which grew so luxuriantly they entwined overhead and canopied the path. She excavated her pocket, cupped her palm around her tiny flashlight. Shining the light on the path, she stepped beneath the canopy and hurried upward, her pulse racing as she climbed.

What she'd thought was the end of the path was actually a sharp bend. She rounded it and came to a sudden halt. Before her was a dark opening that had to be the entrance to Loutra Tis Aphrodite. She moved closer, tiptoed inside, and glanced around the grotto. Her breath caught in her throat, the place was so lovely.

Through a cleft high above, moonlight streamed down, reflecting off slick oozing walls and turning the grotto's myriad mosses iridescent, creating an illusion not unlike daylight. In the cavern's center, a low wall rimmed a steaming, limpid pool, its circumference teeming with colonies of incandescent algae. She moved closer to the pool and drank in the overall effect of the grotto. It felt alive. Refreshing. Fertile. Andrei was right to call the place primeval. She was glad she'd accepted his invitation. Very glad.

Her ears hummed with a sound like the unsteady roar of a waterfall or the roll of the sea at high tide. Tears gathered in her eyes, and she was overcome by a feeling of reverence. Not the vague near-reverence she'd felt at Petra Tou Romiou, but an emotion transcending anything she'd ever felt before. She had no sure name for it, but devotion might come close.

No more resisting. She'd sit right down and get serious, give herself over to the place and the feelings washing through her. She wiped off the dewy ledge rimming the pool, turned around, and plunked herself down upon it. Crossing her legs, she balanced herself and inhaled, filling her lungs with the grotto's pungent vapors.

∞

Appalled he was awake at this ungodly hour, Gregor Danilenko took a seat on a damp wooden bench on a hill half a mile from his hotel. Ten minutes ago, the ruby pendulum clattered to the floor and shattered his sleep. When he picked it up, the impressions it conveyed goaded him out of his warm bed and into the predawn chill to this isolated spot, where he could do nothing more than stare down at the headlands of Khrysokhou Bay.

He slipped off his gloves and held the pendulum aloft. It swung gently, a flickering shadow against near darkness. He had never been much of a telepath, but when he focused on this particular object, he was instantly endowed with enhanced telepathic skill. Not another living soul knew about the pendulum, one of the most arcane items from the Hitler collection. Even with all the handling of the collection he'd done over the years, it had never come to light until he'd discovered, in the spine of Dietrich Eckart's old grimoire, a key that unlocked the case in which the pendulum had been hidden. He rolled the pendulum between his hands, warming it, pressing it to his brow until it started to burn him. Then, balancing it on his upturned palm, he sat back, straightened his spine, and tuned in.

The stone flashed softly, suffusing the darkness with a rich claret glow. He stared at it until his vision blurred and his breathing calmed down, then he closed his eyes and switched his attention to remote viewing mode. Though he should have been fully prepared, he jumped in surprise when Julia Giardani appeared in his mind's eye. His sudden movement almost cost him his concentration, but he held on. A moment later, the mirror of his mind stilled and once again reflected the image of the Giardani girl inside a small cavern, where she sat cross-legged, obviously meditating.

He was dismayed by the depth of her meditation, more than a little alarmed. In the 1970s, disgusted by the paltry written and video data gathered by Soviet parapsychology over half a century, he'd used his position in the KGB to requisition the country's most promising parapsychologists, including young Andrei Ivanovich Anatolin, who unenthusiastically engineered dozens of experiments on the various trance levels and phenomena associated with meditation.

The studies failed to deliver the desired results—reproducible, dependable uses for psychic abilities in espionage and warfare—but they were, nevertheless, impressive. None of them had prepared him for Julia Giardani. She was no emaciated Hindu or Buddhist ascetic, no God-intoxicated Sufi or Christian mystic, either, but there could be no mistaking the depth of her meditative trance.

Every indicator pointed toward the same conclusion. Tony's daughter was an adept, or well on her way to becoming one. Her spine was perfectly erect, her breath completely calm. Her gaze, eyes slightly open and raised, was absolutely still. Her face shone with soft astral light. Indeed, she was surrounded by it. Not a muscle so much as twitched, yet Danilenko had the distinct impression she'd been sitting like that for some time. He knew well the years of concerted effort it took to achieve her level of concentration. He himself had shunned the arduous self-discipline required to achieve it.

The paranormal events of yesterday aside, he'd had no reason to suspect her of being as advanced as she obviously was. If he were classifying, he'd have to group her right up there with the most powerful meditators he'd ever seen, live or on video. His neck tendons knotted into thick, tight cords. He shuddered, needed to cease remote viewing at once, pull his consciousness away while he could yet control himself.

But he was bewitched by the young woman's luminous radiance. He had no restraint when it came to beauty. Like the moth to the flame. Even more irresistible was her power. No mere flame, that. It was a torch. If he couldn't somehow manage to contain it, it would surely consume him.

His pulse started to throb fiercely at his temples, the surest sign he was losing his grip. Dropping the pendulum into his lap, he clasped his hands together, pressed hard, then harder still. His wrists ached by the time he felt fully grounded and disconnected from the vision.

He pulled on his gloves, carefully picked up the ruby pendulum, and slipped it back into its quilted pouch. His heartbeat skittered, and he was gasping for air. He was far too agitated.

The last thing he wanted was for his frenetic PK to reach the girl, alert her to his surveillance. Extra caution would be needed in the future. Extreme control. He'd been wrong to be fooled by Julia Giardani's innocent appearance. She was a real threat to his plans.

It was past time to stop his sentimental swooning. She might not know about her legacy, but she was the Giardani Heiress, which made her his enemy. He needed to remember that. Every minute of every hour until he had what he wanted.

∞

Anatolin gave up trying to sleep at six o'clock. He'd read a while, then walk off some of his agitation along the shore of the bay before heading to Loutra Tis Aphrodite.

Perhaps he'd eventually regain his composure, though it was doubtful, as long as he was anywhere in the proximity of Julia. The woman was a wonder. He had to credit her with a near miracle. She had coaxed from him details of his exile he'd previously refused to think about, let alone discuss with a virtual stranger.

It wasn't that she was telepathic. That, apparently, was not one of her many gifts. She was just a superb listener, acted as if every word he said mattered, as if every thought he expressed was extremely profound. A rare skill in one so young. But then, Julia was a rare creature, overall, as unique as he'd originally assumed, and as charismatic. He'd been on this island for weeks, but he'd never had so many people buzzing around his table as he had last night. People seemed irresistibly drawn to Julia. Around her, they acted a little friendlier, stood a little taller, spoke with more intelligence or soul, as if it were crucial she think the best of them. He'd lost count of the times he'd caught himself doing such things since he'd met her.

He glanced back at his narrow cot, remembered the night of turmoil he'd spent there. He had never felt such unequivocal desire. Too much of his adult life had been lived in the passionless state of detachment required for his personal and professional survival under the Soviet regime. Only his mother, Ilina Mikhailovna Anatolina, had ever encouraged him to experience the intensely erotic unity consciousness she believed was key to the greater mysteries of life. Since 1976 or so, he'd sought unity awareness via the ancient science of yoga, which by definition had little to do with physical desire, at least for someone in his present circumstances. Someone who intentionally had remained single and, moreover, had chosen the path of renunciation.

He glanced at his watch and scolded himself for allowing his thoughts to wander. On the flattened top of his old duffel bag roosted the three books that long ago shaped his philosophy for living—an English translation of Patanjali's *Yoga Sutras*, Sir Edwin Arnold's translation of the Bhagavad Gita, and a first edition of Paramahansa Yogananda's *Autobiography of a Yogi*, inscribed by the great Master's own hand.

Smuggled into the U.S.S.R. in the late 1950s by the legendary Madame Racine, the books had been gifts from his mother when he'd more or less mastered English in his eighteenth year. They had rarely been out of his sight until he hid them in the floorboards of his Moscow laboratory the evening before his arrest. They spent his entire exile there. Fortunately, he'd memorized them years before, for in the dark hours of his years-long solitary confinement, practicing Patanjali's eightfold path as best he could, reciting the Gita's verses to himself, pondering the messages in Yogananda's fantastical stories, had been all that had kept him sane.

As was his habit now that he had the books back, he took up the Gita, leafed through it, and let it fall open at a random page, but he couldn't read. His mind kept straying back to Julia. He listened carefully, but no sound came from the room next door.

Perhaps a good brisk walk would be better for him than his usual routine. If nothing else, the exercise would steady his nerves, help him overcome the sense of impending danger that had come over him during the middle of the night.

SEVEN

The walk along the shore had indeed worked its magic. Anatolin was ready for Loutra Tis Aphrodite. He supposed he sought out quiet places like the grotto because his exile was still too haunting. It had changed him irrevocably. By his third Siberian winter, he'd finally accepted the hyper-sensitivity of his clairsentience, but it was a difficult gift to endure. Being back in the world sometimes felt almost unbearable. Battered by strangers' thoughts and emotions, he was often unable to shut out their more positive energies, let alone their more dominant angers and fears.

He glanced down at the wildflowers that lined the path leading to Loutra Tis Aphrodite. This morning, the sun's first tendrils of pinkish-gold lit the velvet cyclamen petals, the tiny blue squills, and the green spikes of Naples garlic hugging the sides of the path. Closer to the grotto itself, a slight breeze stirred the delicate maidenhair fern, gently bowed the stands of slender spring reeds.

A more intense energy than usual glossed the air. Tiny molecules of light danced before his eyes. Life force. Prana. Whichever he chose to call it, Anatolin had never seen it more clearly than he did right now. Inside, the grotto was positively inundated with life force. Legions of fern and bracken glistened on the grotto's walls. A voiceless, roiling hum amplified its usual trickle and drip. Chills raced up Anatolin's spine.

He scanned the small space, dismayed by how *conscious* it seemed, how even the lilies in its pool seemed to reach toward the woman who sat, poised and peaceful beside them. Julia, immersed in meditation so deep she seemed oblivious of his arrival, oblivious of everything. All around her, the grotto shimmered with her aura's rainbow hues intermingled with rosy gold.

Julia.

Once again the focal point of a paranormal event unparalleled in his experience. But even without a parallel to draw from, it was clear that what happened at the beach was mere prelude to whatever was taking place here.

Anatolin caught a glimmer of moisture on Julia's lashes, noticed tears slipping down her cheeks as she gently nodded her head. Her lips moved, but she made no sound, was obviously absorbed in profound communion with someone or something beyond his ken.

His breath caught in his throat. He tried to tune in to Julia, felt overwhelmed by sensations of joy, a feeling of Divine contact more blissful, more loving, than anything he'd ever imagined. The life force roared in his ears as never before, the unmistakable reverberation of AUM.

He felt suddenly ashamed to think of himself as a yogi. This woman was a true yogi, whether she'd call herself one or not. He was certain she had attained everything he set his heart on attaining years ago, that this very moment, she was experiencing the very deepest level of meditation.

He couldn't be mistaken. Who in the world—?

No, the question wasn't *who*. *What* was she? At the very least, she had to be a great soul, one of those rare emissaries of the Divine who incarnate to accomplish some special task.

He should feel sublimely blessed to have come upon her during her meditation. What he felt was apprehension.

Extreme concern. Not for himself, but for Julia.

She was too trusting. He hadn't realized it before, but she was probably much too friendly, an easy target for others' negativity. And even if she hadn't possessed her charismatic persona, she was much too lovely to be inconspicuous, ever.

These things aside, what made him most worried was her openness, which could be seen as audacity, even recklessness. One of the few personal facts she'd let slip last night now made his blood run cold—she'd never traveled abroad alone before, yet here she sat in an entirely unknown and potentially dangerous, isolated spot in a state of consciousness that left her fully exposed to all manner of harm. She seemed as carefree as if she were safely in her own sitting room.

She was undeniably vulnerable. Excruciatingly so.

He looked away, stared up through the open crevice above her head at the quickly warming, morning sky. In a minute or two, the sun would stream in through the tangle of branches and fill the grotto with brightness. A flicker of ruby-red light drew his attention back to Julia's aura. Something about it confirmed his impressions she was in danger.

He tightened his focus on the ruby light, realized it was not actually part of her aura, but rather an imprint of someone attuned to her energy field. Someone hovering near her. Someone evil. Stalking her, desiring her, or something belonging to her, Anatolin couldn't quite discern which.

Alarm shot through him. Before he knew it, Julia and he would be resuming their separate paths. A few more meager hours. How in the world could he help her learn to protect herself in so short a time?

"Andrei?"

Julia's voice startled him. He stood up. "Good morning."

"Good morning, yourself!" She unfolded her legs and stood up. She was flushed, and she seemed embarrassed. "Boy, did I lose track of time!" She yawned and rubbed her palms over her cheeks. "What a wonderful place!"

"I thought you would like it."

"Thank you for telling me about it." She shook her head, pushed her fingers through her hair, and started toward him, still obviously shaky from her trance but wearing a smile so potent it could melt a granite wall.

Anatolin almost staggered from its force. "My pleasure," he said. How could Julia behave as if nothing of consequence had transpired here? Was it possible she didn't realize anything had? After what he'd just witnessed, she acted like the same ordinary young woman he'd met the day before.

Some strong emotion—admiration, perhaps—overcame him. He quickly cleared his throat. "You didn't mention you liked to meditate."

"What? Oh!" She gazed up at him, smiled again. "Right! My dad used to say I was meditating when I thought all I was doing was day-dreaming." She paused, put her hands on her hips. "I have to tell you, though, this morning was a bit different."

"In what way?"

She seemed not to hear him. She turned and gazed around the grotto as if for the first time. "Actually, I probably should have told you sooner, I've been having pretty strange experiences ever since I got to Cyprus."

Her guilelessness stunned Anatolin. "I've been less than com-pletely forthright with you, as well," he said softly.

She turned and faced him, gave him a lingering stare. "Somehow I have this feeling you're another secretive guy, just like my father."

"A typical Scorpio, I must confess."

"November birthday?"

"Yes. The seventh."

"Dad's was the seventeenth."

She made a deliberately funny face he could only describe as adorable, a thin veneer of mock annoyance overlaying her character-istically sunny smile.

He felt his heart wrench. "What can I say?"

She reached up, rubbed gently at her temples, and gave him a slightly pained grin. "I guess it's time we both started 'fessing up, but after breakfast. I can't think on an empty stomach."

He didn't know what "'fessing up" might mean to Julia, but at least he intended to find some way to convey his foreboding about her safety without seeming like a lunatic. "Perhaps during our drive to Aphrodite's sanctuary."

∞

The road veering up to Old Paphos was bumpy, steep and dusty. Julia gathered her hair up off the back of her neck with one hand and cranked her window closed with the other. It was a shame to shut out the air, but if she didn't she'd probably wind up with a sore throat, and that she didn't need. Her recent psychic experiences had already taken their toll, and this morning's belated revelations about her reasons for coming here and Andrei's former profession had all but finished her off.

Andrei, a parapsychologist.

He could have told her sooner, might have been able to offer the benefit of his professional opinion, or shed some light on her strange experiences as they'd occurred. She had probably a zillion questions she'd ask him if there were time. She turned her head and watched him swerve left and right, struggling to miss the road's worst potholes. His brow was furrowed in concentration. A slight gleam of sweat had broken out on his temple. He seemed a bit worn down, too.

The road leveled off abruptly. Turning wide into an unevenly paved lot, Andrei parked and turned off the engine. Great clouds of dust swirled in the air, obscuring the view. A welcome stillness descended. She leaned back in her seat, let go of her hair, and felt herself relax as the dust settled.

Aside from a few chunks of rough-hewn stone and some dilapidated buildings beyond the crumbling ruins of a small Orthodox church, nothing much could be seen in the direction of the sanctuary. Directly ahead of the car stood a partially restored medieval castle.

Behind that spread a plateau-like promontory which overlooked the sea to the east and, according to Andrei, to the south and west as well.

Glancing sideways, she caught Andrei staring at her and looked away. A parapsychologist, for heaven's sake! She hadn't thought anyone but a few aging ex-hippies in California were still into anything like that, but he'd assured her parapsychology had been taken very seriously by certain factions of the Soviet government, dubious factions still functioning, apparently, in Russia today. They were some of his reasons for making a clean break from both his country and his profession.

He surely had lived a difficult life. She shrugged off her annoyance and smiled at him. "Isn't it amazing that you and I both seem to be starting new lives?"

"Amazing, indeed. Why didn't your father tell you about your legacy sooner?"

"His mother apparently swore him to secrecy." The Anna Giardani Julia remembered was a tiny dictator, demanding and proud, and the saddest person Julia had ever met. "She told him she alone had the authority to pass on the legacy, and he apparently wasn't qualified to receive it."

When her father shared that part, he'd frowned so hard his eyebrows formed a silvery band across his brow, but his frown had seemed more puzzled than resentful. "It seems the legacy has always been transmitted from female to female, regardless of generation."

"Matrilineal inheritance in 1920s Italy?"

Julia smiled. "Dad's explanation was that the family was always eccentric." She remembered his quirky grin, the twinkle in his eye as he'd teased her, felt the knot of grief in her stomach tighten again.

"An impressive ancestral mix, Julia. Not just witches, but community leaders, as well. Two thousand years of them. Maybe more, if your father's estimation is correct."

She nodded and leaned her head against the window. She fanned herself with her father's postcard.

"That must be one of the cards you told me about," Andrei said. His voice sounded strained. Maybe he was as dismayed by her news as she'd been by his. "Might I see it?"

"Sure." She passed it to him.

He propped the card against the steering wheel for several seconds, as if contemplating it. When he turned to her, he gave her the sweetest, most tender smile, his eyes very soft, kinder than ever. "Not only was your father a gifted telepath, he was also a very wise man."

Julia's breath caught deep in her chest as her father's image came clearly to mind. Tears gathered in her eyes, but she fought them back. Swallowing hard, she turned her gaze out the front window. "What makes you say that?" She was glad Andrei had leaned back against his door, as if deliberately giving her plenty of space.

"According to the anthropologists I've read, when a shamanic clan's ancestral tradition suffers a break in the direct transmission of its power, the lineage can be reestablished only by a return to its magical source." He paused, lifted the card. "With this, your father apparently pointed you to the very wellspring of your clan's power, the place of Aphrodite's supposed origins."

"Oh." She stuck her chin out. "I guess my job's simple enough, then. All I have to do is reestablish a sacred tradition dating back, let's see, to some time near the beginning of the Mediterranean Bronze Age." She knew she sounded a bit sarcastic, tried to soften her tone with a smile. "Single-handedly, unless one rapscallion parapsychologist chooses to grant me the benefit of his expertise."

Andrei gave a little nod. "At your service."

"For two measly hours." She looked at him, realized she was pouting, and smiled, feeling more than a little ridiculous.

He glanced at his watch. "Actually, two-and-a-half. The taxi you asked for will pick you up at five this afternoon."

"That's right," she said with a sigh. He'd be heading back to the Paphos airport then, to catch a plane to Athens. Since there were no direct flights between Paphos and Italy, she'd travel in the opposite direction, to the island's larger airport near Larnaca. She cracked the door open and started to get out of the car.

"Wait," Andrei said, placing a restraining hand on her arm.

Her gaze lingered on his hand. It had given her a sharp thrill which quickly turned to a muddle of rapid images—a woman with features exactly like his, stark tundra stretching out endlessly, his undeniable integrity—the inexplicable sense she knew all there was to know about him.

Disorienting. She leaned back and let go of the door handle. "I'm sorry, what did you want?"

"Let's try a test of your father's assumption regarding your PK abilities."

"Okay," she agreed, but the muscles in her neck clearly didn't. They immediately tensed. Her shoulders followed. "How?"

"Relax," he said with a chuckle. "We won't perform an elaborate laboratory protocol, just a simple, straightforward test anyone could try."

He reached up and gently touched her just above and between her eyebrows. "Focus at the spot often called the spiritual eye, and rub your hands together."

She focused then rubbed her hands until her palms grew hot.

"Good." Andrei's voice seemed especially subdued and soothing. "Now stop and hold your hands up, palms facing each other."

She did as he said. Her palms felt odd, as if invisible elastic bands were strung between them.

"Perfect." Andrei frowned in concentration, like a physician in the midst of a diagnosis. He raised his hands and moved them up and down between hers. Taking hold of her wrists, he pushed them together and pulled them apart a few times quickly, then more slowly. With each movement, the invisible bands seemed more clearly defined.

Excitement bubbled up inside her. "Wow!"

"Relax again, please."

"Okay."

"Julia, please focus again on your spiritual eye and turn your palms toward me. Good. Now, keeping your hands absolutely still, concentrate and visualize pushing me backward, away from you."

Push him backward with her mind alone? Well, she'd give it her best. She smiled without opening her eyes and focused hard.

She heard a thump, felt the car jar to the left. "Whoa!" She peeked out at Andrei, sprawled against his door. "Are you all right?"

Rubbing the back of his head, Andrei straightened back up. "Your PK is exceptional. Your father was certainly right about that!"

"Fine, but what on earth am I supposed to *do* with it?"

He looked at her soberly. "When people are given talents like yours, there's always a reason." He glanced over her shoulder at the mostly bare vista beyond her window. "I suspect yours will come clear quickly, once you get to Tuscany."

She frowned, recalling her vision on the beach. Fulfill my heart's desire—forever be my ally . . . those words had started something, but what? And what might happen here, at Aphrodite's most famous sanctuary, let alone in Tuscany? "I hate waiting to find out."

"So I've noticed." Andrei walked around the car and opened her door.

"I hope we have enough time to see the whole site."

"We should have ample time. There's not a lot left here to see."

Julia stepped away from the car door and held her palms out in front of her, remembering when she touched the Holy Belt. She stared at them a moment then dropped them to her sides. "I hope you're wrong about that!"

∞

Anatolin started to direct Julia toward the remains of the site's famous Roman stoa, once an elegant open-faced hall, but then held his tongue. She was headed with an unmistakable sense of purpose for the area of the Bronze Age sanctuary.

At the prehistoric entrance, she touched a large block of carved stone from the sanctuary's earliest days, then suddenly turned and swept down into the pock-marked expanse of the old sacred enclosure. He followed, watching silently. Her footsteps stirred the chalky dust covering the clay, sent it aloft on the fast-returning westerly wind.

She neared the shallow basin he'd always considered the most sacred spot on the site. For him it evoked scenes of ritual lustration, of devotees purifying themselves to encounter the Divine. She stepped between the basin and the block that once held a massive Horns of Consecration, that ubiquitous symbol of Bronze Age religion. Her gaze swept upward, as if she were seeing the ancient symbol in all its former grandeur. She hesitated, then, right before his awestruck gaze, she changed. Subtly but surely, her aura filled with that now familiar radiant rosy gold. It compelled him, drew him toward her.

In a few strides, he stood behind her, his heart thumping against the walls of his chest. He was intensely aware of her closeness, and of something more, some unnamable, illusory "other." Dynamic and enticing. Imperative.

He was spellbound by this latest manifestation of Julia's gifts. After the events of the last twenty-four hours, he should have expected just about anything to happen in her presence, but he felt surprise stealing through him. He took a deep breath, made his mind even more receptive, and changed his opinion. This was no mere manifestation of psychic talent. He'd read about this sort of thing but never imagined he'd see anything like it himself.

There were two conflicting theories to consider. Either some great power was attempting to manifest through Julia, use her as a channel of expression, or else Julia was experiencing some kind of intrusion or bleed-through into this lifetime from one of her previous incarnations. Neither possibility fell within Anatolin's areas of expertise, and given what he'd observed thus far, he couldn't conceive of a third. She bent down between the edge of the basin and a corner of the block, whispering. He leaned forward. Careful not to jar her, he listened closely. Kneeling, she braced both hands on the floor of the basin and closed her eyes.

"Decimated," she said. The voice sounding through her was utterly strange to Anatolin's ears. It had a golden, honeyed richness. Remote, yet fluid and warm. Sensual in the extreme.

Regally, she stood and stepped onto the block. She raised her arms high, as if miming the Horns of Consecration in a primitive salutation. She turned toward him. Her cheeks shone with tears. She brushed them away. The look on her face was ecstatic, filled with wonder—and eerily familiar. "All rubble and dust now, but *I remember . . .*"

Anatolin's arms and neck felt brushed with electricity.

Julia's gaze seemed focused inward, far away. "I remember stately processions through the torch-lit *temenos,* flower-crowned maidens in a ritual circle dance, a solitary prayer curling on incense fumes above an altar once set not far from the holy of holies. Long ago in mortal time, only yesterday to me."

Anatolin's chest tightened. He closed his eyes, lowered his head, his heart pounding wildly. Filled with sudden reverence, he sent up a silent prayer, looked at Julia again. As abruptly as the mysterious spell had descended upon her, it seemed to have lifted.

∞

Julia swayed, almost lost her balance. Another vision, even more astounding this time, and just from touching a few old rocks! Amazing. She steadied herself, jumped down from the pedestal and rubbed her temples, determined to regain her equilibrium quickly.

"If only there was a way to turn the clock back a few thousand years."

"Why turn back the clock?"

"Because it was once so lovely here." She stared out over the dusty plateau, her gaze lingering on the partial columns and foundation stones littering the area. Long ago, according to her vision, they stood proudly in the beautiful ancient courtyard. "Hard to believe, but this was like a garden. Flowers, bright blooming shrubs, meandering vines."

"You've had another psychic episode, I believe."

She smiled.

Andrei smiled back, lifted her hand, and ran his finger firmly over her palm. "What your father seemingly didn't have occasion to note is that you are also gifted with psychometric intuition, generally called psychometry."

"What is that, exactly?"

"The ability to 'read,' usually through the hands, subtle vibrations left behind in material objects."

"Psychometry," she repeated, mulling the word over.

"It's another form of physical psychism which, like your PK, rarely occurs in the degree you seem to possess."

"Terrific." She looked down at the dusty ground, sighed, and glanced back up. "Walk with me?"

"Of course." Andrei walked beside her, letting her set the pace. "You seem less than pleased about your special gifts," he said.

"I guess less than pleased sums it up pretty well." She paused. "My father assured me the gifts would be useful, though, once I learned to control them." She walked to the center of the open space to her right. Scrutinizing the area, she chose a dusty corner and squatted down, her palms against the ground. "I sure hope he was right."

EIGHT

The earth warming her palms, Julia relaxed and concentrated on the spot between her eyebrows until images started to pass before her mind's eye. The images slowed, changed from vague, out-of-focus snapshots to more distinct pictures. She gasped as her mental screen turned from pale, grayed-out hues to something approaching Technicolor. "Oh, Andrei!"

"Tell me what you see," he said in that soothing tone she'd decided was his professional voice.

She wet her lips. "Small altars tucked everywhere, at least that's what I think they are. And Goddess images—all over—different sizes, different shapes. Oh, my!" Julia gasped for air, pushed her hands down harder onto the chalky earth, focused more intensely to make out more detail. "Yes. And representations of male privates— what do the scholars call them?"

"*Phalloi.*"

"Right! Large and small, planted like lilies in the rich, fertile loam all around the garden. They're prayers, Andrei, all the little statues, male and female." Tears started to choke off her voice. She fought them. "Prayers for fertility. For abundance. For peace and safety from harm. For a gracious, happy life."

She yanked up her hands, brushed off the dust, stood. She couldn't handle any more, really needed a break.

"Take some deep breaths, Julia." He sounded oddly shaken, too.

She glanced at him. He started, guiltily, she thought. Breathing deeply, she shook her head. She had to be wrong.

"Seeing all these images is exhilarating, but it's also exhausting. "Maybe we'd better check out what's in the museum, before I get carried away and start touching every last stone out here."

Andrei clasped his hands behind his back and nodded, indicating she should lead the way. She followed the signs pointing to the lower floor of the medieval castle, which apparently housed the artifacts excavated from the sanctuary in recent years.

Stepping into a huge vault-like room, it took a moment to get her bearings. A small, grim-faced man in a blue polyester suit sat reading on a stool in the corner near a large cathedral window. The museum guard, she guessed. The room was huge and sparsely lit. A few track lights accented a small collection displayed mostly around the perimeter of the cavernous space. She scanned the walls then zeroed in on a large black cone-shaped rock on a stumpy pedestal across the room. Before she knew it, she'd crossed the museum and stood before it.

She felt like kneeling, like rubbing her hands over every inch of the stone. She felt, much to her chagrin, like crying, and the realization surprised her.

"Remarkable, isn't it?"

Andrei had come very close but had been so quiet she was jolted by his remark. "Yes, but why?"

"They say a conical stone like this, perhaps this very one, was the main cult idol of the Paphian sanctuary for several millennia."

"I have a hunch something held sacred for such a long time might still be fairly potent." Goose bumps rose on her arms, and she shuddered, but not from revulsion. Far from it. Her hand itched to touch the rock.

Glancing over her shoulder, she couldn't hold back a sigh. The guard was watching her. Like a hawk. "Pretty different from the shapely marbles of Classical times," she said, making conversation to break the rock's spell.

Andrei leaned close. "As different as was the goddess worshipped here from the nonsensical creature of Greek myth. Somewhere along the centuries, men seemed to have mucked up everything related to Aphrodite." He paused, raised an eyebrow. "Probably on purpose."

"Because she was so powerful."

"Precisely. The most powerful of all the old gods, the most difficult to eradicate from the hearts of her worshippers, and, consequently, the most profaned by those lusting for power at the decline of her epoch."

Julia wondered how Andrei had arrived at ideas so similar to those her father shared last March. She wished she had time to find out, but was acutely aware her watch was ticking the minutes away.

She moved over to a small, dusty case displaying pottery shards and statuettes and was immediately grateful for her largely impractical master's degree in art history. She didn't need an archaeological guide to understand, at least in part, what she was looking at.

The small female statues were quaint, their styles ranging from primitive to more Classical. She was particularly taken with the rougher terracottas, especially those whose arms were raised in the gesture she had felt compelled to make outside.

"Look," she said, pointing to a small plaque beside the best-preserved statue. "This says the Goddess of Old Paphos was called *Wanassa*."

"A very ancient and sacred word from the earliest written language of the Greek world. It translates 'Lady.'"

Lady. She might have known! Her neck prickled. She suddenly recalled how her father's nickname had always made her feel like someone other than herself. Clear recollections of many such feelings from her childhood flooded her mind. She had to focus hard to follow Andrei's conversation.

"That pose with the upraised arms was also very sacred. It has been found at numerous Bronze Age sites spread over a vast area." He paused, obviously uncomfortable. "Forgive me, I didn't mean to bore you, again."

"Are you kidding?" She gave him a smile. "Tell me more."

"I wish I could. What I've shared with you is largely conjecture, and I suspect you already know more about this subject than I ever will."

Another statement that closely echoed one her father made last March. She rubbed a tense knot between her ribs. "Why would you think such a thing?"

He dropped his gaze. "I beg your pardon, I've presumed again."

"Don't be silly." She reached out and touched his arm. "We're friends, right?"

He glanced up. "Of course."

His self-effacing smile warmed the blue of his eyes, triggered a feeling in Julia almost like déjà vu. She decided it was best to shrug it off. Glancing over her shoulder, she noticed the guard had climbed down from his stool and was heading through the door leading to the courtyard, a pack of cigarettes in his hand.

"It seems nothing interferes with his afternoon smoke," Andrei said.

Julia waited a moment then couldn't contain herself any longer. She stepped back to the rock, leaned toward it, caressed it. Its cool surface was smooth, exceedingly soothing to the touch, familiar.

Vertigo struck.

Next thing she knew, she stood straight as a bolt, her spine like a lightning rod, charged with heat yet intensely chilled, all at once. She started to panic. "Andrei?"

"I'm here."

She felt his hand, comforting and solid between her shoulder blades, but his hand was about the only thing that did feel solid. The room swam in a kind of whirlpool. She focused hard. Thoughts and images raced through her mind—vague impressions of incense, of perfumed oil slicked on the rock by countless hands, of prayers whispered and chanted in tongues she'd never heard before but seemed, nonetheless, to understand.

Julia leaped backward in time—felt like she'd moved into a different body, female, clad in flax, with heavy jewelry that jingled when she moved. The temple around her stood on a high, windy mound, the blue sea glistening in the distance beyond its door. Her lover stood at the temple's threshold, barred from entering the holy of holies where she sat, her fingers sore from working the sacred loom.

She stood up and crossed the central chamber, ran her hand over the cool black Goddess stone, and rubbed the oily residue of the morning's perfumed offering into her chafed fingertips. Reaching the door, she took her lover's large, sun-browned hand in her own. The vision dissolved.

As if through cotton batting, Julia felt someone really squeezing her hand. "Andrei?"

"The guard has returned." Andrei's voice seemed to come from a great distance. "Breathe slowly and focus your attention back here."

He squeezed her hand again. Reassured by his confident tone, she followed his instructions.

"Thanks," she said hoarsely. She blinked a few times and broke into a smile. "Whew!" She was thrilled by a sense of discovery, by a feeling akin to triumph.

Andrei gave her a slow smile. "I can imagine."

Beads of perspiration had gathered on his brow, and she wondered why, given that she felt distinctly chilled. She shivered. "It's nippy in here. Mind if we go back outside?"

"Not at all."

The courtyard was a modern construction, not part of the

sanctuary. Julia took her time walking there. She needed to be steady on her feet again before getting near more old stuff.

Andrei cleared his throat. "I confess, I've often wished I were blessed with psychometric intuition."

"Do you think all this might be the past-life recall my father referred to?"

"Perhaps in part." Andrei clasped his hands behind his back again. "The average psychic picks up past-life information through numerous means, but you're far from average, by any measure."

Julia had the distinct impression he'd said more than he intended and much less than he probably could have. He blushed, as if he'd guessed her train of thought—or read her mind!

She looked at him and shook her head then dropped it and banged her palm against her brow. How dense could she be? She knew full well what it felt like to have her mind read, but she'd been so intent on her inner experiences she'd overlooked the obvious. She put her hands on her hips, stared at Andrei, shook her head again.

"You, Mr. Anatolin, are not just another secretive Scorpio, as you put it. You're a telepath like my father was, too!"

∞

Anatolin flushed, dismayed that Julia had caught him red-handed. He should have been much more discreet. Now he could only hope she would not raise her protective shield and bar him from the magic of her awakening.

She gave him a withering stare, shook her head in clear exasperation. "You've seen almost every weird thing that's happened to me since coming here and you've understood it all, or at least far more than I understood. But you were too—closemouthed—to enlighten me?"

"Circumspect is the adjective I'd choose."

She only glared at him. He wanted her to understand, which surprised him. Rubbing at his brow, he groped for an explanation he'd never articulated before. "Most people consider telepaths frightening and freakish. So did many of my former colleagues, who should have known better. They often ridiculed their psychic subjects behind their backs. I've never felt I could afford for my talents to be seen."

He paused and sought her gaze, shoved his hands into his pants pockets.

"I'm listening," she said, her frown deepening.

"I have no other excuse. I suppose evasion became second nature to me at a fairly early age."

She scowled again then, seeming to soften, heaved a weary sigh. "All right. I can accept your ambiguity might have been a necessary survival mechanism. From your remark, it sounds like you've been psychic most of your life."

"For as long as I can remember."

"Lucky you."

Clearly not one to harbor a grudge, she turned on her heel and made for the Roman ruins near the other side of the bluff. Anatolin spent the next hour at her beck and call. She soon recovered from her annoyance with him, seeming to warm to his company again as she roamed the entire ancient sanctuary, touching everything, devouring the tiniest details of the site like a starving waif. He tried to convince himself it was enough just to watch her, sharing her pensive moods or listening to her lively chatter, engaging in the banter she seemed to enjoy. It wasn't enough, would never be enough to make him truly happy, but what might make him happy was entirely out of the question. He would always be grateful for finding Julia, for the few brief hours they'd shared beneath the broad Cypriot sky, which—he noted with regret—was now mottled with the russet hues of approaching sunset.

Julia meandered over to the western rim of the sanctuary and stood quietly, hugging her sweater close around her shoulders, her chin lifted high as if waiting for something. The first star of evening, perhaps. She saw him watching her and waved. The sight of her against the horizon took his breath away.

He started toward her, but a profound melancholy swept over him, made him unable to return her exuberant smile. Suddenly needing to burn her image deep into his memory, he halted and closed his eyes. When he opened them a moment later, she'd climbed onto the nearby ashlar block that held half of a massive Horn of Consecration. Her side pressed against the ancient symbol, she'd lifted her arm in a graceful arc that mimicked its missing half.

"Whaddya think?" She laughed, a bubbly contagious sound that lifted his gloom and evoked from him a heartfelt chuckle. "Could anyone ever put it back together again?"

"Perhaps not anyone, Julia," he said. "But you surely could. And shall, I have no doubt."

Seeming far from convinced, she smiled rather sadly and stepped down. She walked to his side, took his arm, and turned him toward the sunset fast staining the distant sea. "So very different," she said with a sigh.

"What's different?"

"Every confusing thing I've learned on this island, everything related to Aphrodite." She faced him, her eyes radiant, brimming with tears. "She's not just some ancient icon, Andrei. She's real, vibrant, here and now, and She wants desperately to be known again, not as our culture depicts Her but as she really is—as Love and as Joy."

"And what do you want, Julia?"

"To help Her any way I can," she said without hesitation. "Carry Her true essence in the world, be Her hands and feet, Her voice. Whatever."

"You'll succeed in this. I know you will."

"Thanks for believing." She shuddered as she slid her hand down his arm and gave his hand a squeeze.

He moved his hand away but kept still beside her, begrudging the inevitable passage of time, unwilling to break the stillness that seemed so natural between them, that melted their psychic boundaries and sailed her thoughts and feelings toward him like leaves on a gentle stream. The thrill of her recent discoveries. Her commitment to serve her Goddess. Sadness about her father's death. Confusion over her attraction to Anatolin, which mirrored his own confusion and made him feel most uncomfortable.

He glanced surreptitiously at his watch, hoping she wouldn't notice.

"I suppose my taxi will be here soon," she said.

"Yes." Her expression turned grave, and Anatolin realized he'd taken her hand, and that his grip was much too tight. He released it and moved a few inches away. "I beg your pardon."

"Lighten up, Andrei. Come on." She patted his arm reassuringly.

He gazed at her against the background of the museum's whitewashed wall, almost gasped as he caught a lackluster smudge of ruby again staining her aura. With better lighting here than in the grotto, he could make out the ruddy energy trailer he should have seen that morning. He spun around and traced the trailer to the east of the Roman stoa and the ruins of the church.

Beside its entrance, Anatolin caught a blur of movement, no more, but he was instantly suspicious. Whoever hid in the ruins had an air about him so sinister and vile Anatolin's memory sped back to the worst men he'd ever known. KGB thugs, Gregor Danilenko and his ilk. Fortunately, Anatolin had watched the general sail away from the island the day before. The farther Danilenko was from Julia, the happier Anatolin would be, especially after he was no longer close by to protect her. He frowned, composing a warning he was certain would fall on deaf ears.

Julia had a twinkle in her eye he wished could banish all his fears. "Are you always so serious, Andrei?"

"Ponderous is the word I've most often heard used."

"There's one question I've been meaning to ask you for the past hour."

"Please feel free."

"I'm pretty stunned by the phenomena I've experienced. I'd like to know if these talents of mine will always be as disruptive as they are now."

Glad for the diversion from his concern, he smiled. "I would say not. They may even seem to go away entirely, from time to time, especially in the beginning." He thought a moment, reviewing similar awakenings he'd observed over the years. "Sometimes, when we need to learn a great deal of information very quickly, information not accessible to us by normal means, some power—one's soul, perhaps—turns up the intensity of one's perceptions for a while."

"Or someone, like a guardian angel, kind of gives you a temporary energy boost?" The sun dropped closer to the horizon, creating a perfect halo round Julia's body.

"Guardian angel? Perhaps."

He gave her aura another quick scan. Indeed, someone did seem to be boosting her energy. Several someones, in fact, though he doubted they were angels, precisely speaking. He focused again, as intently as he could. Unlike the ruby energy of a few minutes ago, the added energy he sensed in Julia's aura now seemed familiar to him.

He couldn't put his finger on exactly why, but it felt rather like the same strong psychic force he'd tuned into late last year and had, in the intervening months, come to regard as a powerful network of highly honorable souls. Sensing this network might not only be boosting Julia's natural allotment of psychic energy but also meant to protect her, Anatolin let himself relax.

He'd never specifically explored reincarnation, but he knew enough of the theory to surmise he and Julia had probably met before, in previous lives. Perhaps that was how they both connected to those in the psychic network. Regardless, Julia wouldn't need his warnings, or any unsolicited lessons from him on psychic self-protection. The cold, tight fist clutching his gut just below the surface of his awareness relaxed for the first time all day.

The blast of a car's horn, abrupt and insistent, drove all but the thought of Julia's imminent departure from his mind. "Your taxi, Julia, and it sounds as if the driver is in a rush."

A glance toward the parking lot confirmed his assumption. The taxi driver climbed out of his vehicle and waved his arms in the air. "Come on!" he shouted. "Hurry up!"

"He's late." Julia looked up from her watch, started quickly toward Anatolin's car to retrieve her bag.

Ignoring her protests, Anatolin carried her bag to the taxi, where the driver stowed it in the trunk then ducked inside the car and settled himself behind the wheel. Anatolin was grateful he and Julia would have a somewhat private farewell. He opened the taxi's rear door, turned, and faced her. The driver started the taxi and revved its motor.

Julia smiled wistfully. "Forget Athens. Come with me."

"I'm sorry. Truly." He shook his head, braced his arm on the open door. "My destination is actually Marseilles, then Paris. For business. Urgent business."

"Then come later."

He focused intently on the dust coating the toes of his boots.

She sighed and tugged at his jacket, forcing him to look at her. "Isn't there a single monastery in Northern Italy you'd care to investigate?"

A friend had invited him to spend some time with a Benedictine community not far from Siena in the coming weeks, but just about anything could happen in Marseilles. Best not to raise hopes—his or hers—when he had no way of knowing where his likely confrontation with Danilenko would lead. He shook his head again.

She took a step back, held out her hand. "Well, then," she said, a sweet, sad smile on her lips. "Thank you for an unforgettable tour and the pleasure of your company. I hope to see you again, some day."

He stared at her hand, blinked hard. A cheek muscle twitched. He meant to shake her hand, had every intention of behaving like the gentleman his mother raised, but before he could stop himself, he'd grabbed Julia by her elbows and pulled her close.

Her eyes widened in obvious surprise as he pressed his lips over hers, then, slowly, they closed. Her hand curled into the curve of his neck for a few moments then flattened over his lapel.

He felt her pushing slightly against his chest, but he couldn't make himself pull away. It took the taxi driver gunning his engine to end the kiss.

Anatolin moved back and met Julia's gaze. "I must apologize. Please forgive me."

Her eyes looked troubled. She reached up, brushed the pad of her finger over his cheek and along his jaw. "Don't be sorry, Andrei," she finally whispered. "I'm certainly not." She turned quickly and ducked into the taxi.

He grabbed the door before she could pull it closed. "How might someone write you in Italy?"

She broke into a beatific smile. "General Delivery, Florence," she shouted as the taxi started to roll toward the road.

"But your family name—what is it?" he asked, jogging alongside.

"Giardani! Julia Giardani, General Delivery, Florence."

He slammed the door closed. The taxi sped off, bumping along the road through the potholes. Dust billowed in its wake. Anatolin waved until dust completely obscured his view.

The museum guard was busily locking the gate. He grunted with the effort. "Closing time," he announced officiously, as if Anatolin might actually want back inside without his lovely companion.

"No problem."

The twilight breeze, balmy only moments before, now seemed parched and cold. Anatolin zipped his jacket closed, flipped up the collar against the chill, and walked to his car.

Julia was gone—headed straight for Tuscany and her legacy. Soon she'd be far from him, and from his care, his sole consolation the belief she would be protected. She would do fine without him, for the time being. But what if her guardian angels could not, in due course, keep her safe?

What then, indeed?

BOOK TWO

THE CALDEROLA

Very great witches . . . when they die

become great spirits who . . .

reappear again in human forms.

This is a rather obscure esoteric doctrine,

known in the witch families

but not much talked about.

—CHARLES GODFREY LELAND
ETRUSCAN ROMAN REMAINS IN POPULAR TRADITION, 1892

NINE

It was the light, Julia decided, that gave Tuscany its special appeal. Unlike the ethereal gold she'd experienced on the beach at Cyprus, this light seemed almost tangible. It all but hypnotized her. Especially up here in Fiesole, on the hill above Florence. Here it seemed particularly resplendent, descending like an iridescent cloak over the hilltown-studded panorama, drifting along on the mist, then receding into the violet-tinged horizon.

She hadn't imagined anywhere on earth could be this dazzling. Only three days in Tuscany and she was hopelessly in love with the place. Not just the famous old Jewel of the Renaissance, with its cathedral, its museums and bridges, but the rolling hills surrounding both Florence and its age-old rival, Siena, greener even than Northern California's in early spring.

Enjoying the beautiful surroundings and refining her Italian had kept her from dwelling on Andrei's unexpected kiss. She missed Andrei. Badly. In the mere thirty hours she'd spent with him, she'd become more attached than she'd realized. Much too attached, given that she might never see him again.

She'd also grown attached to her psychic gifts, and maybe that was what had driven them away. She'd never asked for the gifts, had not even wanted them, but now that she needed them, they seemed to have left her. It was a good thing Andrei warned her the gifts might not always respond on cue, or she might have been worried they would never come back. She'd just have to stay calm until they did. Waiting was frustrating, though. Almost as frustrating as her fruitless search for the family village.

Sighing, she leaned on the wrought-iron railing beside the steps leading down the hill. Beyond the paint-encrusted railing, the hillside dropped off steeply, providing an excellent view from the outskirts of Florence down into the Chianti, the region she'd canvassed earlier today in her small rental car.

She hadn't really expected to find the family roots in the famous wine district, but after days of searching, she'd felt she couldn't afford to skip any area within a fifty-mile radius of the spot her father indicated on his second postcard. Some treasure map that turned out to be. She couldn't imagine why he had not been more specific, who besides her he'd expected to see let alone understand or give a hoot about his cryptic message.

"X marks the spot," she whispered.

She closed her eyes and stood very still, listening, hoping to hear that bell-like laughter, another thing she'd never asked for but wished she could experience again, right here, right now. Maybe then she'd feel somewhat reassured, know she was not as alone with all this as it seemed.

Glancing around to be sure no one else was near, she closed her eyes and recalled as vividly as she could the golden Goddess she'd seen in the vision on Cyprus. She squeezed her hands into tight fists once, then again, then once more. It might be nothing at all would happen, but she had to try something.

"Come on," she whispered softly but firmly. She waited two seconds. Nothing.

She thrust her arms up high into a V over her head and opened her fists, her hands relaxed and slightly cupped. "Aphrodite, *Wanassa*—" She raised her voice. "Lady!" Chills raced up her back. "Whatever you want me to call you, I have a feeling it was you, not Dad, who got me into this mess in the first place. I need your help."

One minute. Two.

She felt a slight tingling in her palms. It grew stronger. She had an urge to turn slowly and face due west. She inched around. The tingling dulled. She opened her eyes to get her bearings, closed them again and inched around to face north. The tingling all but stopped. She gave her hands a good shake, widened her V, rotated to the east. The tingling stopped cold. She started to drop her hands, but had another idea and decided to keep them aloft. She turned and stretched her arms into an even wider V, rotated to the south, mentally reaching beyond the Chianti region to an area west of Siena she'd actually covered without success during the first day of her search.

Forcing herself to breathe calmly and slowly, she stood absolutely still. She felt something—like a feather's touch—travel down her spine and back up again. Her hands started tingling intensely. She dropped them to her sides, took several long, deep breaths, waited for her heart to stop pounding.

"*Buona sera,*" piped a childlike voice.

Startled, Julia scanned the shrubbery along the stairway and spotted a small, dark-haired girl with big brown eyes peeking through the wrought-iron bars of the fence.

"*Buona sera,*" Julia answered.

"*Mi scusi*, I frightened you."

"Not really."

"I did so," the little girl insisted soberly. She leaned back from the fence. "You were starting to fly away into the sunset until I interrupted you."

Julia chuckled, shaking her head in response. She sat down on a step level with the child, wrapped her arms around her knees.

"You can't fool me." The child's eyes grew wide, her thick eyebrows arching eloquently. "I *know* who you are." She raised her right hand and flashed the finger sign for averting the evil eye, *il malocchio.*

Julia swallowed a gasp of surprise. "My name is Julia." She offered her hand, but the child pulled away.

"*Phoo!* You are Bellaria, the *strega bellissima* who became a good fairy long, long ago. My grandmother taught me about you. She even showed me your picture in a book. The book was *very* old, but you haven't changed hardly at all."

"What an imagination you have." Julia chuckled again and shook her head in mock despair. "But at least you don't think I'm a mean witch."

"Of course not," the child said, glancing heavenward with an air of righteous exasperation. "You have always been *very* good, but I have been very bad, talking to a stranger. I must go. *Addio!*" She scampered down a narrow path and vanished into the luxuriant shrubbery that obscured the houses clinging to the hillside.

Dismayed, Julia shrugged her tense shoulders and walked back up to her vantage point. She waited several minutes, staring directly toward distant Siena and to its west, surveying the hilltowns, counting the tile roofs clustered round the larger farms, tracing the roads that meandered alongside the fields until they dipped between the hills. Searching back over her shoulder to be sure absolutely no one was anywhere in sight, she raised her hands back over her head and stretched them wide.

They started tingling all over again. She dropped them and crossed her arms over her chest.

Tomorrow. First thing in the morning, she'd check out of her hotel and head south. The family village had to be down there, somewhere.

SOUTHERN FRANCE

The shimmy of the train braking to another stop woke Anatolin from the first sleep he'd had in two days. He glanced at his watch. Two in the morning. Only hours from the Abbey Notre-Dame de Lérins, the first and most promising of the monastic communities he planned to investigate while Danilenko's slow-moving tankers made their way to Marseilles.

Sickening, the thought of the Nazi hoard returning to Europe after fifty years. According to Ilina Mikhailovna, her Task Force colleagues in Paris were not surprised when Hitler's library officially "vanished without a trace" by the time the Americans reached Berlin in 1945. Neither were they surprised when Ilina Mikhailovna was summoned abruptly to the occupied German capital and ordered to assist with the removal of certain "archival materials" to secure vaults in Moscow.

As a youth, Anatolin doubted his mother's outlandish tale about those final days of the war. As a graduate student, he'd heard rumors that seemed to confirm them. Once he'd become a parapsychologist, he'd actually seen the storage vaults, been authoritatively informed of their contents and allowed to examine them despite his mother's well-known objections to the handling of the events she called the Berlin Affair. Now, he could hardly bear to think of the harm Hitler's artifacts could bring to the world should they come into the wrong hands. Surely the case, if Danilenko had his way.

Apprehension haunted Anatolin's nights. Sleep had become his nemesis, something he fought off as long as he could with twenty-minute rounds of mantra meditation. He'd picked up the technique in the 1970s from a wandering hippie fresh from a Rishikesh ashram. He also employed the technique now because if his mind was occupied with the repetition of a mantra, he couldn't think about how he'd behaved on Cyprus. He'd relived those hours with Julia hundreds of times. He would not indulge again, would not dwell on the desire Julia awakened in him, on his near loss of resolve, that mindless kiss.

Then there was the matter of her family name. He was halfway to Athens before the significance of that broke through his enchantment. Given his intuitions on Cyprus about the karmic nature of his attraction to Julia, Anatolin would not be the least surprised to learn his mother's old Task Force colleague, Tony Giardani, was related to Julia. Indeed, Anatolin would almost bank on it. He'd long ago reached the conclusion there was no coincidence in his life anymore. To all intents and purposes, the world appeared to have diminished in size the instant he took his first conscious step onto the spiritual path.

He rubbed his eyes, tried to focus on the notepad opened on his lap. When everyone else on the train was fast asleep and he could no longer meditate, he was reduced to writing and rewriting a simulated report on Julia's extraordinary talents. It was the only way he'd been able to maintain some objective balance about what had happened on Cyprus, to keep his mind off Julia's face when she'd climbed into the cab.

Utterly beguiling. Open and exceedingly vulnerable.

THE EASTERN AEGEAN SEA

Gregor Danilenko carried a large black briefcase from the lead tanker's deck down three flights of rusty stairs to the depths of the cargo hold. Off limits to the crew, the cavernous compartment was entirely isolated, the perfect place for his last meeting with the bloated scions of the Guardsmen's top echelon.

Danilenko's footsteps rang hollow on the steel floor as he entered the humid compartment and made his way to its core. There, sitting alone in the otherwise empty hold, was the last crate of Hitler's occult collection. He walked to the crate and yanked off its sweating oilskin cover, exposing a sturdy lid sprayed with the Soviet hammer and sickle. The now defunct insignia failed to obscure the black SS swastika branded into the blond boards in early 1945. That brand not only permeated the wood, but bled through the red Soviet symbol from its seat of power in the astral realm, redoubling its shadowy mystique. The crate had long since absorbed the malevolence of its contents and thrummed with energy, at close range overriding the drone of the engines churning in the belly of the ship.

Already centered upon a huge inverted pentagram, the crate would serve as the sacrificial altar for this very special Black Mass. Danilenko removed a large square of onyx satin from the briefcase and spread it over the crate. He unwrapped a heavy pewter goblet and set it in the middle of the satin, pushed two black candles into holders and placed them on either side. Balancing his razor-sharp ritual knife on his palms, he angled it crosswise in front of the goblet, slid it from his hands, stepped back to survey the effect. The liturgical assemblage was almost complete, missing only the sacrifice, which would arrive on Danilenko's helicopter with the Guardsman from Sicily whom he despised above the rest.

Beneath the bare flood light's glare in the center of the hold, the altar looked impressive. It would look even more so by candlelight. Danilenko needed to impress, needed to demonstrate his supremacy beyond all question. He wanted no opposition when it was time to sever his Guardsmen ties, which he'd do immediately after making use of their base proclivities for this final Black Mass.

A pity he would have to share these last precious, untapped Nazi relics with even the few select Guardsmen he'd invited, but when this obligation was discharged, he'd be free of their organization forever—and once again he'd have the vitality he needed to pursue his own goal of finding and seizing the powerful Giardani heirloom, which ought to be a good deal easier with Andrei Ivanovich no longer in Julia's life.

WEST-CENTRAL ITALY

Julia adored outdoor markets. She'd made herself wait to enjoy one in Florence, until her need to find an expandable journal for recording her quest outweighed her urgency to get back out into the Tuscan countryside. She was checked out of her hotel, her car was packed and parked across the Arno, near the quickest escape route from the city. She was all set to leave, but first she'd check out the market she'd heard about the day before.

The arcade that housed the market was hardly more than an alley. Vendors were crammed into precarious stalls, jostled by customers and passersby, alike. Shoppers in their classy, if rather conservative, attire looked like Florentines, not tourists. Inching through the crowd, Julia watched the lively bartering between customers and merchants. She overcame a rickety pushcart laden with embroidered wares, spotted a table heaped with leather goods, and crossed to it for a closer look.

A hand-tooled leather journal caught her eye. It came with two thick, water-marked vellum inserts, enough pages to chronicle the whole history of Italy. Apparently, more inserts were available if she needed them later. She patted the journal. She'd keep amassing information in notebooks, but her thoughts about the information would go here. Her bartering successful, she slipped her purchase into her canvas bag and started out of the arcade.

Directly in her path stood a bookseller's cubicle. Inside sat a man who looked so much like her father he could have been his twin. She stopped in the center of the passageway, the voices of hawkers instantly dimming to a buzz, the background bustle of the city eclipsed by the pounding of her heartbeat. The bookseller had the same wispy silver curls streaked with lingering bronze, the same deep-set green eyes as her father. So often she'd watched her father sit like the Florentine sat now, browsing through some dusty old tome. She thought her heart would break if the bookseller picked up the worn pipe he'd apparently forgotten atop a precarious stack of large art books.

The man noticed her staring at him. He smiled widely.

Julia relaxed. Similarity to her father eroded with the smile, showing teeth that had never enjoyed the benefits of American dentistry.

The bookseller beckoned her to his stall.

She walked over and ran her fingers lightly across a few gilded bindings. "You have a nice selection, here," she said.

"Take your pick. I'll give you an excellent price."

"Not today, thanks. I'm finished shopping." She patted her bag.

"*Sì*, Signorina," he said, nodding his head. "But I have something special. Not for the tourists. I know you'll love it."

He reached under the table and pulled out a small, ornate leather pouch. Opening the pouch, he slid out a stack of beautifully illustrated cards and fanned them over the surface of his table.

"A tarot deck!"

"Very old. Very rare. Absolutely made for you."

Strange, her father had collected tarot decks, but she'd barely held one before. This man assumed she'd be interested in buying those cards. She wouldn't even know how to use them.

They were beautiful, though. "How much?"

He named a figure so reasonable Julia couldn't resist. Without hesitating, she pulled out a handful of lire, counted out the man's price, and thanked him.

"*Prego,* you're welcome, Signorina." He reached for her bag and tucked the pouch inside. "But there's something else, also very old, from the same person who sold me your cards."

"No, really, I can't buy anything else today."

Acting as if he hadn't heard her, he reached under his table again and pulled out an antique shawl. He held it up and stretched it wide. His smile radiated quiet pride. The shawl's colors were muted, rosy, its floral pattern subdued yet stunning. Silk fringe shimmered in earthy shades of copper, gold and verdigris.

Julia fingered the fringe. The shawl was probably way beyond her budget, not at all her style, but she was absolutely covetous, an entirely unfamiliar sentiment. "Sorry," she said. "Maybe some other time."

"But it's yours, you purchased it with the deck!"

"What?" Julia could hardly believe what he'd said.

He reached over the table, whipped the shawl around her shoulders, and tied two of its corners into a graceful loop just below her neckline. "*Bellissima,* Signorina!" He threw his hands in the air, waved them with a passionate flourish. "Elegant! Take it! It's yours! Like the deck, it was positively made for you! Besides, the *strega* who sold me both items insisted they be sold together."

Strega again. Interesting.

A very old woman hovered near the stall, obviously listening closely to the transaction. Julia had been puzzled by the bookseller's blatant attempt to ignore the woman, then to shoo her away. Now the woman seemed to shrink back from Julia's gaze. She held one hand up in front of her face and signed *il malocchio* with her fingers.

Julia flinched. Twice in twenty-four hours. Something was going on here, but she couldn't figure it out right now. It was past time to head for her car. She set her shoulders and walked toward the arcade's exit, where she turned back for a last glimpse of the bookseller.

The man smiled and blew her a kiss. A few steps behind him, the old woman scowled nastily. Her stare made Julia's stomach lurch.

TEN

Crossing the Ponte Vecchio, a sudden chorus of church bells pealing through the air brought Julia to a standstill mid-span. Her father loved those bells, had reminisced about them often. A surge of grief too strong to choke back almost bowled her over. She spotted an open stretch of low wall beneath the arches adorning the bridge and hurried toward it. Relieved to be out of the crowd rushing by, she leaned her elbows on the wall and gazed down at the river's muddy depths. Her eyes burned with unshed tears. Relaxing her fists, she tucked her hands under the shawl.

The grief she'd experienced with the loss of her mother had been so overwhelming it had devastated Julia's adolescence. Since her father's death, she'd tried to keep her grief within bounds, had promised herself she'd enjoy this trip for his sake as much as for hers.

Maybe she should let herself mourn him now, not push away her strong sense of missing him. It was perfectly natural to keep thinking how much he would love being here, natural to be able to envision him readily, especially here. The bookseller's resemblance to him only confirmed how deep the Giardani roots must be, reminded her to slow down and relish each second of her Tuscan sojourn, as her father surely would have, had he been with her.

She stared out over the Arno, her gaze skimming the Renaissance spires and domes of the city's skyline. Her father had known her as only a parent could. He'd probably worried she'd behave exactly as she had—rashly, in true Julia fashion, needing to make something happen before she had all the facts. Well, not anymore. Definitely not anymore.

She gazed down into the river's swirling, yellow tide, watched it course under the ancient bridge. It was time to slow down. Let subtler layers of her consciousness guide her, as she had on Cyprus, only without her new Russian friend's help. Time to dig in here and discover what her father had meant when he spoke of her new life. As soon as she got out of Florence, she would slow down. It wouldn't be easy, but she'd do it.

Toward the far side of the Ponte Vecchio, she spied the old woman from the arcade. The woman cowered against the ornate façade of a jewelry shop, trying to hide from Julia, it seemed, behind a large marble planter packed with pansies and ferns and bright blue lobelia. The old woman seemed more than unfriendly. She seemed hostile, the glint of hatred hardening her eyes.

Wrapping her new shawl more tightly around her shoulders and calling up a smile, Julia walked over to the woman and nodded politely. "*Buon giorno.*"

"What do you want here?" the old woman croaked, her arthritic fingers signing *il malocchio* again, even more frantically, as if to keep every demon in Europe at bay.

Julia ignored the crippled old hands, the gesture that conveyed such aversion. She stepped closer, smiled again. "I'm here because my family lived here a long time ago."

"Yes." The woman shuddered, her curved shoulders twitching as she slumped down against the wall. She eyed Julia up and down. "So I see."

A chill raced up Julia's neck. "What do you see? Tell me, please." Julia moved closer, until she stood looking down on the woman's frightened face. Reaching out, she tried to steady the old woman, who seemed to be feeling faint.

"*Dio mio*, don't touch me!" The woman wobbled dangerously, swatted Julia away. "Get away!" she hissed. "You bring danger upon us and upon yourself. You must leave Tuscany now. Today!"

A crowd had gathered behind Julia's back. She half expected someone to assume she was molesting the woman and shout for the police, but the crowd stayed silent. They were either too shocked or too amused to move, but since no one would make eye contact with her, she couldn't tell which.

"Don't be ridiculous, Signora," Julia said in her most comforting, most conciliatory voice.

The old woman was far from comforted. Her eyes had a wild, threatened look. She raised her hands and waved them defensively. "Be gone from here, *strega!*"

A murmur swelled through the crowd. Julia started to step back, but the woman was much too upset. Julia worried about her.

"Please, Signora, you must let me help you." She bent down and extended her arm. "Take my arm, so you don't fall."

The old woman leaned away, lost her balance entirely. She tipped to one side and collapsed on the pavement, cradling her elbow in her palm.

A man pushed through the crowd. "What's her problem?"

"No problem we can't handle." Julia smiled at the man, held up her hand and signaled she didn't need help. "She's just a little confused."

A middle-aged jeweler leaned out the door of the nearest shop. "Pay no attention to that superstitious old hag, run away from her family again, driving half the town to distraction."

The crowd seemed to lose interest. People moved on about their business. Julia squatted down at the old woman's side, still worried, wishing she knew how to help. Following a hunch, she smiled steadily to ease the woman's almost palpable fear. She took hold of the injured elbow and visualized a current of healing calm passing through her hands, as she'd taken to doing with the children at the shelter. "There now. You mustn't be afraid, you'll be just fine."

"I'm sorry." The woman's trembling ceased. Obviously ashamed, she searched Julia's face. "Please forgive me."

Julia shook her head. "Shush . . ." she soothed, her fingers probing the woman's elbow, then above and below it. The arm would be fine. She was sure of it. "There's nothing broken," she said, helping the woman to her feet, "and no need to apologize. You must have mistaken me for someone else."

"I made no mistake, but you will if you stay here. There is nothing left in Tuscany for you." The woman was bluffing, seemed still quite distraught.

Julia cocked her head to one side and made herself keep smiling. "I wish you'd tell me how seeing me would make anyone afraid."

The woman seemed to vacillate, then suddenly turned fearful again. "I can tell you nothing. Nothing at all." She pulled her arm from Julia's grasp and marched back toward the market.

"Right," Julia muttered to herself. Terrific, to be called a witch yet again, in the most derogatory tone possible. Just what she needed. She brushed back her hair with both hands.

The old woman was either demented or she'd deliberately lied. There *was* something for Julia in Tuscany. Close, within fifty kilometers of Siena, was a village just seething with the ghosts of countless Giardani generations.

∞

Danilenko propped up the most recent Florence edition of *La Nazione* on the caffè bar wall. He had folded it precisely, accordion-style for easier reading in cramped quarters. It would be a challenge to block out the noise of some fifty raucous Italians sipping espressos and cappuccinos, inhaling the local gossip right along with their breakfasts.

He scanned the headlines, flipped over the newspaper, and scanned some more. Though he read almost no Italian, he was sure he'd recognize the story he expected to see. No luck yet, though surely the story would run soon enough. Unofficial word was likely already circulating through Tuscany but he would be the last to hear it. He had to head back immediately to Marseilles, would have to wait until his agent here, the man he'd hired two hours ago, got wind of it and called him.

Italian customs officers had searched his bags in their usual half-assed fashion when he passed through the VIP lounge at Malpensa Airport late last night. Danilenko chuckled. The Italian press would have a field day with the little bundle fresh from hell he'd floated down the Arno a few hours before dawn. Not every day were the bloody vestiges of a Black Mass unleashed on an unsuspecting public, a public that also happened to be one of the most superstitious on the entire globe. No doubt the Church would add to the brew, whip superstitions into a witch-hunting frenzy. Danilenko was counting on it, had made a point of stressing that fact in his transaction with his new assistant.

Anti-witch sentiment would hinder the Giardani Heiress. A hostile environment would keep her from unearthing her legacy before Danilenko could make adequate headway in his own hunt for the heirloom. He folded the newspaper into a neat square, gulped the last pale sip of his cappuccino, and started for the bar's exit.

Near the door, a stunning raven-haired Florentine sent him a come-hither smile that almost brought him to his knees. He lifted his chest, returned the woman's gaze. The woman wore skin-tight black leggings and stiletto heels but it was the genuine lynx jacket that spoke loudest to him of her true nature. She was no older than forty, probably thirty-five. Less than half his age, but thanks to the Nazi artifacts, he could once again hold his own in a room full of much younger studs. He sauntered toward her.

"Buon giorno," she said over her shoulder as she swiveled her sleek flank sideways to make room for him at the bar.

He fitted himself into the tight space. She stared unsmiling into his eyes, rubbed her sharp hip up against him, made him all too aware it had been a damn long time since he'd had a prime cut of perfectly aged Italian tail. His mouth watered. His groin ached. The woman would prove the ideal antidote to Tony's bewitching daughter.

∞

Julia turned off the *autostrada* at Poggibonsi, circled out toward San Gimignano and west to Volterra before looping back and following the side roads to search the hills and valleys west of Siena. Her route took her through some of the most captivating scenery she'd ever seen, past dozens of farmhouses and villas, each surrounded by patterns of green and umber, like tapestries woven in the dark rich earth.

Old stones awash in late morning light, silver olive groves, and budding vineyards beckoned her to stop and enjoy them, but she traveled on. She'd taped her father's postcard to the dashboard for inspiration. The darn thing wasn't good for much else. Even its boldly printed legend seemed to be misleading. Nowhere in the dozen roadmaps and guidebooks piled on the seat beside her had she found a single mention of a district called La Calderola.

Still, she refused to give in to discouragement. There was so much beauty around her, she had to drink it all in. Since her first day in Tuscany, she'd wondered how her grandparents were able to leave. Her grandmother had spoken fondly of her life here, but she'd refused to come back, even for a visit. As far as Julia knew, no one had dared ask why. Anna Giardani's reasons for leaving Italy remained a secret she took to her grave.

Anna was an enigma to Julia. Probably always would be. When Anna first came to live with the family, she'd kept Julia at bay. Only later, close to the end of her life, did Anna start to reach out, share secrets, tell Julia Italian fables and wonderful stories. About her childhood in Italy. About her own mother, Giuliana Giardani, after whom Julia had been named. Those stories were all now committed to writing in the Giardani notebooks, along with every family anecdote Julia could recall. It wasn't much of a memorial to Anna, but it was the most she could do.

Somewhere back a few turns, the terrain had changed dramatically. A gloomy cloud darkened the sun, made the view seem quite stark. Volterra loomed on the horizon, an austere walled town set in an ominous vale of cliffs and rocky slopes.

She circled Volterra and headed south, through the barren fringes of the Colline Metallifere, or Metal Hills, toward gentler country again. The vista here was far from amicable, though. The Tuscans were once a pugnacious bunch, and reminders of their militaristic glory crested almost every peak.

To her left, the fortress walls and towers of San Gimignano glistened against the horizon. Visible from higher elevations along her route were other hilltowns, their bastions and parapets fully described in the guidebooks, clearly designated on the maps. Unlikely her family village was one of these, or she'd have learned something by now.

She glanced at the postcard and wondered again about the Etruscan tomb beside the penned X. She'd tried that line of investigation but discovered that while a few lesser-known Etruscan sites were sprinkled around the countryside, most, like the castles and churches, were meticulously noted. She'd already scoured around every one of them, introducing herself, asking if anyone might remember her family. Nothing had come of her efforts.

She turned at a narrow, unmarked road she'd wandered onto her first day here. There were no noteworthy sites on the road, that much she remembered, but it was a lovely stretch, the kind she especially loved to drive. The farms were larger here, the houses mostly smaller. There were tracts of relatively undeveloped forest and a scattering of empty fields rampant with early wildflowers and unruly weeds.

Unusual for Tuscany. Julia had decided it was the most civilized, most manicured area she'd ever seen. She cruised past another unmarked road she hadn't noticed before. The road intersected a larger one on the right and curved up the hill toward the northeast.

Her heart started to race. Half afraid to hope again, she pulled over and slipped the car into reverse. Both roads were empty. She made it through the intersection easily, slowed to a stop. Yanking on the hand brake, she gripped the steering wheel, told herself to calm down, but she couldn't ignore the knot in her stomach, the tingle of anticipation chasing up her spine.

She got out for a better look. The fresh air smelled divine—green and earthy and spicy sweet, all at once. A derelict field edged the intersection. A butter-colored stone wall lay tumbled to the ground, the abutting shed draped with a chartreuse vine at the peak of its spring growth. Green grass, cool and damp, tickled Julia's calves as she crossed the field and came up to the vine, a passion flower, if she wasn't mistaken.

A dusty pickup truck, the first vehicle she'd seen in the last half hour, puttered around the corner. It slowed to a crawl as it passed, the driver leaning far to the right, obviously checking Julia out.

Italian men. Incorrigible. She chuckled but restrained herself from waving. The man barreled up the hill, his truck sputtering then roaring, emitting a disgusting cloud of exhaust.

A glint of rusted metal caught the light through the vine on the far side of the wall. It seemed the vine had clambered up an old signpost, obscuring a cracked and peeling village marker at its top. Julia stroked a vibrant tendril, enjoying the feel of the plant sliding through her fingers. When she let go, it tumbled off the sign.

That was odd. If the vine had actually grown over the sign, it would have wrapped its tendrils everywhere it could, would be clinging like mad. Julia touched another limb to be sure, and that one, too, slid right off the sign, as if someone had draped it there recently.

Ridiculous, she decided. The sign, once bright-green letters on white, was too faded to read. Why would anyone need to hide it?

She could make out only a few letters of a very long name—an M, an O, and an N in succession, an A much farther along. Aside from its decrepit condition, the sign looked identical to all the other village markers she'd seen in the region. This had to be a village. Mount something, probably, but she'd have to talk with someone who lived up there to find out the rest.

The uphill grade was steeper than it appeared from below. Julia's rented compact strained every foot of the way. She shifted to second gear, then only moments later all the way to first. The road divided into two lanes. She followed the one that veered right. Columns of cypress and poplar rose on either side of the lane. Her heart thumped in rhythm with the alternating sunlight and shade as she drove between them.

She passed a shuttered house. The road leveled off, and she passed two more. Rounding a sharp bend, she came upon a small village clinging to the north face of the mountain. The place had retained a primitive beauty that nearly took Julia's breath away. She snaked upward on its narrow main street.

It was only one-thirty in the afternoon, yet the village seemed deserted. Laundry hung from balconies, evidence women had been hard at work for hours, but there wasn't a single woman in sight. The children were probably off at school, the men to their factories and fields, but at least some of the women should be out in the streets. And the old folks, where could they be?

She slowed down, observing more carefully. Furtive movements behind lace curtains sent twinges of alarm through the knot in her stomach. To her left, a shutter fluttered. Across the street, another angled open, but not so far that anything—or anyone—could be seen behind it.

Turning into the small square, Julia parked beside the fountain at its center, her curiosity warring with an irrational feeling of being unwelcome. She peered out the window, was struck by how unimposing the village was. It didn't even crown the hill. Rather, it perched on a deep ledge about three-fourths of the way up. Behind and above it was dense, green forest. Not only was there no typical hilltown castle here, there seemed to be no duomo, either. Only a small church, relatively modern by Tuscan standards, that huddled on the far side of the square, well off the main street.

A long, terraced loggia, or porch, bordered three sides of the square. Julia sniffed the aroma of newly baked pastries, rosemary-seasoned foccacia and freshly brewed espresso, but as she climbed the loggia's steps, she was surprised to see a closed sign on the bakery door.

She moved closer, cupped her hands on the cool windowpane, peered inside. The tables that probably spilled out onto the loggia when the shop was open had been carelessly crammed together, chairs flung upside down on their small round tops. Near the rear door, one chair still wobbled precariously, as if someone had knocked against it only a moment before.

The loggia should be bustling now, not empty as a graveyard. Julia backed up, noticed the other shops, all five of them, also bore closed signs in their doors and windows, one still whooshing from side to side. Crossing her arms, she raised her clenched fist, pressed it to her lips.

Never had she felt like such an intruder. Clearly, that was precisely how she was meant to feel. It was tempting to just take the obvious hints and head out of town. Not like her, but there was no real pressing need to push herself on the place just yet either. She forced back her disappointment and scanned the village more carefully. Her gaze came to rest on the rear end of a very dusty pickup truck. She had entirely misread its driver's interest in her. He'd obviously warned the village she was on her way up. Amazing. More amazing still, the whole town seemed to have conspired to make her feel shut out.

She walked back to her car and leaned her elbows on its roof. Despite the lack of welcome, there was definitely something special about this place, a sense of familiarity.

Strange. She didn't really want to leave, even if she was unwelcome here. She raised her head and stood up straight.

"I'll be back." She meant to shout, but the words came out choked, hardly more than a whisper.

∞

Just beyond the village, the road dropped down sharply. Julia hit the brakes hard and curved into a hairpin turn. Two hairpins later, the descent tapered off. Past the cypresses and poplars, the lane converged again with the road she'd driven up.

A densely wooded tract stretched along the right side of the road. Looking upward, intent on finding the village, she hadn't noticed it earlier. Half a mile farther down, a much smaller lane headed south over a mossy cobblestone bridge almost hidden it was so overgrown with rose brambles and rampaging vines.

She parked, carried her picnic basket to a grassy spot on the bank of the stream, and sank down, but she didn't feel much like eating. Wrapping her arms around her raised knees, she closed her eyes. Birdsong wafted through the air. Some small beast in the woods across the stream made soft rooting sounds as it moved through the thickets. She refused to let herself give in to a growing sense of rejection. It was too pretty here.

She wished she felt a whole lot better than she did. Her nerves were jangled. Disappointment—no, anger—made her stomach churn, but she wouldn't give up on that village. She'd keep going back until someone gave in and talked to her. They couldn't close up every time she came. Eventually they would learn she was a nice person, no threat to anyone. Perseverance was all it would take.

Something cold and wet touched the back of her neck. She held her breath, turned quickly around. A small white goat leaped away from her, scampered forward again, tossed its head from side to side. Julia was glad she hadn't frightened the little guy away. At least there was one sentient being here who didn't reject her on sight.

She held out her hand. "Come on over here, Cutie."

The goat cocked its head to one side, its eyes shining as if it understood her. Reaching blindly into her basket, Julia grabbed a small apple. She held it out, and the goat inched toward her.

"Good baby," she coaxed, keeping her voice soft but firm. A moment later, the goat snatched the apple off her palm and stood beside her, happily nuzzling her shoulder as he crunched the fruit to bits.

Out of the corner of her eye, Julia caught a patch of red plaid. Near the corner of the bridge, beside its stone culvert, she saw something move again. A child, most likely.

She stood and waved an arm over her head. "Hello!"

A boy, no older than seven or eight, judging from the size of his coveralled body, peeked out from behind the culvert. Muttering to himself, he climbed the bank. He wore the most mischievous expression Julia had ever seen, and she'd seen more than her share.

She smiled and waved again. "Is this your goat?"

The child scowled. "He's a rotten goat. Rotten, rotten, rotten! I told him not to bother you, but he wouldn't obey me."

Julia curbed her smile, sat back down. "What makes you think he's bothering me?" She scratched the goat between its ears, let it nudge her again. "I was feeling a little blue, wishing I had some company."

The boy squinted in the direction of the village. "I saw what they did."

She was embarrassed by a sudden flush. "Pretty rude, don't you think?"

He looped his thumbs through the straps of his coveralls, glared down at his boots and kicked at a clump of grass. "I'm not surprised. They're mean to me, too." He scowled then quickly smiled again. "I hate them."

Julia nodded. "Everyone in the whole village?"

"Well, that depends." Having vented his anger, he seemed to relax a bit. "Not my great-grandmother."

"No, of course not." Julia patted the grass. "Wanna share my picnic?"

"Depends."

"On what?"

"I'm not supposed to talk to you. You have to promise you won't tell."

"That's easy." Julia laughed. "Nobody up there will talk to me, so who can I tell?" She pulled out her sandwich, tore it in half, and balanced it on a napkin on her knee. "What's your name?"

"Vario Andrade." The boy came over and plopped down, cross-legged, facing her. "My parents sent me here from Sicily six months ago to take care of my great-grandmother while my great-grandfather was dying, and now I'm staying forever, I guess, 'cause old women really shouldn't live all alone."

"Right." Julia held out half of her sandwich, which he accepted with a grunt, soon talking again as fast as he could.

"I should be in school today but the rotten old teacher kicked me out because of that goat! He follows me every place and that's a bother, but I have to keep him because I'm growing him up for someone special—so I can't help it if he misbehaves, I have to take good care of him—you see, he's a magic goat!"

"I can tell," Julia said quickly, grateful to get a word in edgewise. She kept her face solemn. "And I can tell you've had a rough time lately. I'll bet taking care of your great-grandmother isn't easy."

Vario wolfed down three large bites of the sandwich then nodded and talked with his mouth still full. "Neither is taking care of this naughty goat, I tell you!" He obviously meant to sound angry, but his eyes gleamed.

"I can imagine."

"You know what else?" he asked breathlessly. "They told me you were wicked, but I didn't believe them—I never do."

"Sometimes grown-ups say very silly things. What's the name of your village?"

"The grown-ups around here say silly things *all* the time. They act dumb about lots of stuff. My great-grandmother's not, though."

"No, I'm sure she's not." Julia smiled and handed the boy a napkin then offered him the other apple she'd brought along. He'd avoided answering her question. She wondered why. "Has she always lived here?"

"Pretty much forever, she says, but even though she swears she's as old as the hills, she still works. She's the postmistress."

"Has she ever talked about a family named Giardani, who may have lived in the village a long time ago?"

"She talks about everyone all the time." The boy steeled his gaze toward the village. "I can promise you one thing for sure, though, nobody named Giardani ever lived in that boring place!"

Julia followed his gaze. "You still haven't told me what it's called."

"I know."

"Why not?"

"I'm not supposed to," Vario said, "but I'm gonna. They can punish me all they want, but I like you—and I sure as the devil don't like them!" He stood, faced the village. "That ugly old village has a prettier name than it deserves."

Julia held her breath.

He cupped his hands around his mouth and puffed up his chest, called out in a sing-song voice. "It is called *Mon-te-cip-ri-ana!*"

"Montecipriana," Julia whispered.

Mount of the Cyprian—Aphrodite's Mountain—the very place Julia had wanted so desperately to find. She swallowed hard. She was sure this was the family village, but why on earth were its people so set against her?

ELEVEN

By four-thirty that afternoon Julia was on a path that curved along the side of the hill above Casa Sergio, an old farm apparently converted to an inn about ten years ago. Her new buddy, Vario, had promised she'd like the rustic inn and the Sergi women whose family had owned it for centuries.

The child was a genius. Julia had enjoyed Florence, but this was the Tuscany she'd been longing for. Apparently, the Casa was the largest of several inns in the region, which Vario confirmed was indeed the Calderola. She'd taken the Casa's smallest room, a split-level space heated by an ample fireplace, before which she'd work on the notebooks each morning and evening, get her most recent experiences recorded and sorted out.

The path above the garden terraces climbed gradually, skirting the woods, which rang with the songs of twilight's feathered sopranos. The sun was still warm, and the grass beneath her feet sent up a delicate perfume. She walked past the inn's kitchen garden. Emerald scallions spiked up between rows of carrot tops and beet greens. Cabbages of all types, from pale-green giants to tiny wine-colored radicchio, squatted beside lettuces of several varieties. Farther along the path, she sat down on a wooden bench at the forest's edge and relaxed.

The earth smelled sweet and musty. It was sunny here, but filmy wisps of lavender fog lay in the deeper gorges of the hills, and a velvet mist hung over much of the distant landscape. She stretched her legs, crossed her ankles, and draped her arms on the back of the bench. Lifting her face to catch the filtered rays of sunlight, she looked out through half-lowered lids. Soon dew was falling, coalescing all around her, on blades of grass and waxy leaves. It was easy to imagine fairies with gossamer wings floating in the mist that glossed the air.

Fairy tales. Anna Giardani had been full of them.

She never told Julia tales she believed had been contrived to frighten people into submission to the rules of the patriarchy or the Church. There were lots of those told in Italy, she'd said, but they would never be told around a Giardani hearth.

Instead she told beautiful stories of love and kindness, of bravery derived from inner strength. Like the fable the little girl in Fiesole had mentioned, about the fairy Bellaria, who outwitted a wicked king by answering the hundred riddles he put to her, thus saving her land from his domination. Or like the tale of Cinderella, who in spite of her life of misery found true and lasting love through the mediation of a kind fairy godmother.

True and lasting love.

Julia chuckled to herself, remembering Andrei and the jolt of pleasure she'd felt when she first looked into his startlingly blue eyes. The sensation had intensified during their trip to the Akamas peninsula, made even stronger by the feeling she'd known him before, as if he were some long-lost love returned after lifetimes of separation. It had taken days for the feeling to fade, and it still wasn't entirely gone.

She couldn't shake the hope she'd see Andrei again, though in light of his intentions to enter a monastery, her attraction to him made her feel like some kind of nutcase. She stood up and hugged her new shawl around her shoulders, let her gaze wander.

These last few weeks, it seemed she was always standing on hillsides, gazing into the distance. Her father would insist that was symbolic of something. Her changing perspective, most likely. He wouldn't be wrong. From Berkeley, her Tuscan roots had seemed a world away, finding them a duty she owed her father. From Cyprus, they had still seemed fairly distant, but she had definitely become engaged by then. From where she stood now, Tuscany felt irresistible. She wanted to wrap the place around her and stay a very long time.

Her gaze came to rest on Montecipriana. She ought to be standing there right now, not miles away.

Mount of the Cyprian.

Not surprising the mountain had no medieval castle, no fortress at its crown. The rocky outcrop above the dense forest was shaped a lot like Petra Tou Romiou, which made it seem all the more emblematic of the Goddess Julia believed it was named for.

Below the forest, Julia made out the houses of the village and the green fields that fanned down the slopes beneath it. She needed to get back there. Get under people's skins. Convince them they could trust her and let her in on whatever secrets they were so intent on guarding. She stared until her vision blurred, wishing she could see more of the village, see into the very soul of the place.

Closing her eyes, she focused between her eyebrows and watched the patterns that formed in her inner vision—distinct yet, like the village, very far away. A star. A figure eight, upright then on its side. A burst of golden light that slowly transformed into the lovely laughing Goddess.

"I need you to help me learn what I must." Julia wasn't laughing, wasn't even smiling. "How can I serve you if you won't show me how?"

AVENUE KLÉBER, PARIS

Madame Racine suddenly felt truly weary. Last night's nonstop meeting in Versailles was grueling. She'd barely muddled through it. All the hidden agendas, political shenanigans. Exhausting, but as necessary as anything she'd ever done.

Helping Julia Giardani was even more necessary. Fortunately, the young woman was right on track, as Tony would have said at this juncture. Racine's contact in Tuscany was optimistic, despite Danilenko's gruesome plot to thwart Julia's progress.

Times like this made Racine glad she'd stayed around, kept her broomstick in the cauldron, so to speak. She'd always despaired for those members of her group who fled from the great work in the wake of the last World War. They refused to believe in what had been foretold, had refused to wait for the young ones to come, Julia and Andrei and all the rest. Already exhausted by the long years of need-less carnage, many colleagues looked into the future and saw only decades of shallow, grasping materialism, years of growing nuclear threat, incessant rape of the planet's resources. One by one, most turned their sainted backs on this dreary century and left for far-off ashrams hidden in the clouds, still connected with the work, but sadly disengaged.

She would never regret staying on here. No, indeed. Neither, she suspected, would her other earthbound Alliance members. They enjoyed working behind the scenes, planting the necessary seeds, guiding those they could reach toward the brighter tomorrow they were certain would come.

Now Racine's duties here were nearly finished. Only one thing was left to accomplish before she could relinquish her obscenely long life, and she had to accomplish it soon. Risking the cohesion of her beloved inner circle would be dangerous, but a positive outcome would be worth any sacrifice.

All the pieces were falling into place. The Alliance was poised and ready to forge ahead with their plan for the new millennium. If Racine could somehow help preserve the Giuliana legacy for future generations, she'd be better than halfway home.

WEST-CENTRAL ITALY

Pale sunshine broke through the mist curling outside Julia's window. Gradually, it lit the loft in which she'd slept. From the sitting area below came the crackle and hiss of a burnt log collapsing in the fire a maid must have started while Julia slept. It would be warm and snug down there.

She heard a polite knock at her door, probably someone delivering the caffè latte the innkeeper, Maria Sergi, had promised the night before.

"Come in!"

The door opened then closed. Scooting to the edge of the tall bed, Julia slid down, landed in her slippers, and reached for her cotton robe, which felt cool where it met her bare skin. She wrapped it about her and started down the short flight of stairs. "Good morning!"

"Good morning, Signorina!" a young maid answered, setting Julia's breakfast tray on the small table beside the fire. She gave Julia a quick glance. "*Scusi*, Signorina, but you need something warmer for the mornings here in the Calderola. Are you not cold?"

"Not too," Julia answered. The maid's gaze reached Julia's face, seemed to freeze, almost as if from fear. Julia continued down the steps and extended her hand. "My name is Julia. What's yours?"

The maid pulled away quickly. "I am Lucia," she said, her voice barely above a whisper, her gaze dropping to the items on the table. It was obviously something of a struggle to compose herself. She took two steps toward the door, reached for the knob. "*Scusi,* I must go now."

"Not so fast."

Lucia faced back into the room. "Please, Signorina." The dread in her eyes made Julia's stomach turn.

"I just wish someone would tell me what's going on here, what people are so afraid of! Yesterday in Montecipriana—"

Lucia drew her breath in sharply. "You have been to that place?" She dropped her hand to her side, glanced out the window, sighed. "They don't like strangers over there. I'm sorry if they insulted you."

"Don't be sorry, just tell me why they'd do that."

Lucia shrugged. She offered a feeble smile. "The old folks say that village was settled by people from the East and they've always been peculiar."

"Xenophobic, you mean?"

"*Non importa,* what word you use to describe them."

"Not important," Julia said, surprised she'd slipped into English, that her voice sounded so skeptical—so resentful.

Lucia looked embarrassed and became a bit rattled. "They aren't important. They know nothing important."

Julia's eyes started to burn. She gulped hard, ran her hands through her hair, crossed her arms and hugged them to her. "At least you seem to have some idea of what's important and what's not. That's a lot more than I've been able to figure out."

Lucia paled. "I can't help you."

"Then who can?" Julia felt like shaking Lucia, calmed herself. "There must be someone here who is willing to help me. At least one person who is able to explain what's going on."

Lucia hesitated, seemed to ponder Julia's suggestion. "In time, this may be possible."

"How much time?" Julia's mind raced ahead.

Lucia suddenly looked even more miserable. "I'm sorry. I don't know what I was thinking. I was mistaken to say anything."

Julia stepped forward. "Lucia—"

"*Scusi*, Signorina Julia, I really must go." Lucia scurried out the door before Julia could stop her.

Julia paced over to the desk tucked into the alcove between the stairs and the doors leading to her balcony. Her father's postcards glared up at her, accusingly, from the desk's polished surface. She'd pushed too hard. The maid had been ready to help her. At least on the verge. She walked back to Lucia's arrangement, picked up the caffè latte. Cradling the cup in both palms, she turned her attention to the spot between her eyebrows.

Focusing intently, she waited.

Impressions came slowly but, thank heaven, they came. Something else, not just Julia's impatience, had stopped Lucia from talking, but Julia could not make out what it might be.

SOUTHERN FRANCE

For all its sea-washed beauty, the monastery at Lérins would never suit Anatolin. It wasn't the community's strict Benedictine rule that didn't work for him. Nor was it the group's devotional focus. Anatolin admired their philosophical and theological work. He could think of no more worthy a life than one emphasizing silent prayer in community, no finer example than that of St. John—ever faithful and persevering under the demands of Divine love. Anatolin yearned for the same goal as these monks, that deepening of the bond with the Blessed Mother, but he'd pursue that end no matter where he eventually found himself drawn.

No, it was none of these aspects that deterred him from joining the small group at Lérins. Perhaps it was the absence of hard physical work that made him shy away. The lack of a place to dig, to nurture the soil, to create new life. The earth energies on the small island were not exceptional, either. For all the prayers sent heavenward here, Anatolin would have expected more evidence of heightened electromagnetic activity.

But perhaps the problem was not a dearth of soil or energy at all. Perhaps the problem was with him, with his own lack of receptivity. He didn't know what was happening to him lately. He knew only that in his dreams, the Blessed Mother now wore Julia's face, smiled at him through Julia's smile, laughed Julia's sweet laugh in his mind as he awakened each morning and drifted off to sleep each night.

It was definitely time to push on, to the Abbey Notre-Dame de Senanque, a few kilometers beyond the village of Gordes. After that, Marseilles and Danilenko's odious cargo, and then to Paris to meet the woman his mother had fondly, and apparently very much tongue-in-cheek, dubbed the "Charlatan."

∞

Ilina Mikhailovna was generous when she named Racine the "Charlatan." Danilenko had tagged her the "Hag of Paris," would go to his grave thinking of her as such. He hadn't set foot in Racine's city since the war and never would again. Marseilles was as close as he got. He'd spent recent days here firming up the pending sales of the Nazi goods. The ships would arrive very soon. He prized the added powers he'd gleaned from Hitler's stash but hated that he needed them.

There was a time Danilenko wouldn't have needed either extra power or crude devices to hone in on anyone's energy field. There was a time when he could be at one with any living soul, effortlessly.

He was only six when he had his first conscious experience of the hidden oneness of nature. He and his mother spent that year at their dacha a few kilometers west of Yalta. His father, a brilliant intellectual unable to cope with a small child's commotion, had abandoned them the winter before and returned to Moscow.

It was a melancholy time tempered only by his mother's poignant tenderness. In those years between the world wars, the Crimea was much more beautiful than it is today. Less developed. Far less polluted. When the weather was good, it filled with crowds. One afternoon stood out from the rest. Sometime during the long velvet season. September? No, October, when weekend refugees from the harsh realities of postrevolution subsistence flocked to the shore for a last respite before another seemingly endless and hungry winter set in.

Danilenko had loved to watch the large families clustered around their picnic baskets on the beach. Bandannaed babushkas cradled babies and tended youngsters playing in the sand. Teenagers skimmed pebbles on the waves or walked, hands thrust in pockets, over densely turfed paths above the shore. Soldiers strolled, clearly sweltering in their dark woolen uniforms.

A café at the edge of the beach had served tea from an ancient samovar, the smell of the brew always on the breeze, the Gypsy seated on the stairs forever strumming folk tunes on a balalaika. All those years ago, yet Danilenko could almost feel the warmth of the air as it came softly off the turquoise waters of the Black Sea, almost hear the laughter and the music, almost smell the sharp scent rising from the samovar.

Was it the plaintive strains of the balalaika that inspired the vision he remembered now, or had it simply been evoked by the day's indolent mood? He couldn't be sure. He recalled only that he'd slipped into a surprisingly deep trance, considering he kept his eyes open throughout.

The beach had teemed with currents of white-gold light, connecting one person to the next, pulsing and flaring through the crowd, generating multicolored ribbons of vital energy. Patterns formed, resembled kaleidoscope shapes magnified to an immense scale. His heart had raced erratically in his chest, and he'd felt the most baffling sensations. Intense happiness. Awe. A desperate need to lose himself in the swirling, rainbow-colored ribbons joining those on the beach.

His mother had noted the changes in his consciousness. She'd tuned her awareness to his, helped him grasp the significance of what he saw. "The web of life, Gregor. What you see is but a fragment of nature's great secret," she'd whispered reverently. Unable to think coherently, let alone speak, he'd simply nodded and continued to stare at the wondrous sights.

His mother had steadied him during the walk home. Beneath an ancient magnolia, she had lifted him up to stroke the tree's trunk and run his fingers over the surface of a low-hanging leaf. The magnolia seemed to respond to his love, gave off a pink light that awakened in him an intense response. His mother noticed. "It is right to feel as you do," she said. "To love beauty with all of yourself is the very best way to live."

Later, her reassurances taught him he could selectively employ his psychic perceptions, could gain mastery over what he let in and when. Eventually, he trained himself to screen out anything he wanted to. Over the years, he turned less and less to mystical insights as guides for living. Now he preferred PK over any other form of psychism. It gave him power rather than overpowering him. He laughed, the bitterness in his tone surprising him.

Cynicism, irony, he could understand in himself, even appreciate, but the bitterness that had become his prevalent attitude was like venom. It ate away at him, consuming him from the inside out.

He'd once been a boy who made love to trees, a youth who dreamed of love that would last an eternity. Then came December 24, 1941. The Crimea under Nazi occupation. His dear mother slaughtered along with eight hundred others of Rom ancestry, no matter how dilute the bloodlines. After that, each Nazi atrocity against the Rom pushed Danilenko farther from his high-minded friends, his thoughts mired in violence—retribution.

And then came Paris, 1943, and the act of vengeance that had cost him his only true love and his honor. Later, he'd become a spy, bent under the thumbs of agency bosses until he had strength enough to bend them under his. He rarely looked closely at the man he'd become.

The occult power siphoned from Hitler's artifacts had rejuvenated and fortified Danilenko's body for an indeterminable yet definitely limited time. Only the Giardani heirloom would afford him a perpetual fountain of youth and endow him with the supernatural vigor that was as close as he'd ever get to genuine, earned immortality.

He had to have the damn thing. Nothing else mattered anymore. He sat up straight, his jaw cracking, then his vertebrae. Slowly, he rolled his neck. Tension. Too much tension.

WEST-CENTRAL ITALY

Julia had spent the last few days steeping herself in Etruscan art and architecture, all but camping out in the region's numerous small museums. She'd toured as many nearby towns and hamlets as she could. Aside from putting in regular appearances at the village of Montecipriana, there was nothing else she could think of to learn more about her heritage.

This morning she was headed not for the village itself but for the bridge on the mountainside below it, where she'd picnicked with young Vario. The place was like a magnet, drawing her there for an hour or so each day. She didn't understand why, but she didn't really need to. Just being there made her feel better, helped soothe her feelings of rejection.

The sky was overcast. A light drizzle glistened on her windshield. She reached the bridge, climbed out, and took a deep breath. Since the grass was too wet to sit down and meditate, she leaned against the car and crossed her arms over her chest. The rain had freshened the air, given it a sweet clover scent that tickled her nose. She loved the way the countryside had turned even greener than it was the day before. In the distance, she heard the rumble of a large farm tractor.

Glancing up at the village, she pulled her antique shawl closer around her shoulders, ran her fingers through its silky fringe, wondering for the hundredth time what the old woman in Florence could possibly have meant when she spoke of danger. Although Julia's father had conveyed, however unwillingly, that he was in danger, he'd never even hinted she might be, let alone that she might somehow bring harm to others. Modern Italy was still predominantly Roman Catholic. Maybe the old woman's *danger* was a religious metaphor. Like endangering one's immortal soul by hanging out with witches.

"*Streghe,*" she said aloud. The plural form of witch in Italian was a harsh word, even harsher than the singular. The sound of it raised goose bumps on Julia's arms.

How proudly her father had always called himself a witch. How especially proud he'd seemed when he announced the family had been hereditary witches in a tradition that dated back hundreds, if not thousands, of years. He'd managed to convey the distinct impression that Tuscany, Catholic or not, would embrace Julia proudly—the Pagan heiress joyously welcomed back home. His belief system had been pretty far out there, but so far out he couldn't know how people here might feel? Julia didn't think so.

There had to be some other explanation for the fear she'd met. Whatever it might be, she'd faced down fear before. Superstition, too. Back in California, the shelter's neighbors had been fearful, at first, about having homeless people living in their midst. Maybe the fear and superstition Julia faced here were of a different sort, but she could deal with them.

She watched a flock of ducks fly by. They squawked loudly, their wings thrumming the air as they skimmed through a low cloud.

When they emerged, she followed their flight, which brought her gaze to the craggy top of Montecipriana. If she took the road leading over the bridge, it might take her through the forest and up to the rocks. Anyway, since the grass was too wet to sit down, the idea of trying to get there seemed altogether better than standing here doing nothing. She started the car and drove across the bridge.

The forest was thicker than she'd expected. The road flanked the stream on her right. To the left, a muddy gully edged the single paved lane. She drove slowly, easing around a long bend. Immediately, the road curved the other way. Around the next bend, she saw the tractor she'd been hearing no more than fifty feet up the road. She gripped the wheel, fought the impulse to jam on the brakes. The last thing she needed was to skid the car off the road. None too soon, she came to a stop and took a deep breath.

The tractor seemed immense compared to Julia's compact. Puffing an obnoxious shaft of diesel fumes into the air, it took up the entire width of the way ahead, and it rumbled unevenly, as if badly in need of a tune-up. Two people in yellow rain slickers and wide-brimmed hats sat up high on the tractor's bench, a yapping dog between them. Leaving the car idling in neutral, Julia cracked her door. She leaned out, stood on one foot. "Good morning!"

One of the people, a man, stood up and put his hands on his hips. "This is private property. Didn't you see the sign beside the bridge?" His Italian was a coarse dialect, probably from the south. He'd ignored Julia's greeting, but she wasn't going to let that get her down. Better to start over.

"Good morning." She double-checked the brake and stepped away from the car, moving cautiously over the sodden roadway. "I didn't see your sign or realize I was trespassing." She shielded her eyes from the glare off the overcast sky, smiled up at the two on the tractor. "My name is Julia Giardani, and I was hoping this road led up to the top of Montecipriana."

"I don't care if you're the pope," the man said, even more agitated than when he'd first spoken. His dialect was all but indecipherable, his gestures emphatic. "I pay my rent here, and I say you may not pass this way."

The other person reached over and took hold of his arm, as if to calm him. "Emilio, Emilio." A woman. She took off her hat, and Julia was struck by her wholesome good looks. "*Scusi*, Signorina," she added to Julia. "My husband is upset because the road ahead washed out during the night. It means much extra work to get it passable again. Perhaps you wish to try again some other time?"

At this, the husband's anger erupted all over again. He spoke to his wife in hushed yet furious tones, his gestures bellicose. All Julia could make out of the argument was the man's name, jumbled in with several mentions of her own. The woman remained clearly unperturbed.

Although she seemed to prevail, the man apparently needed to have the last word. He gestured toward the bridge. "People around here pay attention to signs and respect others' privacy. If you want to get along, you will learn to do the same."

Julia glanced at the woman, who gave her a sisterly shrug and raised her eyebrows at her husband's irascibility.

"I'm sorry if I've upset you," Julia said to the man. "I really did not see any signs. If you could suggest another route to the top, I won't bother you again."

"There is no other way," the man snarled. He shook his wife's hand off his arm and pulled up the collar on his slicker. "It is not a tourist place. It is not visited. Ever." He raised his hand and signed *il malocchio*. For a change, the gesture was directed not at Julia, but at the rock outcrop instead.

"I don't understand, but again, I'm sorry," she said, smiling. She waved to the woman then to the man. "*Ciao!*"

"Good day, Signorina," the woman answered formally, looking pointedly at her husband, who jutted out his chin and kept silent.

Julia got into her car and carefully backed up, the car's reverse gear protesting stridently all the way to the bridge. On the other side, she parked and crossed back over the stream, searching for the farmer's sign.

It took only a minute to find the NO TRESPASSING sign, laying face down near a tall fence post on the right side of the bridge. The muddy embankment all around it was marked with fresh tracks made by a small cloven-hoofed animal and a pair of boots not much smaller than Julia's. Vario and his frisky critter, no doubt.

Julia chuckled to herself. She supposed she should disapprove of the boy's mischief, but what she felt was a sense of conspiratorial pleasure. No use inviting more trouble, though.

She picked up the sign, swished off the mud in the stream. Then, using a large flat rock, she hammered the shiny bare nails sticking out its back into the holes on the post, not at all surprised that they fit perfectly into place.

Back out on the main road, she pulled over and rolled down her window. Wet, heavy fog encircled Montecipriana completely. The rock formation at its crown appeared to loom up like an island in a foamy sea.

So very familiar, it seemed. Beckoning.

Irresistible.

TWELVE

The delicious scents of the midday meal, *il pranzo*, made Julia's mouth water as she entered the Casa Sergio's dining room. With the morning's drizzle turning to a downpour outside, the large windows at the far end were entirely steamed up, making the barrel-ceilinged room seem even more homey than it did in the evenings. Julia chose a corner with good enough light to be able to work on her notebook, sort out her questions about the legacy and about the Goddess upon whom she felt compelled to call more and more.

A cavernous fireplace on the dining room's north wall opened through to the kitchen. Over its flames hung a huge cast-iron pot of steaming bean soup. On a tall pair of fire irons nearby perched a grill chock full of wild game and several varieties of homemade sausage. A skillet of golden polenta, Julia's lunch choice, sat on a ledge near the bottom beside a board lined with lumps of bread dough set there to rise undisturbed for the afternoon's baking.

Lucia apparently worked as a waitress as well as a maid. In a neat black skirt and a prim white blouse, she moved efficiently from guest to guest. Apprehension clouded her eyes when she spotted Julia.

She crossed briskly to Julia's table. "We weren't expecting you for *pranzo.*" She glanced anxiously toward the door as Maria Sergi wheeled her mother into the room.

"The weather drove me back earlier than I'd planned," Julia said. "Will it be a problem to serve me without a reservation?"

"That's not a problem." Lucia moved nervously, as if blocking Julia from the Sergi women's sight.

"Then what is?"

"Nothing."

"Is that so?" Julia's tone hardly disguised her skepticism.

"Sí, Signorina. Nothing at all." The young woman shifted feet. "Would you care to start with today's antipasto? It's very delicious— warm artichoke hearts, some crostini, a wedge of fresh pecorino cheese."

"Fine," Julia answered, more interested now in the elderly Augustina Sergi in her wheelchair than in eating.

Lucia sped away, allowing Julia a clear view across the room, where the wheelchair faced away from her. Disappointed, she turned her attention to her notebook. She finished her antipasto and her second course, lingered over her coffee. Writing and sipping absent-mindedly, she spilled a few drops on the hem of her sweater. Bother. Cleaning the spill meant a trip to the restroom before a stain had time to set.

The nearest restroom was off the lobby. On her way back to the dining room, she spotted Lucia talking with Maria Sergi at the reception desk. Both women seemed upset. Neither spotted Julia, who disliked eavesdropping but sensed strongly she'd best stay put and see what she might learn.

"You must tell her what your mother told you," said Lucia.

"Do you think I want the neighbors more wrought up than they are already? They're giving me a terrible time, threatening me. If Mamma finds out, it will provoke her, no end."

"How much longer do you think you can hide this from her?"

Maria rubbed her forehead. "Not much longer, I would guess."

"I was also warned not to help the American in any way. Threatened." Lucia seemed to shiver. "My grandmother's heart is weak, too. If it helps, I understand why you can't risk letting your mother become too agitated."

"It helps. I hoped you would understand. Run along now, Lucia, back to the dining room. I'll see you later."

Lucia reached out and squeezed her employer's arm then left. Maria moved behind the reception desk and pulled out a folded newspaper, which she spread over the desktop and proceeded to read, seemingly not for the first time.

Julia felt more rejected than ever, but decided it was time to make her presence known, squarely face the inevitable. She walked quickly to the desk.

"Did you have something to say to me, Maria?"

"Yes." The innkeeper seemed startled, but quickly recovered and stood up straight. "I am most sorry, but it seems your presence here is causing our neighbors concern and making some very angry."

"Do you know why?"

"I have some idea."

"Nobody will tell me what's going on around here, why everyone I meet treats me like some kind of leper." Julia caught Maria's gaze and held it. "What in heaven's name are people so afraid of?"

Maria sighed. "Maybe this." She folded the newspaper in half and handed it to Julia.

Julia could hardly believe her eyes as she devoured the headlines then skimmed down the page. Words all but screamed from the page, none of them initially making much sense. *Satanic Mass! Human Sacrifice! Unidentified Infant's Horrible Death!*

A human infant recovered from the Arno a few days before had apparently bled to death, its heart cut savagely from its chest. Found tied with it inside a plastic-wrapped bundle of black satin were a small but extremely sharp "ritual" knife and a bloody pewter goblet splashed with black candle wax, leading the authorities to conclude the dead infant was the victim of a black-magic ritual. The journalist following the story had apparently alluded to several outlawed satanic groups in earlier reports. Now he reported that authorities suspected the bundle was the work of some previously unknown witch cult.

Streghe and infanticide.

Julia's stomach started to heave. She rubbed her hand over it, gulped, forced herself to keep reading. "Terrible, absolutely terrible, but why would your neighbors associate me with something like this?"

"Because you are a witch, *Giuliana Giardani!*" said a gravelly voice from behind her.

Maria gasped. "Mamma!"

Julia spun around to face Augustina Sergi who, though extremely pale, stared at Julia imperiously then proceeded to wheel herself toward the elevator marked PRIVATE at the end of the hall.

Giuliana Giardani. Julia's true name, the one on her birth certificate. Nobody had called her that since Anna died. The sound of it, spoken in an accent identical to Anna's in every inflection, gave her nerves an icy jolt.

She pulled herself up as tall as she could, looked directly into Maria's troubled eyes. "If people here don't realize no member of my family would ever take part in a satanic rite, they don't know the Giardani half as well as they seem to think they do."

"That may be so, but I must still ask you to vacate your rooms by the end of the week." Maria turned abruptly and hurried after her mother.

Julia was too stunned to care. She felt pretty certain the neighbors had already ensured she'd find no other hotel nearby, and there were only three days left before the end of the week.

SOUTHERN FRANCE

Anatolin awoke with a start. He sat up and leaned back against the stone walls of his retreatant's cell at Abbey Notre-Dame de Senanque. Cold, like everything about this abbey but the exceptionally warm smiles of those members of the community he'd been fortunate enough to encounter since he arrived.

The dream that awakened him still made his entire being quake with the force of its subconscious terror. It was not a dream at all, but a nightmare, perhaps the worst he'd ever experienced. Recalling it now made his hair practically stand on end. His heart pounded so hard he could hardly make out the Gregorian chant of the monks celebrating their predawn devotions in the chapel, not far away. He stood and pulled on his jeans, then his boots, grabbed his jacket and left his room.

Closer to the chapel, he found a stone bench and sat down to listen to the monks' first sacred office of the day. Perhaps their soft, deep voices would soothe his jangled nerves, drive his nightmare from his mind. It would have been bad enough if the nightmare had remained the same as it was the first time he'd dreamed it, but it hadn't. In the earlier occurrence, the KGB had cornered him at the end of the hallway outside his Moscow laboratory, one agent pinning him there, starting to rough him up. Anatolin faced his assailant and took a swing. He managed to knock the fellow's hat to the floor, revealing the receding hairline of a dark, husky man—General Gregor Danilenko.

Danilenko's dream image had grinned menacingly, his teeth gleaming as he placed his hat back on his head then summoned two comrades to assist him. The agents took Anatolin to a drab windowless room made of concrete slabs. Even now, starkly awake, Anatolin relived the horrifying hyper-reality of the nightmare, the soulless interrogation, the appalling demoralization of being caged in that dingy room. He wouldn't be surprised to learn he'd cried out loud in his sleep. But what curdled his stomach was the latest permutation in the dream sequence—Danilenko facing toward the corner, removing his hat before taking over the interrogation then swinging back around, his dark hair turned to coppery curls. The unnerving transformation went on until the apparition became a specter of Julia, then a phantom Goddess draped in light and crowned with flowers.

Anatolin had been a fool to think he could continue with his plans after meeting Julia. That couldn't possibly be any clearer. His subconscious was practically spelling it out. Moreover, Julia and Danilenko had somehow become linked in Anatolin's consciousness, a fact that would never make sense, no matter how long he lived. The two didn't belong in the same universe, let alone in the same dream.

If only Danilenko's convoy weren't sailing so blasted slowly. Thank God the ships would finally pull into Marseilles harbor late tomorrow afternoon.

WEST-CENTRAL ITALY

Siena's beauty pierced Julia's heart. Amassed along the ridges of a hill whose deep gorges divided the city into three districts the Sienese called *terzi*, its palaces, houses, and artisans' workshops were all strung together in almost unbroken lines of rich brown stones and rosy tiles. Yesterday's storm had passed in the night. This morning, the sky was soft springtime blue.

Julia hadn't found a single hotel vacancy earlier, but even that couldn't dampen her spirits as she wound up through the medieval warren of Terzo di San Martino. Hard to believe, but the houses were even more crowded than elsewhere. Some were built out over the narrow streets, turning them into sunless tunnels. Walking here was like stepping back into the thirteenth century. Julia had the sense she would find it hard to keep her mind in the present if she spent much time here.

Up ahead, her route opened onto a tiny square on which she hoped to find the herb shop she'd spent the last twenty minutes searching for. She climbed a half dozen wide stairs, stepped around a wheelbarrow heaped with rich pungent topsoil destined for somebody's courtyard garden, ascended the steepish ramp leading into the sunlit square. Blinking against the sudden brightness, she surveyed the façades opening onto the square.

A simple wooden sign hung beside a narrow door to her left. On either side of the door was a small, rather dark display window. In one window sat a chunky antique marble mortar and pestle flanked by hand-blown glass flasks, in the other, a handful of gardening books and herbals.

She checked out the sign, ERBORISTERIA CELESTE. Bells jingled over her head as she entered the shop, so dimly lit she had to stand still a few seconds to get her bearings. A fresh, aromatic scent spiced the air. Most of the light came from the yellowed display windows and a Tiffany-style lamp beside the register on the front counter. Deeper into the long, narrow space, a few bare bulbs dangled from antiquated cables strung along the twelve-foot ceiling. Every inch of vertical space was covered with centuries-old apothecary cabinets and shelves laden with jars and decanters. For all the shop's venerable age, there was hardly a speck of dust to be found.

Halfway down the single aisle, on the right, a cramped stairwell led up toward filtered sunlight. She called out. No one answered, but she thought she heard footsteps overhead. "Hello," she repeated.

"Good morning," said a woman's voice in a lovely and pure Sienese Italian. "I'll be right down."

The footsteps came closer, then Julia heard a soft click. The rest of the shop lit with dim electric lights.

Julia smiled at the stylish woman, probably in her thirties, descending the staircase. "Hello! You must be the proprietor."

"Yes, I am Celeste."

"What an interesting shop."

"You think so?" The woman gave Julia a tentative smile. "This building has been in our family for hundreds of years, but the business was closed for the past eighty or so. I've only recently reopened. It is very old-fashioned, this place."

"That's precisely what makes it so interesting."

"Good." The woman seemed to relax. Her smile was wider now, but still seemed subdued, a bit sad. She wore all black. "I am a widow," she explained before Julia had time to avert her gaze. "My husband was killed in a hunting accident late last year. "

"I'm sorry."

The woman shrugged with admirable bravado. "Life goes on. How may I help you?"

"First, point me toward your books. We'll go from there."

Celeste turned and waved toward several low shelves across from the counter. Julia bent over and studied the titles, her mind on Maria Sergi's ailing mother.

It was easy to empathize with Maria's anxiety for her aging parent. This morning, Julia pulled Lucia aside and asked her to describe Augustina's heart condition. The ailment was widely known as congestive heart failure, a progressive deterioration and weakening of the heart muscle common among older people. Apparently, there was no known medical cure. Julia had immediately recalled a conversation with a fellow student in her midwife's certification course, an herbalist, who had spoken enthusiastically about an herb traditionally used for treating heart problems.

Julia was certain she'd recognize the name of the herb if she saw it in print. Fortunately, the shop had four herbals written in English. She snatched them up and joined Celeste at the counter. "How wonderful you have English titles."

"A gamble, but the university near here has a popular program for foreigners. I was told British and American students would likely find their way to this shop."

Julia smiled. "Your gamble has made my day. Maybe my whole month."

She opened the first book, scanned the index, flipped to the pages on treatments for the heart. There she found the exact herb she'd been trying to recall, hawthorn berry, which this author combined with two other herbs into a strengthening tonic for the heart.

She glanced up at Celeste. "That was almost too easy."

Celeste laughed. "You're just getting started. I've been advised to cross-reference more than one source before arriving at an herbal prescription."

"Book two, then," Julia said.

"The translation from German to English is said to be excellent."

"Good." Julia scanned the index. Once again the preferred herb was hawthorn berry, used in combination with other tonic herbs. "Must be wonderful, knowing about all this."

Celeste nodded her head. "I am not yet an expert. I'll be glad when I know more."

"Hmmm." Julia almost added *me, too,* a thought so surprising all she could do was silently peruse the third book. Tinctures or teas? She supposed a combination of the two would cover all the bases.

She turned and scanned the small drawers of the apothecary cabinets. Lifting the first book again, she opened it to the alphabetical listings of the various herbs and compared the Latin names in the book with those on the drawer labels. A moment later, an urge prompted her to put the book on the counter and hold up her hands, palms facing the cabinets.

Her raised hands immediately started to tingle. When she closed her eyes, she saw bursts of energy, like clusters of tiny bright sparklers that swiftly changed in color and pattern as she passed her hands over the drawers. Fascinating. Even if the novel technique resulted in nothing, she sensed keeping faith with this inner guidance, however far-fetched it might seem at the time, was the only way to proceed.

Another idea came to her. Concentrating at the spot between her eyebrows, she called up an image of Augustina Sergi and sensed a pattern flickering faintly over Augustina's midriff. She held the image in mind, moved her hands from drawer to drawer, came to a stop about a third of the way down the aisle. She reached for the drawer straight ahead.

"Aah! I see you have found the hawthorn berry." Celeste's voice sounded loud.

"I guess I have," Julia answered, glancing at the Latin label. "*Crataegus oxycanthus*," she read aloud, her palm itching to hold the herb.

"A beautiful crop, organically grown and harvested at a local farm. Open the drawer, examine the berries yourself."

Julia pulled out the drawer and ran her fingers through the smooth, dark-red orbs. She rolled one in her palm then closed her eyes, watched its energy pattern, again like bright sparklers, flickering in soft bursts of red and green.

Celeste smiled proudly. "It is not so easy to purchase high-quality herbs, these days."

"Yes. Beautiful." Julia again closed her eyes. The sparklers suddenly condensed into a reddish-brown fluid. "But what I need is the tincture."

"You're in luck!" Celeste snatched a small dropper bottle from among many lining the small shelves behind the counter and gave it a shake. "I tinctured some of this very crop when it came in fresh last fall. Here," she said. Taking Julia's hand and turning it sideways, Celeste dropped a bit of liquid between Julia's wrist and the base of her thumb. "Try it!"

Julia poked her index finger into the liquid and dabbed it on her tongue. The tincture had a fruity flavor, medicinal but surprisingly tasty.

"Nice." She glanced back through the herbals. "How about some of these other herbs?"

Celeste leaned over the books, too. "I have a good balm and linden mixture we can combine with the hawthorn."

"I'd like four ounces altogether, in a dropper bottle," Julia said, feeling a confidence the source of which escaped her. She relaxed against the counter and looked up the herbs Celeste had mentioned. "You must have studied herbalism for quite some time before opening the shop."

"No. Actually, it doesn't take long to pick up the basics. Of course, I'm no *maestra*. A master healer develops her knowledge over many years."

"Or many lifetimes, as my father would say, if he were here."

"I was raised Roman Catholic, Signorina, but I must confess, your father's opinion supports what I've come to believe."

"You know, Celeste, this shop reminds me of something, but I can't put my finger on what."

"These old places have that effect on some people." Celeste smiled serenely as she poured the tinctures through the tiny stainless steel funnel that sat atop a cobalt-blue bottle about four inches tall.

There was an ancient-looking tome at the end of the counter nearest the door. It piqued Julia's curiosity.

"I'll bet this is old," she said, moving toward it. She reached out to smooth the frayed binding. Touching the old leather, she felt something akin to an electric shock.

Celeste glanced up from her task. "The registry of suppliers our family dealt with long ago." She nodded, indicating Julia could open the book.

Julia lifted the cover and turned a few thick, brittle pages of vellum. Much of the ink was too faded to read, but the dates Julia could make out went back centuries. "What a treasure!"

"I suppose it is," Celeste said with her modest shrug.

Julia was so engrossed in the book Celeste's words barely

registered. There was something mesmerizing about the antique script, the ledger-like notations from so long ago.

"*Scusi*, Signorina, your tincture is ready. Will there be anything else?"

"*Un momento*, Celeste."

There was something else Julia needed for Augustina, but she sensed the small yellow flower she was visualizing would not be found in a shop in town. Fresh, she decided. The herb in her mind's eye had to be picked fresh, aged in white wine. But how in the world did she *know* that?

"Can you put together a nice tea to fortify someone with a weakening heart?"

"Aah! But of course."

Julia continued through the registry, carefully turned a few more pages. Stopping at random on a page with a faded header dated 1395, she ran her finger down a column of names. Halfway down, she almost gasped as she made out her own. She blinked her eyes, but there it was still—*Giuliana Giardani!*

The room seemed to shift around her, the scents in the shop to heighten, becoming distinctly medicinal, sharp. She felt herself wearing different clothes, a heavy dress and cape, felt the weight of long hair piled high on her head. The sensations intensified then gradually abated.

Totally disoriented and a little woozy, she felt pulled between elation and caution. Her psychometry seemed to be back, focused and clear as on Cyprus. If Andrei was right about the purpose for such skills, their return had to mean there was something important she needed to perceive. Important for her understanding of the legacy. Important not just for herself, but for her power to do good. In the depths of her mind, she heard golden laughter like she'd heard on Cyprus, sensed hearing it validated her speculations.

She felt a subtle change in herself, recognized the signs of a new commitment building within her, increasing eagerness to serve whatever—or Whomever—was causing these transformations. She closed the book and moved abruptly away from it, wishing Andrei were here to help figure out why this experience felt pivotal. Later. Maybe she could sort this all out on her own. Later.

THIRTEEN

Julia's days of stopping briefly in Montecipriana's main square, then driving on, were past. She decided that earlier in the herb shop. She pulled up beside the fountain, got out of the car, and started walking.

Today, she wasn't just putting in an appearance. Today, the villagers would acknowledge her. Climbing slowly, deliberately, she wound her way through the cobbled streets. The townhouses were nowhere near as impressive as Siena's but they, too, were tall. Ivy and ferns had etched out shallow root-holds in their walls. Their steep and mostly unadorned façades seemed completely secure, as if they'd still be here unchanged in another five hundred years.

At one intersection, she encountered a young mother with babe in arms. Instead of answering Julia's greeting, the young woman crossed the street then turned silently into the nearest courtyard. At another, Julia came face to face with an old man stumbling along on bent legs, a bulging string bag hanging from each hand. For her smile she received a morose stare before the man vanished behind a heavily carved door.

A few minutes later she came across a half dozen rosy-cheeked children playing ball in a small, nearly sunless square. The children glanced at her curiously, but didn't clear out of the square, as she half expected them to do.

Bundled in bright knit sweaters, suspendered woolen shorts, and colorful knee-high socks, they clashed with the seeming austerity of the town. Their shouts and laughter lifted Julia's mood. She recognized their game, had actually played a fair bit of soccer since starting the shelter, mostly with the immigrant children. When the ball wound up in the vicinity of her feet, she gladly accepted the wordless invitation to join in.

One boy, about eight years old, had clearly assumed the captain's role. He orchestrated the flurries of movement with finesse, pointing across the square, where a six-foot-wide stairway lined with the children's discarded jackets and book bags comprised a makeshift goal. Julia laughed as she moved with the children, her shouts blending with theirs each time the ball was passed through the crowd.

Suddenly the ball skidded over the cobblestones in her direction. It was her chance to take possession of it, and she wasn't about to hesitate. Using some fancy footwork she'd picked up from a Salvadoran refugee, she stopped the ball with her right foot, put her toe under it and popped it up a couple of feet, then toed it through the astonished players, setting up a shot the captain couldn't miss.

His kick sailed into the stairwell to a lusty, "G-o-a-l-l-l!" The children circled the captain, then Julia, congratulating her for setting up the play, asking where she learned the game. It felt great. The adults of this village might continue to shun her, but its children had definitely come around.

"Is this where you always play?" she asked the captain.

"No," he answered. "We usually use the big piazza, but we were supposed to stay out of sight."

A little girl with long, black braids squeezed in beside Julia and looked up at her. "Nobody expected you would walk all over town, big as day!" she said, her eyes round and gleaming with indignation. "The adults will be angry with us for playing with you, but I say we didn't do anything wrong."

The captain cut her off. "Eh, you shut up!" The children murmured in agreement.

"Everyone, take it easy." Julia raised her hands. "The adults can blame me if they want, but I won't let them be angry with you." Before she could say more, Julia heard footsteps approaching the square, a muted whimper, a child's whispered, "No, I can't! No, please!"

The children near Julia fell silent. From behind her, the soccer captain clicked his tongue. "The new Jesuit," he muttered as a man in an old-fashioned dark cassock led a small, red-haired girl down the lane, his hand gripping her arm much too tightly.

The little girl resisted him, her face puckered, her eyes awash in dread.

The man yanked the child into the square. "Do it!"

"I can't, Father." The child stumbled to a stop and burst into tears. "Please, don't make me!"

"Do you want your friends to know what a sinner you are?" the man growled. "Do you want your parents to know?"

The child twisted in his grip, her sobs tearing at Julia's heart. Julia walked over and laid her hand on the priest's arm. There wasn't another sound in the square as she spoke. "This child is too frightened to do as you ask."

"How dare you touch me!" The priest tried to shake off her grip.

She held firm, though her palm started to burn, sending images and sensations vibrating through her as if she were some kind of stringed instrument. Suddenly, she knew full well what so-called sin the child had committed, knew precisely the threat the priest held over her head. Julia looked the man in the eye, gave him an intransigent smile, moved her hand from his arm to the little girl's shoulder. "Please let her go."

The child whimpered again, but there was no response from the priest, who just stared at Julia, aghast she would challenge his authority.

"Now!" She pried his hand off the child's arm, dropped it. The man moved backward several steps, but Julia didn't give a hoot what he did anymore.

She encircled the child's shoulders, scooted her a few steps farther from the priest, squatted down to face her. "Are you okay?"

"He told me to curse you," the child sobbed, "but even if you are a *strega*, I don't believe you're as evil as he said."

"No, of course not." Standing again, Julia pulled the child behind her and squared her shoulders, stared calmly at the priest. "I think you should leave now."

The man's jaw set in a hard line. As if following a previously determined plan of action, he lifted the crucifix dangling from his belt and, holding it up between his eyes, took two steps toward Julia. He muttered in a language she assumed was Church Latin. The little girl shrieked and burrowed her head into the backs of Julia's legs.

Still holding the crucifix high, he started slicing symbols through the air. A cross, Julia thought. A pentagram. The children cried out. Julia waved the rest of them behind her and stood her ground. "Stop muttering that medieval nonsense! You're frightening these children."

He stepped closer. Still enunciating, he swiped the crucifix much too close to her brow. "*In nomine Patris et Fil—*" He stepped closer, his voice rising. The little girl gave a sharp scream.

"You are no man of God!" Julia scooped up the terrified child with one arm, raised her other and pointed at him. "Doesn't your own scripture say you should not use the Lord's name in vain?"

The priest came to a dead halt, stared at her, his mouth agape, his eyes growing fearful. He shook his head, seemed entirely stunned.

"Get away from us!" Her voice rasping, Julia took a step toward the priest, who retreated in kind. "Leave—now!"

The priest said nothing. Clearly dazed, he let the crucifix drop to the end of its cord, signed *il malocchio*, ducked into the nearest alley.

Julia sighed. Glancing around, she noticed several adults had entered the square. They watched her intently. The old man she'd seen earlier approached her cautiously. "You were disrespectful to the priest in front of the children."

"I suppose I was." She looked down, shaking her head. "I don't know what came over me."

The old man seemed embarrassed. "That man acts like no priest I've ever met. He must be substituting for our usual one from the diocese. I had never seen him before he said Sunday Mass here last week."

A woman spoke up. "I'd never seen him before, either." She shuddered. "I certainly hope we don't see him here anymore." Several other mothers murmured their agreement.

Julia gave the villagers a distracted smile. There was only one thing on her mind. She dropped onto one knee, hugged the red-haired girl, then pulled back and held the child at arm's length. The priest's loathsome energy still impinged on the child's emotions. With all the force of her will, Julia tried to replace it with impressions of tenderness.

"The priest was mistaken, *cara*," she said aloud. "You're a good girl." Silently but emphatically, she continued, *What he told you was evil was something entirely natural. It is not a sin to touch your own body.* Then she smiled. "Do you understand?"

"Yes, Signorina. *Grazie.*"

"All right, then," Julia said. With the crook of her index finger, she nudged up the child's chin, gave her cheek a soft kiss, and stood.

Two men marched belligerently into the square. The youngest, stocky, about twenty-five, spoke harshly to an expectant mother then pushed her ahead of him down the lane. Julia didn't like what she saw, but she held her tongue. She'd spoken out of turn quite enough for one day.

The villagers began to disperse. Julia waved good-bye to the departing children and started to walk away.

"You! *Strega!*"

Julia turned back. It was the bullying husband, approaching her quickly, his fist clenched above his head, his face looking fierce. At the edges of the square, the other villagers sent the children off and stood quietly, obviously curious.

The husband kept walking toward her. The way he'd said *strega* had sounded so filthy it almost made her stomach turn. He came to a stop only inches from Julia, his fist almost touching her chin. She fought back a shudder as the man spat vile curses in her face. The only other sound in the square came from the old man, who shuffled from foot to foot.

"Makes you wonder what the priest is holding over *his* head," he said to his closest neighbor.

The husband swung toward the old man. "Shut up, you old snake!"

He grabbed Julia by one arm and spun her toward the lane leading down to her car. That was all it took to shake her from her state of shock. Her arm tingled wildly where he held it. Impressions sped past her mind's eye.

She pulled out of the man's grasp. "You may bully your wife and get away with it, but touching me was a huge mistake! You just gave your secrets away."

"What do you mean?"

"You heard me." She lowered her voice so only the husband could hear her. "I know everything the priest knows, more, and I understand why you obey him, why you are harassing me." She willed the man to listen to her. She hoped his wife never had to learn about the mistress stashed five kilometers east of Montecipriana.

"Are you threatening me?"

"I have no intention of doing so. Nor will I act as your conscience." She sighed and brushed her hair behind her ear. "You know what you need to do. Tend to your business and leave me to mine."

The man glared and stepped back. "Go on, *strega*, get out of here!" he said, but there was a change in his tone of voice. The villagers continued to stare, stone faced, from the edges of the square. Julia turned and walked away, the unexpected use of her gifts leaving her a bit woozy and more than a little depleted. The village was absolutely silent but for the sound of her soft-soled boots upon the cobblestones. She'd never felt so alone in her life.

She walked to her car and opened the door, but instead of getting in, she leaned her arms on the roof and gazed up at Montecipriana. A door opened on a second-story balcony to her right. The little red-haired girl appeared, her mother behind her.

The child waved. Julia could swear she heard a sweet, soft *Thank you, Signorina!* flit through her mind. Her spirits lifted.

She scanned the perimeter of the village, carefully tracing a route up the streets and onto a path leading into the forest. What had she been thinking, to feel she was alone with the Mount of the Cyprian right beneath her feet, with her family's ancestral home so near she could almost see it? She stood up, slammed the door closed, and started right back up the street she'd just come down.

At the second intersection, she turned right and walked quickly to the edge of town then skirted the backs of the houses, ducking into the forest on the path she'd spotted from below. Her heart was pounding—from traveling so quickly straight up or maybe from sheer excitement.

Regardless, she felt wonderful, more optimistic than she'd felt in days. She stood still to get her bearings under the dense canopy. From the way the moss clung to the trees and the rocks, she was definitely headed south. She squinted up the slope, trying to get a glimpse of the route, but she couldn't see far with late-afternoon shadows obscuring the thicket. Just ahead along the path, the brush had recently been roughly hacked, as if cleared in a hurry by someone whose skill didn't match his enthusiasm.

Careful not to snag her sweater on the sharp branches, she started walking again, wending farther south. She soon came upon a small stone foot bridge encrusted with a dense carpet of deep-green moss.

Not much used. Twenty yards past the bridge, the canopy overhead thinned, and the path forked.

There were no signs of recent traffic leading down the hill to the right, but there were fresh tracks on the trail leading left, which she hoped went all the way to the top of the hill. She continued upward. The path was steep, slippery from recent rains.

Twilight came on quickly, riotous birdsong marking the hour. Just a few more minutes, and she'd have to start back. Over a crest, a large, fairly level ledge cradled a meadow overgrown with wild-flowers and tall, virgin grass. *Mostly* virgin grass, Julia corrected herself, spying a small white animal grazing along the meadow's edge. The goat lifted its head, spotted her, and hoofed the ground, tossing bits of grass hither and yon.

A moment later, Vario Andrade popped up from the grass, both hands full of flowers. Vario didn't seem half as pleased to see her as she was to see him. He tucked a wildflower bouquet into each side of his coveralls' bib and walked toward her, scowling all the way.

"Hi, there!" she said. Past him across the meadow stood a large, moss-and-vine-covered mound that reminded her of something she'd recently seen. She searched for a path leading beyond the mound but saw only dense overgrowth shaded by the rocky outcrop she'd hoped to reach.

Vario frowned. "How'd you find this place?"

"I saw the path from down there." She pointed.

"I told my great-grandmother that path should stay overgrown."

"Why?"

"So you couldn't find it, of course. Our neighbors will be furious. If they say one mean word to my great-grandmother," he added, shaking his fist under Julia's nose, "I tell you, I'll—"

"Hey! No need to get all red in the face about something that hasn't even happened." She tousled his hair then plucked a wildflower from the right side of his coveralls' bib. "What's this called, Vario?"

She examined the flower in the dimming light. It resembled a yellow primrose, but was much smaller than any variety Julia had ever seen.

Vario shook his head in obvious despair. "It's a cowslip, silly."

There could be no doubt about it—this was precisely the herb Julia needed for Augustina Sergi's heart wine. "Where did you find it?"

"They're all over this pasture. There's scads of them here. Always have been, according to my great-grandmother. I'm taking these to her for a nice cup of tea. She's been funny all week, happy as can be one minute, down in the dumps the next."

"Too bad. Maybe she should have come with you. Being here makes me feel absolutely terrific." Julia closed her eyes and smiled, realizing how true her words were. "You never know, this place might cheer her up. Or better yet, take her up to those rocks. That's where I was headed. I'll bet it's even prettier there."

Vario looked at Julia as if she were totally crazy. "You just don't get it, do you? Nobody visits either place, ever."

"You're here."

"I'm already sorry I came." He scanned the meadow, obviously worried because darkness was falling quickly. "We better get outta here, fast." He whistled, and the goat trotted to his side.

He clipped some kind of leash on the animal's rope halter, looked grimly at Julia. "Give me your hand." He clearly wasn't going to tolerate any argument.

Julia let him guide her down the hill. Puzzled as she was by his disclosures, she was glad Vario seemed to like her, at least enough to lead her down the path. Thank heaven for him, and for the other children of Tuscany. And for a certain Russian parapsychologist. Without the insights Andrei shared before they parted, she wouldn't have guessed how to relax and make use of the strange energies that kept surprising her when she least expected them.

She sure wished he'd been able to come with her. It would have been terrific to have at least one grown-up ally here. Someone interested in her exciting discoveries. Someone who wouldn't be put off by the strange, unpredictable, almost magnetic vortex her psychic gifts seemed to have made of her life.

SOUTHERN FRANCE

Marseilles reeked of smog made even more noxious by the stench of a dirty port at low tide. From a fire escape on the second floor of a converted brick warehouse, Anatolin could survey the entire harbor.

He held a Styrofoam cup of coffee to his lips but dared not savor its aroma. Even strong French roast couldn't overcome the smell drifting up from the waterline. The port's rank aura made Anatolin's skin crawl. It seemed an altogether fitting backdrop for Danilenko's cargo, scheduled to arrive soon at the wharf directly below.

When he'd been close to Hitler's artifacts for the hour or so of his inspection years ago, the energy they gave off had literally made him ill for days. Even the few moments on Cyprus when he'd been near them had affected him for several hours. He dreaded getting close to the collection again, but it couldn't be helped.

Earlier Anatolin had learned of the convoy's docking time from a stalwart French matron staffing the reception desk in the harbor-master's office, where he'd overheard talk of Danilenko's leasing a metal-roofed building on the nearby wharf. In the hours since Anatolin took up this post overlooking the wharf, he'd seen little action below, but a few hefty types had shown up. They loitered now near the wharf, most drinking what appeared to be beer, chain-smoking cigarettes.

A decidedly rough-looking bunch, one Anatolin would be wise to avoid.

AVENUE KLÉBER, PARIS

Madame Racine covered her cheeks with both hands and sighed. She might have guessed young Andrei would attempt to follow Danilenko and the artifacts. He had his reasons—*certainement.* Nevertheless, it was exceedingly worrisome, him heading off all by himself, on the trail of those reprehensible artifacts.

Not unlike Danilenko, Racine recalled all too well, on that fateful night of November 9, 1943. Charging alone out of Racine's townhouse on his mission of revenge. So filled with hatred for the Nazis, he'd been. So determined to get an inside line on the Thule Society's enclave in Paris. Not listening to reason, but throwing caution to the winds, behaving like a bloodthirsty maniac.

She might have seen that coming, too, but she hadn't. None of them had.

Picking up the telephone receiver, Racine dialed a number she'd called often of late. An operator answered and informed her the extension she wanted was busy. Racine hesitated a moment but agreed to hold.

Danilenko. That dreadful night, his sorry misuse of his PK had disqualified him from the Task Force. His diabolical interrogation of the young Thule initiate, his use of brutal, forbidden tactics were more suited to Hitler's colleagues than to Racine's. Dani's mindless deed made it impossible for him to continue serving the Allies with honor. The Task Force had barely averted a scandal. Terrible. A nightmare for all of them.

And now, Ilina Mikhailovna's only son was in harm's way as never before—a dire state of affairs, one that promised to become much worse. It was definitely time to reshuffle the deck.

FOURTEEN

Julia made her way to the Casa Sergio's top floor, the pretty gift bag containing Augustina Sergi's herbal tea and tinctures swinging from her arm. She'd come upon Augustina enjoying the sunny enclosed porch several mornings this week. Hopefully, the elderly woman was a creature of habit, and Julia would find her there again.

Unfortunately, Signora Sergi's wheelchair was not in its usual spot. Maybe Julia had come too early. She glanced from her watch to the double oak doors that led to the family's apartment. It was barely eight o'clock. Augustina might yet show up.

Julia set the gift bag on the low chest that served as a coffee table and took a seat with her back to the windows. Even though a slight overcast dimmed the sunshine, the porch was a pleasant place to wait, with its cozy wicker furniture, plumped chintz pillows, the old treadle sewing machine lined with photos and other memorabilia pushed back into one corner. She settled back and enjoyed the homey ambience.

Through the wall she heard muffled voices. A conversation, or maybe a breakfast party, she mused, her mind wandering back to the episode with the priest the day before.

No use second guessing how she might have avoided the fiasco. No use kidding herself, either. If she saw any man treat a child with such a heavy hand, she'd do the same thing again, priest or no.

She started at the sudden, harsh sound of a man's voice raised in anger. A second man shouted down the first. Several female voices, also clearly perturbed, chimed in all at once. She suddenly realized she could be accused of eavesdropping. She stood, decided to leave the porch, forget about seeing Augustina Sergi. Maybe Maria could present the herbs to her mother later in the day. Whatever. Julia picked up the gift bag.

The Sergi's apartment doors slammed open. A man—the farmer Emilio—muttered obscenities as he brushed past Julia and stomped away down the hall. Through the open doors, Julia saw Augustina slumped back in her wheelchair. She was surrounded by people Julia had encountered at some point during the week. Lucia and Emilio's wife stood to Augustina's left. The old man who had spoken to Julia in Montecipriana and the pregnant woman with the bullying husband stood to Augustina's right. Behind the wheelchair stood a very spry older woman who, judging from her postal service uniform, was probably Vario's great-grandmother.

Maria, her arms full of packages, charged up the hall toward the porch. Her face aflame, she glared at Julia, then rushed to her mother's side. "Mamma, what is this?"

Augustina arched her neck proudly. "A meeting. I called it."

Maria propped her packages against the wall. "Emilio Greco almost knocked me over on the stairs. Someone must have upset him."

"He does not matter!" Augustina rapped her knuckles once on the armrests of her chair, gave a preemptory wave. She craned her neck around and looked at Emilio's wife. "I'm sorry, Silvana, my dear, but I speak the truth as I know it. Emilio is not one of us, may never be, if he keeps this up." She motioned her daughter to one side and wheeled toward Julia. "This one," she added with a nod at Julia, "*is* one of us, whether certain people like it or not!"

She continued out onto the porch and backed into her usual place. "Come, let's all be seated, so we can continue."

Everyone did as Augustina ordered, whispering among themselves as they moved wicker chairs into a close semicircle. A moment later, Julia was the only one left standing. She quaked with excitement.

Motioning to Lucia for the empty bolster beside her, Augustina orchestrated its placement opposite her chair. She lifted her cane from its spot by her side and tapped it on the bolster. "Sit, Giuliana. Listen." She tapped the floor. "Everyone, listen."

The group fell silent as Julia took her seat.

Augustina tucked her cane away and stared at Julia. "You must realize something, Giuliana. For us the past is very much a part of the present. History hangs around our necks like leaden crosses, whereas, I take it you know very little of your own family, of their past in the Calderola."

"Mostly only what my father told me right before he died last March."

Augustina frowned. "I am sorry to hear he is gone, but for shame. For shame," she said, shaking her head.

"I came here to learn whatever I could, but people seem afraid to talk to me. If even half of what my father said was true, the Giardani must have been eccentric, but I refuse to believe they were bad."

"Some might have considered them eccentric, but bad?" Apparently, the question was rhetorical. Augustina stared at Julia, her gaze coming to rest on the gift bag Julia held on her lap. "What have you there?"

Julia raised the bag. "Some herbs I hoped might help to strengthen your heart."

"I see. And you see, don't you?" she asked, scanning her neighbors' faces. "Have we forgotten how to recognize goodness? 'By their works you shall know them,' I believe Christ said. By this young woman's deeds she defines herself, just as the Giardani have always done! Healers. Helpers. Good-hearted, considerate neighbors."

The pregnant woman pointed at Julia. "Yesterday, she stood up to the strange priest to protect our children."

"Francesca's right! I saw that," said the old man. "And as I tried to tell Greco before he left, Giuliana also helped my poor, addled cousin recently when she took a fall on the Ponte Vecchio."

"Yes, thank you, Urbano," Augustina said. Shifting from her imperious demeanor to a grandmotherly posture, Augustina dabbed her hanky over her moist upper lip then took her time tucking it inside her cuff. "I called everyone here because I think it is only right to share what we know about the Giardani with this young one."

Several others in the group murmured their agreement. Julia's gaze moved around the semicircle, her heart thumping in her chest.

"I shall start." Augustina cleared her throat. "For generations before I was born, a Giardani woman was present at the birth of every child in my family, for everyone in these parts knew the Giardani were skilled midwives, gentle with both mother and child."

"Midwives?" Julia asked, a thrill charging through her. "I'm a midwife!"

"Of course. You would be. But let me finish."

Julia bit back a rush of questions. There'd be time for them later.

Augustina's gaze traveled over Julia's face, assessing her, it seemed. "The Giardani were feared, as were all who still practiced as they did, for their old-time wisdom gave them powers others did not have. The power to heal, to restore the balance, to calm the frightened mind. These things were mysteries to the simple folk of these hills." She scanned her neighbors' faces again, grinned. "It seems some of us may still be rather simple."

Old Urbano chuckled, a bit self-consciously.

"There were other healers, other midwives, in those days." Augustina's expression grew solemn again. "Not all were so kind, nor nearly so wise. The reputation of the Giardani even spread far beyond the Calderola. They were known as teachers as well as healers. Certain families sent their brightest daughters to train with them."

"I remember!" Urbano interjected. "My eldest sister always complained that she'd begged to be sent, but my parents refused, and then Anna was gone, and it was too late."

"Middle-class girls seldom were sent, but some might have liked it better if we had been, for the Giardani lived an interesting life, very different from ours. They kept ways that hadn't changed in countless generations."

Julia leaned forward. "That's exactly what my father told me."

"I cannot speak of their ways, for they are not part of my direct knowledge." Augustina hesitated, seemed to make up her mind about something. "Their traditions were so old they were steeped in a world that had long since met its death except in a few very old family lines."

Julia felt her heart sink. "I'd hoped someone here might know of them."

"I couldn't say if any of the old ways survive today." Augustina glanced at Lucia then turned back to Julia. "I only know when I was young they were still kept by some." She looked at the postmistress. "Did the Andradi ever speak of this, Fiorella?"

"Yes," Fiorella answered. "Stories of those families were also told in our home, but never were shared around the fire during the winter months, when we gathered for the *veglia*. You know of the vigils, the night watches of the Tuscan family?" she asked Julia.

"I've only read about them," Julia admitted.

Augustina took over again. "The *veglia* brought us together back then, to share riddles and fairy tales around the hearth, our solidarity protecting us as we passed the long winter nights. They supposedly kept evil spirits and witches away, another old tradition that dies off now."

Fiorella piped up again. "Stories of your family were told when the men and boys were away in the hills or the fields. As we sewed or cleaned, did the women's work, that is when we spoke of our friends, the Giardani."

"Friends?" Julia glanced from Fiorella to Augustina.

"Friends." Augustina's gaze softened. "Your grandmother was present at my birth, Giuliana. She was no more than a child herself then, of course, but everyone always reminded me Anna Giardani was the first to hold me and care for me when I came from my mother's womb."

"Me, too." Fiorella said. "That's not something one forgets." Her voice cracked. "I met Anna a few years later, at the birth of my youngest brother. She impressed me with her kindness, her gentle understanding." Fiorella glanced toward the windows. Her eyes had a faraway look. "I never forgot Anna Giardani. She was special to me for the rest of my life. Through all the years of my youth, I dreamed of being like her, proud and strong."

Augustina looked at Julia. "I was sad when Anna left us," she said. "There was no one like her when Maria was born, or my little Alessandra, the child I lost. Only the doctors with their hard, cold instruments, their pompous attitudes."

"There is something else you should realize, Giuliana. It's important," Urbano said. "Here we all know well the ancestral bones rattling away in our neighbors' closets. There are few families in the Calderola whose history has not overlapped with yours at some time or another, some more honorably than others."

Augustina leaned toward Julia. "That's how it is, when people live so close for so very long. Your father understood this, I think. Did you know he came here to help us during the war?"

Julia nodded. "Yes, he mentioned that last March."

"Not happy for us, the war years." Augustina shuddered. "We suffered then as we have always suffered in war. Terrible. We knew your father used the strange talents inherited through his family to fight against Mussolini and the *Fascisti*. His actions were secret, even from us, but we considered him a hero. We couldn't comprehend much of what he did here, but we understood enough to know we should shelter him. I myself kept him for a week, hidden in our root cellar."

"I kept him for two," Fiorella said.

Augustina settled back into her chair. "He brought your mother to meet me in 1980. He was a good man, proud of his family, especially proud of you. I can't understand why he didn't prepare you for coming here."

Julia attempted a smile. "That's a long, sad story, Signora. I'd rather hear the rest of yours."

"We don't know the whole story. There are others with whom you must speak."

"Who are they?"

"I don't know them, only of them. You will need to find them."

"I wonder if they'll know who I am."

"Rest assured," Silvana Greco said with a wide smile, "anyone from around here would know your identity the instant they saw you. No other family in the long history of this region has ever given birth to copper-haired women with eyes the color of yours."

Urbano gave Julia a toothless smile. "One old story says the eyes of the Giardani were once as famous as the gold of Florence."

"My grandmother always said their hair color came from the alchemists, a magical mixture of copper and gold," added Francesca.

Julia felt a blush spread over her cheeks.

"Forgive our teasing, Signorina Julia," Lucia said softly, "but anyone here really will know that you are a *true* Giardani."

Julia remembered her father had used the same phrase last March. "I sure hope you're right about that."

"Of course we are right." Augustina held her head high, as if defying anyone to contradict her. "Now. I shall tell you a story I once heard in our kitchen, as I worked beside my mother and my aunts. Let me see . . . how did it go?"

"I know the one you mean—" began Urbano.

"Hush, I recall it, now!" Augustina gave the old man a silencing frown then glanced back at Julia, humor lighting her eyes. "One of my great-aunts was jealous of a Giardani girl. The aunt was complaining to her sisters about how pretty the young woman was."

"Your mother's Aunt Francia, I'll bet!" Urbano slapped his hand down on his knee. "Never much to look at, they say, but a wonderful cook."

Augustina sent Urbano another stern look. "So my mother said, 'I heard the men of Tuscany have always desired the fair Giardani, but only those who would forsake their fathers would marry into that clan, for the Giardani women keep their own family name, no matter who they marry.'"

Francesca stood and pressed her hands into the small of her back, pushing her round, heavy belly forward then straightening as if to relieve some strain. "That's right," she said. "I remember something like that. 'Only a man with no pride would marry a Giardani, for it is known in that family the woman rules the man, according to the oldest ways.'" Her gaze looked a bit dreamy. "I'd forgotten that."

Augustina glanced soberly at Julia. "The young men around here have decreed no one should help you. They have blustered and threatened, spoken lies about the *streghe*, but I for one know how much I owe your family. I felt it was important to warn you."

Maria Sergi sniffed. "I just wish it had not been necessary to take such a blatant stance against those men, Mamma."

"Me, too." Julia rose from her chair and turned to the window. Outside, the morning mist still muted the view. "I promise you, though, everything will turn out fine." She was probably jumping way ahead of herself to say such a thing. Even with all she'd learned today, Julia knew she'd barely grazed the surface of the puzzle that was her legacy. She lifted her hands, stared at her palms, clasped them firmly together behind her back. "As I learn more, I know I can find some way to help your men live with all this."

"We have always lived with it, Giuliana," Augustina said with a sigh. "Those of us who scorned it and those of us who practiced it, we have always lived with *la Vecchia Religione*." She wheeled her chair to the window and took Julia's hands in her own.

"The Old Religion," Julia's whispered almost breathlessly.

"Every Tuscan, whether a *strega* or not, always had the Old Religion to turn to when all manner of Christian prayer failed." A frown wrinkled Augustina's brow. "Yet another ancient tradition lost to us forever, I fear." Her grip was firm, as if holding Julia's hands tightly would keep the past from slipping away.

Julia suddenly sensed precisely where her ancestral home lay. Not in the village, but just outside it, below Montecipriana's rocky outcrop. She closed her eyes, clearly envisioned a small cottage. She looked out the window. "My home is right over there, isn't it?"

Silvana looked tentatively at the others. "It is, Giuliana. You can't see it from here because it is on the south side of the mountain, around the hill from the village. You were on the property when you met us the other day."

"It's a farm."

Lucia joined Augustina at Julia's side. "It's called 'the Gardens.'"

Augustina smiled. "When your father came here in the 1980s, he learned the farm was still registered in the Giardani name. It belonged entirely to him. Now, I suppose, it belongs to you."

Maria gave Julia a moment to let the news sink in. "There were rumors that taxes on the Gardens were long overdue, that the place was a burden on the village of Montecipriana. No one knew what to do about it, so they did nothing until Tony came back."

"Not true," said Urbano, resting his elbows on his knees. "We scraped the tax money together every year for decades, struggled to keep the property from being sold. I think some feared the wrath of the old gods if the place fell into the hands of strangers, or worse, if it were sold to foreigners who wouldn't respect it and care for it properly.

Julia sighed. "I have so much to thank you all for."

"Don't thank us, thank your father." Urbano made a pious Sign-of-the-Cross. "Bless his soul. You can imagine how relieved we were when he took responsibility for the place and put right the long-standing debts."

Augustina nodded. "Tony said he could never come back here to live, but he wanted to preserve the family home. I assume he had you in mind."

Maria walked to her mother's side. "He wanted to set up a trust fund here in Italy to maintain the farm, so I gave him the name of our lawyer in Siena. The fields had been sporadically worked by distant relations of the Giardani when your father first hired Emilio to share-crop the farm."

Silvana nodded. "The Gardens themselves, famous in this countryside for generations, were entirely overrun. I have felt privileged to bring them partly back to what they once must have been."

Maria shuddered a bit, cleared her throat. "No one has lived in the cottage since the family left. No one besides your father has been inside it since then, either, so far as anyone seems to know."

Lucia put her hand on Julia's shoulder. "Old legends surround the Gardens, Signorina Julia, the kind that make people respect a place but fear to live there themselves." She paused. "In your grandmother's time, it was a famous *poste del streghione*."

"*Poste del streghione*," Julia whispered, gazing out at Montecipriana. "Meeting place of the witches."

FIFTEEN

Julia approached Montecipriana, swung left, and crossed the vine-covered bridge. Winding through the forest, she passed the place where she'd encountered Emilio and Silvana on the tractor.

This morning, the road ahead was empty. It continued to curve southward, inclining up a gentle slope and widening into a two-lane driveway that disappeared between two mammoth barns. The rock-built barns were joined by an arch wide enough to contain some kind of room, to judge from the pair of shuttered windows at its midpoint.

Beneath the arch, both doors of a wide, wrought-iron gate stood ajar, as if to welcome Julia inside. She stopped a few feet from them and jumped out of the car, thrilled by the beauty everywhere she looked. From under the arch, she saw a cobbled courtyard, stone garden walls awash in morning light, the sunny eastern face of a modest stone cottage, its eastern porch smothered in dark-green vines.

She had come to adore Tuscany, but this seemed more enchanting than any other place she'd seen. Even the breeze here felt softer than elsewhere. It had a signature quality she couldn't quite define. According to Silvana, the cottage stood about two-thirds of the way up the wedge-shaped Giardani property, which tapered from mostly level fields skirting a mile-long stretch at Montecipriana's base upward to a small plateau that abutted its cliffs.

Apparently, it was a large farm by local standards. The lower terraces were exquisitely sculpted, Tuscan style, into the contours of the mountainside with that air of cultivated near-wildness Julia had decided was unique to the Calderola. Above them, freshly tilled terraces gave way to a dense stand of forest, the outskirts of which Julia had obviously barely penetrated when she ran into Vario the evening before. All hers. Almost unbelievable. It had taken only minutes to present her passport and driver's license to the lawyer and walk away with the keys for the Gardens' gates, the barns, the house.

She patted her jacket pocket. The heavy keys clanked against each other reassuringly. She had never cared much about possessing anything, let alone real estate. This felt different, though. Entirely different. Ownership wasn't what mattered here, didn't even enter the equation that made up the Giuliana legacy. Ancestral home of the Giardani clan or *poste del streghione,* the Gardens was about responsibility—ancient responsibility.

She opened the gate wide, walked back to her car, stood a moment more to take it all in. Overhead, doves circled in the cloudless sky. In the silence of this peaceful place, she heard the soft rustle of air through their wings. Fanning out, the doves broke formation and dipped beyond the fringe of trees surrounding the rocky mountaintop. Julia ducked back into the car. She had so much to learn. Why her grandmother had left the Gardens. What the Giuliana legacy might once have been. Even more crucial, what it might be again, might bring to her own life and the lives of those in her community, whatever that might be or become. There was nothing left but to pass through the gates and enter the *strega*'s world.

She drove under the arch and into the courtyard. Compared to the barns, the tightly shuttered cottage seemed small but well suited to the gently curved terrace on which it stood. It was built low in front and rose to a second story toward the rear. In addition to its vine-covered eastern porch, two other deep overhangs with low walls and graceful arches stretched along the loggias on the north and south sides.

Unlatching the gate that led down to an enormous herb garden, she passed beneath a rose trellis from which drooped a few early blooms. In the damp morning air, the scent of herbs was pungent, the perfume of citrus blossoms heady and alluring. Mounds of green and silver herbs lined the flagstone paths. Taller bushes sheltered small stone statues of *folletti*.

She walked on, her attention honed to take in every detail. Several small buildings flanked the herb garden, forming part of the stone wall that marked its lower boundary. The terraces farther down held row after row of vines, a few thin olive groves, and freshly tilled fields bounded by trim rows of trees, looking for all the world like a scene from a Renaissance landscape. How lovely the pond in the garden's center would look filled with water, the stone birdbaths scattered around the grounds filled, the feeders that hung on rusted chains from the larger trees all bursting with seed. She imagined the place must have been even more lovely in her grandmother's day.

Anna Giardani. Proud and strong, Fiorella had called her. Julia could see how her grandmother might well be described in those terms, but the people here had never seen Anna's golden eyes turned a lusterless, milky brown, or the unparalleled sadness that had seemed night and day to wrack the old woman who moved to Berkeley when Julia was nine years old.

Surrounded by the loveliness that was the Gardens, Julia finally understood that sadness. No wonder the kind *strega* had died somewhere between Tuscany and Ellis Island, been transformed into the self-contained, immigrant grandmother Julia had known. Anna Giardani had been torn from her garden. Uprooted.

No wonder, either, that Julia had felt indifferent toward her father's house in Berkeley after his death. This was home to her as truly as if she'd been born here. The place was part of her makeup, she was sure of that now. This was where she was meant to live and work and grow—the garden in which she was meant to continue to "blossom," as her father doubtless would have said.

She looked back up the hill. The cottage seemed to call her, to pull at the strings of her heart. She'd love to press herself against the walls of the old family home, run her hands along the curves of its brick-trimmed arches, but above the cottage loomed the top of Montecipriana, and the urge to find out what was at its summit was stronger than ever.

SOUTHERN FRANCE

Anatolin gripped the pitted iron of the fire escape overlooking Marseilles harbor. He was more than worried. There had been no sign of Danilenko on the lead tanker, no sense of him anywhere nearby. An astounding fact. The general should have appeared right along with his shipment. That he hadn't was cause for the gravest concern, but it also meant Anatolin could check on the artifacts more easily—and sooner than he'd expected, from the looks of the crew below. They were taking off their work gloves, donning their coats, leaving.

Anatolin climbed down the fire escape and walked slowly to the wharf, passing unseen through a dark, narrow alley. Listening as the boisterous crew dispersed. Watching an emaciated cat scurry beneath a pile of soggy newspapers. Keeping an eye out for Danilenko, though he was certain the general would not show up now.

Anatolin came round the side of the metal-roofed building and stopped in his tracks. One of Danilenko's men, apparently left behind to guard the cargo, leaned against the front of the building beneath a canvas awning that had seen better days. Fishing with his index finger for one last cigarette in an obviously empty pack, the guard seemed frustrated and preoccupied, unaware of Anatolin's approach.

Anatolin lifted the collar of his leather jacket, pulled down his stocking cap, then turned and silently headed back toward the alley. The cat he'd seen a moment before had apparently followed him. The scrawny thing chose that moment to yeowl and hiss.

"Hey, you!" the guard shouted, coming to attention then stepping briskly from under the awning. "*Gavnó!*" the man added, a nasty Russian epithet. He had either taken Anatolin for one of Danilenko's crew or this was some kind of trap.

Anatolin tuned in but received no clues. He'd have to take a chance. "What!" he shouted, trying to match the guard's lowbrow snarl. Praying the ruse would work, Anatolin assumed an appropriately defiant arrogance as he sauntered back toward the guard, who pointed toward a brightly signed convenience store two blocks south of the wharf.

"Go get me some smokes—Gauloise—and make it fast!"

"Get them yourself!" Anatolin set his jaw, shoved his hands deeper into his jacket pockets.

The man scowled then broke into a slow, conspiratorial smile. "So, you will give me a short break?"

Anatolin shrugged. "Suit yourself, but be quick about it!"

"What's your rush?" The man guffawed and tossed Anatolin a heavy key ring. "They say French whores, like honest taxis, don't start their meters until you get going."

Anatolin raised an eyebrow, forced a sour grin, nodded away from the building. "Get going yourself, before I change my mind." He breathed a sigh of relief as the man scurried in the direction of the convenience store.

Huge metal doors, no doubt electronically operated, sprawled across the building's front. Off to Anatolin's left was a small, inconspicuous entrance. He hurried toward it, flipping through the keys as he went. The largest fit the lower lock. He jiggled it, gave it a turn, heard the lock click open. The deadbolt above was not as cooperative. It took three tries before yielding.

Adrenaline screamed through Anatolin's veins. His heartbeat was probably off the charts. He detested this kind of thing, positively hated the way his pulse raced, the way his breath came in short, ragged gasps. He'd never make a good spy. Inside the windowless building, he searched for a light switch, found one, flipped it on. Rats scuttled. Bulbs dangling from long cords barely lit the large space. Fortunately, he didn't need much light to identify the artifacts. Their heavy pine crate stood in the center, isolated from other cargo. He recognized the crate's markings as he stepped closer, confirming what his intuition already knew.

There was something wrong. Very wrong, indeed. He felt dumbfounded. The crates were not making him ill. Not even uncomfortable. In fact, he felt nothing but intellectual aversion for the uses to which the artifacts historically had been put. He had braced himself to block out their vibrations, but there seemed nothing to block. Nothing! Infuriated, he slammed his fist down on the crate, flattened his palm against its rough surface. Even without Julia's psychometric ability, he could tell the artifacts' energies had gone utterly flat.

Impotent. This was the explanation for Danilenko's absence. There was nothing that precious left here to guard. Though the artifacts would still have significant collector's value in the right circles, they could no longer command the incalculable price they once might have. Nor could they do the world much harm. They'd been drained, somehow, of the occult power they'd carried before.

How the bloody hell had Danilenko accomplished it? Some magician's trick. A Satanic rite, perhaps. No rite could have taken place at Limassol harbor. There'd been only minutes between Anatolin's examination of the cargo and the time the convoy set sail. The filthy business must have transpired on the open sea.

Anatolin felt like kicking his boot through the side of the crate, had to struggle to contain his frustration. He had prepared himself for an encounter, had even psyched himself up to confront his longtime adversary, if need be.

Not only was he disappointed, he was also gravely concerned. That the general was not here could mean only one thing. Having assimilated these artifacts' powers, Danilenko was already pursuing a prize even more powerful than Hitler's infamous collection.

Certainty chilled Anatolin to the bone. The old fox was more treacherous than ever, more dangerous, as well. Beyond any doubt, he was headed for Tuscany—and Julia.

WEST-CENTRAL ITALY

Julia cut up through the Gardens' terraces of newly planted vege-tables, crossed over a small stone bridge and into the forest. The climb was more taxing than it had seemed from below. Her ears rang as she left the woods and stepped into the meadow she'd come upon the evening before.

This morning, the sun shone brightly, illuminating the meadow's far side. With better light, she could just make out what might be a path leading farther upward. To get to it, she'd have to cross the marshy pasture. Carefully, step by step, she picked her route across.

Near the mound, she slipped and grabbed a handful of vine for support. She pulled herself up, lost her balance again, then banged up against the mound, which wasn't a mound at all, she realized, but some kind of structure. Reaching blindly for a handhold, her fingers brushed against cold metal. She pulled back her hand, but not before vertigo struck her.

Staggering, she braced herself against the solid bulk of what seemed to be a metal door. Images sped past her mind's eye. None of them made any sense. She felt sick to her stomach. Faint. Wrenched along on a riptide of images, resisting.

Resisting.

Stop resisting. She took a deep breath. Her knees felt like buckling. She locked them, stood firm. The images slowed.

She could follow them now, make some sense of what she was seeing. A copper-haired woman had stood long ago in this very meadow, her arms overflowing with fragile wild roses. A young boy had watched the woman from the edge of the forest, his mind calling out—*Lady* . . .

Julia concentrated but missed most of what the woman, Lady, answered.

In the next instant, Julia felt herself merge with the woman's body, her awareness sharpened by the musky scent of roses, the bite of thorns into arms that felt sturdier though smaller than her own.

The woman sighed and sent a silent message to the boy.

He answered—*the people . . . scared.*

Julia gasped. Astonished to hear so clearly, she pulled back from the experience. Her curiosity battled with her confusion. She centered herself, stood very still. The sense of being someone else returned, more heightened than before.

The woman frowned, bit down hard on her chapped lower lip. *Lead them far from here. Hurry! Don't return to the Gardens until the warriors tire of pillaging, until the mountain is peaceful again.*

The boy's resignation came like a moan—*Lady, we love you.*

The woman watched the boy disappear into the woods, her fear gnawing at Julia's mind, the woman's thoughts on the hours she'd just endured, on her concerns for the future—not her future but her people's. Lady was here to meet some invader, a warrior king, to offer herself so the women of her clan would not be brutalized. Julia shuddered. Lady believed her death was imminent. The baby she carried would die, too, but something sacred was hidden, safe. The boy would carry the legacy forward, his children would bear the gifts of the Goddess.

Julia couldn't take any more. She had to distance herself from the woman's thoughts and emotions. She went down on her knees, pushed the palms of her hands hard into the ground, but it did no good. She was trapped. Struggling only made it worse.

Why was this happening—why couldn't she stop this vision?

Panic seared Julia's mind as coarse, hairy arms seized the woman. Hot, sour breath, the stench of unwashed flesh—brutal hands and teeth ripping at the woman's body while Julia's senses screamed.

Stop! Enough! The woman's cries or her own?

Crude jokes rose from the warrior band as they trussed the woman up like a piece of game over the low end of the battering ram they'd dragged up the mountain. Lady's belly scraped over the splintered trunk. Her hands were bound tightly around it, her legs spread wide, each ankle tied roughly to a wheel on either side.

Julia was desperate for release, but Lady stayed calm in the midst of her pain, her small body limp, her mind repeating one thought like a mantra as she endured violation after violation. Blood dripping from the torn nipple of Lady's breast stained the pale rose petals scattered in the shadow of the battering ram. Jeers rose from the circle of animal-men in the glade as the iron tip of a spear thrust between the legs below, pierced womb and heart.

Release came in the next heartbeat. Julia's awareness, still mingled with Lady's, hovered above the ravaged body on the battering ram, but the pain was over. Triumph rang through the warrior band. The priestess of this puny mountain had no power after all. Her Goddess was impotent, as feeble as their priestly king predicted. The warriors' victory cries faded.

The space around Julia suffused with rose-gold light. Tender, healing light, dispelling all confusion. She felt suspended, outside of time. Gradually, she started to feel better.

She heard something—a familiar, honeyed voice, echoing Lady's mantra through the bruised recesses of Julia's mind—

The legacy goes on, unbroken.

Suddenly, Julia again felt the marshy ground beneath her. She was panting softly, tears streaming down her cheeks. The ringing in her ears was deafening, the prickling at the back of her neck electric.

The air all around her seemed to whoosh like a fast-spinning ceiling fan, then gradually everything slowed. Beads of moisture trickled down her brow. Her body ached, felt icy. Her knees were soaked, her hands covered with mud, but she was back. Back in her own body, her own time, kneeling beside the mound in the meadow above the Gardens.

Using handfuls of grass, she wiped the mud from her hands and stood up. The mound loomed taller than she'd estimated from across the meadow. Still trembling, she yanked away a heavy cloak of vines, revealing the massive expanse of the metal door, skillfully cast with a pair of winged lions holding a Victorian-era scroll inscribed GIARDANI.

The structure the lions guarded had to be the family crypt. Julia backed up a few feet, paced to her left for a better view. Crossing her arms over her chest, she stared, clarifying angles and contours, gauging height and depth. She'd seen enough photos and drawings of this kind of thing these past few days to recognize the one in her own backyard. No doubt about it. Behind the more recent architecture of the crypt was an ancient Etruscan tomb. She didn't need to touch anything to know the woman in this vision—her ancestress?—was buried in the depths of that tomb.

Too woozy to climb farther now, Julia sighed and headed back down toward the cottage. Emerging from the forest, she paused and looked down on the farm. A prickle of anxiety registered at the back of her neck.

While she'd been up by the crypt, someone else had obviously been down below—might even be there still.

BOOK THREE

THE GARDENS

What is remarkable . . .

is the fact that so much antique tradition

survived with so little change. . . .

But legends and spells

in families of hereditary witches . . .

have been kept since 2000 years.

—CHARLES GODFREY LELAND
ARADIA, GOSPEL OF THE WITCHES, 1890

SIXTEEN

Julia dashed across the courtyard. The intruder had apparently watered the vegetable garden and left. The gate under the arch, which she'd left open as she'd found it, now was closed. Beyond the gate, about to curve around the north rim of the hill and out of sight was a green pickup truck heading quickly off the property.

The house seemed undisturbed, but several items had been piled on the hood of her car. The most prominent was a well-used dust mop with a note taped to its handle. Beside it sat a box-style, high-power flashlight and a pair of heavy workmen's gloves in a smallish size. A cellular phone bearing a property label from the Casa Sergio had been tucked inside one glove, a square cotton scarf in the other.

The note was from Maria Sergi. She had sent the items over with Emilio Greco, whom Silvana was "fast whipping into shape." Silvana herself, with Lucia in tow, would be at the Gardens in less than an hour. Julia was to keep the phone for as long as she needed it, "Mamma insists."

"Bless you, Augustina," Julia shouted in gratitude.

She tied the scarf around her head, pulled on the gloves, and grabbed the flashlight and the mop. She crossed to the kitchen porch, where a massive door seemed to be the only entry. The huge padlock securing it looked old, obviously made to withstand the tests of time and the Tuscan elements.

She closed her eyes and thought of her father standing here years ago. She'd still been a child when he'd clicked this lock closed the last time. With a sigh, she pulled its gigantic old iron key from her pocket, fit it into the keyhole. She rocked the key back and forth, gave it a clockwise turn, and heard a grating sound then a clunk as the lock came open in her palm.

She pushed hard against the door, which slowly gave way, exposing a wide, deeply worn stone threshold. Billowing dust entirely obscured the view inside. Grabbing the dust mop, she cleared the cobwebs from the doorway and shined the flashlight into the darkness. Immediately across from the entrance stood an old-fashioned kitchen workbench. She perched her light on it, crossed to a pair of French doors that obviously opened onto the south loggia. She unlocked one door, then the next, tackled the tall, heavy shutters. One by one, they creaked open, dust motes dancing on the rush of fresh air.

The main room, a combined dining and living room, stretched almost the length of the house on her right. She walked to her left, where the room curved into a deep recess around a wide hearth beyond which a door led to a rustic indoor bathroom. The ground floor's ceiling beams were blackened with age, its stucco walls a splotchy grayish yellow. A shadowy loft loomed overhead. Beneath it stood a desk against the rear wall. Bookcases formed an L in the corner, their glass doors intact but laced with spider webs. Past the bookcases another doorway opened onto a small enclosed porch. Clearly a later addition, the room was lined with cupboards and a long counter.

Julia climbed the stairs and opened the windows and shutters on the loft's far wall. From the wall to her left, a rock-built bed frame jutted out, its slats stacked on the floor inside. Niches for small oil lamps curved into the stucco at table height on either side. Off the landing below, she found a small second bedroom, stepped inside and flung open its shuttered windows, continued downstairs.

An albino scorpion, obviously annoyed at Julia's intrusion, scuttled across her scuff marks in the thick coat of dust on the bottom stair. She stepped around it, feeling almost as if she should apologize for disturbing its peace.

Back in the living area, the huge hearth was a masterpiece, its stucco mantel and base trimmed in dark wood. A swipe of the mop revealed charred bricks that formed a grate at the back of its deep ledge. Moving more slowly, Julia examined the furnishings left behind when her grandparents closed the house. In addition to the desk, the bookcases and the kitchen workbench, there were several large cupboards and a long dining table with chairs. Some low storage chests were pushed up against the walls. That was about it.

Even in its present sorry condition, the house was a charmer. Surely, no place her grandparents could afford for years after emigrating to America would have been this fine. Something must have driven them away. Something terrible. Julia needed to learn what could have been that awful. But first things first. She moved back up to the landing and sat on a step, her arms wrapped around her knees. Abandoned all these years, a place this old could have been in far worse shape. She hadn't anticipated there wouldn't be electricity. Without it, cleaning up would be pretty tedious. Still, Julia felt lucky.

Or maybe luck, like the matter of ownership, didn't enter into the equation here at the Gardens. Maybe, like some living matrix of stucco and stone, the house had been holding itself together, just waiting for her return. She knew there were mysteries to be solved here, but she'd been hoping for some material aspect of her legacy, and now she had at last one concrete task she could roll up her sleeves and tackle.

She stood up and brushed off the seat of her jeans. Hands on her hips, she gazed once more around the house. It was time for the spiders and scorpions who had guarded this place for so long to move aside.

She didn't know how she would handle her remaining

responsibilities in California, but she was here to stay, meant to live the rest of her life on this small mountain, on this land, in this very cottage. Her certainty surprised her, but at some very deep level, the cottage felt solid, rooted, gave her that sense of bedrock foundation she'd lacked since her mother died long ago. She wouldn't spend even one more night at the Casa Sergio. Ready for habitation or not, this was home.

She marched back up the stairs to the loft, glanced around. To the right of the empty bed frame was a small dark door, a key dangling from a chain looped around its handle. She opened the door, gasped at the sight of a small room illuminated by unshuttered windows. The high wall to her left had a large arched niche in its center. On her right, the roof sloped down to a point just above her head, where it joined a whole wall of pastel stained glass.

Though streaked with dust and dirt, the glass had been finely worked in a pattern of sea and sky. The large rock near the center of the scene was unmistakably meant to represent the one at Aphrodite's Beach on Cyprus. Across from the door, another row of windows, short and wide with lovely amber panes, opened to frame the view of the rocky outcrop atop Montecipriana.

The room felt special. Holy. Its only furnishings, two straight-backed chairs with a small chest between, faced the niche from the center of the space. She ran her glove over the seat of the nearest chair, swiped off its carved back, imagined the pretty niche aglow with candles.

She sat down in the utter stillness. Alone though she might be, the last Giardani in Tuscany for all she knew, she had a clear idea of how this room had long been used. It could take a while to learn the precise prayers—or whatever—employed by her ancestors. Until she did, she'd improvise. She couldn't imagine any other way to attune herself with the smiling, unpredictable divinity at the heart of the Giuliana legacy.

∞

A few minutes later, Julia heard a car pull to a stop out front. She hurried downstairs and out to the courtyard. Silvana and Lucia stepped from one of the Casa Sergio's housekeeping vans.

"*Ciao!*" Silvana called, using the informal, neighborly greeting Julia had yearned to hear addressed to her. "I came to help any way I can, and Maria says Lucia is yours for as long as needed."

"Terrific!" Julia answered. "There's so much to do!"

Lucia cracked the sliding door on the side of the van, revealing a barrage of buckets, mops, a vacuum cleaner, other cleaning paraphernalia.

"Is it terrible inside?" Silvana asked.

"Not half as bad as I expected," Julia said, pitching in to unload the van. "Aside from the larger bedroom upstairs, which I'll need cleaned completely by bedtime tonight, we should try to get started on the worst of the mess, clear away enough of the accumulated dust and grime to see what refurbishing needs to be done right away." She looked longingly at the vacuum. "May as well leave that here. There's no sign of an electrical outlet."

Silvana gave Julia a grin. "Your father had electricity run to the barns in the eighties," she said. "Emilio keeps an extension cord in the barn. It reaches to the house."

Julia watched, speechless, as Silvana lifted the Casa's industrial-strength vacuum out of the van and wheeled it toward the cottage.

∞

Danilenko had rented the villa on the eastern perimeter of old Volterra because it provided a superb view of the Calderola. It was a cold house, with milky antique window panes that turned the brightest sunshine a dim, chalky gray. He had taken to wearing his overcoat indoors and still spent much of his time chilled to the bone. But who cared. Creature comforts would come later. After he possessed the Giardani heirloom.

The view was what mattered now. Not that he could actually make out the farm the priest had called the Gardens, but it gave him a sense of power to gaze across the hills and know the object of his desire was within his view.

There was a knock at the door. The villa's sole servant hesitated at the threshold. Danilenko sighed. "Well, what is it?"

"There's a Jesuit downstairs, sir. Says he has an appointment with you."

The world was full of incompetents and fools. "Show the good padre up." Danilenko almost choked on his words. The so-called Jesuit had managed to muck up a thoroughly elementary assignment. Danilenko could barely force himself to look the moron in the eye. To make this appointment as brief as possible, Danilenko had ordered the man to prepare a short list of likely replacements for himself among the Giardani girl's neighbors.

Danilenko hoped the list could be trusted. Hitler's ruby pendulum was fast losing the girl's impression. The link to her was beginning to fade. Danilenko needed another associate, hopefully someone smarter, someone who could get closer to Julia Giardani than a priest ever could.

∞

Julia and her helpers sat around the large stone table on the kitchen porch, enjoying the picnic lunch and lemonade Maria had sent along with the van. Julia was ravenous. Keeping up with Lucia and Silvana had been a challenge. "Neither of you seem the least bit afraid of being here at the Gardens," she said as she tore a piece of bread from a large crusty loaf.

Silvana looked out at the courtyard. "I've been working outside for years. I've never felt anything but happy to be on the property."

Julia leaned toward Lucia. "What about you? Not the superstitious type?"

Lucia blushed. "I suppose I must tell you a secret." She took a sip of her lemonade. "Not a very well-kept one, I'm afraid."

Julia smiled. "I'd like to hear it."

"I, too, inherited *la stregheria,* three years ago, when a great-aunt passed."

Julia chuckled. "So that's why Augustina looked at you as if you knew something I needed to learn."

Silvana sliced a few pieces of cheese and passed the plate to Lucia. "Tell Julia how *la stregheria* came to your family."

"It happened in the mid-1800s," Lucia said. "My mother's family owned a small palazzo near Dante Alighieri's house. There was this priest, rather a country bumpkin who hated being posted to a grand city like Florence." She paused and took a sip of lemonade, continued. "One day, he was called to an old woman who was *in extremis.* But the woman refused the last rites. Eventually, the priest coaxed the woman to explain. 'I have this inheritance, silly priest, and I cannot die until I have found someone to accept it.' 'No problem,' the priest answered, 'give me the inheritance and I will pass it on to our Mother the Church.' 'Not to the Church!' the old woman argued, fighting to rise, but falling back, exhausted. Of course, the priest couldn't allow the woman to jeopardize her soul. He agreed to accept her inheritance himself—and so became a *stregone!*"

Remembering her stubborn Tuscan grandmother, Julia imagined the scene as clearly as if she herself had been through some similar experience. Eerie. She brushed the sensation aside. "He must have resented being fooled into receiving a gift like that one."

Lucia smiled. "Apparently, he despised the gift for a while then practiced *la stregheria* alongside his priestly duties. Many years later, he told my aunt he didn't regret the old woman's trickery, that the craft had enriched his life and helped him become a better person. This priest and my aunt had a strange alliance. Under the guise of discussing linens for the parish altars, they met often. When the priest was on the brink of death, he called for her and begged her to take *la stregheria* from him so he could enter his Catholic heaven unencumbered."

Julia smiled and pushed her unease aside. To judge by Lucia's behavior, Italian witches stood by one another. With even one other, Julia wasn't as alone as she'd assumed.

A silver Lancia zoomed through the gate and purred to a stop in the courtyard. Out of it climbed Maria Sergi and a ruggedly handsome man of fifty or so. The man's stride was exuberant. His face broke into a friendly smile. Maria introduced Giorgio Conti as the contractor who almost single-handedly converted the Casa Sergio. Maria had brought him over in case Julia wanted to make renovations.

Julia smiled at Giorgio. "I've admired everything you've done at the Casa. I'm surprised you'd even consider a small job like this."

Giorgio waved her compliment aside. "I've wanted inside your family home all my life. The old legends say the Giardani always married artistic men and put them right to work improving this place. Your grandfather, Antonio, was considered a craftsman in the tradition of the masters."

Maria laughed. "Giorgio's always looking for lost tricks of the trade." She stopped in her tracks, looked embarrassed. "Of course, we assume you've decided to keep the property. We will all be thrilled if you do."

"Of course I'm keeping it," Julia said. Regardless of how extensive the renovations might be. "Giorgio, please come, tell me what needs to be done."

The contractor stepped over the abandoned vacuum cleaner in the kitchen and brushed his hands over the bricks. Silently, he thumped old copper pipes above the sink, probed around the adjoining pantry, nodded. He went down the narrow stairwell leading to the cantina and came back up, his expression grim, his eyebrows raised. Julia watched him tensely, the other women's anxious glances compounding her apprehension.

Moving into the living room area, Giorgio poked at stucco, checked window sills and door frames for moisture, examined a sampling of terracotta floor tiles. He stuck his head up under the hearth's mantel, jiggled the flue, pulled back just in time to miss a huge cloud of dusty ash. In the bathroom, he ran his gaze over the rough marble covering its walls and floor, peered at the joins, examined the fixtures and checked out more pipes.

Julia rubbed the tight spot just below her ribcage, clasped her hands and held them close against her body. If Giorgio didn't say something soon, she was going to scream.

Near the hearth, Giorgio finally stopped pacing around. He crossed his arms over his chest, leaned against the mantel. "This house is in superb condition," he pronounced. "Absolutely superb!"

Julia almost collapsed as relief flooded through her. The women cheered in unison, smiles lighting each face.

Giorgio grinned. "I think we'll need only a couple of days to freshen the paint, Julia. I suggest you put a small butane cook stove in the kitchen." He rubbed a gnarled workman's hand over his jaw. "And I think you will want two butane water heaters, one here in the kitchen and one in the bath. Now, these are trivial tasks, half a day's work. Central heating and the electrical work will take longer."

"How much longer?"

"Permits will be needed, and so on, requiring a *geometra*—"

"A middle man," Maria quickly explained. "To deal with the bureaucrats."

Julia's hopes for speedy renovations plummeted. She caught Maria's unspoken warning not to ruffle Giorgio's feathers, but she simply couldn't wait months to get the place livable. She didn't have months, knew there was absolutely no time to waste, though she couldn't have said why if her life depended on it.

"Can't we keep things simple and focus on painting and whatever else can be finished quickly?"

"As you wish, but you realize it will cost much more on the whole to paint again later?" Giorgio asked, as if he thought Julia was not very bright but was too polite to say so. "I can have a crew here by eight o'clock in the morning. In only a few days, you can move in."

"Terrific." Julia tucked her hands into the back pockets of her jeans, her thoughts racing ahead. Visions of the house alive again flooded her mind. "But I've already moved in."

"In that case, we better get busy." Maria stepped over to Giorgio and guided him back toward the kitchen, talking with her usual animated authority. "It's only one-thirty," she added. "There really is time to get started today. Julia, you'll need to get into Siena and do some shopping."

"We'll see." Julia loved her neighbors' take-charge attitudes, but she really didn't want to leave the Gardens, even for two or three hours. Her father had been a wise man, overall, but he'd been positively enlightened when he said Julia's legacy would become her first passion.

She'd been devoted to her work for the shelter, but this felt different, touched more than her head and heart. This touched a level of herself she'd hardly sensed before Cyprus, but which seemed much more a part of her since coming here. Maybe her father's and Andrei's predictions about the awakening of her "inner knowledge" were actually coming to pass.

∞

The niche in the small upstairs room had faded to an uneven pale blue, giving it a softly mottled look folks in California paid small fortunes to reproduce. Julia dusted it only lightly then continued washing the room's ceiling and walls. The tile floor was already done. She'd scrubbed it earlier, not once but three times. Silvana and Lucia were proceeding apace in the bedroom. Stepping through the door, Julia gave them each a smile. "Heaven help the scorpion who decides to resume residence up here!"

"*Boh!*" Silvana exclaimed. "Scorpions do not live with people. Those who made it clear of the vacuum cleaner will not come back."

Lucia moved to the armoire and started buffing it with wax. "The shops in Siena open for the evening in twenty minutes, Julia."

Sometime during the afternoon, Lucia had dropped the signorina before Julia's name. It felt wonderful.

Silvana stood up. "We'll be working even harder tomorrow. You'll never have a better time to fit in your shopping."

Lucia opened the armoire door, grabbed a clean wad of paper towels, and polished the old beveled mirror on the inside. "Don't worry, there will still be much work left when you get back."

Julia weighed her need for a few essentials against all that remained to be done. She caught a glimpse of her own disheveled reflection—and of someone who looked like her twin standing in the doorway behind her. She spun around but found no one there. It struck her that while the scorpions might be gone for good, any Giardani ghosts hanging around the place likely wouldn't be. They had no reason to leave. Far from it. Silently, she walked over and locked the small room's door. Pushing the key into her jeans pocket, she peeled off her gloves.

"Okay, you two, consider me gone." She gave Lucia a hug, patted Silvana's shoulder as she passed her. "Thanks, again."

Out in the courtyard, Julia leaned against the car for a moment and gazed back at the house, remembering the woman she'd seen standing behind her. After the frightening experience earlier at the tomb, the idea of coming face to face with her double ought to make Julia nervous, ought to make her dread the time when her helpers would go for the night, yet she could hardly wait to have the house to herself.

SEVENTEEN

METRO CHARLES-DE-GAULLE-ETOILE, PARIS

Anatolin climbed the stairs leading up from the metro station. Paris was wet, as Marseilles had been, but the City of Lights was characteristically vibrant even in this dreary weather. He'd watched over Danilenko's cargo last night and half of today, done the best he could, for the present. Now it was time to set aside his concerns about Danilenko for the moment and enjoy his long-awaited first meeting with Madame Racine, who had been elsewhere while he was finishing his postgraduate studies in Europe years ago.

His mother had spoken of Madame Racine as a powerful, behind-the-scenes political figure of fairly wide repute. A woman of apparently indeterminate age and unaccountable wealth, Madame Racine had taken on mythic proportions in Anatolin's imagination. The letters she wrote to him at Utrecht, enigmatic, filled with whimsy and intrigue, had heightened his urge to meet her, but he'd needed to return to Moscow before he'd had the chance.

Anatolin slowed his pace as he approached Madame Racine's address on prestigious Avenue Kléber, a wide street lined with dignified townhouses. He strolled calmly now, exactly as he'd often imagined himself doing if he ever got to Paris again. Although there was no direct sunlight, the avenue gleamed. When he'd made his one previous visit to Paris, he'd been a member of the Soviet intellectual elite. A demigod, almost, as were all Soviet scientists educated abroad, even briefly as he'd been. Quite a contrast to his present state. Former exile. Recent expatriate. Mystic in search of a home.

Before he knew it, he was standing before Madame Racine's narrow four-story house, reaching for the shiny brass knocker on her carved and burnished door. Ceramic pots brimming with bright cyclamen in bloom welcomed him as he knocked. A brisk butler admitted him and led him up a spiral staircase to the second floor. Ushering him into a huge library, the butler offered him a chair near a crackling hearth and left him to await his hostess.

Anatolin scanned the lovely room, noting the leather bindings on the books that lined every wall. More books sat piled on long, polished tables. What he'd give to own such a library. There were many rare volumes long forbidden in the former U.S.S.R., the kind that would probably cost a Mafia kingpin's ransom in today's economically devastated Russia. Beneath tall windows lining the south wall, he spotted photographs clustered on a cabinet. He was tempted to examine them but decided to hold off until Madame Racine joined him. He sat back in his chair, crossed his leg over his knee.

Turning his attention to the fire, he gazed into its multicolored flames, wondered what the elusive Madame Racine would be like when he finally came to know her.

Would she present herself as the savvy international diplomat or the daring former clandestine? Anatolin grinned to himself, rather hoping she'd reveal the facet of her multilevel personality his mother had most loved—the sagacious and inimitable occultist, Ilina Mikhailovna's "Charlatan."

He didn't have long to wait. The door behind him opened, and he rose to greet a charming vision in a flowing velvet caftan of deep emerald green.

"Mon cher!" Madame Racine said, her voice high, her accent refined. Her hair was swept up and bound at the top of her head in a fanciful arrangement of honey-colored curls and opalescent pearls that complemented the wide silver streak to the left of her deep widow's peak. Ropes of pearls swung across the front of her caftan as she walked swiftly toward him. "At last we meet."

"At last, indeed." Anatolin bowed and brushed his lips over the slender gem-studded fingers Madame Racine extended toward him. The Charlatan, no doubt about it. *"Enchanté, Madame."*

She arched her head back and met his gaze. "Oh, dear!" she said. "I think your mother must have told naughty stories about me, *n'est-ce pas?"*

"I'm afraid so."

"Well, it can't be helped." She extended both hands and took his in a firm grip then pulled him toward the chairs. "I am so happy you have come to Paris. Your mother loved it here." Madame sighed. "I have missed her every day for more than fifty years."

"I think you were one of the few people on earth she really loved." Anatolin wasn't exaggerating. His mother had adored Madame Racine without reservation. He looked away and spotted the butler, standing patiently by the door, holding a heavy silver tray laden with crystal decanters and glasses.

"Mon Dieu! James, I forgot about the tray in my excitement." She waved the butler inside. "Please leave it on the table. Then you may go. Andrei will pour for us, won't you, my dear?"

He glanced at the butler. "Certainly."

"Very well, Madame." James smiled politely and left the room.

Anatolin leaned forward. "Before we start, I need to thank you for engineering my release."

Madame Racine was silent, a poignant smile on her lips, her gaze directed toward the photos across the room.

He braced his forearms on his legs, his hands clasped. "And for maneuvering my invitation to Cyprus."

"How did you learn I was responsible?"

"I guessed."

Slowly, she faced him. "Your mother was my dearest friend, Andrei. It was clear from the moment she returned home after the war there was nothing I could do to save her, but I've been trying for years to obtain your freedom." Her voice quavered then she lifted her chin and gave him a mischievous grin. "Then this year—*Voilà!* I suppose the timing was finally right." She clasped her hands tightly in her lap. "But, my dear, you did not come directly from Cyprus."

"No. I stopped in Marseilles."

A frown puckered her brow. "Andrei," she said soberly. "It was unwise to think you could take on Gregor Danilenko without assistance."

"You know about Danilenko?"

"And his contraband."

"How?"

She hesitated, as if measuring her words. "Your mother became aware of his smuggling activities in the mid-1980s. You know, of course, about your mother's involvement with the items that later came into Danilenko's possession?"

"I first heard the story when I was thirteen."

"Good. Then you understand why Ilina Mikhailovna might remain sensitive to the artifacts, why it was only natural she'd be the first to intuit when Danilenko started shuffling them about." Madame Racine moved to the far side of the room. "I have a young friend with Interpol. I have invited him to join us after dinner tonight. He'd love to discuss the Berlin Affair with you, I'm sure."

The Berlin Affair. Anatolin had never heard anyone but his mother use that tag for the disappearance of Hitler's library. "Hard to believe someone from Interpol knows about that."

"Not only does he know, he cares. We first became friends when he interviewed me about what I knew of the Nazis' occult collection and its confiscation." Madame Racine rubbed her hand wearily over her brow.

Anatolin didn't like the way she looked. "You're tired."

"I'm fine," she said, dismissing his concern with a toss of her head. "You, *mon ami,* are the one who is tired, I think. We shall catch up a while, rest *un peu,* then dine in tonight."

Suddenly, he felt as if his lack of rest had finally caught up with him, as if worrying about Julia had finally taken its toll. He'd go along with Madame's plans for the time being, wouldn't launch into his decision about going to Tuscany just yet. He wanted to be at his best when he put Julia's case to Madame Racine.

WEST-CENTRAL ITALY

By six-thirty that evening, Julia was on her way back to the Gardens, her car filled almost to overflowing with purchases from Siena. At Maria's favorite bed-and-bath boutique, Julia found a blue woolen rug and matching seat cushions for the meditation room and most of the linens she'd need, sheets and cozy wool comforters for the beds, simple floor runners for the bedrooms, kitchen, and bath, some thick white Egyptian cotton towels.

Maria had promised mattresses for both beds and other odds and ends as needed but, following Silvana's suggestion, Julia also checked out the general emporium near the Piazza del Campo. There she picked up a shiny stovetop espresso maker and a can of Illy, her favorite espresso blend. She also bought a small, sleek radio/tape deck with excellent speakers, a few essential kitchen gadgets, and a nifty recharger to handle the wide variety of batteries her new appliances would need.

Driving home across the Gardens' bridge, she felt a surge of excitement that grew more intense as she climbed the grade and pulled into the courtyard. Funny, while she'd been pushing and rushing about, relatively little had happened. Since she'd slowed down a bit, listened to the small inner voice she was coming to know, things were happening fast. Almost too fast.

Inside the house, Giorgio was leaving. The plastic sheeting he'd used in the kitchen was all folded up. The vacuum propped open the door as he carried equipment to his truck. Even in the oncoming twilight, the vaulted room seemed several shades brighter, the brick and stone like pale cinnamon and nutmeg instead of the muddy gray-brown they had been when she left.

"The walls look wonderful."

Giorgio leaned back into the kitchen, gave her a proud grin. "These old places are nice without five or six centuries of cooking grime."

"I hardly believe the walls will look even better tomorrow."

"Believe it." He transferred the plastic to the porch, the corners of which were heaped with the kitchenware removed from the kitchen shelves before he began. "See you at eight tomorrow morning."

"Terrific!"

Heading for his truck, he called back over his shoulder. "You'll have hot water to start washing things up by ten."

"Meanwhile, we have paper cups," Lucia said as she refilled her coffee. "You got back just in time. Silvana has found the linen closet."

Smiling to herself, Julia followed Lucia to the closet, a roomy nook tucked under the loft beside the enclosed porch. She leaned against the closet's doorjamb, caught a whiff of cedar, another of camphor.

Silvana had already inventoried the best preserved items. She would drop them in Montecipriana to be laundered the old-fashioned way. "I would never have expected these old things to look this good," she said. "Amazing, but somehow I'm not surprised."

"I'm not either," Lucia looked at Julia. "It's as if this house and everything in it were just waiting for you."

A chill raced up Julia's spine. "That's pretty much what I felt when I first got here this morning." She surveyed their progress, noting the damp but clean plaster walls, the tiles scrubbed and splotchy with residual moisture, the furniture pushed to the center of the room for the painters but already polished with Lucia's special blend of lemon oil and beeswax. She hadn't guessed they'd accomplish so much so quickly.

Thirty minutes later, her car was entirely unloaded, the cleaning supplies stashed in Maria's van, and her bed was made. She glanced from the small oil lamps beside her bed across the room to Lucia. "Maria, again?"

"Yes." Lucia nodded. "We found Anna's lamps carefully packed away in a corner of the cantina, but there wasn't time to clean and fill them tonight. There are two more of Maria's in the living room and one on the commode in the bathroom."

"I really am going to have to find some way to thank Maria and her mother."

Lucia smiled. "For years, Maria has wanted to build a spa at the Casa, but the large matched pieces of marble she's wanted have been far beyond her means."

Julia crossed her arms. "You're thinking she'd like the marble flooring from the north loggia?" The large marble slabs looked entirely wrong out there, and, earlier, Julia had discussed replacing them as quickly as possible.

Lucia nodded. "I saw her eyeing the marbles before she left. Perhaps you could offer them to her at a price she can afford or trade her for something you need."

"She has some nice furniture for sale," said Silvana. "Items her decorator ordered custom-made before the latest change in the Casa's color scheme. Ask her about them tomorrow, if you're interested." Being invited into the local bartering network felt very significant— gave Julia hope that someday soon she might really belong. The hope kept her going until she was finally alone.

After such a long day, she was more than ready to call it a night. She rubbed her forehead, brushed her fingers through her hair. She'd had no chance to look in a mirror since the afternoon, couldn't help wondering what Andrei might say about the uncanny resemblance between herself and the apparition she'd seen upstairs—her own hopefully friendly Giardani ghost.

AVENUE KLÉBER, PARIS

Madame Racine was even more charming at dinner than she'd been in the afternoon. Anatolin was amazed and delighted by her. Throughout their meal, she seemed intent on keeping the conversation light and breezy. She coaxed him into a spirited discourse on occult philosophy then steered the conversation to his work.

Her knowledge of his field amazed him. When she started grilling him about his research on military applications of psi, however, he grew uncomfortable and closed his mind, employing the special technique he'd developed to resist involuntary disclosure. Eventually, the subject changed and he relaxed again. Soon after, Madame Racine led him back to the library.

For the next hour, over fine, aged cognac, Madame regaled Anatolin with tales that put his mother's old war stories to shame. What a wild bunch the Task Force had been—and if Madame was correct in her conjectures, what a service they had performed for the people of Europe and the rest of the world. Anatolin was happy to learn his mother had been so valued.

Madame Racine took him by the hand and led him over to the photos. She pointed out several images of his mother and Tony Giardani from the 1940s. "They were wonderful together, those two. The very best of friends, no more, though I think Tony always wished for more. So young and full of life, they were. Dedicated to a better world for all." She ran her hand lightly over the tops of several frames, but her gaze never left the photo of herself with Giardani and Ilina Mikhailovna.

"My dear Ilina Mikhailovna—you must have been proud of her, Andrei. She was a noble woman."

Anatolin had heard his mother described by many adjectives during his life. Noble had never been one of them. The Soviets called her demented. Schizophrenic. They'd bumped her from one prison camp to another all through his adolescence then into a so-called hospital ward for the criminally insane. His eyes filled abruptly. Caught totally off guard, he looked away from Madame Racine and cleared his throat. Madame Racine also averted her gaze, lightly dusting a few frames.

Anatolin was grateful for her tact. Once he'd regained his composure, he noticed several other intriguing photos. A couple of American presidents. Several European statesmen. Aristotle Onassis. Rudolph Nureyev. All posed beside Madame Racine, who appeared in numerous guises.

"My collection of former paramours and old political cronies," she said, her chin held high, her eyes glittering. "Never mind which was which. In a life such as mine, more subtle distinctions become blurred over time." She turned toward him and took both of his hands. "You are very upset—and worried—I think, but not about anything we can remedy tonight."

Before he could answer, Anatolin caught sight of another group of photographs sitting unobtrusively on the cabinet to his right. His gaze riveted on a particular series in hand-painted porcelain frames. Julia. She was Tony Giardani's daughter, after all, practically her entire life arrayed before him in chronological order.

His heart in his throat, he turned back to Madame Racine. "You already know Julia Giardani."

"I know of her from Tony but I've never met her."

He had the answer to his question but asked it anyway. "Surely, you realize she's in trouble and needs both of us to help her?"

"Yes, Andrei. The young Giardani Heiress requires all the help we can enlist."

The door burst open.

Madame Racine smiled. "Interpol, I believe."

Through the door walked a man Anatolin had not seen face to face for almost twenty years. He surrendered to a full-bellied laugh, the kind he hadn't experienced since the postdoctoral program at Utrecht, where he first met the often funny, always brilliant Rafael Gibbons.

Rafael's afro was gone, as were his wire-rimmed glasses and tie-dyed clothes, but aside from those minor details, the tall, lanky black man hadn't changed. "Madame Racine," he said with a nod in her direction as he flourished an invisible top hat.

"Good grief," Anatolin said, shaking his head. "This fellow is no more prepared to be an Interpol agent than I am."

Rafael beamed his smile and closed the door softly behind him. He crossed the room and pulled Anatolin into a monumental hug. "Last I heard, you managed to wind up in the slammer."

Anatolin held Rafael at arms length, chuckling. "With a little help from my friends." Rafael and an Italian colleague, Vittorio Mansanto, were Anatolin's Western counterparts in the information exchange that had led to his exile.

Rafael grinned. "Guess that press conference you called pretty much blew your career to smithereens back home. Too bad, 'cause it's slim pickings these days for former parapsychologists. If Interpol or anyone else makes you a serious offer of work, I suggest you sign on."

Anatolin was sorry to sound a serious note only moments after their reunion but it couldn't be helped. "Actually, Rafe, I was just about to make one very serious offer of work, myself. Now I'll make two."

Madame Racine put her hand on his arm. "Try not to fret, Andrei, dear. There are others already in Italy safeguarding Julia. She will likely be fine for another day or two, while Rafael and I make arrangements to get ourselves to Tuscany."

Perhaps two days longer. Anatolin tried not to scowl.

He hoped Madame Racine was right that Julia was protected, but dreaded what could happen if she wasn't. He knew only too well Danilenko was not a man one could afford to underestimate.

WEST-CENTRAL ITALY

It was two in the morning when Danilenko approached the bridge leading to the Gardens. The villa's servant had driven the landlord's limousine. He would drop Danilenko at the side of the road then rendezvous two miles away in thirty minutes, precisely. Parking the huge limo anywhere near here was out of the question. It might be the middle of the night, but Danilenko didn't want his reconnaissance of the Giardani farm to be observed.

His luck might have taken a turn for the better in one aspect of this operation. The new assistant he'd hired to watch the Giardani woman was decidedly more competent than the priest. More observant, as well. The instructions for the drive to the Gardens had been flawless. Nevertheless, Danilenko knew better than to trust anyone else's observations. Making this trip himself had been inevitable. When he really needed to know the lay of the land, especially when there was much at stake, he'd long ago learned he could trust only himself.

He stepped out of the car, was momentarily shocked by the chill in the air. His breath was visible. Bad luck the moon was almost at the full, but he couldn't have put off this job until it waned—couldn't have put it off a single night. Waving the driver away, Danilenko stayed crouched until the car's tail lights were completely out of view. Then he stood, clasped his hands over his head and flexed his biceps a half dozen times. Since the Black Mass, he had been growing stronger and more youthful every day. Now, there was probably not a soul in Italy who would recognize him, a fact that made him feel like laughing.

Instead, he pulled down his dark stocking cap, pulled up the collar of his turtleneck, then slipped across the bridge and onto the Giardani property. It didn't take long to get a sense of the lay of the farm. He only wished the Giardani girl hadn't chosen to sleep that night in the cottage. His new assistant had made quite a point of Julia Giardani's determination. He needn't have. Danilenko was getting a clearer picture of his opponent's strengths every day.

He paused for a moment directly beneath the only visible second-story window. Her bedroom window, he decided, grinning to himself as he turned and started away from the farm. Tonight, his heightened psi had warned him there was strong protective energy surrounding the young woman. But he'd come back another time.

Oh, yes. He would come back.

EIGHTEEN

Lucia arrived promptly at seven-thirty in the morning with a loaf of fresh bread, a huge pot of Tuscan beans for lunch and a large thermos of coffee to start the day. "Did you sleep well?" she asked.

Julia smiled. "I was so exhausted I fell asleep the instant my head hit the pillow." She'd awakened at dawn, her journal and the Giardani notebook still open and lying face down on her bed.

"I'll pour us some coffee before we start to work."

"Hurry, though. Giorgio will be here with the crew before we know it."

Lucia didn't answer. She looked preoccupied as she poured the coffees and carried them over, not partaking in Julia's excited chatter about the upcoming work party, as if she anticipated some kind of trouble. Finally, she settled beside the large chest Julia earlier had tugged into the sunlight, a low ten-foot-long monster that had been none too easy to move across the room.

The chest's contents, large rolls of faded Byzantine silk rugs, soon shook Lucia from her preoccupation. Another, smaller chest held lovely old wall hangings, also rolled, woven in muted shades. The tapestries were obviously authentic, most likely Renaissance era, the rugs somewhat newer.

Lucia hoisted an armful and opened them over the dining table where the light was best. "*Sono bellissimi,* Julia!" She ran her hand over the smallest. "This must have been in your family for generations. They all must have."

"Let's get those smaller chests emptied."

"Yes. Then everything goes outdoors to air. By this evening, they will smell nice and fresh."

Thirty minutes later, the rugs and tapestries were all hung outside. Julia glanced at her watch, sighed. There was still so much to do in the cottage, and now the crew would be getting a late start.

Lucia took her by the arm and led her back inside. "You and I can push some of the chests out to the loggia. We can start spreading the plastic sheets for the painting."

"Right." Julia squared her shoulders and got to work.

By nine-thirty, they had run out of plastic, and Julia had run out of patience with the tardy contractor. She grabbed the cell phone to call Maria for his number, then set it down when she heard a truck pulling into the courtyard. Lucia had cleaned out Anna's old coffee-pot and had filled it with water. She hoisted it onto a large hook over the fire and followed Julia out the kitchen door.

Giorgio, obviously fuming, stood alone in the courtyard beside his heavily laden truck. His scowl stopped Julia in her tracks. "*Porci!* Stupid pigs, Julia. Nothing but idiot peasants around here—sometimes I don't know why I ever set up shop in this part of Tuscany."

"What is it, Giorgio?" Julia asked, though she'd already half guessed the answer had to be yet another attempt by the younger men to make things difficult for her.

"A disaster! No one will even talk to me about the Gardens, let alone come to work here. I can't find a single *geometra,* cannot pull together a crew for the life of me. Not only that—I was threatened—for helping you! Don't those fools know who I am? They can't threaten me!" Muttering to himself, Giorgio started unloading his truck.

Julia exchanged glances with Lucia and realized this was indeed what her young friend had anticipated. She kept quiet about her own frustration, the hurt feelings she refused to let anyone see. At least she had a few hard-working women to support her, and now her own contractor. She was glad Maria brought Giorgio, blustering and huffing and spewing angry vibes though he might be.

Several large cans of paint mounded with supplies, two water heaters, and a small gas stove later, Giorgio seemed to run out of steam. "I gave you my word, Julia, and now I must take it back."

"I understand." Julia crossed her arms over her chest and raised her chin.

"I don't want you having trouble because of me."

"I will install the water heaters and the stove, finish the kitchen myself. Then I must leave until things improve. I can't say when I'll return."

"I can live without central heating or electricity indefinitely—my family did for centuries. And I've painted before. I'm prepared to do it again."

"*Mea culpa, mea culpa!*" Giorgio muttered, striking his fist on his chest several times.

"Never mind. I'm grateful for your friendship. The rest will sort itself out in due course." Julia stared down at the small mountain of paint, rollers and brushes. If she was half the *strega* she ought to be, her words would eventually prove true.

∞

Julia was amazed. By ten-thirty, Giorgio had the bathroom's new water heater installed and was starting on the one in the kitchen. Silvana had arrived shortly after Emilio, who was unloading a large truckload of firewood and stacking it neatly at the corner of the north loggia.

Silvana commandeered Lucia to help unload her car—a roomy station wagon, apparently brimful of homemade farm goods for Julia's pantry—then breezed through the door juggling two shopping bags.

"Your father arranged for this, Giuliana. Almost everything you should need. Every year we've been prepared for you to come. When you didn't, we had your father's permission to sell your share of the crops at the market in town. This year, you came. It is good," She handed Julia the heavy basket she carried.

Samples of the Garden's produce gradually filled every shelf of the pantry. Fresh fruits and vegetables efficiently stacked in modern wire bins. Canned fruits and syrups, like bright jewels in their clear glass jars. Stewed tomatoes and homemade sauces. Honey, jams and jellies. Several large crocks of olives and four jugs of last winter's oil, each different variety neatly labeled. The final items—several cheeses, a bottle of milk, some thick sweet cream, and a chunk of unsalted butter—Julia deposited in the coolest corner of the pantry below a bowl of fresh brown eggs.

"Thanks to you and Emilio, I won't have to shop for weeks, except for simple things like spaghetti."

Silvana smiled as Lucia returned from the car with yet another bag. When she put it down, the bag tipped over. Out fell packages of dried pasta, rice, and the inevitable assortment of beans.

Julia threw up her hands. "You have thought of everything."

"Exactly as we should have."

Silvana gave Julia a hug and went back to work. By the time the women were ready for a late-morning break, Giorgio had finished installing the propane cooking stove.

He guzzled a cup of coffee, gave Julia a perky smile. "You can't use the kitchen yet. You must all stay out of the way while I spray my trademark cotta wash on the walls and ceiling." He tossed his cup into an empty shopping bag and hurried off for his gear.

"He is happy again." Lucia said.

She had taken the coffeepot out to the kitchen porch, then had come back for paper cups. She glanced at her watch and gave Julia's arm a squeeze on her way back outside.

"Are we expecting someone else?" Julia asked, following with Silvana.

"You never know, around here." Lucia smiled as she poured the coffee.

Emilio came around the side of the house, stopped in front of the table, and pulled off his cap. He gave Julia a polite nod. "What would you like me to do next?"

Silvana started to answer but stopped when Julia put a hand on her arm.

"Emilio," Julia said. "You have been in charge of things here for the last few years. Maybe it's best that Giorgio won't be able to continue this job right now. I wonder if you'd consider taking over for a while."

Emilio exchanged glances with Silvana before answering. "I am not a contractor, but I will do what I can to help."

"Good." Julia smiled. "Won't you join us for coffee?"

"Later. I must talk to Giorgio now." He nodded and walked away.

Julia smiled. It might be a while before she could safely call Emilio a friend, but at least he was no longer blatantly hostile and surly. She'd known he would change after getting to know her a bit. Eventually, the other men would, too.

∞

Julia had almost finished rolling her first coat of creamy white paint on the bedroom walls when Giorgio came up to the loft to say good-bye.

"You have done a fine job."

"I'll do the bedside niches last." Julia glanced toward her inner sanctum, which she'd locked again as soon as she'd painted its stucco walls. "The wooden doors will have to wait until I have time to prep for enamel." She smiled and held out her hand. "Thanks, Giorgio. For everything."

He shook her hand, said he'd drop a bill in the mail, then turned and headed for his truck. Julia followed. In the courtyard, he paused, rubbed a rough hand back and forth over the stubble on his chin.

"Be careful, Julia. I don't like some of the things I saw and heard in town this morning."

"I'll be careful. This trouble will all blow over as soon as people realize they can trust me."

Giorgio started to say something else then shrugged and smiled as he climbed into his truck. "*Arrivederci!*" he called out, waving as he drove away.

Julia made it only as far as the cottage door before another truck, large and dilapidated, puttered into the courtyard and stopped. Its open back held several men of varying ages, all dressed for heavy work. Lucia flew out of the house, smiling and waving at the elderly passenger seated in the cab of the truck.

"More friends, Julia. *Streghe* from all over Italy." Lucia looped her arm through Julia's. "I wanted to surprise you." Her smile radiant, she pointed at the old woman who sat beside the truck's driver. "That is Isabella Banfi from Calabria, a living legend. Call her Signora Isabella. She prefers that."

The driver, a sturdy young man with curly blond hair lifted the old woman out of the truck and gently set her down in the courtyard.

"*Buon giorno,*" the man called out with a ready grin.

"*Buon giorno,*" Julia answered.

He approached Julia boldly, blatantly assessing her. "Aha! You are as beautiful as we expected you would be!" he said in a north country dialect.

"Hush, Marco!" Signora Isabella's plum-colored coat was tattered, her darned hose sagged over vintage 1920s high-topped shoes, but she held herself with great dignity. "Welcome home, Giuliana Giardani."

"*Grazie*, Signora Isabella." Julia moved closer, excitement gripping her. The old woman's watery stare seemed grim at the moment, but Julia had warmed to her instantly.

"We anticipated trouble, so we brought help."

Emilio appeared at the porch, his body language awfully terri-torial, considering he'd been promoted only an hour or two before.

"We have more helpers, Emilio," Julia said. She turned to Marco. "Maybe you could introduce your friends to my foreman, Emilio Greco."

Marco waved the men down from the truck, gave Emilio a hand-shake, and introduced each man by name and by village of origin. Julia took one of Signora Isabella's mittened hands and tucked it into the crook of her arm.

"Come inside," she said, turning toward the kitchen door. "Things are still a mess, but we can have some coffee."

"No!" Isabella didn't budge. "We meet here in the courtyard, the *poste del streghione*, where we have always met. I will not stay long today."

"Then sit a while at the table on the porch." Julia helped Signora Isabella to a bench, drew over a low stool from the far corner of the porch, and sat beside her.

"Brush back your hair, child," Signora Isabella ordered.

Julia complied, a bit perplexed.

"So it is true," Signora Isabella reached over and caressed the cen-ter of Julia's forehead. "You are the Giardani Heiress. You wear the mark of the rose upon your brow."

Julia touched her forehead, gave it a rub. "This is the first I've heard about any mark, let alone a rose."

"It is the sign that Anna actually passed the legacy to you. I was fully prepared to see it there," Signora Isabella said. "No matter how disheartened Anna might have been at the end of her life, she would never have failed to perform the *strega*'s final obligation to the One she serves."

Julia covered her mouth with her hand, glanced quickly at Lucia and shuddered. She suddenly recalled her grandmother's passing and a simultaneous vision so traumatic she must have suppressed it. Years later, she'd remembered something, vaguely, but had assumed it was nothing more than a typical childhood nightmare. Now, for the first time, she clearly recalled her dying grandmother's image, heard again Anna Giardani's ragged voice—and her harsh command. "You shall serve henceforth, not I! Turana lives on in you!"

Julia swallowed hard, closed her eyes. "Of course." Like the reluctant priest from Lucia's story, Julia had unwittingly inherited *la stregheria*. "I didn't understand what my grandmother meant at the time, Signora Isabella, but she certainly did fulfill her final obligation."

Signora Isabella shook her head a bit sadly. "Many times over these many years I have dreamed of gathering here once more— many times I have pined to see again the golden eyes of a Giardani woman, though I had no reason to hope I ever would."

She paused and wiped her teary eyes with a faded pink hanky, then looked toward the garden. "I lived here once, in one of the guest cottages down there. During your great-grandmother's time."

"My *great*-grandmother's time?"

"Yes, indeed," Signora Isabella said proudly. "I trained with Giuliana in the healing arts. I knew your grandmother, too, of course, watched her grow up to become a lovely woman and a fine *strega*. Then I left to marry far from here, down south. I seldom returned to this region." She squinted at Julia. "You resemble Anna to some degree, but your heart and soul are more like Giuliana's, my beloved teacher and the last of the truly magnificent *streghe* in all of Italy, immortalized for her good works even in her own time."

"I am ignorant of my family and their ways." Julia bowed her head, wishing what she'd just admitted wasn't true.

"Their wisdom will return to you, Giuliana!" Signora Isabella said. "You are the chosen servant of the Goddess, of that you can be sure," she added softly, for Julia alone to hear. "Listen to your heart and all will be revealed in time. The rose will bring you true visions to teach you what you need to know."

What I need to know. Julia remembered her father saying those very words last March.

The old woman raised her voice to include Lucia. "By today's standards, Giuliana is still young. Before long, she will be as strong and as wise as any other Giardani witch!"

Then she chuckled and relaxed back in her chair, a capricious smile lighting her milky eyes. "Now, where is that boy?" She clapped her hands. "Vario?"

Instantly Julia heard a clatter from the back of Marco's truck. Vario Andrade stood up, his head barely visible over the truck's railing. "Here I am."

Stunned, Julia watched the child jump down from the back of the truck. Vario, with the *streghe.* Amazing.

"His great-grandpa was an old friend." Signora Isabella smiled merrily. "Well, young man, are you going to bring Giuliana her gift basket or not?"

"*Sì,* Signora." Vario hauled a large wicker basket from the truck.

When Vario set the basket beside her chair, Signora Isabella sat up straighter. She took off the towel covering its contents and pitched two homemade cheeses, one at a time, onto Julia's lap. "Those are from Marco's mother, my granddaughter, who lives up in Milan." She pulled out a brown paper bag. "And here, the finest pistachios grown in all Italy!"

Julia took the bag and poured a few pistachios into her palm.

"Wait!" Signora Isabella leaned over and clutched Julia's arm. Her misty blue eyes issued some kind of challenge. "Vario, find a broom!"

Vario grabbed the broom someone had earlier hung from a rusty hook beside the kitchen door. "We must not allow you to become bewitched, Giuliana," he said, his usual mischief in his eye.

Signora Isabella wagged a finger at Julia. "This boy is wise for one so young. Now, there are good *streghe,* and then there are those who are not so nice. Which am I?"

Julia chuckled. "A good *strega,* of course."

"So you believe, but have no certain way to tell. To find out, you must do as Vario instructs."

The boy took Julia by the hand and led her across to the outdoor bread oven, to the left of the kitchen door. "Repeat after me," he said solemnly.

Julia barely followed the archaic Italian, then slowly grasped the meaning of the phrase, an incantation to ensure the food had not been cursed by a vile and wicked witch. Vario motioned Julia to toss a few pistachios into the fire. She did, and he continued.

She was to strike three blows with the broom—one to the chimney, one to the window, and one to the door—to guarantee no wicked witch would ever enter her house. The idea tickled her funny bone, and she couldn't keep from laughing as she followed her instructions. By the time the incantation was completed, everyone was laughing. Julia took her stool and reached for Signora Isabella's hand. "Thank you so much for coming."

Vario tugged insistently at Signora Isabella's sleeve.

"What is it, *caro?*" Signora Isabella asked.

"You know!" he exclaimed, exasperation in his voice.

"Oh! Giuliana, Vario has a gift for you, too. He's so young, I actually forgot he became a *stregone* last year when his great-grandpa died. All right, Vario, go get it!"

The boy ran through the courtyard and past the gates, returning immediately with the little white goat, which he led by a pink satin ribbon attached to a big bow tied around its neck, against which the animal tugged a bit indignantly. Julia walked over and dropped to her knees beside the goat, gave his ears a good scratch.

"It's you I was growing him up for," Vario said proudly. "He's been running away from me and coming here for the past three weeks. He must have known you were coming home, Giuliana. That's what my great-grandmother said, and Signora Isabella said the same thing, too, when I told her. 'Those Giardani have always had a special white goat,' she said, and this goat is very special, you shall see."

"I already have." What she would do with a goat Julia couldn't imagine, but she wasn't about to say so. There was nothing to do but accept the gift. She stood up, put her arm across Vario's shoulders, and turned back to the porch.

Signora Isabella and Lucia stood, obviously preparing to leave. "I'll take Signora Isabella to the Andradi's and come right back." Lucia started toward her car.

Julia walked over, gave the old woman a hug, and walked beside her to the car. "I hope I will see you again. Soon."

"Sì." Signora Isabella smiled. "Maybe a day. Maybe two."

"Giuliana," Emilio called from the kitchen door. "Sorry to interrupt, but we need you inside."

"Un momento." Julia sent him an absentminded smile, turned back and helped her elderly guest into the passenger side of Lucia's car.

Signora Isabella leaned out the window and smiled wryly. "So! A stranger I came, but a friend I go. Remember, Giuliana, although there are fewer of us each year, the streghe are your extended family, and we will come any time you need us."

"I'll remember."

"But will you remember to be careful, cara? I am aware of the trouble here. I don't understand it, but I understand this—when we open to the blessings and talents from the past, we must also be willing to take up the unfinished business from then, as well." She frowned, then glancing up over Julia's shoulder, dropped her voice to a near whisper. "I see your joy, share it, but you must not forget to be cautious."

Julia sighed. How could she balance the need for caution against her more urgent need to keep searching? There weren't just mysteries to be solved here. There were mysteries within mysteries, and always some outer intrigue yanking her out of the far more compelling inner quest that drew her deeper with each discovery.

∞

Julia was glad Giorgio hadn't been able to hire a *geometra.* The idea of the house remaining pretty much as it was in her grand-mother's day gave her an unexpected sense of pleasure.

By three o'clock, Marco had the fire blazing brightly in the hearth and the windows and doors opened wide to vent paint fumes and dry the linseed oil spread over the tiles on the floors. Masculine voices drifted from other corners of the house.

Emilio took off in his pickup to irrigate a recently planted field and run some errands, but before he left, he predicted the initial renova-tions would indeed be finished by sunset. With the hearth roaring full blast, even the enamel and varnish the men had freshened would likely be dry by then.

Silvana had refilled the large coffeepot. Carefully, she crossed the trail of towels spread over the tiles and lifted the pot back onto the hook above the flames.

"Everything's under control here, Julia. Maria called while you were outside vacuuming the rugs. I told her you might be interested in some of the furniture she wants to sell. She's expecting you at the Casa within the hour."

"Did you tell her about the marbles?"

Silvana gave Julia a wide smile. "And spoil your bartering power?"

Julia went around the house to the bathroom's rear door. Inside, she glanced wistfully at the shower, decided there were too many strange men bustling about to feel comfortable showering. She pulled on the culottes and matching sweater she'd worn to see the lawyer and glanced into the mirror. She looked a mess, but she also looked every bit as happy as she felt.

She grabbed the soap she bought in Siena the day before and gave her hands a good scrub, splashed soapy water onto her face, and quickly rinsed it off again. The new cotton towel felt thick and luxurious against her skin. Running her fingers through her hair, she untangled a few curls and fluffed her bangs then noticed an odd reflection on her brow.

She blinked hard, lifted her hair with one hand, cupped the other over her mouth. Blazing in the middle of her forehead, in the place Andrei taught her about, was a golden rose. In constant motion, the rose pulsed from bud, to bloom, to bud again. She concentrated, felt a subtle vibration, wondered how long it had actually been there.

If Andrei had noticed it back on Cyprus, would he have said anything or would he have left it for her to discover? Blast the man! She hadn't heard a word from him since they'd parted. Daily, she waffled between feeling he would come to the Gardens soon and fearing she was merely caught up in wishful thinking.

She focused again on her forehead, gasped. Standing close—smiling into the mirror behind Julia's shoulder—was the woman she'd seen the day before. Julia blinked again.

The woman had vanished before she could smile back.

∞

Too impatient to stay a moment longer in Volterra, Danilenko had set off on his own in the limo and toured the valley around Montecipriana, then made his rendezvous with his new assistant at the Casa Sergio. He'd also determined to get another glimpse of the Giardani Heiress, however brief. He finally encountered her rental car headed back toward the Gardens behind a lumbering truck loaded high with furniture.

Pulling in behind her, he watched her drive, the ruby pendulum in his palm fairly effective at such close range. Why should he be surprised she would buy furnishings? He knew for a fact she'd let nothing stand in the way of what she wanted and, obviously, what she wanted was her ancestral home habitable as quickly as possible, making it that much more difficult for Danilenko to search undetected.

There was no denying the young woman's powers had grown. Impressive. He almost wished he and the Giardani Heiress weren't contending for the same prize. He suspected his new assistant might be equally impressed with his tender young foe. The man had seemed awestruck as he'd recounted Julia's effect on all who came within her sphere of influence. The way people immediately came to her aid. Put themselves on the line without a moment's hesitation. But best of all, the unwitting fellow had confirmed what Danilenko had most needed to know—the chink in his enemy's armor—the inevitable Achilles' heel.

According to his new associate, the Giardani woman was dangerously optimistic and much too trusting, too willing to see only the best in those around her. Danilenko had already suspected as much. He could only hope she continued to do so. It would give him an incalculable advantage—one he desperately needed.

NINETEEN

Julia's trip to the Casa Sergio had resulted in a happy neighbor who finally would build the spa of her dreams and a truckload of furniture that couldn't have been more perfect for the Gardens if it had been made to order. Emilio turned up unexpectedly at the Casa, but his pickup had been too small to carry anything more than three carefully crated boudoir chairs and a thick roll of carpet padding. Marco wound up bringing the marbles in his larger truck and transporting most of Julia's new furniture back to the Gardens.

She pulled into the Gardens behind Marco and parked at the far end of the courtyard, well out of the big truck's way. Marco's workers lounged at the table on the kitchen porch. Smiling proudly, they waved her through the door. Inside, the house positively glowed from ceiling to floor. Tears sprang to her eyes but she fought them back as the men filed into the kitchen behind her, everyone talking at once about how pleased they were with the fruits of their labors. Lucia stepped out of the small bedroom and started downstairs. Silvana came in from the north loggia with the man replacing the floor tiles.

Julia returned each person's smile. "Everything looks beautiful. Thank you all, very much."

Marco stepped forward. "I say we keep right on going until the guest cottages also are cleaned and painted. By the time we are done, your contractor may have the permits needed to finish what we can't."

Julia turned to Emilio. "Could the farm spare you that long?"

"Up to you," he answered with a shrug.

"I like your idea," Julia told Marco. "But let's talk it through tomorrow. Right now we need to get the trucks unloaded so we can call it a day."

Under Lucia's direction, the workers cut carpet pads for the antique rugs and rolled them into place. Before long, the new furniture was inside, the packaging removed, and Silvana and Emilio and most of the *streghe* had gone. Marco and his *streghe* friend, Niccolò, said their good-byes as soon as the heavy lifting was finished.

Julia was relieved to have the commotion over. She spun slowly around. The cozy sofa and chairs, upholstered in rich linens and wools of apricot, deep copper, and verdigris, were splendid complements to the softly faded old rugs. The new stools, painted in deeper hues, added bright notes to the kitchen. Everything fit even more perfectly than she'd envisioned. She glanced excitedly at Lucia. "The tapestries!"

Lucia broke into a smile and rushed after her. The next thirty minutes were spent in nearly silent concentration. The painters had left the tapestry fixtures in place. Julia and Lucia needed only to match each piece to the right hardware, easy enough since they had been rolled on their wooden rods.

The largest tapestry, a rustic design depicting the countryside at harvest, fit perfectly on the landing. Once hung, the muted tones of its autumn landscape warmed the whole downstairs. The other large rectangle, a flowering garden with the Giardani family tree at its center, fit over the sofa between the two small wells that held the fluted oil lamps Lucia found in the cantina. A long table runner in a bold pattern of fruits and vines Julia placed down the center of the dining table, just where her father had always used its twin back in Berkeley.

It was getting dark. Julia lit the lamp hanging above the table, and the whole dining area filled with a delightful homey glow. Lucia retrieved a large bowl from the kitchen and filled it with fruit. She put the bowl in the center of the table and stood back, admiring the effect. Beside the door to the western addition, which seemed to have been used exclusively as an herbal workroom, Julia hung a narrow tapestry done in slightly darker shades of rose, gold and peach. Beneath it stood the family's old walnut desk, which Julia had rubbed to a high sheen with Lucia's lemon oil-and-beeswax concoction.

"Astounding, how much we managed to get done," she said with a sigh. Even more astounding, though, was how much was left to do, to learn, to understand. And to find, like the keys to the bookcases and the one to the chest in the small room upstairs.

"It was worth every effort, to see the place look like this." Lucia yawned.

"You are worn out."

"No, just happy."

"Me, too." Julia gave in for a moment to the awe that had been building all day as the old house came alive before her eyes.

Lucia headed toward the door. "You'll thrive here. I guarantee it."

Julia followed. "My father said that." She choked up. "I'm so grateful to him, and to you. I don't know how I'll ever repay you."

"That's easy. I'll tell you how." Lucia stopped two feet from the door, turned back to Julia. "I want you to become my teacher."

Julia couldn't have been more shocked if someone had asked her to swim clear across the Atlantic. "And teach you what?"

"To develop my psychic talents. To heal the Giardani way—not just with herbs but the energy way. You know."

"That's the problem, Lucia." The young woman's remarks pushed every one of Julia's buttons. "I don't know."

"Perhaps not now, but you'll learn, then you'll teach me."

Julia frowned, remembered all the times she'd poked fun at

teachers of psychic development. She wondered if this conversation might be an instance of what her father had jokingly called "karma with a vengeance." Regardless, in good conscience, she'd have to decline Lucia's request. "Dear Lucia," she started, fumbling a bit for just the right words.

The oil lamp on the desk across the house flared and illumined a silhouette in the doorway to the herbal workroom. Dressed in a long gown from a much earlier age, the silhouette held her index finger to her mouth and signaled Julia not to say what she'd planned.

She chilled from head to foot. She must have shivered, too, because next thing she knew, Lucia was holding both her hands, rubbing them and apologizing for bringing up such a serious matter at the end of a grueling day.

"Signora Isabella is eager to share stories of the old times here," Lucia said. "First thing tomorrow, if possible. I told her we would talk in the morning."

"Good."

"I'll call you early to arrange the best time."

"Thanks, Lucia."

"*Prego.*" The young woman hurried out the door.

Julia scanned the house, aching for something she couldn't define. There was no sign of the lovely silhouette, in the doorway or anywhere else. She closed her eyes, focused on her feelings, realized there was something about her ancestress that evoked a love and longing akin to what she'd felt for her own sorely missed mother.

QUAI AUX FLEURS, PARIS

Anatolin left Madame Racine's early and walked briskly to the bench beside the Seine where Rafael would meet him. Rafael and a

handful of Interpol agents earlier had flown to Marseilles in pursuit
of Danilenko and the artifacts. The whole morning was utterly
wasted. Not only had Danilenko vanished again, eluding Interpol
entirely, but when Rafael and his cohort reached the warehouse, they
learned the artifacts themselves had been spirited away. The operation couldn't have gone any more awry if Danilenko had planned
specifically to confound them.

"You ever hear of sunburn, White Boy?"

Anatolin was momentarily thrown back to the first time he ever
heard Rafael Gibbons say those words, one bright autumn day at
Utrecht. He looked up and met his friend's sardonic smile. "You've
always had the most disconcerting habit of appearing out of
nowhere—without warning." He stood.

"Hey, don't lay that on me!" Rafael exclaimed, his smile growing
wide. "Can I help it if you're such a heavy thinker?"

Anatolin smiled. "I'm glad you were free." He extended his hand.

"Good to have a few hours off. I needed it, after Marseilles." Rafael
shook Anatolin's hand, strolled over to the low wall overlooking the
Seine, and leaned against it.

Anatolin joined him. Madame Racine had been detained in
Versailles, still trying to arrange her schedule for the trip to Siena, so
he and Rafael would share an early dinner.

"We haven't had much chance to talk alone," Rafael said, rubbing
his eyes. "I'm hoping to get in some quality time this evening, catch
up on your last hundred years."

"There's not much from the Moscow days you don't already
know. After that, only a boring decade-plus in Siberia. Nothing much
happened out there, I'm sure you can imagine."

Rafael grinned. "What I want is the *inside* story, what happened to
change you so unequivocally."

"You noticed."

"Anybody with a lick of sensitivity would. What is it, clairsentience?"

"Yes."

Rafael pushed away from the wall. Anatolin did the same, heading south across the Pont de L'Archevêché beside his friend. The damp Latin quarter streets gave off that special scent he remembered from years ago. The mist draping the city muted the discordant sounds of traffic, restrained the normally hectic tempo of the crowds.

Anatolin had not known many good friends. It felt wonderful to talk with Rafael about Lake Baikal's wild beauty, the silence of the Siberian taiga in winter, how, pulling his iron tether as far from his shack as it would reach, he'd scraped a patch of garden from the frozen soil in the impossibly short growing season. Moreover, Rafael was one person who could understand Anatolin's fascination with Mother Earth and her hidden electromagnetic power grid, which Anatolin had always thought of as *ley lines*, but which an East European colleague had recently given the odd name *vril*.

According to Rafael, funding for parapsychology faculty seats and laboratories, always scant in the West, had apparently dried up early on. Most parapsychologists had struggled for a time on the few available research grants, then pursued their research as an avocation, using whatever other work they could to support themselves as they researched in home-built labs pulled together from donations. Not Rafael. To finance his endeavors, he got involved in computers. Briefly, he'd led a Silicon Valley start-up firm that flourished. The sale of the company allowed him to retire at the ripe old age of thirty-five. His voice crackled with humor as he described how, having achieved it all, he'd fled the rat race. By then, parapsychology had lost its luster, so he hit the road, took a trek through the Himalayas, then a tour of the Balkans in the months just before war erupted there.

He'd wound up in the Czech Republic at the helm of a second start-up. Slogging through international security issues while helping develop what would later become the Internet had brought him his first contact with Interpol. The refugee work, intercepting information on arms smuggling, all the rest of his Czech Republic pastimes apparently soon became ancient history.

Rafael loved the excitement of the international scene, the feeling of accomplishment when, unlike yesterday's debacle, some Interpol action succeeded in impeding the efforts of evil, self-aggrandizing opportunists. "It's time to move on, though, I can feel it in my bones," he added.

Anatolin and Rafael crossed back to the Ile de la Cité, walking along the river again, and headed toward Rafael's favorite restaurant. They paused and faced back toward Notre-Dame. The old cathedral reached gloriously toward the Paris skyline, its spires and buttresses and windows of stained glass a harmony of elegance and mass.

Anatolin stared up at the its highest pinnacle. "Our Lady."

"Yep. Call her Blessed Virgin, Divine Mother or Goddess, she's all around us, always has been." Rafael chuckled. "Hidden in disguises acceptable to society, but also in the trees and grass, the waters of the Seine."

And in Tuscany, Anatolin added silently. Especially in Tuscany. Julia, the Lady incarnate. Never far from his mind, anymore, the woman or the phenomenal awakening he'd been blessed to witness. Incarnate, he stressed to himself. Not objectified like the lofty spires and soaring buttresses of the cathedral. Not a disembodied power or transcendental image of the sort that had so readily of late evoked his aspirations and devotion.

Incarnate—and all too vulnerable.

Rafael glanced from the cathedral to Anatolin and pointed toward the nearest intersection. "Apparently, right before he was kicked off Madame Racine's Task Force during the Occupation, Danilenko tortured a young Nazi occultist about a block down that street."

Anatolin's head snapped backward as if someone had slapped him. Stunned, he tore his gaze from the intersection. "Gregor Danilenko was with the Task Force?"

Rafael looked almost as shocked as Anatolin felt. "Sorry, old buddy, we assumed you knew."

Anatolin hadn't known, hadn't even suspected. But he should have. He most certainly should have.

WEST-CENTRAL ITALY

Julia stood on the south loggia, inhaling the lovely scents rising off the herb garden. By the time all her helpers left, she'd missed the sunset, but the indigo sky full of stars was very lovely. The house was quiet behind her, a serene, softly lit oasis. Beyond the loggia's arches, small bats jetted like tiny missiles to and fro. Farther off, a chorus of cow bells played on the breeze, broken now and then by the muted barks of distant farmyard dogs.

If she didn't have the hostility of the Calderola's testosterone set to deal with, everything would be pretty much perfect. Earlier, Marco had installed a new deadbolt on the kitchen door. Before he left, he'd made her promise to lock the house up tightly when she went to bed, though the last thing on her mind now was sleep.

She had hours of work to catch up the Giardani notebooks, but a nice soak in the tub was her first priority, her next a good meditation. Without that, she knew she'd never effectively handle the constant revelations, the new responsibilities and commitments, her expanding psychic gifts—what her father must have anticipated when he'd spoken of her new life.

She closed the porch shutters, carefully locked them, and walked to the bathroom. Her tub, hand-fashioned of old pink marble, quite wide and deep, was already full, all steamy and inviting. Once the candles in the sconces were lit, she hung her robe on the hook behind the door and stepped into the tub. She sank deep in the water and watched the candlelight dance on its gentle waves.

For a moment, she felt again that tingling she'd first experienced at Aphrodite's beach. She let her mind drift to memories of Andrei and how she'd felt around him. Remarkably comfortable, as if she'd known him forever. He also made her feel more womanly, more desirous than she could remember having felt before. She couldn't help wondering if she'd feel the same way if he showed up here.

As if she needed the distraction of desire when she already felt thoroughly overwhelmed by the whirlwind her inheritance had become. She laughed at herself. Laughing, holding on to her sense of humor, was more important with every hour that passed. The pressure of everything happening all at once was more intense than anything she'd experienced in her hectic life back in California.

∞

Danilenko sat half undressed on his bed in Volterra, the ruby pendant clutched tightly in his right hand. Completing his reconnaissance last night had been the right thing to do. Tonight someone—surprisingly not the Alliance—had erected an all-but-impenetrable protective shield around the Gardens' perimeter. If he'd waited, he would have been hard pressed to breach it without certain discovery and he wasn't ready for confrontation of any sort, psychic or face to face.

He held up the ruby pendulum, focused. He could see the Giardani girl clearly, feel her growth almost tangibly, a steadying and strengthening of her inner resources. He also felt perilously ensnared. A web of connectedness bound him to Julia Giardani, to what end he could not fathom. Her unsophisticated beauty confounded him.

She bathed now in a womb-like alcove lit by pale candlelight. She stood and stepped out of the water, silver droplets slithering down her body, accentuating her figure. Elemental woman personified, she was an enchantress—Venus rising from her bath. She turned, reached up to dry and fluff her silky hair, and all her glories were revealed to him. The graceful arc of her neck. The curve of her breasts. The delicate flare of her slender hips and the tight, tufted bronze triangle high between her thighs.

Fire in his loins catalyzed him. A fever of craving swept him. He fought back the fever, called up his will. Before his lust touched her mind, alerting her to his scrutiny, he clenched his fists. He stood, pushed open the doors to his balcony, and gulped the cool night air.

Dangerous, the effect this young woman had on him. Though the pendulum's link grew more tenuous with every hour, the vision tonight still was clear enough to push him almost beyond the limits of his control. Julia Giardani's innocence twisted his gut, whipped at the tatters of long-forgotten dreams. He was disgusted with himself. Had he no more honor than a common voyeur?

His eyes burned. Long-stifled pain nearly choked him. Mindlessly, he flung the ruby pendulum across the room, realized too late what he'd done. He gasped as the pendulum smashed into the hearth and shattered into ruddy dust.

∞

Julia unlocked the door to her meditation room and tied the key back onto the doorknob where she'd first found it. She wouldn't lock the door again, probably never should have bothered. Inside stood the last unpacked bags from her shopping spree in Siena. She scattered the nubby white cotton throw rugs and pillows around the bedroom, positioned the new boudoir chairs over near the banister and sighed in satisfaction. When her grandmother's ivory Damask bedspread returned from the laundry, it would provide the final touch.

In the meditation room, she lit her new candles and placed them on the ledge of the niche, one on either side. Between them she put her father's wedding band, still on his gold-plated key chain. The wedding band was all she'd brought along to remember him by, and this small room, already her favorite, was probably where he'd most enjoy being remembered. Beside the ring, she put the pink heart-shaped stone from the beach on Cyprus, which had come to be linked in her mind with Andrei. Sitting, she closed her eyes and relaxed, gradually becoming aware of the tempo of her breathing then of a deep sense of calm that smoothed around her like a gentle cloud.

Some twenty minutes later, the watch in the pocket of her robe beeped the hour. She opened her eyes. The candle flames jumped and flared, splashing patterns onto the old blue paint inside the niche. From her chair, she could just make out a pale, golden star right above eye level.

She stood and walked over to examine the center of the niche more closely. Sure enough, in the middle of the blue was a slightly raised design—a five-pointed star about nine inches high—she had not noticed earlier.

Stepping back, she studied the niche again, as if for the very first time. It had a shallow scalloped edge all around its wide arch. She ran her bare fingers around the edge, stopping abruptly at about two o'clock. Her hand started tingling fiercely. Up inside the scallop, she felt a small hollow, gasped as her index finger met cold metal. A key. She pulled it off its tiny hook and held it close to the candles. It was small and slender, made of brass, badly tarnished. Smiling, she flipped it over on her palm.

Bending in front of the chest, she opened its lock. Inside the top drawer, two more brass keys shared a small porcelain dish. Toward the back were two small tins, several sable-tipped paint brushes, and an obviously well-used stencil of a five-pointed star. One tin contained a fat sheaf of antique gold leaf, the other a small cake that looked and smelled like dry glue.

She had no doubt about what to do next. By the bed, she'd left a glass of water. She brought it in and mixed some glue with one of the brushes, covered the floor with flattened shopping bags. Her heart racing, she held the stencil up to the wall. Aligning it carefully over the earlier image, she quickly filled in the pattern with glue.

The old stucco absorbed the moisture like a sponge, soon turning the glue nicely tacky. Exchanging the stencil for the tin of gold leaf, she used the brush to lift one sheet at a time, blowing gently at the filmy gold as she dabbed sheet after sheet into place. She prayed she'd adequately covered the glue, brushed the gold carefully, feathering from the center of the star to the tips of its points.

Bits of gold floated in the air, caught on Julia's hair and eyelashes, on the tops of her arms and hands, but the star looked great. She gave her hair a good shake, then brushed off the sleeves of her robe. Something about the procedure she'd just followed felt familiar, comforting even, as if she'd freshened that star dozens of times. More.

Two minutes later, the mess was all cleaned up, the supplies tucked away in their drawer. She pulled open the second drawer. Inside were ancient votive objects much like those she'd seen in the museums of Cyprus. She dared not touch them. She was too weary to deal with the inevitable impressions such old objects would convey. Fatigue was fast overcoming her desire to catch up on her journal, too, and there were still the bookcases and desk to check out downstairs. Yawning, she patted the pocket of her robe, jingled the small keys.

Tomorrow would have to be soon enough to see what was waiting among her family's books and papers. She knew she'd made the right decision the instant she climbed into bed. Her body suddenly felt like limp spaghetti, her yawn like a magnitude-seven earthquake. She wondered how much happiness a person could experience in one day without going into overload, suspected she'd already passed that point.

Reaching over to blow out the lamp, she caught a glimpse of a now-familiar silhouette by the foot of the bed. If she had any sense she might be scared, but she wasn't. All she felt was a deep sense of gratitude that rose up from within and made her eyes burn and get so bleary she could hardly see anything at all.

"Thank you, whoever you are," she whispered into the darkness. "Thank you for everything."

The response, if it was a response and not an effect of her overwrought imagination, came immediately as she closed her eyes and drifted off to sleep.

Prego, cara mia, prego . . .

TWENTY

Madame Racine had awakened in that heavy, drugged state which must be endured when one works late into the night. She was still paying the price. She'd spent most of the early morning catching up on correspondence, declining engagements she doubtless should have accepted, all the while worried about the young ones, Julia and Andrei, and absorbed by her final arrangements for joining them in Tuscany.

From the door of her salon, James discreetly cleared his throat. "Might I say, Madame, you look quite splendid in that particular shade of blue?"

"*Merci.*" Racine smiled, brushed her palm over her suit's sleeve, tugged at a cuff. "Dior called it royal peacock. Too bad I feel more like a spent canary." Designer original or no, James in a more playful mood would have said she looked a bloody fright, and rightly so.

"A note from the young gentleman, Madame," he said, extending a plain white envelope on an engraved silver tray.

If only Racine had been more clear with Andrei about Danilenko, he might not have dashed off all alone. She sat down beside the fire, took the envelope. "When did he actually leave?"

"At dawn."

She snapped open the envelope. Andrei's note was terse, a polite salutation, a thank-you for her hospitality. He promised not to proceed to Julia's until after Racine and Rafael arrived in Tuscany, provided they made it by nine tomorrow morning. If they did, it would be a miracle.

James cleared his throat. "I imagine you're eager to contact Tuscany."

"*Mais, oui!*" Madame glanced at her watch, hoped it wouldn't take long to put through a call to the monastery south of Siena.

"Feeling rather impatient, are we not?" Smiling soothingly, James snapped the phone jack into the outlet beside Racine's chair, patted her hand. "There, there, dear, I've already got the good Brother on the line."

She took the receiver he handed her. "*Buon giorno,* Brother Vittorio!" Quickly moving through the pleasantries, she masked the anxiety fast eroding her confidence. She and the Alliance's inner circle had been sending protective energy to Tuscany from the moment Julia arrived there, but it was Vittorio who had insisted on tracking Gregor Danilenko's movements. When she'd first accepted the help of the Benedictine brother, she'd not known precisely what they would be up against. Yet, even now, Vittorio wanted to help. "You've discussed this with your abbot?"

"But of course, Madame."

"You realize aligning with Julia and Andrei could place your whole monastic community at risk?"

"The abbot wishes to remind you that our friendship with the Giardani and their circle predates the monastery's foundation by many centuries. Our devotion to Our Holy Mother mandates we do our part."

Racine herself should be closer to Julia this very moment. Taking a proactive stand, as dear Tony would say if he were still with them. And Andrei would need her support as much as Julia. His sensitivity could become a toy in the dark master's hands.

The diplomatic urgencies of the day would have to be muddled through without her involvement this time. "Brother Vittorio, I hope to see the abbot when I arrive in Siena."

"Excellent! I'll arrange it. When shall you join us?"

"Immediately." Racine suddenly realized an ancient wound had lost its thick and blackened scab. She feared it would require all who witnessed the wounding to purge the foulness and bring about full healing. "I'll ring you from my villa as soon as I get there."

WEST-CENTRAL ITALY

Firenze. Anatolin felt the heartbeat of the city immediately, sensed the preoccupation of the Florentines bustling through the streets. The coffee bars he passed were packed with customers hastily gulping espressos, too hurried to sit down, even if there had been room. A dense cloud obscured the sun, mirroring Anatolin's mood. In his present state, another crowded city was no place for him. He'd be relieved to get out to the country, where he could meditate a while, prepare himself for seeing Julia again.

He headed through mostly residential streets, moving steadily toward the artisan's district of Sant' Ambrogio, where Vittorio Mansanto had arranged to meet him beside the old church. Making his way through the market near the church was like plowing through molasses. Anatolin spotted his friend at a vegetable stand, handing money to an old farmer. Slinging both of his bulging shopping bags over one shoulder, Vittorio scanned the crowd and, smiling, started in Anatolin's direction.

Anatolin dropped his duffel bag between his feet, held out his hand, and took hold of Vittorio's. "*Buon giorno,* my friend!"

"Welcome to Tuscany, Andrei! I am very glad you came."

"Where's your religious garb?" Anatolin raised an eyebrow. "I expected a roman collar, at the very least."

Vittorio glanced down at his scruffy American Levi's, his flannel shirt open at the neck and rolled at the cuffs. "Home." He chuckled. "We choose not to draw attention to ourselves in public."

Anatolin lifted his bag and slung its strap over his shoulder. "Who'd have thought the flamboyant, urbane Mansanto would ever look so right in the company of farmers?"

"Yes, well, I'm a farmer myself these days, when the need arises. As you'll soon see. By the way, we won't be staying at the monastery. I hope you aren't too disappointed." Vittorio steered him away from the heart of the market.

"Not at all."

"Good, because my elderly charge, Brother Orlando, has been ailing and requires the quietude of our small hermitage near San Galgano." Vittorio paused, seeming to size Anatolin up. "From the looks of you, Andrei, I'd say you do, too."

"The sooner the better. I admit I'm still rather overwhelmed from Paris."

Near the old churchyard, Vittorio stopped beside a shiny new minibus. He opened the rear door and deposited his shopping and Anatolin's bag between the back seats, slid the door closed. A minute later, Vittorio merged the minibus into the slow snake of traffic headed out of the city.

"I suggest you rest on the ride south to San Galgano," he said. "Have no fear, the sisters will keep *pranzo* warm until we arrive."

"Sisters?"

"Our Order is what you might call coeducational." Vittorio turned his attention to navigating through traffic as the minibus approached the *superstrada*. "Separate residences, of course, but at San Galgano, more often than not, we work, take our meals and make our devotions together."

"Sounds quite egalitarian."

"So it's meant to be." Vittorio ground the minibus into passing gear and zipped into the stream of vehicles speeding toward Siena. Finally, he smiled. "I think you'll like it."

"I'd envisioned a musty cloister of dark-robed monks. Ascetics. But I guess even monks have been forced into the twentieth century."

"Many religious feel they have been. Despite how we may seem, though, our little enclave has remained much the same since its foundation in the thirteenth century. We're an uncomplicated Order, somewhat detached from Church hierarchy, you might say. Perhaps that is why we fell out of fashion long ago." He gave Anatolin a quick grin. "By the way, we've always worn white robes. But you shall see, my friend. You shall see."

Anatolin relaxed back into his seat and turned his attention to the countryside. The cloud that had hovered over Florence dispersed as the vehicle continued south. Rays of sunshine lit the forests clustered around the gentle hills, glanced off the crumbling castles at their peaks. Vittorio pointed out the stony ruins of abandoned monasteries they passed along the way. Anatolin smiled. Vittorio had obviously found where he belonged, which was more than Anatolin could yet say for himself. Especially with his concern for Julia growing each hour, almost an obsession now.

He rested his head on the seat back and stared out the window. It was hard to accept that Danilenko was out there somewhere, amidst all this beauty.

∞

Signora Isabella seemed eager to get started sharing her memories. Julia was eager to hear them. With luck, she might learn how and why her grandmother had "dropped the ball," as her father put it last March. Today, she might finally learn how to begin making up for her grandmother's failure, how to bring back the ancient traditions of the

Giardani clan, as her father had surmised she would. It was hard to calm the pounding of her heartbeat, she was so excited.

The old *strega* perched stiffly at one end of the sofa. Lucia sat beside her at the other end, attentive and ready to spring to assistance should the need arise. Julia took the chair beside Signora Isabella's, where she would be free to pour tea and pass the plate of crusty, fruit-laced *panforte* Lucia brought from Siena.

"As I said before, you look very much like Giuliana." Signora Isabella began then paused, causing Julia to squirm under her scrutiny. "She wore her hair much longer, though, in the fashion of those times, swept up and held in a braided knot at the back of her head. Giuliana's face—*Bellissima!* More narrow than yours, with higher cheekbones, a longer, more slender nose, the kind we used to think only aristocrats had. She worked far too hard to be thin. Giardani magnetism or no, she was a woman to take the breath from any man. I believe Giuliana was fifty-one when I first came to the Gardens. I was eleven. That was 1911."

Julia started. "Signora Isabella, are you saying you were born in 1900?"

"I don't look too bad for such an old crone, eh? Giuliana told me my life would touch two centuries. I found it hard to believe, but now the second one is here and I'm still around!"

"Thank heaven for that," Julia said.

Signora Isabella shrugged. "Your grandmother, Anna, was fifteen and very jealous of me when I came." She gazed into the low flames flickering in the hearth. "I can speak about that awful jealousy now with a smile, but back then it hurt, because I dearly wanted her to love me." She dabbed her hanky under each eye. "Anna and I became more like rivals than friends. I mourned that fact for years before I accepted it was our destiny to vie for Giuliana's attention— but that is a tale for another day."

Julia reached over and squeezed Signora Isabella's hand. "I hate to think sharing your memories might make you sad."

"The past is always tinged with sadness, *cara*, but there is much happiness back there, too, especially as regards my training. For the *streghe* the new year began at All Souls' Eve, so my training began then, too. That day, we baked small cakes together. We cleaned the pond and lifted the slab that blocked the duct, so the hot spring water could blend with the cooler water from the well and make the pond warm for my ritual bath."

Tears had again gathered in Signora Isabella's eyes. She wiped them and went on. "It was a night to remember, a night no young girl could ever forget. Giuliana did everything in her power to make me feel wonderful, powerful and wise—and that took a lot of love, I'll tell you. After that, the years passed quickly. Giuliana, Anna and I, sometimes others, too, wildcrafted herbs, tended those that grew at the Gardens, made remedies we shared with peasants and rich folk alike. Everyone was very busy then, all the time."

"Farm life must have been terribly hard."

"Especially so for Giuliana. By day she lived much like every farm woman, but by night her life was completely different, for she worked at her desk very late. We considered such behavior strange in those days, since many of us could barely read and write, let alone for hours at time."

Julia glanced at the bookcases. "I found her books, old letters, goodness knows what all, but I haven't had time to look over them yet. Do you think they'll contain anything about the craft?"

"I don't know. She didn't teach from books. I learned more about the craft only as I learned more about myself. That was how it had to be, Giuliana insisted, when I complained. 'The power comes as the knowledge to handle it comes,' she always said. I now know I had little inborn talent. However, I tried, and eventually I became a fairly good *strega*, after all."

Lucia leaned forward. "She's too modest. She's a wonderful *strega*."

"You can say that only because you never met Giuliana," said Signora Isabella with an adamant shake of her head. "In all the time I knew her, I never learned a single curse. When I asked to learn them, Giuliana always laughed and said she simply didn't know any curses, I'd have to learn them from some other *strega*. I never did, never cared about them, after her. As one season sped into the next, we marked the sacred turnings of the year in keeping with the old calendar of those who came before us. Giuliana taught me to love the earth, to revel in its splendor." Signora Isabella looked down at her hands.

"How many years did you live here?"

"A long time. I was not especially pretty, and I had no desire to marry young. I was here until I was twenty-three, more than a year after Giuliana's death, almost until your grandparents left."

"Then you must know what happened to make Anna leave Italy." Julia took the old woman's hand. "Please, Signora Isabella, tell me what it was."

"I have never told a soul about that, child. I haven't even thought of it in years, have deliberately tried not to."

"I'm sorry if asking about it distresses you, but it may be important."

"It *is* important." Signora Isabella sighed and scooted to the edge of the couch, then stretched up as tall as she could.

"You're tired," Julia said, changing her mind. "I should not have pushed you. We'll stop for today."

"Don't fuss over me. I'll decide when I need to stop."

Julia glanced at Lucia, who took a soft pillow and plumped it behind Signora Isabella's back.

"Perhaps a fresh pot of that good lemon balm tea will lift all our spirits," Lucia said. "Then we can go on."

∞

Anatolin could readily see why the region around the ruined Abbey of San Galgano had encouraged one of the most intense monastic flowerings of the Middle Ages. Though most of the monks had left centuries before, it still offered the profound repose that fostered deep contemplation.

Vittorio's hermitage would be a fine place to stay here in Tuscany. Perhaps for good. He'd enjoyed meeting the other monastics currently in residence, but his urge to get centered was so acute he'd come outside as quickly as civility allowed, ostensibly to explore the ruins and become acquainted with the countryside. The crumbling shell of San Galgano's once-breathtaking Gothic church dominated the valley's landscape. At the top of the hill above it, the soldier who became Saint Galgano long ago thrust his sword into the rock, renouncing warfare to take up a life of peaceful service.

Built around the still-standing sword was a round, twelfth-century chapel. Anatolin climbed to the chapel, circled its portico, and came to a stop facing north. He closed his eyes, imagining the valley below as marshy wetlands, the old indigenous clans who thronged here to hunt, the later Etruscans and other settlers from distant lands, then the Romans. Gradually, he relaxed, became attuned to the great force he'd learned to revere in his exile, the force he'd come to think of as Divine Mother.

Across the valley stood the rocky cone of Montecipriana, aligned on an almost-perfect axis with the abbey ruins. The Calderola's vital energy grid, that invisible, usually imperceptible manifestation of the Mother's power, seemed extremely strong. Perhaps stronger than that surrounding his cabin on Lake Baikal.

Thoughts of Julia—of seeing her soon, hopefully tomorrow, flooded his mind, and he was again consumed by concern for her safety. He took a seat on the bench at the edge of the portico. The trees on either side of his view framed an area due west of Siena almost to the sea and from San Gimignano's towers in the north to the valley below his feet.

Anatolin sensed Danilenko's proximity. The monster was out there, somewhere.

Stalking Julia. Closing in on her and whatever it was he sought.

∞

Lucia seemed enthralled by Signora Isabella's story of her years at the Gardens. Sometimes, Julia noticed the young woman staring at her, particularly when Signora Isabella spoke about learning the old healing arts from her teacher. Then another strange new responsibility weighed on Julia's shoulders, one she wasn't at all sure how to carry.

Having shared poignant memories of the last Giuliana's untimely death, Signora Isabella's voice grew choked and harsh. "Things were never the same for Anna after her mother's passing. Anna tried to carry on, but she never seemed to think herself worthy of the Giuliana legacy. I lived here still, but by then I was a woman full grown, and I came and went as I pleased.

"In the spring of 1921, Anna told me she was with child, her first, for she had seemed barren until then. I was happy for her. Of all the things Anna had wanted in her life, she'd particularly wanted a child of her own. Though she was old for a pregnancy in those times, while carrying that child Anna became more radiant with each passing hour. Then Anna was called to Florence to attend to a woman who was having a difficult birth. She didn't return for several days. When she did come back, she looked tired and sick, had bruises all over her face and arms, probably others I couldn't see."

The old woman gripped the sofa, her knuckles white, her voice barely more than a whisper, her face far paler than before. "I soon realized Anna was no longer expecting. She refused to talk about why. It took me many years to learn the truth. I had to piece it together from fragments of gossip heard here and there as time passed, as old guilt faded and old wounds healed."

Julia glanced at Lucia, who was obviously as worried about the old woman as she was. Lucia gave Julia a nod but kept silent.

Signora Isabella took a few long, deep breaths. "The woman Anna was called to help in Florence had been in the hands of another *strega,* a mean woman whose specialty was fortune-telling. Not a midwife at all, she had coveted the gold the pregnant woman paid her, so she kept her ignorance to herself. When the labor was clearly not going as it should, Anna was finally called. By the time she arrived, the mother was half dead, and the child had not yet been born. Anna struggled to save the lives in her care, but the baby was deformed, the mother hemorrhaged and died. Soon after, Anna was almost dead herself. An angry mob had formed, urged on by the wicked *strega,* whose pride was badly tarnished. The mob followed Anna, heavy with child herself, from the dead woman's palazzo to the doors of the famous Baptistery. There they cornered Anna, stoned her, left her for dead."

Julia felt half sick and so worried about her elderly guest she could hardly sit still, but Signora Isabella pushed on.

"Later, a local woman dragged Anna to safety and nursed her back to consciousness. They say Anna's aborted babe was born with a full head of copper-colored hair, that her skin was transparent as fine porcelain and smooth as silk. They say she lived long enough for the half-conscious Anna to hold her just once. Anna was inconsolable. Worse, she refused my sympathy, didn't want anyone's help but your grandfather's."

"I never met him," Julia said softly. "He died years before I came along."

"Antonio was a gentle, green-eyed *stregone* from Benevento. He loved Anna beyond all reason. Month after month, I watched him care for her. In time, Anna found she was pregnant again. When she told me, she rubbed her still flat stomach and announced this one was a boy."

"My father." Julia glanced at the fire.

"Yes, *cara.* Now, I don't know if you are aware of this, but male children in your family are almost unheard of."

Julia nodded. "My father told me."

"Antonio was overjoyed about their son, but not Anna. She believed she'd failed to bring into this world the daughter she'd longed for, the Heiress it was her duty to provide."

Julia shook her head. "What a tragic error in thinking."

"It was tragic," Signora Isabella agreed. "But we must not assume it was an error in thinking. There may have been some element of truth in Anna's shame, some old sin haunting her from the deep past."

Julia shuddered. "My father would have agreed with that conclusion."

"Yes, undoubtedly, he was schooled in such matters. Though Anna clearly felt shamed, she swore she'd give her son as much of her family's knowledge as she was free to pass on." She shrugged. "Who am I to say, eh? I've always felt Anna sensed more about that than she'd ever share with me."

"I wonder if we'll ever know," Lucia said with a wistful sigh.

"Never mind. Let it stay Anna's secret or not, as the Goddess wills," said Signora Isabella. "There is plenty more I can tell you. That very winter, we were hit with a terrible epidemic. Children and old folks got sick first, but by the fourth week everyone was deathly ill." Signora Isabella shuddered. "All the *streghe* worked very hard throughout that plague. Anna and I worked day and night, picking herbs, grinding them, cooking them down in her large copper vat. We walked for miles each day, distributing what we had made. Because she was with child, Antonio begged her not to go far from Montecipriana, but she went farther, anyway, taking her remedies to all who needed them."

The old woman sighed, her bosom heaving with the obvious burden of her memories. "Then there were rumors in Florence—the *streghe* were suspected of starting the epidemic. Someone claimed an angry *stregone* had called down a curse on the town, the result was somehow the fault of all who practiced *la Vecchia Religione*, that it was their wicked spells assailing the countryside."

Julia's mouth turned sour. "The *streghe* became scapegoats."

Lucia frowned. "In the twentieth century—I can hardly believe people could have acted so superstitiously."

"Even today some would act thus. Even today!" Signora Isabella answered.

"I suppose you're right," Lucia agreed, giving Julia a sympathetic smile.

"Humph!" The old woman shook her head. "In those times, rumors spread like wildfire. Innocent healers were hounded and hurt. Antonio exploded into rage. He didn't want to live in this place anymore. Tuscany was too backward, he ranted, Italy a land of fools. He insisted the influence of the *Fascisti* had grown since the Great War had ended. It would become even more dangerous, he said, for those who practiced the Old Religion in a country that would soon have a godless regime. The *Fascisti* would try even harder than the Church to eradicate *la stregheria*."

"Was he right?" Julia asked.

"He may have been, but he also wanted to go to America, where he believed he would have a chance of providing their unborn son a good education and greater opportunities. Anna finally agreed to leave with Antonio as soon as the baby was born. She must have known she would be missed here, but she had never performed the full offices of the Giardani Heiress. There were things she couldn't bring herself to do, take her mother's role in the community, wear the mantle of authority to which she was heir. She wouldn't get near the holy things, let alone touch them—use them the way Giuliana had."

Julia put her hand on Signora Isabella's knee. "What holy things?"

"You have not found them? In the little room upstairs?"

"In the chest!" The items had seemed so innocuous. Julia's stomach knotted. "How were they used?"

"Some were worn, on the holy days only, I think. Some, I suspect now, simply focused the mind. I was too ignorant to be trained in such ancient matters. Anna was too scared. Giuliana must have despaired of us both." Signora Isabella sighed. "But let me finish. Those last few weeks Anna and I spent together we grew closer than we had ever been. Eventually, she confided in me. With no daughter to train, she would never bring another woman into *la stregheria*— practicing the craft correctly brought every flaw, every small mistake to light, made a *strega*'s life too difficult to bear."

Lucia shook her head. "Her training died with her, then. Such a loss."

"So I felt once. Now I feel differently." Signora Isabella frowned. "One day, shortly before I moved away, Anna pulled me aside. She told me she'd had a dream, had been shown that in the future the fear and loathing the people felt about *la stregheria*, and especially about *la Vecchia Religione*, would ease."

Julia sat up straight. "Did she explain what she meant?"

"No. When I asked her how and when this would come to pass, she apparently couldn't answer me, except to say this would not happen in her lifetime."

Signora Isabella asked Lucia for her handbag then pulled from it an old photo in a wrought-iron frame. "This is Giuliana."

Julia took the photo and gasped at the similarity between her eyes and those gazing back at her from the photo. But there was an energy, a strength of spirit Giuliana conveyed that Julia couldn't hope to measure up to in a million years. No wonder her grandmother had felt inadequate to carry on.

"You will not fail, young Giuliana, as Anna failed. Do not even entertain the thought." Signora Isabella sniffed and pulled out a second frame. "Anna had this picture taken just before the family sailed from Genova. Antonio sent it to me a few years later, but I never heard another word from them after that."

"Anna never wrote you herself?" Julia asked, staring down at her grandmother's youthful image, so very sad, even then.

"Not once. But those days are *passati!* In the past. We live now." Signora Isabella leaned forward and peered at Julia closely. "I believe Anna lived exactly where and how she was meant to live. I believe the same is true for you and will be even more true in the future. There is enough blame in this world—especially self-blame. Giuliana always said that was precisely the source of our greatest evils."

Julia sighed. "Again, thank you, Signora Isabella."

"One last thing, *cara*. That time your grandmother dreamed of—" The old woman's stern gaze made Julia's stomach flip. "You need to prepare yourself quickly, for I believe it has come."

TWENTY-ONE

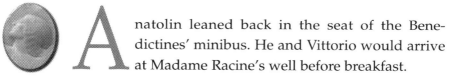natolin leaned back in the seat of the Benedictines' minibus. He and Vittorio would arrive at Madame Racine's well before breakfast.

Vittorio glanced quickly in his direction, smiled. "You seem to enjoy the portico outside the chapel. Is it the quiet you like or the view?"

"Both. The valley between Montecipriana and San Galgano seems unique, rather—active for such a rural area."

"It is called La Calderola."

"The Cauldron." Anatolin smiled and looked toward Montecipriana. "An apt name. Eloquent, even."

"You have seen the earth energies, I take it."

"Extraordinary. I've never seen anything like them before."

"Neither had I, though I'd heard all the legends."

"Tell me about these legends."

"Later," Vittorio said, negotiating another sharp curve in the narrow road. "When I don't have to drive. But the phenomenon you saw just started up again last week after decades of dormancy. Very faintly at first, growing stronger each day. Heaven knows what it will be like when the Giardani Heiress has fully awakened."

"You're proposing it's linked to Julia?"

"I'm not proposing anything." Vittorio smiled. "I'm telling you that's what the old tales say. The Cauldron contains the Witches' Brew—when the great *strega* Giuliana returns, magic roams the land once again."

∞

Julia had barely rested the night before. Her visions of Anna and Giuliana had been too haunting. In her one or two short hours of actual sleep, Julia had dreamed of the Giuliana legacy in its glory days, or at least, how her unconscious mind projected it must have been. Despite the lack of sleep, she'd awakened fully energized, ready to meet all challenges head-on, starting with Giuliana's volumes in the bookcase, spread now all over the kitchen workbench.

It seemed the Victorian folklorist, Charles Leland, had once been a friend of Julia's family. A first edition of his *Etruscan Roman Remains in Popular Tradition* was inscribed in 1897 with a lengthy note to Giuliana Giardani, apparently in Leland's own hand and in English no less. Beside that were two of Leland's other works, also annotated by the author, each liberally laced with references to families of hereditary witches and to the enduring power of their traditions, which he'd traced back over two thousand years.

Julia leafed through the eccentric scholar's largest book while she waited for her new espresso pot to cough up her mid-morning cup, which she'd started drinking straight up, Italian style. Leland's work was fascinating. She scanned one brittle page after another, absorbing the theories, tales and incantations he recorded long ago. He had even identified and discussed to some extent the Etruscan Aphrodite, known as Turan, and sometimes Turana. Reading those ancient names raised goose bumps on Julia's arms.

Once she might have scoffed at Leland's sentimentality, might even have considered his conclusions nonsense. Now she found herself devouring each detail, wondering how many of the *streghe* traditions he ferreted out a hundred years ago might still survive. Some definitely had. Vario's incantation with the broom was almost identical to something Julia read only an hour before.

Her thoughts turned to the small chest upstairs. She'd relocked the drawers with barely more than a peek at their contents. This morning, she'd have a better look at the objects Anna had been unwilling—or afraid—to touch.

∞

Madame Racine's villa on the outskirts of Siena faced south over a chalky expanse toward Mount Amiata. Anatolin had chuckled when he heard the villa's name, chuckled again when he heard its story. Il Calice Zolfo, the Sulfur Chalice, apparently was a hangout for a number of alchemists from Ficino's day to the close of the nineteenth century. How and when, precisely, it had come into Madame Racine's possession remained a mystery, but if one chose to believe the tale circulated at San Galgano, it had passed to her from the heirs of one of the University of Siena's most infamous alumni, the fabled Comte de St.-Germain.

Breakfast was superb, as Anatolin had fully anticipated, with no mention of the grim circumstances that had brought them together. Now he could see Madame Racine bracing herself for the inevitable discussion of how to protect Julia and defeat Danilenko.

She leaned forward, her elbows resting on the table, her fingers clasped below her chin, and looked at Anatolin then Vittorio. "I spent all day yesterday canvassing the Alliance for support. I have the worst possible news to share."

Vittorio frowned. "Let's hear it."

"The group will not act with us on Julia's behalf."

"They are adamant?"

Madame Racine dropped her hands to her lap, fidgeted with the rings on her fingers. "Memories of earlier failures have made the inner circle overly cautious, I think."

Anatolin folded his napkin in half and draped it over his crossed knee, unsure he was catching the gist of the conversation. "Would you care to elaborate on their problem?"

Vittorio shrugged. "It's the age-old injunction not to intervene in worldly affairs, not to risk affecting individual free will."

"The inner circle's conservatism is a huge disappointment." Madame Racine shook her head. "I'd counted on their help. Now, it seems, they may even decide to withdraw their protection of Julia."

Anatolin sat up straight. "You must not allow that to happen."

"You misunderstand my role in the Alliance." Madame Racine lifted her chin. "Leadership in that sphere is more subtle than one might imagine from the outside looking in. What I want, personally, is the last thing I'd be free to press upon others. Then there is the matter of individual karma. Yours and mine, to be specific, in relation to the Giardani Heiress." She gave him a wry look. "Not to mention whatever karma there might be with Gregor Danilenko."

"Do you think for one moment this is a simple matter of personal karma?"

"*Mais non*, Andrei." She smiled again. "Not at all. In fact, I feel the great ones themselves have a stake in this matter. A considerable stake. I believe they want me to help Julia directly. If I did not believe this, I would not have been willing to step down from the Alliance leadership."

Vittorio sprang to his feet. "Step down?"

"For a time."

"Blessed Mother, wait until the abbot hears about this!"

"It was upon his suggestion I acted—and upon his agreement to take on my duties for the duration of this affair with Danilenko."

Vittorio seemed to calm down quickly once Madame's response registered. "How, then, should we proceed?"

She rubbed her fingertips in small circles at her temples. "With all the love and trust we can muster among us, each of us watching Julia as closely as possible." She looked at Anatolin. "You have seen the Witches' Brew?"

"Yes." Anatolin's pulse raced, just thinking about it. "Remarkable."

"And dangerous to endure at close hand unless one is scrupulously genuine and aware of his feelings at all times." Madame Racine narrowed her gaze and stared at Anatolin. "It amplifies any confusion one might have, sensitizes in ways very difficult to predict, and you are already more sensitive than anyone should have to be. You may rest assured Danilenko will twist any and all unplumbed feelings to his own advantage, given half a chance."

"Is this a warning?"

She smiled. "No more to you than to myself and Brother Vittorio— and the good brothers and sisters of his Order. If we work together, all should be well."

James entered, a concerned frown wrinkling his brow. "Excuse me, Madame."

"Yes, James?"

"There is a package, from America. Apparently, it arrived here the other day, addressed to Julia Giardani. At least the caretaker had the good sense to accept delivery of it until he could check with me." He paused. "I have a sense it may be important."

Anatolin stood and helped James shove the large cardboard package into the room. "I wonder why Giardani didn't send this directly to Montecipriana?"

Madame Racine joined Anatolin beside the package. "I suspect because he couldn't risk it falling into Danilenko's hands before Julia could receive it herself. It is no coincidence it arrived here. Tony used an old Task Force trick," she said with a wink.

She reached down and yanked off the label bearing her address. Beneath it was another, made out to Julia, General Delivery, Montecipriana.

"Perhaps, Andrei, you would prefer to ensure its delivery to Julia directly? And I suggest you stop at the post office in Montecipriana, make it known to the villagers that Julia is no longer so completely on her own."

∞

Anatolin liked the village of Montecipriana the moment he laid eyes on it, though his heightened clairsentience made him painfully aware of the small community's economic woes, its almost palpable sadness, its all-but-futile attempts to hold itself together in a rapidly changing world.

Unsettling. To ground himself, he made straight for the bakery and enjoyed the best morning pastries he'd had in years. Then he browsed the shop windows opening onto the main square, paying particular attention to the stationer's, which apparently doubled as the local postal office. When the elderly postmistress crossed the square, Anatolin sensed he would find in her a soulful ally.

Not five minutes later, she flipped the CLOSED sign on her door to OPEN, glanced at him, and gave him an instantaneous and guileless smile. "Come in." She held the door open and waved him through. "Please do come in."

Anatolin walked beside her to the counter, which she slipped behind, folding her hands on its immaculate surface, then assuming an efficient stance. "How can I help you, sir?"

"I am looking for an American woman whose family came from here."

"An American, you say."

"Yes, that's right."

The postmistress glanced down at her hands. When she looked back up, her gaze was guarded, her eyes had lost their open look. "I'm afraid no Americans live in this village."

"I was told I could get directions to her nearby farm from you."

The postmistress raised her eyebrows, looked at him down her long, slightly bowed nose. "Aah!"

"The young woman is a friend. I have something belonging to her."

"I don't understand, sir. This is the postal office. Perhaps there is something you'd care to mail somewhere—a letter perhaps?"

"No, I don't care to mail a thing." Anatolin reminded himself to smile. "As a matter of fact, I intend to take something to Signorina Giardani that was delivered in error to a villa near Siena."

"Siena?" The woman leaned toward him. "Which villa, might I ask?"

"Il Calice Zolfo."

"Aah!" The postmistress gave him a quick nod, her guard banished, her smile wide and friendly again. "You say a letter went astray?"

"Not a letter, a rather large box."

A small boy peeked through the doorway at the back of the shop. He stepped forward, looped his thumbs through the straps of his coveralls, stretched up onto the toes of his muddy boots. "I saw the box on the seat of his car."

"You naughty boy." The woman clicked her tongue. "You're supposed to be in school."

"This is more important than anything that dumb teacher has to say. The box, you see, is from Giuliana's *babbo!*"

The postmistress became clearly flustered.

Anatolin leaned toward her. "The young man is correct, Signora. The matter may be quite urgent. If you can give me directions—"

"Never mind that," the boy interrupted, holding up his palm. "I'll show you the shortcut from here." He inclined his head toward the woman. "This is my great-grandmother, Fiorella Andrade." He walked to Anatolin, his hand extended. "I am Vario Andrade, Giuliana's friend."

"Anatolin, here. Andrei Ivanovich Anatolin." He smiled seriously, shook the boy's hand.

He was suddenly aware Vario was reading his aura, scanning his mind to determine his intentions, confirm his sincerity. It seemed imperative to be as forthcoming as possible.

"I promised Signorina Giardani I would visit during my stay at the hermitage near San Galgano. When I learned of her father's package, I offered to deliver it, since I was coming here, anyway."

Vario frowned, nodded, and took Anatolin's hand. "Let's go."

Anatolin let the boy lead him to the car then followed, Julia's package in his arms, as the boy retrieved a squat wagon parked at the edge of the forest. At Vario's insistence, Anatolin put the box into the wagon and followed behind, ready to take over if the gently climbing path became much steeper. Montecipriana's forest was the most alive place Anatolin had been since leaving his Lake Baikal cabin. It felt wild, untrammeled. Pristine. If he spent much time here, the place would quickly get under his skin.

The air resounded with birdsong, smelled rich, pungent with the scent of the forest's life cycle. Death, decay, transmutation, rebirth. The endless wheel. He shoved his fists into his pockets and strolled behind the wagon, enjoying the added boon of the boy's thoughtful company.

At a small, ancient-looking bridge, Vario stopped. He dropped the wagon's handle then squatted at the far side of the bridge and squinted up. "I think I like you." He reached down, grabbed a handful of flat stones from beside the stream. Standing, he skimmed one back into the water, held out the stones.

Anatolin selected a couple and followed suit. "Do you always make up your mind about people before coming to know them?"

"Depends. I liked Giuliana immediately." The boy scowled. "You are not her lover," he added with a pout.

Anatolin wondered about Italian boys. This one seemed decidedly young to question a man about his love life. He hoped his psychic shield concealed his plans to become a monk and didn't betray so much as an inkling of the kiss on Cyprus, which before coming to Tuscany he'd determinedly vowed he would not repeat. Instead, he'd resolved to transmute his desire, strive for the yogic ideal of Divine friendship, as any self-respecting renunciant would. If Divine Mother intended more than friendship between him and Julia, hopefully, She would make it evident soon enough. "No, I am not Julia's lover."

"That *really* is too bad!" Vario reached up with his free hand and patted Anatolin on the back. "Our Giuliana could use a strong man around her place, night and day." He slid the stones back onto the stream bank and resumed hauling the wagon along the path. A few steps later, he turned around and stared drolly at Anatolin. "You'd sure be a whole lot better than any of those other men."

Anatolin's chest contracted. He swallowed hard. "What other men?"

∞

Julia heard a tinny squeak and rattle coming from near the court-yard, male voices, one young, one older—and familiar. Sliding from her stool, she stepped out the kitchen door and gave a delighted yelp.

"Andrei! Yes!" She clapped her hands, dashed across the courtyard, and opened the gate. "What in the world took you so long?" Andrei didn't answer, except to give her his sweet, lopsided smile. She wanted to throw herself into his arms but, of course, she couldn't.

She grabbed Vario and gave him a hug. "You darling boy," she said, ruffling his hair. "Just look what you've brought me, now!" She held out her free hand. "Welcome to the Gardens, Andrei."

"It's good to be here." Andrei returned her gaze and took her hand.

His touch shot to her very core. Heat flared there, stealing her breath. She went utterly still. Everything went utterly still. Except her heart, which thundered and made her eardrums pound.

Her attraction to him was stronger than she remembered it being on Cyprus. Definitely stronger.

It took a moment to realize Vario was speaking. She had to close her eyes to break away from Andrei's gaze, regretted doing so the instant she had, but it couldn't be helped. Vario had mentioned her father, said the box in the wagon was mailed from America. "Oh, my!"

The boy looked up at Julia, tugged on her right hand. "It got delivered to the wrong address, you see."

"Let's take it to the porch."

Andrei stepped forward. "Allow me," he said, lifting the box.

Vario muttered again. Andrei seemed to hear what the boy said, looked momentarily appalled. Then he gave Vario a wink, walked across to the porch, and settled the box on the table.

Vario grabbed Julia's hand and held it, chattering about the package going astray, all the way to Siena, then south to some villa named the Sulfur Chalice. He'd guessed something was up when Andrei first arrived in Montecipriana, he said very seriously, so he'd stayed away from school to help.

Julia knelt down, brushed back the boy's unruly curls, leaned her forehead against his. "I really appreciate your help, *caro*." She tipped up his chin, gave him a kiss on the cheek. "Will you come back later this afternoon, after school is over, and teach me how to take our goat for a walk?"

He beamed her a grand smile. "Absolutely!" He turned to Andrei. "Good to meet you, sir."

Andrei nodded and smiled.

"Humph!" Vario tipped his head in Andrei's direction as he crossed back to the gate. "Watch out for that one, Giuliana. He doesn't talk much, but I'd say he's a stealer of hearts."

Waiting for her blush to cool before she dared look back at Andrei, Julia watched the boy scamper toward his wagon and pull it away. She let her gaze return briefly to Andrei, a huge mistake, had to close her eyes and take a deep breath before she could continue.

"Am I ever glad to see you," she said. "I have so much to tell you, show you. Discuss. I hope you plan to stay a while."

"I certainly can." He crossed his arms over his chest and leaned back against the porch wall, one ankle crossed over the other. He seemed pleased to see her again. Maybe even more than pleased. "I like your new name," he said in perfect classical Italian. "Giuliana."

"I'm so glad you speak Italian. But of course you would. You speak just about everything." She was talking too much, but she didn't dare stop or she'd just drown in the sheer joy of being in Andrei's presence. She didn't know how to deal with the heat slowly melting her thighs, hadn't thought at all about the practicalities of being attracted to a would-be monk. "It would be wonderful if you could help translate some of the stuff I've found in this place. Stacks of letters from numerous scholars tucked into the bookcases. Old tomes with margin notes jotted in English, Greek, and Latin, even a few in German."

"Sounds extraordinarily multilingual for the family of peasants you expected to find when you spoke about them on Cyprus."

"That's putting it mildly."

"Somehow, I'm not surprised."

She glanced at her father's box, tried to push aside a growing sense of being overwhelmed, but to no avail. And now, she also felt this monumental attraction to Andrei. Somehow, she had to keep him here at the Gardens.

His eyes were so kind, so fabulously blue. She hadn't forgotten, but they stunned her, nonetheless. "You know, I can hardly wait to catch you up on all that's happened since we parted."

"You seem very happy, Julia."

"I am." She stepped over and took his arm, motioned toward the house. "Come inside."

"Your farm is beautiful," he said, looking back over his shoulder as she pulled him toward the door.

"So is the cottage. I still have trouble thinking of it as *mine*, though. You're the one person who wouldn't think I'm crazy to say I've never wanted to own anything for myself, certainly nothing as fine as this."

Inside, Andrei glanced around then took a deep breath, as if dismayed. "This is a fine house, in the truest sense of that word." He smiled down at her. "It suits you."

"Thanks." Suddenly acutely aware of being alone with him, Julia dropped her gaze to the floor, straightened the fringe on the nearest rug with the toe of her shoe, noticed the smell of burning coffee. "Oh, dear, the espresso!"

She was glad for the diversion the bubbling pot caused, glad for something to do while she got hold of herself. Andrei took a seat on a stool by the workbench, accepted her offer of a cappuccino, and sat quietly, watching her bustle about as she cleaned the pot and started over. He was even more handsome than she'd remembered, but he still had that familiar, unobtrusive way about him that made him so easy to be with.

"How did you ever find this place?"

"That's quite a story."

She smiled. "I don't have jet lag this time."

He crossed his leg and propped a knee against the workbench. "It seems you and I have a mutual connection. While I was in France, I learned your father and my mother worked there together on an Allied task force during World War II."

Julia covered her mouth as shock rocked her. It seemed too strange that their parents had known each other. "Isn't it odd you and I would meet like we did?"

"Indeed." Andrei seemed as unnerved by the coincidence as she was.

She thought a second then gave him a grin. "Actually, though, it's not any odder than the rest of what's happened these last couple of weeks."

"I gather your gifts have continued to unfold at their usual clip."

"Oh, definitely."

"I'm not surprised but I'm sure you must be, from time to time."

"Constantly. Stunned, really." The coffee gurgled up in its pot, sending its sharp, nutty scent into the air. While she steamed the milk for Andrei's cappuccino, he went out to the porch and brought the box from America inside. He balanced it on a stool beside Julia's, pulled out a pocket knife, and slit the tape all around. She poured the coffee, sloshed the silky foam over Andrei's, glanced back over her shoulder, her excitement intense. She moved closer. "I'll bet that's my father's research on the legacy, and I haven't even had a chance to digest a fraction of what I've already learned."

Andrei opened the flaps on the box, stood aside to let Julia take a look. Inside were several large books and a tower of photocopies, what looked to be articles, separated by neon-colored sticky tags. The bottom of the box was lined with her father's prized tarot collection, the sight of which brought on a fresh pang of grief.

"Looks like my father had lots more to share than I ever suspected. No wonder he regretted I hadn't had years to prepare for coming here." She sighed, shook her head. "I keep telling myself I'll be able to handle everything. At the same time, I keep feeling like I'm going into overload."

Andrei's eyes looked especially kind as he nodded. "I can imagine."

"Can you?" She put their coffees between them, sat, and leaned both elbows on the workbench. "That's terrific, because I'm sure a good imagination will be as crucial as your scientific training in solving this riddle called the Giuliana legacy."

"Fortunately, the hermitage where I'll be staying is not crowded. I won't have to hurry off to make room for someone else."

"Hermitage?" It took a moment to realize how disappointed she must look. Thoroughly embarrassed, she closed her mouth and eased back from the workbench, her stomach sinking. She'd hoped to invite him to stay at the Gardens but she should have anticipated he'd make other arrangements, ones he'd consider more suitable, given his vocation. "Is a hermitage the same as a monastery?"

"Actually, this one's much smaller and closer to the Gardens than the monastery where I had originally planned to stay." He smiled gently, as if sensing Julia's dismay.

His sensitivity only added to his appeal. So rare in a man.

∞

Andrei cleared the lunch plates off the kitchen workbench and stacked them carefully in the sink. Julia poured him another glass of fresh lemonade, topped off her own, and sat down. He had just finished telling her horror stories about a Russian man he'd recently learned had served with their parents during World War II.

Apparently, this man was a real bad apple, had set out to destroy both Andrei and his mother. "No wonder you're upset by the thought of Gregor Danilenko serving with our parents," Julia said.

"It's not only that, Julia." Andrei frowned. "If Danilenko learned of your family's history in Tuscany from your father, which is likely, he's probably come here to steal one of your family heirlooms."

Like he'd stolen Hitler's disgusting artifacts. Even the idea of them made Julia shudder. "The contraband you followed to Marseilles consisted mostly of holy relics, right?"

"With a few loathsome exceptions, yes."

"So, what I need to watch for is something the family considered holy?"

"Yes. An extremely powerful something."

"Powerful in what way?" Julia thought of Giuliana "using" the holy things, of Anna not wanting to touch them.

"Objects exposed to intense psychic or sacred energies accumulate psi in much the same way batteries accumulate electricity. Danilenko's specialty, of late, seems to be draining off the psi from such objects and using it for his own nefarious purposes."

She leaned back on her stool. "What does Danilenko look like?"

"I'm not sure, anymore. It's been ten years since I've seen him. He's a big man, probably well into his seventies by now, who looked more and more Slavic the heavier he got." Andrei leaned back on his stool, gave her a questioning glance. "Why do you ask?"

"Just wondering if I might have encountered him already. There was a heavy-set older man I noticed on my way to Cyprus." The memory made her shiver. "The guy gave me the creeps."

"I hate having to say this, but that could have been him. I hope you'll use extra caution until Danilenko can be curtailed."

Julia tensed. Yet another threat to her legacy, one she obviously dared not ignore or underestimate. Her unwanted admirer on the plane had loomed so large above her. Like a bear mooning over an empty honey pot, the Cypriot beside her had teased, an image that might help her cope with the apprehension even the thought of the big man evoked. "I'll definitely try to be more careful."

"It's important, Julia."

"I know." She squeezed her shoulder blades together. "Actually, you're not the first to warn me of danger, but you've been more specific about its source. I appreciate that." At the same time, she didn't want to get all worried before she'd figured out how to remedy the situation. Things had worked out fine up to now, probably because she'd been meditating enough to stay calm. Besides, no matter what came her way, her most urgent need now and for the foreseeable future was to find out as much as possible about the legacy. If that meant taking calculated risks in order to forge ahead with her father's entreaty to revive the family traditions, so be it.

"You seem different here."

"How?"

He gave her an appraising look. "More authoritative."

"Hmmm." He probably meant headstrong but was too polite to say so. Julia leaned on her elbows and propped her chin on the heels of her hands. "Please tell me more about the woman in Paris."

"Madame Racine." He said it with a Parisian flair.

"Funny name. Racine." Julia felt a tingle chase up her spine, followed by an icy chill. "*Ray seen* is how my father pronounced it." She closed her eyes before tears could escape them, took a deep breath, and let it out. "Just minutes before he died, he said 'Ray seen. For help. Ask!' I couldn't guess what he meant."

"I'm sorry, Julia."

She shook her head, tried to smile. "Thanks to you, another mystery bites the dust. What is Madame Racine like?"

"Quixotic. Opinionated. Delightful. No one knows for certain how old she is, but when our parents met her during World War II, she appeared to be about sixty, precisely how old she appears to be now."

"She sounds fascinating, and like someone I'd like a lot."

"Yes, I believe you will. She has asked me to invite you to tea tomorrow afternoon. Are you interested?"

"Absolutely!"

"Good. She apparently loved your father like a son, says she's looking forward to meeting you."

"What luck—meeting two legendary women in one week." Julia smiled. "Signora Isabella was wonderful. I have to get her memories of living here in the old days recorded in my notebooks."

Andrei lifted an eyebrow. "Notebooks?"

"I needed some way to keep track of everything I was learning, so I've started writing it all down. I'm way behind, though." She glanced at her father's box. His papers would have to be read and summarized, too, a task she'd relish if only she had more time. "It'll take me days to catch up. Maybe longer." She glanced up at the loft, her stomach tightening into a knot. "I'm so glad you're here, Andrei. There's another discovery I need to check out upstairs, and I wasn't looking forward to doing it alone."

TWENTY-TWO

Julia jumped off her stool and pulled Andrei up the stairs behind her. He chuckled softly, but he didn't balk. When they reached her inner sanctum, he fell silent and bowed his head, his hands clasped behind him. At this hour of the afternoon, the room glowed with the sun streaming in through the stained glass, tinting the room an unforgettable Cypriot blue. "You like it here. I thought you would."

"Very much." Andrei walked over to the niche and leaned toward the star. "Did you discover the star like this or do it yourself?"

"Both. The star had faded. I found the supplies to freshen it in this chest." Julia patted the top drawer of the chest.

"You did a nice job."

"Thanks. It was fun. I found some other things in here, but I decided to wait to study them. Then yesterday, Signora Isabella called them 'holy things,' implied they were important."

"Let's take a look."

Inside the chest's second drawer, the artifacts still lay exactly as she'd found them. From beneath them peeked an old envelope she hadn't noticed earlier. It was quite large, labeled in faded ink. She slid the envelope out from under the artifacts and slanted it toward the light. *Exploratory Excavations: Turan of Montecipriana.*

"What is Turan?" Andrei asked over her shoulder.

"The Etruscan Aphrodite, according to Charles Leland, an American folklorist learned in things ancient and Pagan."

Inside the envelope were brittle pages of text and pen-and-ink sketches, mostly of the terracotta and bronze objects in the drawer. The pages of text comprised a report on three small test excavations performed in 1920 on the Giardani property, one of which was on the north loggia, which had soon after been reburied under the marble slabs Julia had traded to Maria.

Andrei carefully lifted the objects from the chest and arranged them in an arc along the edge of the rug. Five small terracottas, each depicting a seated musician, were worn and chipped with age. A circle of lively dancers in the same material was broken in three places but all the pieces seemed to be there. A terracotta rose arbor was also in fragments. Following one of the sketches, Andrei pieced it together. Several crude bronze figurines of animals were not very interesting, but a corroded bronze tripod caught Julia's fancy.

She started to reach for it but suddenly grew wary and changed her mind. "Let's put these back in the drawer to keep them safe."

Andrei grimaced. "Unless I'm badly mistaken, nothing is likely to be terribly safe here, Julia."

She sighed. "Safe from Danilenko."

"Yes." Andrei's expression was stone serious.

She glanced away. The only thing that might neutralize Danilenko's menace was a better grasp of her legacy, some sense of what Danilenko was after. Tired or not, wary or not, she had to see what further information she could glean from these ancient objects.

Her brow was already burning. She gave it a rub, pushed her hair back from her face. Her breathing slowed as she calmed. The rose appeared in her inner vision. She picked up the tripod. Closing her eyes, she cupped it in one palm and traced the engravings on its legs with the index finger of her other hand. The tripod brought back the image of the meadow—the rape—the violent death she wished she'd never witnessed.

A moment later, the vision was upon her again. Her stomach churned. She felt Andrei's hand on her shoulder, felt his breath on her cheek as he gently braced her from behind. "Only images this time," she told herself aloud. "Impressions, but no pain."

"That's good, Julia." Andrei's voice was soothing, strong.

She braced herself, centered her mind again on the images, slowed them. "I've seen this scene before," she whispered. "There must be another lesson in it—an important one. I sure hope I can get it."

"You will."

Julia's mind again merged with Lady's, but this time the ancient woman's wisdom buffered most of Julia's trauma. Quickly, another angle on the meadow took form. The warrior king had arrived at the glade, his slave beside him. Lady was already dead. Lady had known the slave, had loved him. She'd also recognized the king, although she'd never met him.

This made no sense. Julia shook her head. Never mind, she scolded herself, relaxing her brow.

The scene replayed. Lady *knew* the king, although she'd never met him! And the king *knew* Lady, *revered* her! The slave's despair at Lady's death, his pain at arriving too late to help reeled through Julia's mind, followed by the king's remorseful fury—his dishonor—his intense self-contempt.

Julia took a deep breath. Impressions only, she repeated silently but firmly to herself. The strong emotions dimmed, and Julia's calm returned. She perceived subsequent images as if from a great distance: Lady's body draped over the cumbersome battering ram, her long copper tresses now shrouding her nakedness; the slave returning to the dark and empty glade, freeing Lady's corpse from the crude iron chain, his tanned muscles straining as he dug a deep grave at the edge of the glen then dragged stones for her burial from the nearby spring; the slave's own savage death as the warriors discovered his rebellious monument; and last, the warrior king's mock ceremony, his embittered smile as he ordered the slave interred beside the woman the king had loved forever but, in this life, had never known.

Julia wrapped her arms around herself and collapsed over her knees, that dreadful sense of "too late" weighting her mind. "Did you get that?"

"Some of it." Andrei looked badly shaken.

"It doesn't make any sense." She sat on her heels, pushed her hair back, caught sight of a vague darkish smudge in the center of his chest.

"I'm not convinced it doesn't make sense," he said. "It may not be a simple vision. It may be a past-life flashback. Don't force yourself to sort it out now. Give the information time to process."

He took a deep breath, lifting his chest. There was no dark smudge after all, must have been an illusion caused by the light. She felt a surge of gratitude for his support, his priceless friendship. "Thank you for coming." She held out her hand.

He took it, his smile filling his eyes with kindness. "I couldn't have stayed away."

"I really need your help, your expertise. All this is beyond me."

"It won't be for long."

"So you've said." She took another deep breath. This day had stretched her to her limits. She felt exhausted. The support Andrei instinctively gave made the discomfort of her attraction to him seem a small price to pay.

He leaned toward the chest. "What's in that last drawer?"

"I haven't a clue." She unlocked the drawer and pulled it open. There was only one object inside, a heavy chain attached to a large iron key ten inches long. The pattern on the top of the key was familiar, a pair of winged lions holding a scroll engraved with an ornate G. "I found the family crypt in the meadow where I had the first part of the vision we just saw." She lifted the key gingerly by its chain. "The pattern on its door matches the one on here." She put the key chain back and started to close the drawer. "Guess that's all."

"Wait! There's a false bottom in that drawer!" Andrei pried up an all-but-invisible tab, lifted off the false bottom and set it aside, then pulled out a faded purple velvet pouch embroidered with golden roses.

Julia could barely contain her excitement. She took the pouch and poured its contents into her hand.

A golden necklace curled in her palm. She gasped and held the necklace up between her hands. It was made of delicate gold links with tiny golden topaz-hearted roses laced through the length of it. From its center hung a larger rose surrounded by filigree leaves.

Her heart skipped a beat. "What a lovely large topaz!"

"That isn't a topaz, Julia. It's a quite extraordinary diamond."

"Oh, my." She spread the necklace flat against her palm and stroked it. "All those years in that chest, a treasure like this." She slid it onto her lap, searched the pouch, and pulled out a small rolled parchment covered with faded lettering. "Can you read this? It looks like Latin."

Andrei took the parchment. "It is Latin. I'm not sure how much I can make out. Let's see." He squinted at the antique scroll.

Julia scooped up the necklace, slid it into her pocket, stood. "The light in here isn't good enough. Let's go downstairs."

Andrei followed her through the house and out to the herb garden, where the sky was still bright. He held up the old manuscript.

"Brace yourself, Julia. It says *November—1498—Firenze* . . . *Workshop of M-A-R-S* . . . something . . . I can't make out the entire first name, but the second is Ficino." His voice sounded tense. "Marsilio Ficino was a master alchemist, one of the most celebrated of the Renaissance!"

∞

"Witches and, now, an alchemist." Julia seemed truly overwhelmed. Concerned, Anatolin studied her face and decided to postpone his translation. "I'm afraid my skills can't do justice to the poetry of these phrases. The manuscript is badly faded and should be treated by an expert. It may be quite valuable."

"Signora Isabella said some of the things upstairs were worn on holy days."

"A necklace is worn."

A worried frown dimmed the excitement Julia should have had the chance to savor. "I don't think this could be the heirloom Danilenko is after."

"Does it give you a strong reaction?"

"Not especially. Nothing compared to what I felt touching the tripod."

"Danilenko's greed is insatiable, but, regardless of its monetary value, if the necklace doesn't contain an inordinate amount of occult power, it's not likely to be what he seeks."

"I find it hard to believe anyone is as power hungry as you say he is."

"Of course, you would. Most people can't conceive of how thoroughly evil can twist a person like Gregor Danilenko."

"It seems you had to learn about Danilenko's evildoing the hard way." Julia took his hand, tilted her head up. "Tomorrow I'll go into Siena and see if I can rustle up a safe-deposit box."

She was distracted by the reappearance of young Vario. Leading a white goat on some kind of leash, the boy called to Julia from the path above. "Oh, dear! I need to spend some time with Vario. Can you stay a little longer?" she asked with a dazzling smile.

Under the dazzle, he felt her anxiety, her sense of being torn between the desire to continue their reunion and her loyalty to the child. He'd felt her stress mounting since he'd arrived, knew she was all but done in by the day's events, perhaps needed him to stay on for a while. "Of course I'll stay."

She smiled again. "Terrific!" Her shoulders seemed to relax. "I haven't had a chance to check out the barns or see what condition the farm is in. I'd sure value your opinion."

He chuckled. "I'll start now."

"The keys are on the hook inside the kitchen door. They're labeled." She reached over to a basket sitting on the low porch wall and pulled out two small apples, which she juggled expertly in the air. "See ya in a bit!"

He admired the sparkle in her eye all the more knowing the effort it cost her to keep it there. He was speechless from strong emotion, could only stare as she turned and strolled toward the gate where Vario waited.

∞

Anatolin meant to survey as much of the property as he could while Julia was with her young friend. The farm fanned all the way down the hill to the road that cut through the Calderola's central valley.

To Anatolin's right, bordering the forest, was a long line of linden trees. Below them began olive groves, their trees hoary, with short gnarled trunks. To his left, wrapping down the face of the hill, were trim vineyards, their borders studded with taller fruit trees, the young green grasses beneath them shot through with wildflowers in bloom. Sweetness spiked the air.

Spring was bursting her seams here, the Witches' Brew noticeably on the rise. Dousing rods might have made his foray slightly more eventful, but with his clairsentience, he could become a fairly accurate receptor if he could find a way to neutralize the widely varied energies to which he'd recently been exposed.

Two minutes later, near what seemed to be the edge of the property, he found an abandoned length of old galvanized wire coiled over a corner fence post. He lifted it off and carried it to a level patch of open ground, where he set it down then stepped inside the hoop.

Instantly, he felt himself energized and balanced in the cleansing column of energy created and contained by the coiled wire.

A moment later, he felt relatively static free, better able to tune in to Montecipriana's effervescent power. He looped the coil back over its post and continued down the hill, following the *vril* line created by the old fence, mostly made of loosely stacked stone sometimes two feet thick, timeworn and ageless, patched here and there with more modern posts and wires, themselves decades old.

There were random gaps where the boundary was not fenced at all. He selected one, stood back and examined it in relation to its overall environment. A gully yawned to the left of it, the line of linden stretched from above, a large oak marked its right. A huge boulder curved from below almost into the gap, rather like a sickle. Interesting.

He walked into the space and attuned himself to the vibrational frequencies passing through it. The energy flow, its speed and its power, called to mind the arterial web he'd seen from above San Galgano. The Gardens may once have fed energy to the entire Calderola through arteries like this. In fact, he would bank on it. He stepped through the gap, off the Giardani property. The energy stratified, slowed, consolidated. He moved back into the Gardens, clear of the gap, and felt patterns coalesce there, as well, but differently. Within the flow itself, the energy was supercharged, brimming with potentiality, chaotic and neutral, as befitted a threshold place.

Anatolin cut diagonally across the center of the property to trace the flow from this gap to its counterparts. He could locate them readily now that he knew what to look for. He stopped abruptly in the middle of the terraced field. Beneath his feet he felt the distinctive sensation of swiftly running water. An underground stream, not very deep.

He closed his eyes, slowly gazed out at the air directly in front of him, turned his head steadily left then right. Negative ions filled the air, barely visible, almost indistinguishable from the *vril*. Darting and colliding, bouncing off each other in no particular rhythm, they danced like bliss-drunk Sufis in a crowded square.

Anatolin smiled and started back up the hill. This was the finest farmland he had seen in years. Far finer than he would have expected in twenty-first-century industrialized Europe. He climbed up a few more terraces, came to a spot that afforded him a good view all the way to the top of Montecipriana. He stood quietly, watching the *vril* flow as if from some intricate fountain.

How magnificently Nature had put this small mountain together. It was a genuine power spot of the highest order. What he would give to have such a place to study, a living laboratory of exquisite complexity. He could hardly wait to tell Julia what a treasure her mountain was, what a sacred jewel.

Moving toward the center of the property, his eye caught a flash of bright turquoise in the vicinity of the small cottages near the border of Julia's herb garden. A man, large and burly, was snooping around the farthest of the cottages directly below Julia's. He leaned against its shutters, his hands cupped around his eyes, clearly trying to peer inside. Anatolin quickly climbed the hill.

Closer, he could tell the man was perhaps Julia's age—not Danilenko, thank God. The tension between Anatolin's shoulder blades eased. Closer still, he saw the man's hair was curly, close-cropped, streaked with blond, the man's face bronzed from working in the elements, no doubt. There was a name for men who looked like this, but the American slang expression eluded him. The young man moved to another window and peered inside. He seemed not to notice Anatolin's approach. Whatever he was doing, he obviously was completely engrossed.

Anatolin cleared his throat. "Looking for something?"

The young man started. His bright-turquoise eyes darkened as he took an aggressive stance, well-articulated muscles bulging every-where. "Who the hell are you?" Brute force and plenty of it, but no real malice.

Anatolin extended his hand, smiled. "Anatolin here. Andrei Ivanovich Anatolin, a friend of Julia's."

"Aah, *sì!* Me, too." The young fellow even had articulated muscles in his neck. He beamed a wide smile, his very white teeth flashing. "My name is Marco."

Anatolin's nerves relaxed. "Signora Isabella's great-grandson."

"Yes. I hope to help Giuliana clean and fix up these guest cottages. It would be a great honor."

"Indeed." Anatolin glanced around. Still no sign of Julia and Vario. Anatolin had time to look over the barns. "Nice to meet you, Marco."

The young man didn't answer, seemed distracted by something going on down the hill toward the far boundary of the farm, where Anatolin had not yet explored. He followed Marco's gaze and spotted another man, ostensibly irrigating a field.

"Emilio Greco." Marco seemed unhappy to see the man here.

"Julia's foreman."

"He troubles me, that one," the young man said, tipping his head in Greco's direction. "I would really like to know what he's doing. He's been working that same irrigation ditch for the last twenty minutes."

Anatolin pushed his hands into his pants pockets. Was Marco surveilling the foreman? If so, why? The muscles across Marco's chest rippled, those in his neck strained, and he cracked the vertebrae in his spine as if to release some annoying stress. The fellow even had muscles in his jaw, which delineated as he gritted his teeth, then glanced at Greco again. "My great-grandmother does not like that man, and neither do I."

∞

Twenty minutes later, Anatolin felt reassured on one score: Julia's foreman, for all Marco's suspicions, had indeed been a conscientious

tenant. The barns were in exemplary order, the equipment antiquated yet impeccably clean and oiled. Back in the courtyard,
Anatolin heard soft laughter, glanced up and noticed Julia heading
down toward the house with Vario. She and the boy strolled arm in
arm, their heads together as if sharing some deep secret. The
immaculate goat brought up the rear. At the gate, Julia kissed the
boy's forehead and sent him off in the direction of the village, goat in
tow. She came toward Anatolin, looking more radiant than she had a
while ago.

"Thanks so much for waiting. There's still lots I'd like to discuss
with you."

"There are flowers in your hair." He touched one. "Forget-me-
nots, I believe." The small flowers suited her utterly. Their loveliness
made his chest ache.

"Oh, right!" She chuckled. "Vario."

She gave her head a shake, and a sprinkling of tiny blue and pink
blossoms drifted down onto her shoulders. One stayed nestled in a
ringlet below her ear. He untangled it, then, feeling self-conscious,
handed it back to her.

"What did you think of the barns?" Smiling up at him, she tucked
the flower into the buttonhole on the lapel of his jacket, finished by
giving the center of his chest an absentminded pat.

His heart leaped in response, strangely energized. Her PK, obviously, working on him without her even seeming to notice.
"Magnificent, in superb condition," he answered quickly.

Glad for the diversion, he described the barns, told her about the
room that joined the barns over the gates. A perfect sentinel's post,
he realized as she took hold of his arm and steered him back into the
house.

∞

Julia was fascinated by Andrei's discussion of the Gardens' earth energies, even more fascinated by his visionary ideas about how she could employ the energetics-based agricultural theories he'd developed in Siberia. His innovative ideas were thrilling.

Too bad it was time to end their reunion. He stood quietly beside her on the south loggia, halted on the way to his car by the sight of evening deepening over the Calderola as the sun quickly edged toward the horizon. The sky was too clear for an exciting sunset, but the air had taken on that misty, lavender tinge Julia loved.

While helping unpack her father's box, Andrei convinced her to photocopy everything related to the legacy—letters, margin notes, her spiral notebooks and summaries of the neighbors' stories, her recollections of the visions she'd experienced. He even insisted on helping make the photocopies, starting tomorrow, on their way to Madame Racine's. His sense of urgency made Julia feel tense. She was delighted he had joined her in Tuscany, but Danilenko or no Danilenko, she hoped Andrei wouldn't fret all the time. If she wasn't careful, his apprehension coupled with her concerns over the hostile neighbors could easily keep her in a nervous jumble.

"Julia," Andrei began, then cleared his throat. "I really think you need a full-time bodyguard, someone brawny, like that chunk, Marco Banfi."

"Chunk? You must mean *hunk!*" She gave a small, dismissive wave.

"He's good bodyguard material, whatever you'd call him. In my opinion, you would benefit greatly from keeping someone like him close by."

Since he'd broached the subject of employing a man about the place, she'd give him her two cents on the subject. "Thanks, but I think I need a visionary, preferably a scientifically trained *Russian* visionary. Someone who can see himself serving somewhere like this, growing things." She met his gaze. Inadvertently quoting the very words he said to her on Cyprus gave her an intense chill.

"Here?" Though he'd clearly fallen in love with the farm, he seemed entirely caught off guard by her suggestion, as if the thought never would have occurred to him.

"Yes, here. Can you see yourself reconditioning this land? Helping me turn the Gardens back into the working herb farm it was long ago?"

He hesitated, not answering, clearly stunned.

She started off the loggia and through the herb garden toward the courtyard. He followed. Near the rose arbor, she stopped and fell silent. The scent of the antique roses abloom was intense, almost intoxicating. Earlier, she had learned from Silvana the variety derived from the Crusaders' old Autumn Damask. She picked a half-open bud and twirled it between her finger and her thumb.

"Honestly, I'd really love your help with the farm." She reached over and exchanged the rose for the wilted forget-me-not in his lapel. "Think about it, Andrei. I wasn't kidding."

"Neither was I. I believe you really do need a bodyguard." He took her hand, a strictly friendly gesture, so strictly friendly it seemed he was determined to control himself with an iron resolve. A shame, in her opinion, but he hadn't led her on. One kiss should never have caused her to hope he might change his mind about becoming a monk.

He looked at her oddly, his steady gaze making her feel uncomfortable. "What are you staring at?"

"Not at. For. Any sign of Danilenko's psychic intrusion. I've been watching all day long and am relieved I haven't sensed his energy anywhere near you. You'll be fine without someone guarding you tonight."

He said it, she thought, more to convince himself than her.

∞

Anatolin could hardly bear to drive away from the Gardens and leave Julia standing there in the courtyard, stubbornly resistant to his suggestion of a bodyguard and seeming rather forlorn. He stopped beyond the arch, got out of the car and secured the large lock on the gate, then proceeded down the hill, fighting the urge to look back. Near the bridge, he spotted a man in coveralls who seemed to be loitering there, deliberately. It was Emilio Greco.

Anatolin pulled off the road, parked a few yards from Greco, set the hand brake. He got out and leaned against the car.

The man strode toward him, a belligerent frown on his face. "*Buona sera.*" There was nothing friendly in his tone.

"*Buona sera,*" Anatolin answered, extending his hand. "Name's Anatolin. I'm a friend of Julia's."

Greco ignored his hand. "Are you leaving now?"

"Yes. Are you Julia's foreman?"

"I am." He didn't offer his name.

"It's late to be working."

"I'm not. From the village to here makes a perfect after supper stroll."

The man was lying outright. He was working, just not for Julia. Danilenko's vileness tainted Greco's aura.

Whether Julia believed she needed protection or not, Anatolin meant to do his best to keep her safe. If she wouldn't take Marco on as her bodyguard, Anatolin would have to accept her offer to help with the farm. Then, at least, he'd have a legitimate reason to draw Emilio Greco into his scheme for the Gardens, keep him so busy he wouldn't have time to make trouble. He'd find ways to keep Julia's attention diverted, as well, from Marco's muscled splendor. And he'd have to work on curbing this nascent jealousy. His protectiveness of Julia could easily become possessiveness, an emotion wholly unsuitable for a renunciant.

He drove away from Montecipriana, doubled back to the village, soon located a metered telephone in the caffè bar, Il Gatto Nero, the main square's sole open establishment. Aside from the miniskirted *barista*, the place was empty. He dialed the number Vittorio had given him for the hermitage. Luckily, Vittorio answered. Anatolin quickly summarized his plan, which required his friend to gather the needed gear and meet him halfway to Montecipriana as quickly as possible. The silences on the other end of the line grew markedly longer as Anatolin talked.

Vittorio sighed. "So, you intend to break this news to Julia over the telephone?"

"As soon as you and I hang up."

"Coward."

Anatolin didn't flinch—he'd called himself the same and worse since the moment he'd made his decision, but he'd had trouble enough withstanding Julia's charisma earlier. He wanted some distance between them when he announced his decision.

When he didn't respond, Vittorio continued. "This room over the gate sounds terribly Spartan."

"The accommodation is at least as comfortable as the cell I was given at the hermitage. With the bedroll you're bringing, it will more than suffice."

"I suppose you'll be better off than you were in Siberia."

Anatolin pulled Julia's rose from his lapel, held it up to his nose, savored its scent. "Frankly, I'd be far better off if you were staying there with me—if your whole community were."

"Aah! The Giardani Heiress must be very beautiful."

"Beautiful, indeed. Undeniably beautiful."

BOOK FOUR

RECOLLECTIONS

I believe I am not quite accurate

when I call this "Etrusco-Roman."

For in fact, the religion, such as it is,

which forms the real faith of the streghe . . .

goes back to a time of which

there is no record.

—CHARLES GODFREY LELAND
ETRUSCAN ROMAN REMAINS IN POPULAR TRADITION, 1892

TWENTY-THREE

Julia and Andrei finished the photocopying much earlier than planned and had everything neatly filed in new three-ring binders before Julia knew it. "Mind if we make a quick stop to pick up another herbal or two?"

"Not at all."

"Terrific." She took Andrei by the arm and hurried out of the copying shop. The bottom floor of the building next door was a bank. Out through its doors trooped several men Julia had seen around Montecipriana. Francesca's husband was among them. They looked angry and very unhappy.

Ordinarily, Julia would have waved and sent her new neighbors a smile to cheer them up, but they seemed intent on giving her the snub. She sighed when she realized Andrei had noticed. "This way," she said, starting toward the narrow street leading up toward the heart of Terzo di San Martino.

Inside the erboristeria, Andrei went immediately to the end of the sales counter to check out the old ledger she'd told him about. He quickly started poring over the pages, a frown of intense concentration on his brow. Julia squatted down and perused the shelves of books.

"*Scusi*, Signorina, but are you not Giuliana Giardani?" Celeste asked.

Julia smiled at her. "News spreads fast here." She stood up.

"I thought so the first time you were here." Celeste came around the counter and took hold of Julia's hands. She smiled brightly, her eyes shining. "Welcome home."

"Thank you." Julia turned to Andrei, who glanced up from the book. "This is Andrei Anatolin, who has agreed to help me revive the Gardens."

"*Favoloso!*" Celeste turned to Andrei. "You will grow herbs again?"

"Yes."

Celeste put her hands on her hips. "Organically, I hope?"

"Of course."

"There is tremendous demand, you know."

Andrei smiled, clasped his hands behind his back. "We have a great deal to learn. Perhaps you could point us toward a growers' association?"

"*Sì,*" there are several." Celeste walked back to her side of the counter and pulled open a drawer. After searching a moment, she took out two business cards and handed them to Andrei. "Contact these groups first. They are connected to everyone else you might need."

"Wonderful." Andrei slipped the cards into his jacket pocket.

Celeste turned back to Julia. "When I was born, my mother's aunt predicted I would be the first Brunetti in generations to study with a Giardani Heiress. I was despondent when I grew up and learned the Giardani had moved to America. I thought I'd come along too late, but I see the old witch was right!"

While they copied the Giardani papers, Julia had discussed with Andrei her dismay at Lucia's expectations of apprenticeship. He hadn't seemed surprised by Lucia's request and clearly wasn't by Celeste's, either. He gave Julia his trust-yourself look.

"As my friend indicated," Julia said with a sigh, "we have a lot to learn. It may be a while before anyone at the Gardens does any teaching."

"No hurry," Celeste said. "Now you're home, we have the rest of our lives, right?"

Julia just smiled. She wasn't willing to commit herself to teaching anyone anything yet, but she was truly delighted to make another woman friend. Too bad the Calderola's younger men weren't even close to giving up their preposterous resistance. Their wives likely would not be permitted to speak to Julia for some time to come.

Was it her return to the Gardens that bothered those men? Or was it who—or maybe what—she was?

∞

As villas go, Il Calice Zolfo was relatively modest, but Madame Racine was pleased Julia was enjoying her tour. They had come to the gallery, a long colonnaded rectangle with a pink marble floor and scrolled travertine walls. From deep in the arches between the columns smiled a baker's dozen of the world's most notorious alchemists. Racine's favorite of the marble busts, that of her benefactor, the Comte de St.-Germain, reigned from the tallest pedestal at the end of the room, but Julia had stopped in front of Marsilio Ficino.

Racine's taffeta caftan rustling, she crossed to Julia, who faced her and smiled. A delightful young woman.

"These mosaics are breathtaking." Julia pointed behind Ficino's bust at the bright jewel tones glittering on the wall. "Did you commission them?"

"*Mais, non,*" Racine answered with a shake of her head. "They came with the villa. I've been too busy, have seldom had occasion to enjoy them."

"Your work sounds exciting, though."

"*Oui,* at times it has been." Racine chuckled. "And other times, *non.*" She slipped her arm through Julia's and walked beside her.

Julia paused in front of St.-Germain and glanced up at the quote over the old master's bust. "Woe unto him who misuses the gifts of heaven to serve his passions." She lifted her eyebrows. "Now that's a heavy warning."

"One I wish the young Gregor Danilenko had taken to heart."

"I find it hard to believe he was ever anyone's friend, especially my father's. The Tony Giardani I knew was a fairly astute judge of character."

"It was part of our training, an extremely necessary part, to give each other the benefit of the doubt, up to a point. Dani was a decent man once, though he had come into this life with a heavy burden of old guilt." Racine sighed. "It is this, I now believe, that broke through and eventually broke him."

Julia's shiver was answer enough. Racine glanced toward the salon. It had taken an extra day to secure permission for Rafael to continue tracking Hitler's collection. He'd arrived only minutes before Andrei and Julia. Knowing Racine wanted time alone with Julia, Rafael had offered to keep Andrei entertained.

Racine smiled. "I wonder if the men have yet tired of my laptop."

"Probably not," Julia said with a chuckle. "I've heard the Internet eats up a tremendous amount of time."

"Then it won't matter if I show you my favorite garden before we rejoin them." Racine led Julia out to the villa's large boxwood maze. "While we walk, you will tell me all about what you have found at the old family home."

She listened attentively to Julia's discoveries in Tuscany, clicked her tongue when she heard of Julia's troubles with the Calderola's men, but those troubles paled to insignificance when further probing brought out Julia's visions of death in the meadow above the farm. Racine abruptly turned Julia back toward the villa, her blood turned to ice.

Her fears were confirmed as the young woman went on to explain she thought the visions might hold some sort of karmic message. How much more Julia was adequately prepared to know was unclear, as was how much Racine might be free to discuss—even if her recollections were completely lucid which, unfortunately, they most certainly were not.

Julia's own past-life memories soon would become far stronger than Racine's dangerously blurry ones. There was precious little Racine could do to help. All she knew for certain was that Anna's failure to assume the Giardani mantle had opened a well of old trouble Julia, as the designated heir to the Giuliana legacy, would now be forced to work her way through. "I'm glad Signora Isabella was able to share her memories with you, *ma cherie.* They will be useful, I am sure."

"Maybe they will, once I get them all sorted out. Plus, Andrei says there's an elderly monk who has memories to share with me, too."

"*Très bien.*" Racine had managed over the years to scrape together a sizable stash of Giardani letters. She pulled out the bundle she'd tucked earlier into the sleeve of her caftan. "Even more to sort out, I'm afraid. Letters I retrieved from Charles Leland's estate and from that of Giuliana's English friend, the archaeologist Jane Ellen Harrison, whom I met long ago in Athens. Also, Anna's very few letters to me, from Italy and then from America for a while."

"Good heavens!"

Racine put the bundle into Julia's hand. "I wish I had more to offer you, *ma cherie.* Hopefully, these will fill in a few gaps and provide some insights you might otherwise have missed." Racine couldn't ignore Rafael's hearty laugh, booming from the salon.

Julia seemed not to notice. She pulled an envelope from the top of the bundle and stared at it, then at Racine. Shaking her head, she slipped the letter out, and glanced at the salutation. "You knew my great-grandmother?"

"Don't even attempt the math, Julia," said Rafael, who appeared with Andrei outside the salon. "The woman's age has baffled the finest minds on the planet. The years never have added up. Never will, I suspect."

Racine rolled her eyes and hurried toward the salon.

Julia followed, still holding the letter up. "But—1915? How?"

"Listen up, old buddy," Rafael said, giving Andrei a jab in the ribs. "This is one we have to hear."

Julia seemed flustered. She looked pointedly away from the joking men and gave her head another shake. "Madame Racine—"

"Really, my dear!" Racine stopped in the center of the room, her caftan swishing around her legs as she pivoted to face the three young people, who had followed her through the door. James was bent over the sherry glasses, studiously pouring two ounces of liquid gold into each. Racine noticed his shoulders shaking with mirth though his lips were pursed, his expression deadpan as always. She glanced from the butler to Rafael then to Julia. "I assure you I never tell my age—and—I never volunteer my secrets!"

"Volunteer?" Rafael grinned. "You couldn't wring secrets out of our Madame Racine."

"There are no secrets to wring," Andrei continued the teasing as he walked to Julia's side. "Obviously, Madame is a highly advanced yogi."

"Naw!" argued Rafael. "It's gotta be alchemy. She found the elixir of eternal youth, probably hidden for centuries here at Il Calice by a previous owner who shall, with all due respect, remain nameless."

Julia glanced up from skimming through the letter in her hand. "Well, according to my great-grandmother, one Mademoiselle Racine seemed inherently adept when it came to Italian witchcraft."

"Let's say I am knowledgeable about the occult and leave it at that, shall we not?" Racine raised a sherry unsteadily to her lips.

Rafael grinned and lifted his glass into the air. "I'd say a toast was in order. To Madame Racine—and her secrets."

∞

A sanctuary of Aphrodite Turan at the top of Montecipriana, the very spot that had been calling Julia all along! She climbed quickly toward it, photocopies of Madame Racine's letters tucked into the pocket of her sweater. Without those letters, Julia might never have learned of the sanctuary. No doubt it was the crowning glory of all the marvels she'd discovered thus far. When Andrei had given her his usual locked-doors lecture on dropping her back at the Gardens earlier, she'd been so flustered she forgot to tell him she meant to investigate her very own sanctuary as soon as she could get there.

Of course, a sanctuary couldn't belong to any person, only to She in whose name it was consecrated, however long ago. Julia, like generations before her, was merely the latest of those chosen to preserve the memory of the sanctuary's existence, if no longer its full purpose. She only hoped she hadn't come home too late to do whatever it was Turana expected of her.

She passed the family crypt and picked out a narrow path up the steep incline. Her breath caught in her throat as the path suddenly widened, becoming a roomy staircase with small lamp wells set every five feet or so into the mossy stones. She continued up the stairs then stopped where a small, mostly circular plateau spread out before her.

To her right was a wide, raised area that seemed almost like a stage. Behind it curved a high rock face carved with niches. Tall trees continued the circle, forming a natural cathedral wall that sheltered the high plateau from the wind. Moss seemed to grow everywhere the thick spring grasses didn't, softening every angle. Immediately ahead, the rocky outcrop tapered down to about waist-high. She approached and cautiously extended her hand. Beneath a coat of damp prickly moss, cool stone met her fingers. She held her hand there, slowing her breathing, then tuning in to the rose on her brow.

Sensations came. Coolness. Dampness. A lovely image—lilies dancing in a shallow basin fed by crystal-pure water—the old sacred spring. More images swirled in her mind's eye, memories not from this life but hers just the same, fleeting memories, probably insignificant. A child's skinned knee bathed clean in the icy cold spring. The sacred enclosure lit with torches for some evening procession. Lilies in the flame-lit basin framing the pale reflection of a copper-haired woman's face. The chants of a crowd filing past the sacred spring, prayers rippling the water.

Julia walked to the level area, crouched down, and searched until she found a sharp-edged stone. She used it to scrape the moss, peeling then rolling away a dense carpet of green. She closed her eyes, touched. Here, long ago, devoted hearts and loving hands had set large paving stones into place, creating a platform for the sacred dance.

She glanced around, saw a mound near the center of the circle, the ancient altar, she realized, even before she touched it. The altar squatted low, no more than knee-high, directly in front of a stocky, conical form that jutted forward from the platform. She retrieved her flat stone and scraped at the conical form. Sure enough, the cone was a large uncarved rock like the holy stone from Old Paphos. She scraped the altar, touched it, and her mind filled again with images. Honey and oil offerings for the Lady. Frankincense and myrrh rising high on flower-scented air. Tears spilled here when love was sacrificed to duty or when joy brimmed over.

She stood and brushed off the knees of her leggings. The larger shapes at the far end of the circle were covered in raspberry vines, but when she touched the altar, the impression she'd had of the sanctuary intact gave a sense of a building in that very spot, maybe a small temple.

Leaning against the platform, she pulled out the crisp new photocopy of an especially beautiful letter from her great-grandmother to Madame Racine, read it aloud:

> The Giardani Heiress lives in the Gardens. She keeps the joy of life foremost in her heart and shares it graciously with the world in which she lives. She knows the name and the meaning of the Goddess she serves, and she keeps alight in her mind's eye the sacred flame that burns in the shrine high above.
>
> Her life is a living altar from which that eternal flame draws its earthly sustenance, never dampened in the midst of all manner of fear and travail. She is *strega*, yes. But she is more than that. She is also priestess.

The old Lover of Mortals, whom the jealous warrior God forced into uneasy slumber long since shall reawaken— and with her the Giardani Heiress—ready to speak Her true name for all to hear once more, ready to reestablish Her altar again beneath sun and stars and to rekindle Her eternal flame atop Sacred Mountain, for all to behold.

Julia swallowed hard. She was the Giardani Heiress. She would be so with joy. Tears burned her eyelids. She didn't even try to fight them back.

Ruin though it was, this sanctuary was a treasure. No great monument, here. No ornamental grandeur. Just the simple planes and dimensions of an old seat of Pagan worship so precious generations of Giardani had pledged their lives to keep it intact.

Julia would clear the weeds away immediately, set the stones straight where she could, fill the sanctuary with flowers. She'd scrape clean the old basin and let the sacred spring fill it with sparkling water, find some water lilies and root them there.

Moving onto the platform, she felt crushed moss underfoot. She centered herself in front of the altar, not far from the ancient rock cone. She longed to lay face down to embrace the mountain itself, but because the ground was growing wet with fast-falling evening dew, she knelt instead. Overcome by reverence so profound it shook her to the core, Julia prayed.

Reaching into the recesses of her imagination, she called up images of the Giardani who had worshipped at this site through the ages. She raised her arms above her head, her fingers outstretched, her chin held high. It was time to pledge herself to the old One her ancestors had always served, the One whose true name Julia knew she would learn someday.

The first glow of sunset stole softly over the sanctuary. She focused on the golden rose pulsing wildly on her brow. An invocation seemed to form from some wellspring deep within.

O, Most Great and Holy Goddess—hear my prayer! I, Giuliana, have returned to serve you. Abide with me and guide me in all I do, as you have always guided the Giardani.

Bright rose color suddenly lit the sacred precinct. Julia gasped as bolts of highly charged current shot through her, passing down her uplifted arms, rumbling and churning deep within, speeding down her legs into the earth, only to pass upward again, colliding with the incoming force and purging any residue of resistance from its path.

She couldn't focus. She closed her eyes, prayed for balance, opened them again, and gazed out over the sanctuary. She blinked. A vision crystallized around her. The platform beneath her feet was polished clean, the altar glistened with oil, and the little temple stood erect and tall, as if Julia's incantation had turned a key, opened a doorway to the distant past. The vision shimmered a moment then dissolved.

Julia rubbed her hands together, steady resolve taking hold of her. *Strega* or priestess, if she was one, surely she was the other. She'd do whatever she needed to do to fulfill her role—even if that meant teaching psychic development. She felt commitment swell within her, glow like a flame rekindled from long-buried embers. She was thrilled by the discovery of the sanctuary, delirious almost, but she knew beyond any doubt that the powerful something still missing from her legacy, the object Danilenko sought, was the key to the future. Not just her future, but her new community's future, as well. Her father had obviously hidden the key to protect it, like Lady's brother had hidden the sacred object she died to protect.

Whatever was it that Julia needed to search for, protect? Aside from her father's indecipherable third postcard, she didn't have a clue. His hasty message seemed clearer than it had before, but only slightly. She walked to the ledge above the old crypt, crossed her arms, scanned the darkening meadow.

"Where the grove is pleasantest, by precincts sacred to you." She was supposed to "take a seat there" and wait for "thoughts of her ancestors." Her father had to have been talking about the crypt, but she was going in circles, again, not making any headway. And there was Signora Isabella's warning to think about.

Sunset slashed the clouds with breathtaking, fiery streaks, and the evening star had just peeked through, a favorable sign, if Julia ever saw one. She wouldn't worry over whatever "unfinished business" this latest blessing might bring down on her head. All she wanted to think about was her own special Goddess and how insistently She'd called her up here tonight. Maybe Julia had found the place too late to save her family's entire tradition, but she'd forever be glad she'd at least answered the call.

∞

Danilenko waited in the woods below the ancient stairwell for Julia Giardani to cross his path on her way back down to her cottage. He'd followed her this far on her trek up but, with no way to shield himself from observation, he'd been unwilling to go any farther.

Since the moment he first set foot on the Gardens' soil, Danilenko had been affected by a bizarre confusion of a sort he'd never before experienced. It was unpredictable—devastatingly so. Now he was a wreck.

The night he'd viewed Julia in her bath, it had come to him that mating with the Giardani Heiress would give him access to her subconscious mind, to her repressed memories, even to her genetic memories and past lives, eventually disclosing the whereabouts of the treasure he sought. The idea was making him crazy, hounding him day and night. Not even a bout with his raven-haired Florentine had banished it, though he still wore the marks of her last vicious stiletto-heeled ride and would for some time.

He couldn't think straight, and he shook from his first waking moment each day, as if with some lethal palsy. He couldn't plot, anymore, from a distance. It made him feel weak, which was unacceptable. Worse, he couldn't contain his desire. The merest hint of Julia Giardani made him strain against his trousers like an eighteen-year-old.

He'd barely controlled himself while she dallied above, but now—finally—there she was again, only meters away, her supple body moving freely, hugged by soft leggings and a clinging T-shirt under her long cardigan.

To hell with waiting for her to locate what he sought. To hell with waiting for the full return of his youthful good looks or for his immortality. To hell with waiting for anything. He had to have her, afterwards worry about finding her precious heirloom.

He started for her then stopped in his tracks.

What was he thinking? If he took her now, he'd lose more than his chance at the Giardani heirloom.

He wasn't thinking—and he needed to think. Needed to muster every power at his disposal, before it was too late.

Too late. Her thought, he realized, not his. He grabbed at her free-floating anxiety as if it were his lifeline.

His confidence returning in leaps and bounds, he magnified her thought, elaborated on it, projected it back forcefully—*It's too late for you, little girl. You're too late, inadequate to the task, ineffectual and weak. A powder puff, nothing more.*

TWENTY-FOUR

alfway down the stairs, Julia felt a shadow fall over her. She guessed she was pretty pooped. After all, she'd just given her life to a sacred cause, probably should have anticipated some sense of letdown. Maybe she wouldn't feel quite so heavy had she prepared herself better, but it was too late now. She already felt depleted.

She started across the meadow, slowed just beyond the small bridge near the crypt, where the gray, postsunset gloom made silvery mirrors of the meadow's large puddles. Slowing further, she glimpsed herself in one after the other. How pale she looked, how small and frail. Half dead and already defeated, with no chance to do what she'd been brought here to do.

She pulled her gaze from the hypnotic pools, but a sense of despair already possessed her. *Too late.* Maybe she had indeed come too late. Her greatest fear, unconscious though it might have been until now, really couldn't be ignored any longer.

But it couldn't be true. Couldn't be.

Fighting off a feeling of hopelessness that almost immobilized her, Julia passed the crypt and came to the crest of the hill just as Andrei's car sped back into the courtyard. She was surprised, hadn't expected to see him until much later in the evening, when he'd finished supper with his friends at the hermitage. Apparently, he'd changed his mind and come back early.

She stopped, stood a moment, watched him down in the court-yard, pacing, a bit frantically, she thought. He'd be furious when he realized she'd left the house. She lifted her arm and waved.

"Andrei!" she called, her voice piercing the silence that lay over the farm.

He turned around, clearly had heard her, but seemed too panicked to realize where she was.

Waving again, she raised her voice. "Andrei, up here!"

The poor guy looked hysterical now. He bolted through the gate and up the hill, started shouting halfway to her.

"Where have you been? The house was locked, so were the barns. Your car was parked in the courtyard. I couldn't sense where the bloody devil you'd gone!" When he reached her, he grabbed her by the shoulders. For a moment she thought he might give her a good shaking. He didn't, but neither did he smile. "You're safe."

"Of course." She saw his pulse pounding in the vein above his collar, put her cool index finger on it. He seemed to shudder but he didn't pull away. She dropped her hand to her side. "Look at you, all riled up," she said, as calmly as she could. "Must be that darned Witches' Brew, getting to us both."

"I wish it were that simple." Andrei smiled, but the gesture didn't warm his blue, blue eyes. He let go of her. His gaze kept her riveted where she stood. "Madame Racine told me something this afternoon I didn't know but should have suspected. Danilenko was responsible for your father's death, as he was for my mother's."

Julia gasped. "What are you saying? I was there!"

"Not when the fire started."

"Danilenko started it?"

"Close enough." He softened. "His accomplice apparently lit the match, but your father might still be alive if it weren't for Gregor Danilenko."

She shivered, too stunned even to cry.

He reached out and tucked her hair behind her ear. "I'm sorry, Julia, but you need to know the truth. There's something else I wish I didn't have to tell you—Danilenko was here just now."

Julia blinked. Her stomach turned. "Where?"

"Not fifty feet from you. I sensed him very near when I spotted you."

Her throat closed. Unable to talk, she shook her head, shivered again, hugged her arms closer, then shrugged at the knot that cinched her shoulder blades together. Maybe she had made a mistake coming up here alone, but the urge had been so strong. Like a magnet. She doubted she could have stayed away if she'd tried.

Andrei walked to her left, came to a stop a few feet away. "Look, a footprint. It's large. Deep, as it would only be for a very heavy man. I should never have left you alone."

She didn't like Andrei feeling responsible. She walked over to where he stood, still looking down. "Nothing happened. I'm okay." Her voice sounded small, like a little kid's. She made herself speak up. "I lucked out. Or the Goddess called me so *She* protected me— something. Nobody's to blame here, Andrei, least of all you."

She felt the truth of that, a certain, undeniable knowing that fought against the dread evoked by the muddy impression left by Gregor Danilenko's boot.

∞

Too much, too fast, Julia had said to her father last March, but she had no idea back then how much too much her legacy might eventually seem. She'd practically lost it earlier on the hill. Now she was all pink and warm from her bath but she still felt far from her best, felt, in truth, like her circuits had shorted, like she'd barely make it to bed, where she wanted to curl up with her newest photocopies to read for a while and settle her nerves.

She sighed, pulled back the covers, and glanced around her lovely bedroom. So much nicer than Andrei's chilly office in the passageway over the driveway, into which he'd moved abruptly the night he arrived. Even the guest room would have been nicer, but he'd refused her invitation to sleep inside the cottage, had insisted he'd be fine out there between the barns.

A real bed would at least be more comfortable than sleeping on the floor, bedroll or not. Tomorrow, Julia would ask Marco to put together the old bedstead and add an extra mattress and bedding to the Casa Sergio hand-me-downs he'd be picking up for the garden cottages.

She turned her attention to the letters, highlighter pen in hand, marking things she especially wanted to note for more careful future study. Twenty minutes into her task, she came upon a mention of May Eve. It was vague, a mere reference in the context of the *strega's* year, but it triggered the memory of her father's voice, of the look in his eyes when he mentioned that date on their last night together.

Serious. Encouraging. Hopeful.

She read on, skimming the pages more quickly. Almost missing a reference buried in Giuliana's chance remarks about needing more lilies for the sacred spring, Julia slowed down and continued with care. The payoff came when she found a whole paragraph that spoke of a May Eve celebration in 1919, the first in five years because World War I had made gatherings difficult and unsafe.

She ran downstairs, snatched her journal off the desk, and was back to her bed in a flash. In only an hour, she'd made three pages of notes. May Eve was only two weeks away. She'd have to scramble to prepare the sanctuary, get the word out to whoever might care to know. The real challenge in pulling off this year's May Eve celebration, though, would be learning everything a Giardani Heiress needed to know to make it the great event Julia sensed it had always been, wanted it to be once again.

She hoped the *streghe* would come if she asked, maybe help spruce up the sanctuary. Maybe Signora Isabella would move back to her cottage in the herb garden for a time, lend support while Julia worked her way through the riddle of May Eve. Maybe Lucia would consider moving here, also, and sharing a bit of ritual know-how, modern or otherwise.

With Andrei here, Julia already felt much safer. Having more people at the Gardens would be better still, might discourage Danilenko from coming around. At the very least, it would certainly cause him some difficulty in sneaking up on her again. Slipping the journal into her purse, she closed the binder, scooted it to the far side of the bed with the others, and snuggled down under the covers.

Thanks to Andrei, she could finally let down her guard a bit. She might find his mental telepathy bothersome sometimes, but she was sure glad he had sensed she was in trouble up in the meadow, already the site of one fatal event Julia knew of. The close call there with Danilenko had rattled her more than she'd wanted to admit, even to Andrei.

As if she could hide how she felt from a telepath.

She hoped his gifts, like hers, came and went. If her true feelings for him were entirely transparent, she'd be humiliated. Lately, she spent a fair amount of time wondering why the universe worked the way it did. How could she have fallen this hard for a man who might care for her, maybe even desire her, but who had no intention of letting their friendship blossom, become the intimate relationship she would now, after nine years of almost total disinterest in men, leap into without batting an eye?

Her first and only love affair—her "big disappointment"—had taught her well what she wanted in an intimate relationship. She'd decided back then she'd never settle for less than the qualities she'd earlier observed in the beautiful glow of her parents' love for each other. True friendship, respect, consideration, passion fueled by something more than mere physical attraction—the very qualities she'd experienced so seldom with the young men she'd met in the last nine years.

She had never regretted her relative lack of experience in matters of the heart. She'd gotten along fine, up to now, but her confusing love for Andrei had her in a muddle, which made her feel like crying.

She knew what she felt. No question.

She loved him.

And she sensed his feelings for her had grown far beyond friendship, even the Divine friendship about which he often spoke. But he'd promised himself elsewhere, and because she intensely wanted his happiness, she had to accept that. It felt wrong to try to dissuade him from a course he clearly still believed was the right one for him.

Sighing, she wiped her teary eyes on her nightgown sleeve, rolled onto her side, and curled her hand under her damp cheek. Her other hand tucked close over her heart, she finally drifted off to sleep.

∞

After fretting over Julia's near encounter with the general for half the night, Anatolin had awakened in a gloomy mood. Fortunately, Julia's infectious sense of discovery and her eagerness to meet her Benedictine neighbors had lifted his spirits, making the drive to the hermitage on the mild April morning delightful. He savored each fresh perspective as he steered through the hilly terrain, Julia's voice all but chirping as she described her latest plans.

Her idea to fill the property with activity was sound, though the thought of living day to day surrounded by the bustle of all those people gave his exile's soul quite a shock. He'd get over it, he was sure, if the extra population at the Gardens helped keep Julia safe. And it might, in a way his admonitions clearly couldn't.

That Julia, left to her own devices, would never exercise adequate caution to suit him had never been more certain. Her natural audacity seemed to have grown more extreme since coming here, as if fueled by some naive, irrational belief that a Giardani Heiress could suffer no harm within the magical nimbus of the Witches' Brew. Now, it appeared she'd surrendered whatever good sense and caution she might have retained to the enigmatic promptings of her Giardani Goddess.

Worse yet, the magnetic force of Julia's optimism all too often eclipsed Anatolin's native wariness, just as his pleasure at being in her company and aiding her cause were fast eclipsing his desire for all else and utterly eroding his inclination toward monastic renunciation. This last once again weighing heavy on his mind, he pulled into the hermitage grounds and parked. He desperately needed to set himself right. He'd head for a meditation on his bench beside the chapel as soon as he saw Julia to the reception area, where Brother Orlando would meet her.

Her expectations for the meeting were obviously high. Hopefully, they would be not only met but exceeded by whatever the aged monk wanted to share with her in person.

∞

Premonitions gripped Danilenko as he climbed up Montecipriana. His shoulders were in knots, his mind a morass of confusion. He was bewitched by the Giardani Heiress, obsessed by desire for her yet beset by shame for thinking he could seize her.

This morning his assistant had reported Julia's discovery of the so-called holy things and where to find them. Despite his turbulent state of mind, Danilenko was determined to do so. Apparently, it would be his last chance to search the Gardens for at least two weeks, perhaps longer.

From the edge of the forest, the Gardens' courtyard appeared to be empty, its huge lower gate padlocked. He continued up the property line, found the south-facing garden gate also locked, but the small wooden gate to the north posed no obstacle.

A moment later, he stood before the cottage door. An obviously new deadbolt lock glistened against the door's dark wood. It would be a breeze to tumble with PK. He grabbed the door latch, felt pain sear through his hand, jerked it away. Stepping to the window on his left, he cupped his hands around his eyes to peer inside. He leaned forward. His hands touched the windowpane. Searing heat again shot through them, as if the perimeter of the cottage had been hot-wired. Impossible. This could only be some kind of spell.

He zeroed in on it. Yes. A rudimentary warding-off spell. Childish and quaint. Hardly the kind of protection one would expect to find securing the home of the Giardani Heiress.

Someone would receive the shock of his life when Danilenko returned the spell to its maker—rather enhanced by the added PK he'd have to call up to break the crude ring-pass-not and enter the cottage. He backed into the courtyard, took a good long look, and gradually made out the lines of subtle force. Like fine silk filament, it surrounded the structure, was especially thick near the kitchen door, where it seemed anchored in an old broom. From there Danilenko would remove it.

Retrieving the broom, he braced it against his knee, cracked the handle in two, and let the pieces fall to the pavement. He extended his hands before him, fingertips aimed at the door. He visualized the net in his mind's eye and took a slow deep breath, drawing the net's force toward him as he inhaled and bent the almost tangible energy to his will, pressing it into the shattered wooden handle of the broom. Finally, muttering a two-syllable word of power, he carried the broom pieces back to the porch and slammed them forcefully into the corner, sending the protective energy back to its source.

An instant later, he discerned the impact of the spell hitting home.

∞

Seated in the warm reception room at San Galgano, Julia held on her lap the first and only illuminated medieval manuscript she'd ever seen outside a museum. Apparently, it was hers. It was a large book covered in Florentine marbled paper, roughly sewn together with silky twine.

The Giardani Herbal.

The gilded title delighted her each time she caught a glimpse of it. She trembled all over with joy and excitement, had to struggle to keep following the gist of the old monk's rambling conversation. "I'm sorry, Brother Orlando, did you say you didn't know my grandmother?"

"I regret, my child, I did not know her," he said with a sad little nod of his head. "You are the first Giardani Heiress I have ever had the pleasure of meeting." He chuckled, his eyes sharp and clear. "In this lifetime, that is."

Julia cocked her head. "Is that a reference to reincarnation, sir?"

"Could be."

She raised her eyebrows. "I didn't think anyone affiliated with the Church would speak in terms of reincarnation."

"Aah! But there are affiliations and there are affiliations, is this not so?" He winked. "Now before this old body completely expires, are there not other questions you wish to ask me?"

"Only about a thousand," Julia said, tickled by Brother Orlando's sense of humor. She hoped he was kidding about expiring soon. She sensed there was much she could learn from him, even if he hadn't personally known her family. "How did you come to possess *The Giardani Herbal?*"

The monk leaned back in his chair, toyed with the long, heavy rosary beads hanging from his belt. "My old master in the healing arts entrusted it to my keeping when he left this world sixty years ago. Dear Brother Arturo." Brother Orlando sighed and rubbed at a spot of dried pesto on the threadbare sleeve of his otherwise immaculate off-white robe. He smiled. "It was he who knew your family."

"Did he speak to you of my grandmother?"

"Not much. He barely knew her, but Giuliana had been his lifelong friend. Apparently aware of the friendship, Anna asked him to safeguard *The Giardani Herbal* when she left for America."

"I see." Julia frowned. "Do you think it is valuable?"

The old man sat up straight as a rod. "It is priceless!"

"Valuable enough to incite someone to violence?"

"Aah!" He shrugged. "Now I understand." He rubbed his chin. "Probably not, though it would certainly fetch a substantial sum in the antiquities market if you—"

"No!" Julia interrupted, hugging the manuscript to her chest. "I wouldn't dream of selling this if my life depended on it." She shivered and gazed out the window, decided the old herbal's charge of psychic energy was probably too slight to interest Danilenko, sighed. "I was just wondering if, in fact, it might."

∞

Danilenko glanced desperately around the Giardani girl's bedroom. Even though his assistant had directed her workers to the outskirts of Florence to purchase their supplies, Danilenko had searched for so long, he now had only fifteen minutes left until they were due to return.

Aside from one small bronze tripod, the so-called holy things were useless junk. None of them was a precious relic. More important, none possessed much occult power. He'd realized that immediately. Searching twice, he had failed to find the object for which he'd come—or any indication that any such object had ever existed. Another search would be futile.

He shouldn't have come here again. Returning to the farm had been worse than a waste of his time. He'd become even more distraught than he'd felt earlier this morning, even more acutely aware of his own despair. His mortification. There was too much joy, here. Too much love. It gagged him, how charming the cottage was, reminded him of its irreproachable owner, of her obvious nobility of spirit.

He glanced at her bed, covered in white like the walls of her room. A few thin three-ring binders, dark blue, were piled on the bed's left side. She probably slept on the right. He pulled back her quilt, lifted her pillow to his face, drank in her scent. Sinking onto one knee, he sniffed the musty sweet impression of her body, which had remained vaguely in her sheet, left unsmoothed when the bed was made. He ran his hand along its amorphous curves, its soft indentations and shuddered, had to close his eyes to steady himself.

There was no lust left in him. For the moment it had fled, leaving a vacuum into which coursed a worshipful reverence he'd experienced only once before, and that, long ago. Clutching the edge of the bed with both hands, he struggled against a tide of yearning, knowing he would only profane it, as he had the adoration he once felt for his little Magda.

He forced himself to stand then skirted the bed. His hands still shaking, he picked up a binder, perused it, and cursed to himself. He'd been an utter fool. The information in the binders obviously could have been useful in his search. He should have examined them when he first came upon them. He'd have to take the pages with him.

Leaving evidence of his burglary was sloppy, showed too damn much of his hand, but a glance at his watch confirmed there was no time to cover his tracks, regardless. He had barely enough time to get away from the Gardens unseen. He snapped open the first binder and hurriedly removed its contents, did the same with the next.

The unmistakable sound of a vehicle starting up the Gardens' drive gave him an adrenaline surge. He couldn't ignore the vehicle's approach. He'd have to leave without the pages in the final binder. He folded the papers he already had, stuffed them into his inside coat pocket.

Backtracking to the room with the niche, he snatched the tripod off the shelf and tucked it away with the papers. No time now to exit the way he came in. He raced down the stairs, headed for the route he'd earlier charted, through the porch on the north side, where he'd have the cover of the forest. He only hoped he could make his way off the farm undetected.

TWENTY-FIVE

Julia did not seem to mind that Anatolin had monopolized the conversation all the way back from San Galgano. Cradling the lovely old book on her lap as if it were fine blown glass, she was obviously too distracted to pay close attention to his plans for the farm. She'd hardly said a word, and they were already winding up the road to her cottage.

She glanced out the window. "I'm really glad both Rafael and Brother Vittorio will be able to help us reestablish the herb farm. This place will serve as a powerful example to the whole community by the time we're finished. That makes me happy."

"Even before we are finished, if you have your way, right?"

"Right!" She patted *The Giardani Herbal.* "Maybe you and I can study this for a while after lunch. I have a strong feeling there may be useful stuff in here, information that might help us decide what we want to grow right away and how to go about getting started."

"I hoped that would be the case." Anatolin smiled as the car climbed the final grade and rolled into the courtyard.

Marco's truck was parked in its usual place, but there was no sign of Emilio's. Anatolin glanced down at the guest cottages, spotted Marco and his friend, Niccolò. Each had selected a cottage to work on and had obviously gotten a reasonably good start, despite the trip to town for supplies.

Anatolin pulled up beside the kitchen porch, heard Julia draw in her breath. "What is it?"

"Something's wrong," she said. "Terribly wrong!" She was out of the car before he could stop her, had reached the door before he could even call out her name.

He banged his head getting out of the car. "Julia, wait!"

She was already inside. Panic hit him in the gut. He practically hurdled the car and raced through the door behind her, his heart pounding wildly against the walls of his chest. Impressions sliced through his mind. He couldn't slow them, but he knew in the next instant Julia was safe. She stood between the end of the hearth and the foot of the stairwell, a blank, startled look on her face. The aborted threat had left him shaking like an aspen in the wind. He heaved a huge sigh as he crossed the room and took her by the shoulders.

"Dear, darling Julia," he managed to start in a reasonably calm voice, "if you don't stop chasing headlong into danger I am going to wring your lovely, obstinate neck!"

"He was here, Andrei. Danilenko was here."

"Yes." He pulled her close, manuscript and all, and held her tightly. Her anger was palpable as was her fear. They tore at Anatolin's heart, made him wish he could banish them from her experience forever.

"Dammit!" he whispered in frustration, remembering too late how she hated to hear people swear. *"Dammit!"* he repeated more loudly, for what reason he couldn't have said, except that it made him feel better. She didn't even seem to notice, a clear sign of her distress.

Still clutching the manuscript, she pulled away and climbed the stairs. He followed her through the bedroom and into her meditation room, where she crouched in front of the chest, touched her free hand to its surface then rested her forehead upon it.

"He mauled everything in here, smeared his ugliness all over. And he stole the ancient tripod." She gave a small sob. "How *dare* he invade this space! How dare he touch the holy things!"

Anatolin stood at the door, unable to answer for the fury ripping at his gut. He wanted to hurl something, but knew doing so would only make matters worse. He gripped the doorjamb and, with effort, composed himself.

"Consider your warnings vindicated." She stood up and brushed at her tears.

"You're angry with me."

"Not at all." She sniffed. "Only with myself for not listening to you."

He stepped back from the door. "Let's go downstairs, make a cup of coffee. There's nothing we can do up here."

"Right."

She centered the old manuscript on the seat of a chair, brushed past him, then stopped so suddenly he ran into her. He fought off another impression, this one so disgusting he prayed Julia wouldn't perceive so much as a hint of it.

His prayer was in vain. Her gaze was riveted on the bed. Her anguish hit his solar plexus like a wrecking ball. Her fear felt like ice water down his spine.

"He touched my bed!" she whispered, obviously repulsed. "My bed, that freak!" Her voiced cracked, her eyes again filled with tears. She stepped toward the bed, fell to her knees. "This is not how I left it this morning."

"Julia." If only he could drive the knowledge away. "Don't."

She shook her head, crossed her arms over her chest, and rocked back and forth. She pressed her knuckles against her lips, started to stand, her knees buckling as she glimpsed the obviously empty binders. "I'm sure glad you insisted on extra copies of the notebooks. I guess he took mine." She shook her head. "I really don't know what I'd do without you."

He helped her up. "My dear, that's nothing to be worried about now." That Danilenko had Julia's papers and soon would know everything she'd learned was what worried Anatolin.

Keeping her close in the shelter of his arm, her steered her toward the stairs. He felt her tension recede, if only slightly, as she gave a sigh and dried her cheek against his shoulder.

He dared not name how he felt.

∞

Abhorring Danilenko's intrusion, Julia felt resolve building even stronger within her. The only way to stop Danilenko from repeating his violations of her space was to make sure she—and only she— found the family heirloom he had to be after. She'd tried every way she knew how to figure out what it might be. Now she'd just have to pray harder that the answer would come to her in time.

A shrill beep cut into the sound of their footsteps on the smooth stone stairs. Julia tensed and pulled out from under Andrei's arm, fished for the cellular phone in the depths of her purse. Finally, she found the obnoxious device and flipped it open. She pressed the ON button, started to relax, but the caller's news sent a new terror through her.

"Oh, Lucia—not Vario!" She dropped her purse to the floor, grabbed Andrei's hand, and listened to Lucia's explanation of what had happened. "Yes. *Ciao*." She clicked off the phone and dropped it into her pocket.

"What is it, Julia?"

"To get into the house, Danilenko apparently reversed a protective spell Vario taught me the day he came here with Signora Isabella. I thought the spell was only a gag, a funny skit the *streghe* put on for my entertainment, but I was wrong." She shuddered at the fury that registered in Andrei's eyes as he apparently grasped the import of what she was saying. She lowered her voice, grabbed his other hand, held it tightly. "When Danilenko returned the spell to its source, a fairly common magical procedure, Lucia says, Vario was struck down. At school. The teacher didn't know what to do for him. There was no indication of illness or injury, so they just took the little guy home."

"Is he conscious?"

"No. He's in some kind of coma." Tears came again against her will. She brushed them off on her sleeve without letting go of Andrei's hands. "I can't bear the thought of him suffering because of me. There must be some way to help him!" She bit her lower lip. "I better call Marco. He knows the way to the Andrade's."

Andrei's anger suddenly gave way to some other emotion. If she didn't know better, she'd have suspected he was jealous. He broke away from her grip. "I'm glad Marco can drive you to Vario. I presume he'll also stay with you and escort you home?"

"Marco is driving *us*, Andrei—you and me—I'm not going anywhere without you until further notice." She started toward the kitchen door, turned. He was jealous, whether he could admit it to himself or not, but she couldn't force the knowledge on him. "Providing you don't mind, of course."

She walked back to him, straightened his mussed jacket, leaned her forehead briefly on his chest, where there truly *was* a dark smudge, however vague and transient it might be. "I'd say an expert parapsychologist might be just what Vario needs right now, wouldn't you?"

∞

Looking from Signora Andrade's kitchen out toward the converted sun porch, Anatolin watched Julia at Vario's bedside. She was huddled close to the bed, gently stroking the boy's fine, dark curls, holding his hand and talking very softly so as not to excite him while she supplemented his energy with her own. Vario had returned to consciousness twenty minutes earlier. He was extremely weak and disoriented, but aside from that he appeared to be fine.

Anatolin was deeply relieved. Julia would have been inconsolable had the child suffered lasting injury. Her concern for her new neighbors' welfare only increased his admiration for her. Her commitment to this small community surpassed any logical expectation, was obviously grounded in the love she expressed so effortlessly, almost lavishly, for everyone she met. She was his opposite in that regard. There was nothing circumspect about her.

"She's good with him," said Fiorella Andrade, who apparently had come up behind Anatolin while he was lost in thought.

"She's good with everyone." His voice husky, he cleared his throat.

"A healing presence, as you are, Dr. Anatolin."

"Thank you, Signora." He accepted the old woman's compliment with a slight bow. "I'm pleased I was able to help."

He'd recalled a procedure learned from a West African shaman, back in 1980 or so. It involved linking energies with a person in deep shock and bringing them back to awareness via positive images and affirmations. Julia, a natural trance healer, had done most of the work. Anatolin had merely made suggestions and guided her imagery.

"I hope I'll be seeing more of you, once Isabella moves back to her old place at the Gardens," Fiorella said.

Signora Isabella had accepted Julia's invitation the instant she'd received it. Lucia agreed to take the cottage next door to the elderly *strega*'s. On the drive over, Marco had reported the guest cottages would be ready by noon tomorrow.

Anatolin smiled. "Julia is fortunate to have made so many trusted friends in such a short time."

Fiorella gave him a humorless grin. "Isabella says not all Julia's new friends can be trusted. I hate to admit it, but I must agree. Surely you've arrived at the same conclusion, have you not?"

"I have indeed." With the events of this day, his vow to protect Julia had become an all-consuming passion. Henceforth, he would stay close by her side, no matter that she might resent it. And he would add to his daily meditation routine a prayer that Julia's Goddess might show him the way to keep her safe.

Julia. . . . He could hardly breathe at the mere thought of losing her.

∞

Back at Volterra, Danilenko again cursed himself for a fool. He tossed the Giardani papers down on the table, leaned heavily on his elbows, and held his throbbing head between his hands.

How had he not recognized the acute degeneration of his self-control since first going to the Gardens? How had he not guessed Montecipriana's powerful *vril* could turn him into a raving lunatic? Finally, his actions these past few days were comprehensible. As was his obsession. Given time, he would regain control of them both, but only if he stayed away from that mountain, away from the Calderola entirely, until he was back in balance and had concrete knowledge upon which he could act. Knowledge of how to resist the irresistible Giardani Heiress, how to bend the mountain's treacherous force field to his own ends. Knowledge of where the Giardani heirloom was hidden and how to secure its possession.

He gazed across the room at the small tripod, which he'd removed from his pocket only after pulling on his thickest pair of gloves. Though he'd never been one to perceive much psychometrically, especially unaided, the tripod had blasted him with intense emotions from two clear, consecutive images as he slipped it into his pocket back at the Gardens. He wouldn't touch it again until his control was fully restored, which could take several days, given his present state of agitation.

Danilenko felt sick, infected. That insidious Witches' Brew. He hated it as surely as Andrei Ivanovich, with his devotion to the earth-bound vagaries of the Divine Creatrix, must surely love it.

∞

An almost-full moon lit the hillside below Julia's cottage, where Anatolin meandered slowly from terrace to terrace. He'd recently done his best thinking on his feet, and he had a lot to think about, tonight. Not the least of which was the way his entire being rejected any hint of the life he'd wanted before meeting Julia.

He wondered now why he hadn't seen this coming, why he hadn't thrown in the towel long before this. He'd lost himself to her the first moment he'd seen her on the beach in Cyprus, but his Scorpionic fixity must have blurred the obvious. That his destiny was with Julia. That he could just as readily achieve his highest spiritual goal—complete mystic union notwithstanding—at her side as in any monastery. She was indeed his most precious friend, Divine or otherwise.

Divine friendship. By her actions toward him, she'd come to embody what had previously been an empty thought form, an ethereal ideal. But now he had another problem he'd never anticipated. He felt too deeply for her to enter an intimate relationship carelessly and he didn't at all trust his control over the desire she stirred in him. To help keep a grip on himself, he'd taken to walking the Gardens every night before going to bed, which had become increasingly later over the last few nights.

He barely let Julia out of his sight now, and given she stayed up working then meditating late, so did he. They'd enjoyed a few short days of relative peace, with no sign of Danilenko. No sense of him, either. The general had obviously made a strategic but surely temporary retreat.

Emilio Greco was Danilenko's man, whether or not Julia could bring herself to acknowledge it. Anatolin had tried to convince her she was blinded by her friendship with Silvana, Greco's unmistakably honorable wife, but Julia refused to accept Greco's betrayal, let alone permit Anatolin to call him to task. Her resistance had made it difficult to keep the foreman's treachery within bounds, though eventually, Anatolin had done just that.

Under the guise of needing his advice, Anatolin now managed to keep the farmer constantly under his thumb throughout the day.

Rafael stayed on Greco's tail at night, not retiring to Madame Racine's until long after the Greco house went dark. Interestingly, the farmer had met only once with Danilenko after the break-in, and that had been the very next day. Since then, nothing.

The longer Danilenko stayed away the better. It gave Julia time to stabilize, intensify her quest for an object that might possess the power Danilenko craved. It gave Anatolin the relative tranquillity of mind to concentrate on reviving the farm, Julia safe. The land already seemed different, and he and Vittorio had barely started to inoculate the fields with biodynamic preparations, hadn't even begun to incorporate compost into the soil or to plant the fallow acres with cover crops. Anatolin felt wonderful at the end of each day of hard work, alive and stronger than he had in years. Vibrant, like the Gardens' trees.

He glanced up at the skyline to the east, caught the bright corona rising off the fast-budding birches and, behind the lindens, the oak and laurel and old bristly pines that thickened as they climbed up the hill. The Witches' Brew was exhilarating. He was pleased it seemed to have responded to his ministrations, though he imagined it was the incessant quickening of the Giardani Heiress that sustained and fed its awe-inspiring expansion.

Such a quickening Anatolin had never dreamed possible. Julia's talents were more formidable than ever, yet on the surface she seemed entirely unchanged. Entirely unaware of the implications of her latest awakened ability, as well. He'd been observing her carefully, watching her healing PK in action on all those lucky enough to cross her path.

Her friendly handshakes, little pats, rubs and squeezes carried tremendous healing force. He'd seen it happen more times than he could count, had himself experienced that very force, from his first evening at the Gardens. He'd come to realize she was intuiting and working with people's energy blocks—long buried, in most cases totally unconscious—like the one in his own heart. And now that he knew about the blockage, it was incumbent on him to work with it, too.

TWENTY-SIX

Julia finished organizing the books along the counter in the herbal workroom, then walked out to the south loggia. She was thrilled the old farm now swarmed with new friends. Signora Isabella and Lucia seemed happy as clams in their neighboring cottages. Marco and Niccolò shared the third cottage and had joined the other two with a lattice breezeway, transforming them into a temporary kitchen and dining area for feeding the *streghe* arriving daily from far and wide in response to Signora Isabella's call.

The *streghe* were generous and warm, every one. Some helped Andrei and Brother Vittorio with the farming, but most had pitched in on the heavy clearing work needed up in the sanctuary, which was where Julia planned to head in the next fifteen minutes.

She heard a child's voice, some footsteps approaching the herb garden. The gate opened, and through it came the little red-haired girl from the village, whom Julia had learned was named Graciela, accompanied by her mother.

Julia smiled, sat down on a heel, and held out her hand. "Hello, there! I'm so glad you came to see me!"

Graciela broke away from her mother's grasp and ran toward Julia. "Everybody talks about the Gardens all the time now," she said. She ignored Julia's hand and gave her a tight squeeze around the neck. "They say it is safe to come here again, that the old curses are gone away now you're home."

"How about that!" Julia kissed Graciela's cheek then stood to greet her mother. "Welcome."

The woman smiled. "I couldn't have kept that child away an hour longer." She lowered her voice as her daughter crossed the loggia and peeked inside Julia's cottage. "Signora Andrade believes Graciela needs your help. Her appetite is off, and she can't seem to sleep through the night."

"Why don't you have a seat?" Julia pointed the mother to the table and chairs on the loggia then looked at the child. "Somebody brought me some giant goldfish. Wanna see them?"

"Oh, yes!"

"They're down in the pond."

Graciela bounded down the steps. Julia followed, deep in thought. When the mother had spoken of the child's symptoms, Julia had instantly seen something flicker across her mind's eye. Just the faintest of impressions, but it had resonated deep within her. She took a seat on the bench by the pond and waited a moment while Graciela acquainted herself with the fish. Observing carefully, Julia noticed a dark energy smudge above the child's left elbow, where the priest had held her. Another seemed to linger around the child's upper back, in the vicinity of the liver. Words formed in her mind.

Black bile. Shame held in the body creates black bile.

In the next instant, she knew what the mother should do. But first things first. "Come, tell me how you've been," she said, patting the bench.

"Not so good, Giuliana." The little girl ignored the bench, scooted up onto Julia's lap, and rubbed her cheek against Julia's shoulder. "The bad man still gives me the creepies. My tummy gets all sick." She leaned away and looked dismayed. "It feels icky!"

Julia opened her eyes wide, poked softly at Graciela's tummy. "You think maybe the bad man's meanness is stuck in there?"

Graciela wrinkled her nose, shuddered. "Must be."

"Like some hard little marble?"

"A whole bunch of them."

"Yuck!" Julia, hugged the child close and positioned one hand over Graciela's liver, the other at the crown of the child's head. She held perfectly still while her palms burned then cooled, then she pulled back and smiled. "Do you trust me enough to do as I suggest?"

Graciela clicked her tongue, shaking her head in obvious disgust. "'Course I trust you."

"Good. Then I'll tell Mamma how to make you a special drink. It will taste kind of funny but not too bad. I'll bet it washes that man's ugly meanness right out of you."

"And I'll be all fixed!" Graciela stood up, pulled Julia off the bench and started climbing the steps toward her mother. Halfway up, she stopped. She stood several steps above Julia, almost at eye level. "I'm going to be ten years old soon—in only a couple of years." She gazed down at the cottages. "In town they say by then it will be like the old days here, with girls coming to stay—to learn to be like you." She reached over and took hold of Julia's chin. "Don't you forget me, Giuliana, when that time comes." Without waiting for Julia's reply, the child turned and all but flew up the steps.

Julia glanced out over the garden. Her gaze rested on the cottages, and she chuckled to herself. Maybe she was meant to fill those cottages with little apprentice priestesses, to turn the Gardens back into some kind of modern-day academy for training in the Mysteries.

Amazing! A thought that once would have caused her great distress now made her intensely happy.

She turned and climbed the stairs, stopped in front of the worried parent. "Graciela seems to have a bit of liver congestion, nothing serious unless it goes untreated." Not knowing where the recipe came from, Julia told the mother how to mix up the simple household ingredients that would do the job and how to administer them to the child. "She wants to get well, so she's promised to drink everything down, right?" She winked at Graciela.

"Right!"

Five minutes later, mother and child had gone. If only the local men had warmed to Julia the way the women and children had. She still hadn't a clue how to turn their hostility around, though she'd mulled the question over every time she'd had a moment to spare since she'd come to the Gardens. She knew there had to be some answer. She frowned in concentration, but soon reminded herself to let the matter be. She refused to allow frustration to spoil this lovely day, especially not on her way to the sanctuary.

At the meadow, she stopped to admire the job the *streghe* had done cleaning out the stream near the crypt. If the stream was kept clear of debris, the meadow might not flood again next winter. To the left of the small footbridge, where she'd had to pick out precarious steps from the hillside, the workers had exposed the entire lower staircase, carefully crafted of old stones like the one Julia had found above. Silvana said it was probably Etruscan.

Dear Silvana. She'd made the sanctuary refurbishing her personal project. The other workers took their directions from her, which made Julia's job of uncovering the sanctuary's ancient features much easier.

Climbing onto the plateau, Julia smiled at the sight of the ceremonial platform all scraped off, its granite slabs glowing in the soft sunlight. Under thick brambles along the platform's rear, Silvana had found more antique roses, several rambling varieties. New trellises across the back now held a profusion of buds bursting their seams. Newly planted around the platform's front three sides was a short hedge of small-leafed myrtle with violets, yarrow and columbines beneath it, all apparently sacred to the Giardani Goddess.

Farther on, the rampant vines and accumulated debris had been stripped away from a blossoming quince, a gnarled and knotty fig tree, and the little temple that stood between them, its fallen stones awaiting Julia's attention. Cutting the grass to the edge of the forest revealed toppled boundary stones, which were easily righted. The rusty old chains once swagged between them were sanded and oiled, an arduous task but well worth the effort, as it turned out. On May Eve the chains would mark off the perimeter of the ritual circle.

To the left of the entrance, a group of *streghe* were setting several tall junipers into the ground. Around them would cluster vervain and feverfew and beneath those, the wild strawberries and lady's mantle plants Brother Orlando had sent over from the monastery garden south of Siena.

And then there was the sacred spring.

Julia crossed to it almost reverently. Silvana had personally trimmed the mugwort and thinned the pennyroyal and horsetail growing beneath its basin. Now you could see the basin's walls, with their carved reliefs of doves and roses in interlocked rings.

Silvana joined her. "Look what I finally found." She pointed to the wheelbarrow parked in the shade of the nearby elderberry trees.

Julia gasped. The wheelbarrow held tubs of water lilies.

"My dear, you are an angel. I'll plant them in the basin later, after everything else is done. Thank you—for the lilies and for your support and your help. I don't know what I would have done without you."

Silvana gave Julia an earnest look. "Nor do I know what I would have done had you not come home. It is beautiful to have a sweet new friend. It's exciting to be part of a myth in the making, to see it unfold before my eyes." She looked away. "Now you have even won over my *stupido* husband."

Julia started to protest.

Silvana put the pad of her finger to Julia's lips. "You have never complained, but don't think I haven't seen how his behavior has sometimes hurt your feelings. That is over now. Today, I heard Emilio defending you in the village, telling his buddies how kind you are, not at all the selfish American they assumed you would be." She leaned over and gave Julia a kiss on the cheek. "I don't think he deserves a medal, I just wanted you to know he's changing."

"Silvie, you are a wonderful friend."

"And now, Giuliana, this friend must get back to work."

Silvana headed across the plateau. Pulling on her work gloves, Julia returned to the entrance, smiled at the *streghe,* knelt and started to work beside them. The simple melody the men hummed was a ritual tune she had recently learned from Lucia. They seemed pleased when she joined in.

The breeze was fresh and soft, the sun gentle yet warm. The earth smelled damp and sweet and full of life. Julia felt like she was in heaven, for sure, and she worked with no thought of anything but the task before her. A while later, she looked up and realized someone was standing beside her.

Someone very pregnant. Young Francesca from the village, seemingly unescorted. Julia slid her trowel into the earth, brushed the dirt off her gloves and stood up. "I certainly hope you didn't walk up here alone."

"No, Signorina Julia."

"Good." Julia took off the gloves and tucked them into her jeans' back pocket. "Welcome." She took the young woman's hands in her own. "This old place is starting to look pretty good, don't you think?"

"Very nice." The young woman seemed sincere but distracted.

"What is it, Francesca?"

"I have a favor to ask."

"Okay. I'm listening."

Francesca heaved a sigh and rubbed at her heavy belly. "Our midwife has taken ill. She won't be able to deliver the baby, which is just as well because I want you to do it—the Giardani Heiress—like the old times."

"I'm flattered." Julia smiled sincerely but shook her head. "But I'm certified to practice in California—and even if I could practice here, I was trained to work several weeks with expectant couples, so everybody knows each other well by the time of delivery."

Francesca's eyes teared up. She clasped her hands under her belly and hugged it close. "Please—don't say you won't help us."

"I'm sorry, but I'm not sure what's involved, legally. Besides, we have your husband's feelings to consider. I don't think he cares much for me, and it wouldn't be good for you or your baby if we arranged something that would only upset him."

"That will not be a problem, Signorina," a man interjected from behind Julia's shoulder.

Francesca's husband wore a much friendlier expression than the last time she'd seen him. His eyes conveyed his unspoken apology. He walked to Francesca's side and put his arm around her shoulders. "My wife knows everything now, including how you tried to help and protect her. There are no more lies or mistresses between us. We both hope you will help bring our child into the world."

Though she was relatively new at it, being a midwife was one of Julia's all-time favorite experiences. She eyed Francesca more carefully. "I'd say you're about six weeks from delivery, am I right?"

"*Sì*, Signorina. June 18."

"We might have time." It would be wise to get plugged into a professional network here, anyway. Midwifery seemed an important part of her legacy. "I'll start investigating the legalities on Monday. You keep looking for another midwife, just in case I can't help, after all."

Francesca beamed. "At least one of our dreams for our life here might finally come true."

Her husband squeezed her shoulder. "When we moved back from the city to the family's old farm, we had such high hopes. To return to the land, to the simple life. But everything's gone wrong, so far."

He obviously needed to unburden himself. Julia forgot the planting, took Francesca's arm then the husband's and strolled between them, listening to the story of their difficulties since returning to Montecipriana. Apparently, these two were not alone. Several young families had come back to the land, but their dreams had been bigger than their pocketbooks. It hurt but made total sense when Francesca's husband explained how blessed and effortless Julia's return to the Gardens had seemed.

With the realization of why the young men of the region were so frustrated dawned an idea of how she and Andrei might be able to help. One of her pet projects back at the shelter had been a community garden, which had provided the homeless and transitioning families vegetables for their tables and a sense of belonging as well. Her mind made a leap, transposed the phrase community garden to garden community.

Well, why not?

The scale would be different, but the two were similar enough in concept. She glanced around. The sanctuary had really come alive, was once again the Lady's own garden. She'd seen visions of the ancient sanctuary at Paphos, essentially a sacred community garden. The prayers whispered and chanted and planted in that holy space had been simple—requests for fertility, for grace, for life close to nature—the very things this couple was trying to manifest on Montecipriana, today.

It wouldn't be hard to extend the Lady's garden from this plateau down and around the slopes of Montecipriana, throughout the whole neighboring region, for that matter. Maybe that was precisely what Julia had been meant to do all along.

∞

Anatolin stood in his office at the Gardens, watching the early spring sunshine travel across the roof of Julia's cottage. He had heard his own share of stories about young would-be farmers running headlong back to the land in the wake of the European union. He'd seen their faces when they spoke of being crushed by the harsh economic realities of competing for market shares in a global economy.

Julia's idea of a community-wide farming collective was brilliant. Without a second thought, he'd taken it on as if his own, and he hadn't stopped running since. Rafael had immediately agreed to help develop the business and marketing plans and a prospectus for start-up financing. Vittorio had set right to work researching additional organic farming resources, seed and plant information, and more about the latest developments in appropriate technologies.

Rafael and Vittorio practically lived here, these days. They were both now bent over their respective tasks, and it was only eight-thirty in the morning. There were more time-critical duties to be performed than the three of them could hope to accomplish, even putting in twelve-hour days. One thing was immediately clear from Rafael's initial market research—the only way to make a go of the collective Julia envisioned was to develop an integrated philosophy then capitalize on it from every angle they could.

The relative lack of development in the Calderola quite naturally presented an almost unique solution to their market philosophy. With the Internet, Rafael assured them, other hurdles like distance and obscurity would virtually dissolve. His expertise was already proving invaluable. He'd promised a marketing plan and preliminary Web-site mock-up before the week was out.

That their approach extended Julia's vision for the Gardens was an added advantage. Each time Anatolin gave her an update on their progress, usually at least twice daily, she grew more attentive to the plans, seemed more thrilled, more committed—and bloody hell—more enchanting.

"He's broodin' again, Brother Vito." Rafael glanced up from the computer screen. "What are we gonna do with him?"

"Ship him back to Siberia?"

"Only if you can figure out how to bundle up this farm and ship it there with him, including its owner, of course, preferably packaged in bubble wrap and little else." Rafael grinned. "I can see the headlines now." He held up his hands, framing an invisible line of news type. "*Mysterious glacial meltdown floods the Siberian tundra!*"

"*Sì*, quite an image."

Anatolin failed to grasp the humor. He'd meant for days to ask Vittorio how his Order dealt with monks' erotic impulses, if their doctrine employed methods similar to the yogic sublimation and transmutation he'd been using with some success. He would have to broach the difficult subject soon, if he couldn't keep hold of himself.

"Don't forget, you are not a monk, Andrei." Vittorio had obviously caught his train of thought.

"But—"

"No, no, my friend!" Vittorio waved Anatolin's concerns away. "Already, you channel your creative energies s-o-o-o effectively! Everything you do, pouring yourself into this farm, giving your all in honorable service to others, these are precisely the sorts of activities our abbot would advise."

"Only thing you gotta watch out for is denial," added Rafael.

"I am not in denial!"

"You admit you love the Giardani Heiress?"

"Of course I do, who doesn't?"

"And that your feelings are hardly spiritual?"

Vittorio raised his head. "I'd say his feelings are intensely spiritual, Rafael. As spiritual as they come."

"Well, they certainly aren't platonic."

Vittorio smiled serenely. "Neither are they remotely brotherly, I'm sure."

"Odds are, he hasn't bothered to tell her, either." Rafael looked Anatolin in the eye. "Don't you think she ought to know?"

"One goal takes precedence now, and this discussion is not moving us closer to it."

Rafael turned serious. "Using work to avoid dealing with a problem is a tried-and-true recipe for trouble, Andrei."

Vittorio gave Anatolin a sober frown. "I regret I must agree."

Anatolin knew his friends meant well, realized Rafael was absolutely right. Anatolin's feelings for Julia had become a stormy sea, but he couldn't spare the time or the energy to sort things out anytime soon. His sweet taskmistress had decided to call a community meeting to introduce the collective concept to her neighbors, and Anatolin had accepted full responsibility for the presentation.

TWENTY-SEVEN

Women filled the living room of the cottage, Julia's new friends, come together to hear about her progress with the Giardani papers and to contribute anything further they might know about the family history, which was finally beginning to emerge from obscurity. Julia carried her grandmother's large ceramic teapot from the kitchen. Mugs and a plate heaped with luscious *panforte* already sat on the chest she had put to use as a coffee table. Her things were stacked in her corner of the sofa. Everyone else was already seated.

Madame Racine had perused the notebooks before taking one of the boudoir chairs Lucia had earlier brought down from the loft. Next to Madame Racine, side by side in matching armchairs, Signora Isabella and Fiorella Andrade chatted quietly, as did Maria and Silvana, who had settled in among the cushions on the long chest below the windows. Lucia seemed comfortably ensconced on a pillow on the floor beside Celeste, who was curled up at the far end of the sofa. Only Augustina had been unable to attend.

Julia sat down and picked up her journal, three hundred handwritten pages of historical conjecture and huge jumps of intuition no one could ever fully prove or disprove.

The women fell silent, obviously eager to hear what Julia had to say. She thanked everyone for coming and got right to the point. "When I first came to the Gardens, I thought of this farm in terms of centuries, but if the things I've read in the Giardani papers tell of historic events, not fictional fancies, I was seriously in error."

She summarized the most important contents of the letters, in which both Giuliana and Anna wrote of events they believed happened millennia ago. Their correspondence with experts in various fields corroborated their beliefs, especially the Charles Leland letters, those from a student of his who lived in Siena before World War I, and the ones from Jane Ellen Harrison, whose works on ancient religion were the most heavily annotated in the cottage's old bookcases. The research Julia's father provided substantiated the earlier works with more recent scholarly evidence.

Madame Racine smiled. "You have gathered so much information so quickly! Incredible, *n'est-ce pas?*"

Julia rubbed a hand over her eyes. "It is pretty incredible, but I had the letters to guide me—and the benefit of my father's research. Not to mention the Goddess-culture theories he made sure I couldn't miss. Without them I might have struggled for years to synthesize everything I have here."

Julia had learned Celeste sometimes took feminist courses at the university and was fairly familiar with the Goddess-culture theories. Celeste picked up one of the binders and leafed through it. "Extraordinary," she said. She'd earlier browsed the photocopied excavation reports of Aphrodite's sanctuaries, which Julia had compiled with Andrei's annotated translations from ancient authors and copies of selected letters that seemed to confirm or clarify the family legends. "Absolutely extraordinary!"

Lucia came up on her knees and peered at the binder but looked baffled. "Would someone mind translating all this for the uninitiated?"

"I guess I should start at the beginning." Julia sat back, collecting her thoughts and wondering how to distill all she'd learned into a few simple paragraphs.

She curled her legs under her and leaned against the arm of the couch, her heart racing at the prospect of telling even the little she knew of the Giardani saga aloud for the very first time. "Most of you know my family's teachings were always transmitted from mother to daughter in a strictly oral tradition. But around 1890, my great-grandmother apparently came to believe the family secrets were in danger of being lost. She broke all the rules and wrote about things that had been passed down only from mouth to mouth for about three thousand years, since our family originally arrived in Italy."

Lucia sat straight up, her eyes wide. "I knew the Giardani were an old family here, but three thousand years?"

"That's what their stories say," Julia answered. "Or at least, that's how my great-grandmother timed it all. Apparently, Anna tried her best to confirm the timing. After her mother died, she worked with an American scholar who knew a lot about early Mediterranean history. They pieced together the fragments of the old tales and came up with the idea that the family arrived in Tuscany about 950 B.C.E."

"Give or take a few decades," Madame Racine said, a twinkle in her eye. "There was not enough research completed back then to corroborate their conjectures, especially since Anna wasn't sure from where the Giardani might have sailed."

Signora Isabella looked thoughtful. "Old legends say the family came from a big island southeast of here. I think Giuliana once mentioned Crete."

"What I found out this week may verify her speculations. In the last few years, archaeologists have unearthed a sanctuary in southern Crete that may be the one we came from."

"I remember now!" said Signora Isabella. "Giuliana always said the Giardani called their original seat of worship Sacred Mountain."

"That's right," added Fiorella. "Years ago, you told me she said that."

"Well," Julia said with a smile, "I found the first mention of a Sacred Mountain in Anna's letters. Then I started digging through my father's photocopies and found this." She reached over and held out the report.

"Was this site in Crete called Sacred Mountain?" Celeste asked.

"According to the excavator, it was. Our oral legend says the family worshipped at Sacred Mountain 'from the beginning,' but then terrible things happened. Their island was invaded again and again. Each time, a small group formed from the community and set out for distant shores, spreading their religion far and wide. Apparently, the outposts kept in touch through the centuries, especially the one on Cyprus, made infrequent pilgrimages back to the old seat of worship. My family, the hereditary 'keepers of the lineage' stayed longer."

"That fits with the feminist reading of prehistory," Celeste said.

Julia sat forward and continued excitedly. "This is where it really gets interesting for me. Eventually, an Heiress of the old lineage at Sacred Mountain took a 'priest/consort' from an island even farther East, an artist who wanted to move to the metal-rich lands to the west, closer to the materials he used in his work."

Madame Racine went to sit on the arm of the sofa. She leaned over Celeste's shoulder to see the report. "As I recall, the whole Mediterranean basin was on the move during those years. Does the tradition make any reference to the mysterious raiders they call the Sea Peoples?"

Julia shook her head. "None that I've found. All I know is, it was that migration which established my family in Italy. We were a clan of artisans and musicians, it seems, and were welcomed in Etruscan territory because the people here passionately loved art. Eventually, we were absorbed into the existing culture."

"Fascinating," said Silvana softly. "Such a rich history. But your family's religion is so different from what other Tuscan *streghe* practice, according to the little I've picked up over the years."

Lucia laughed. "For every other *strega* in Italy, Diana is supreme, but not for our Giardani. For them, the Old Gods rule, especially Turan, the spirit of lovers, of peace and love and, of course, the Goddess of beauty."

"Humph!" said Signora Isabella. "My old granny had a special name for the Giardani's odd ways. She called it '*la Vecchia Religione Antica.*'"

"The oldest old religion," Julia said with a smile. "I like that!"

Madame Racine stood again, paced back to her chair. "I believe Giuliana once used the phrase *la Stregheria Antiquata,* if it's any help."

"Everything helps," Julia said. "Apparently, our religion was what set our settlement off from other Etruscans, especially our Goddess who, as Lucia said, was known locally as Turan. Later, Greeks came to Italy and recognized Turan was the same as their Aphrodite, so She became Aphrodite Turan. It seems Her worship was preserved intact in the family tradition, its ritual and symbology changing only slightly over all those centuries."

Madame Racine chuckled. "A terribly conservative bunch, your family."

Julia smiled. "So I've learned."

"That's part of the wonder of all this," said Celeste.

"I agree." Julia gazed out the window toward the uphill slope of Montecipriana. "Following the old ways, the mountain the family settled was itself considered holy. The legend doesn't say when it became known as Montecipriana, only that a few latecomers had rejoined the clan from far-off Cyprus, but the sanctuary at the top of the mountain here seems to be very similar to the one uncovered in Crete."

"What's your next step, Julia?" Celeste asked, the excitement in her voice unmistakable.

Julia leaned back against the sofa. She stared at the hearth, thought of the still missing family heirloom, took a sip of tea.

"There's only one thing I can do," she answered. "Continue doing my best to reconstruct the ritual before May Eve."

"Three more days." Celeste shook her head. "That sounds tricky."

"It will be," Julia agreed. "But at least I have some of you to help me, in addition to this information on the artifacts uncovered at Sacred Mountain in Crete, which I believe may provide the strongest clues to the family's original worship." And the heirloom, once she'd found it—and she *would* find it.

Signora Isabella raised her chin. "We've been doing pretty well with the reconstruction thus far, I'd say."

"Are you almost finished, Julia?" Madame Racine seemed dismayed.

"Don't I wish." There was still so much Julia didn't know, couldn't even imagine, but they were making headway. She knew that deep inside. "With Lucia's and Signora Isabella's help, I now have a rudimentary grasp of Pagan ritual. We've searched all the letters for references to the later Giardani tradition, started working backwards through the centuries via these archaeology reports. Hopefully, we've managed to make a few right connections, but we still have a long way to go."

"It's been fun, like reweaving an unraveled tapestry," Lucia said.

Celeste looked skeptical. "Fun before perhaps, but probably not for the next three days." She gave Julia a sympathetic, almost despairing look.

Julia would meditate day and night and work on the plans till she dropped, and she wouldn't give in to despair. She might never learn everything that once constituted her family's magical religion, but she'd never stop trying to live the joy she now firmly believed was the essential foundation of the Giardani path.

∞

The women stayed on for another hour, talking about the notebooks, exclaiming over the cottage, discussing the general excitement and rampant speculation in the neighborhood about the community meeting Julia and Andrei had called for this evening. Many of Julia's hostile neighbors seemed ready to give her the benefit of the doubt. Hopefully, the collective would cinch their conversion from near enemies to friends.

By six o'clock, everyone but Madame Racine had gone home. As a major benefactress of the collective, Madame Racine had stayed behind for the meeting. She would sit beside Julia during Andrei's presentation. Julia had been watching Madame Racine closely since the discussion. There was clearly something on the older woman's mind. She'd looked nervously at her watch half a dozen times. Sipping a glass of sherry, she perched elegantly on a stool across the kitchen workbench from Julia, waiting to leave for the meeting, rather impatiently, in Julia's opinion.

Madame Racine smiled at her. "I have excellent news for you, *ma cherie*." She pulled a paper from her pocket, unfolded the headline page of the most recent *La Nazione*, Florence edition.

Arno Baby Identified!

Julia took the paper, holding her breath as she read. The authorities in Florence had identified the dead infant found in the Arno as the abducted child of a minor Sicilian Mafia underling. Local or otherwise, *streghe* were no longer under suspicion. The police investigation was pursuing other lines of investigation.

"Gregor Danilenko is clearly losing his touch to allow his Sicilian associate to come under suspicion." Madame Racine squeezed Julia's hand. "It is a terrible shame the child, abducted by a feuding family, was doubtless murdered for Danilenko's gain, but at least the witch hunts will subside, and just in time for your May Eve celebration."

Julia's heart ached for the innocent little tyke, but there was something in Madame Racine's tone that turned Julia's mind toward another train of thought, entirely. "You seemed a bit dismayed to hear of our recreation of the ritual," she ventured. "It just occurred to me you actually might have attended one."

"I did. I was very young, of course."

"Too young to have relatively clear memories?"

"Mais, non. Not at all." Madame Racine was twinkling again. She cocked her head to one side. "Memories . . . I have many, but then so do you, *n'est-ce pas?* Perhaps even clearer than mine?" She gave Julia a wink.

"You're speaking of past-life memories."

"Oui."

Julia couldn't imagine gleaning information about May Eve from the experiences she'd shared with Madame Racine. They'd mostly been frightening, even violent. Nevertheless, from their first meeting Julia had sensed Madame Racine never said a thing without reason. What was she suggesting now?

"I'm suggesting you ask for help. For insights." Madame had read her mind, but Julia was learning to take that in stride.

"Ask whom?" The instant the question was out of her mouth, Julia knew the answer. Madame was staring over her right shoulder, as if fascinated by the tawny enameled pantry door.

Julia kept perfectly still. "You see her," she whispered. "I'm so glad someone else can see her!" Slowly she turned to face the pantry. The woman didn't vanish instantly. She stood there smiling a moment then faded slowly from sight. It was the first time Julia had been aware of the woman's presence since Danilenko's attempted attack. She'd missed her.

Madame smiled. "There has been much activity here, many people. These things make communication with one's inner guide most difficult."

"Is that what she is—my inner guide?"

"She is many things to you and for you, *ma petite.*" Madame seemed suddenly rather sad. "She has missed you, too, and wants you to know she is always close, will come whenever you call her from the depths of your heart."

"You mean in prayer?"

"*Oui,* and in meditation."

Julia felt reassured, better than she had in days, but Madame Racine still seemed troubled. She glanced at her watch yet again, and the smile she gave Julia was tinged with sadness, or maybe it was resignation.

∞

Danilenko had only been back in Tuscany since late morning. He was impressed by the excitement pervading the area. He'd expected the countryside to be tranquil as before, but instead the atmosphere for miles around seemed electrified.

Although Danilenko had made a concerted effort to lay low, the one time he'd stopped for food he'd heard excited speculation that he might be yet another foreign *stregone* gathered for the May Eve ritual. On his way out of the restaurant, he'd caught an old woman making a surreptitious Sign-of-the-Cross as he passed by.

He hoped his appearance in the nearby town wouldn't draw Greco's attention. He had come to doubt Greco's loyalty and he didn't want word of his return getting back to Julia Giardani's associates. There were things he still needed to figure out, the most pressing being what might have triggered the spate of deep trance-like visions that had kept him from sleeping for three days in a row after his search of the Giardani cottage. Unnerving, to say the least.

In the first, he rode a proud stallion beside an army on the march. He knew he possessed great valor, immense wealth, high station in life, yet he desperately wanted something more, something he feared he would never possess. The soldiers were lackeys and dolts, not at all dissimilar to the incompetents and fools he'd encountered all this life. They had bungled his orders badly before, seemed doomed to bungle them again, as if mired in some predestined course. The one man he admired abhorred him. That man, it just so happened, was his slave.

The second vision, a scene of total devastation, made Danilenko's blood practically freeze in his veins. Again, incompetents and fools— only now the wanton and shameful desecration of one he held most dear—one whose love he'd craved from the depths of some far-distant age. The rampage that followed on its heels had sickened him when he'd first had the vision, indeed sickened him still when he let it come to mind.

At first, he'd thought the visions were caused by touching the bronze tripod he'd taken from the Giardani girl's niche. After reading her papers, he'd decided her mountain's *vril* had simply gotten the better of him. It would take incredible skill to approach Montecipriana again without succumbing. He dreaded even the thought of returning there, but return he must.

TWENTY-EIGHT

Madame Racine walked with Julia from the Gardens to the community meeting, which was about to begin in Montecipriana's main square. The square was packed by the time she and Julia arrived. She was shocked to hear Brother Vittorio announce more people were on their way.

On a makeshift speaker's platform sat a row of straight-backed chairs. Roughly center stage stood a rough wooden podium. Julia took the chair beside it. Racine took the next.

Andrei, Rafael at his back, was down working the crowd, shaking hands, throwing smiles like an American politician. He couldn't have recently learned that bearing, that innate sense of timing. He acted like he'd been born to it.

Andrei was a man of more talents than Racine had ever suspected. His efforts here would bring much-needed economic relief to the Calderola, could well turn the region into a beacon of environmental harmony for the new millennium. She couldn't help but wonder what had happened to the reclusive man she met only weeks ago in Paris. Seeing him in action tonight made Racine feel positively inspired.

How might he respond if she asked him to someday assume her role for the Alliance?

Her life had been extended overly long, and this afternoon she'd learned she'd run out of time for choosing her replacement. She'd be joining Tony and her dear Ilina Mikhailovna on the other side all too soon. She hoped only to experience the supreme satisfaction of living long enough to witness Julia's ultimate triumph over Danilenko.

∞

Julia turned to see who had leaned against the stage behind her. It was Brother Vittorio. "There are over 150 farmers here, many from quite far away," he said over the din in the square. "Counting their families, we have probably three hundred all together, a much better turnout than we hoped for."

"Good," Julia said. "If we can bring even 10 percent of them into the fold, we'll have enough to launch the collective." She was trying to stay calm but was intensely excited by the size of the crowd and by the waves of obvious enthusiasm and goodwill swelling through it.

"Andrei is about to start," Brother Vittorio said. He moved away from the stage, joined the others from the hermitage near the center of the audience.

Rafael leapt up onto the stage, checked the volume and height of the microphone, then took the seat to Madame Racine's right. Andrei bounded up and stepped behind the podium. The crowd's sudden, attentive silence marked the degree of respect he'd garnered in the Calderola. Julia tensed but needn't have. Andrei began strongly, greeting the crowd and waiting for the initial applause to die down before continuing.

"We promised when we invited you here to make this presentation short and we shall," he said with a smile, pausing for another quick round of applause. "Our plans have gotten around, so many of you already know at least part of what Signorina Giardani has had us working on."

The two front rows clapped politely. Someone near the back sent up a sharp cheer, but most of the crowd waited quietly as Andrei outlined the basic principles of the collective's marketing angle. He stressed the unique opportunity the Calderola offered, how its largely undepleted land would lend itself optimally and, for the most part immediately, to organic farming.

"I've heard some of you complaining of being too poor to exploit your farms, too poor to afford modern chemical amendments and pest controls, but your so-called poverty actually gives us an undreamed-of advantage. Most of you won't have to wait to detoxify your soils to qualify for the 'organic' designation. Those who do will find the task easier because your neighbors won't be polluting the water table with heavy metals and harsh fertilizers, won't be contaminating the air with pesticides. With the collective to support you during the detox process, you won't have to wait until your lands are clean to participate in the profits."

"How does that work?" someone shouted.

Andrei outlined the incentives aspect of their proposal and its communal labor pool, sketched their expanded credit union concept. He stepped back from the podium and pulled Julia to her feet.

"Signorina Giardani has insurance money from America that constitutes our core funding. Others, like the owner of Il Calice Zolfo and our entrepreneur friend, Rafael Gibbons, have added more funds and are working on securing additional venture capital."

He gestured to Madame Racine and Rafael, who each stood briefly and waved as Julia sat back down. He paced over to the large poster display Rafael had worked up for investors, switched on Rafael's laser pointer, and aimed it at the map in the display's upper corner.

"We hope to reopen as many of these abandoned neighborhood olive presses and grain mills as possible, promote their products abroad along with anything else you want to sell, handmade cheeses and preserves, for instance. Unlike conglomerates, which turn whole regions into single-crop monstrosities, the more diversity we have the better. Most herbs, the collective's core product, are forgiving to grow, indeed actually flourish in less-than-optimal conditions. There is bound to be something for everyone, depending on each person's resources."

Old Urbano stood near the front of the crowd. He stepped forward. "My land is so steep and dry, all we've ever been able to grow are potatoes."

Andrei smiled. "Good ones, Urbano?"

"The best!" his neighbor shouted.

"Then we need them," Andrei said, his voice gaining strength and conviction, "for the organic vodka we'll use to make the Gardens' herbal compounds. I'll bet the good Brothers from San Galgano might even be willing to help you design your still if not run it for you themselves."

Brother Vittorio smiled. His fellow monastics nodded their heads as a few farmers shouted encouragement. Andrei paused, seemingly searching for someone in the crowd. From Julia's angle it seemed his gaze came to rest on Emilio and Silvana Greco.

"Our point is," Andrei said, emphasizing his words with firm slaps on the hollow podium, "we want all of you—your land, your labor, or just your ideas if that's all you have to share—no one who wants to participate should feel left out!"

Julia was in tears. Andrei was in his element, his heart wide open, his love and vital energies flowing as never before.

∞

To Julia, the Gardens by the light of the moon looked more lovely every night. Too excited about the upcoming ritual to sleep, she'd slipped from the house fifteen minutes before. She was on the trail of a mandrake plant Signora Isabella assured her grew somewhere within a hundred meters of the cottage. The old woman had explained how to locate the supposedly wily plant and pull it from the ground when the waning moon was passing between two zodiac signs, which according to Lucia's almanac would happen within the next half-hour.

Crossing from the herb garden through the upper gate, Julia went a little way up the hill. She slowed down, alternately concentrating on her brow and watching in the beam of her pocket flashlight for the mandrake's large, five-pointed leaf. She felt drawn toward the path to the village, or more precisely, to the stream bed that crossed it. At the edge of the stream bed, she finally found the odd plant.

Signora Isabella had told Julia to sit and talk to the plant. She'd give it a try. She chose a perch on the low footbridge, put her cushion on the dewy stones, and sat down, but instead of focusing on the task at hand, her thoughts wandered. She gazed out over the Gardens, glad she needn't be afraid of walking out alone at night anymore. Campsites rimmed the perimeter of the property. There were already forty *streghe* families gathered here, waiting for May Eve. Signora Isabella said a hundred more were on their way and others could easily materialize as word of the celebration's revival continued to spread.

Julia was thrilled by her crash course in priestessing, though she hardly felt up to people's expectations. She knew, no matter what, she would give her very best to the ritual. There might come a time when she would feel fully competent in her role, but until then, she simply had to hope she didn't let anyone down too badly.

At least the sanctuary was coming together beautifully. Cutting the tall grass in the sacred precinct, or *temenos,* as Signora Isabella called the flat, open area, had caused a profusion of wildflowers to burst into bloom. The May Eve celebrants would dance on a dense, fragrant carpet of rosy creeping thyme and fairy-blue iris.

This morning, Signora Isabella had insisted on climbing up to the sanctuary, where she ordered several men to rearrange the boulders up on the cliff. Only then had Julia learned the boulders had been shifted after the last May Eve gathering to disguise the cliff's secret ritual features.

Moving the boulders revealed what Signora Isabella called the Altar of the Greater Mysteries, with its cave-like grotto on the ledge of the cliff's sheltered south face. Inside the grotto were more carved niches and some well-preserved reliefs of Turan with a consort. Beneath them, a lovely granite fountain poured hot spring waters from the mountain's core into the pool at its center. A lovely spot, so reminiscent of Aphrodite's grotto on Cyprus, it gave Julia a thrill when she first saw it, which was probably how she'd missed where to light the oil and ignite the Sacred Flame.

She'd also been preoccupied by her search through the numerous votive objects tucked away up there. Not even a Sacred Flame was more important than finding the Giardani heirloom before Danilenko could find it. This wasn't a matter of pride, simply her duty to the One she served.

Deep down, she knew the Goddess was guiding her, but with so much at stake for all the lives Julia sensed the legacy's full return would eventually touch, she knew she couldn't relax until the sacred heirloom was in her hands, where she could protect it from being defiled or abused.

She stood and stared up at the outcrop. She'd love to go up to the grotto for a moonlight meditation like she did weeks ago at Loutra Tis Aphrodite, but she'd promised Andrei she wouldn't go beyond the tree line unescorted. She wouldn't break her word.

Andrei. Moment to moment now, her heart and mind were full of him, her body exhilarated simply by his nearness. Sometimes her attraction for him stretched her to her limits, but her love and respect for him always seemed to prevail. She was trying her best to accept that though his love and devotion were obviously huge, they were simply nonpersonal, and though there seemed to her a clear contra-diction between his head and his heart, he seemed oblivious to it, and still apparently set on his monastic calling. She wouldn't deny herself loving him, regardless. What she felt was hers, he needn't return it.

If it was some kind of sin to love a future monk, she'd go to her grave a sinner, simple as that, for it was his very longing for the Divine that she found most appealing. Not his wish to become a monk per se, but that core of spiritual craving that motivated his vocation, this was what drew her to him, would leave her forever wanting Andrei Ivanovich Anatolin and no other.

The poor guy had been hovering again.

It had taken an act of sheer will to keep from getting all put out with him for shadowing her every move, even after he announced Danilenko was back in Tuscany and was probably holed up nearby. That Danilenko was now acting far more furtive made Julia nervous, and seemed to make Andrei more intensely protective than ever.

Lately, Julia suspected Andrei of hiding his confused erotic responses from himself behind overprotectiveness, an emotion a would-be monk would find less reprehensible than the intense desire she was now certain he struggled against, just as she did. Her own desire had sometimes brought her dangerously close to employing her Giardani magnetism—risking all to bring him closer—even rejection.

The real tragedy was, if Andrei weren't headed for the monastery, he would have been the one man she'd met in this life who could probably handle her passion and sensuality, the emotional fire that had so terrified most of the men she'd known and sent them running headlong for the blandest, most placid females they could find.

For all his telepathic skill, Andrei could sometimes be as dense as any other man. He often clearly felt hurt by her insistence on her own autonomy, couldn't disguise that any better than he could his desire. And he also didn't seem to get it that she couldn't afford to be wholly dependent upon someone who might up and leave at any time. To become a monk or not, leaving was leaving.

Regardless of the reason, when he eventually did go it would tear her to shreds. She stared unseeing at the garden gate, too preoccupied to notice when the breeze blew it shut.

∞

The garden gate—clicking closed in the dead of night! Panicked, Anatolin jumped up from his computer. He grabbed his turtleneck, pulled it on, tucked it into his jeans as he crossed to the window.

Outside, a waning crescent moon hung low over the cliffs, lighting the whole side of the mountain and casting deep shadows onto the courtyard below his window. He heaved a sigh of relief when he spotted Julia sitting alone and safe on the footbridge. His heartbeat calmed. He bent and pulled on his boots. A moment later, he stood in the courtyard, breathing in the rich scents drifting up from the herb garden, the sweet cinnamon perfume of the latest vintage rose to bloom prevailing over the rest.

Julia's long white nightgown glowed against the dark shadows of the forest. Her large, filmy shawl draped over her shoulders, its pale fringe shimmering as it danced on the breeze, she looked as enchanting as a panel from a medieval triptych.

Gradually, Anatolin slipped into a deep meditative trance. He saw the golden rose pulsing on her brow, saw magical symbols floating in her aura that hadn't been there the last time he looked.

Suddenly, her features changed then changed again. A dozen times, she transformed, each visage subtly but clearly distinguishable from the one before it, and each familiar, sparking memories, fleeting and uncanny. He blinked them away, shook off the meditation, and started toward her.

She saw him and waved.

"Hi, there." Her voice was deeper and sweet, the way it got when she emerged from an altered state. "I'm okay, wasn't thinking of going farther from the house than we agreed."

"I realized that."

"Terrific." She pulled her shawl closer, tied its ends into a loose loop, and started down toward the gate. "Actually, I'm glad you're here. I have something important to tell you, since you're awake, anyway. You are awake, aren't you?" She smiled then quickly turned serious. "I mean, if you're too sleepy, if you want to go back to bed, its okay. We can talk in the morning."

"I wasn't asleep." Anatolin sensed her nervousness, knew he must seem taciturn and cold, which was far from how he felt. It was all he could do to keep himself from kissing her. He trusted his control less than ever. If he kissed her tonight, he feared they might both go up in smoke, and Julia needed her all her energies concentrated now far more than she needed a lover.

"Really, Andrei, we can talk tomorrow."

"No." In the distance, he heard what had to be the *streghe* sentinels changing shifts, which meant it was about two o'clock. "A talk would be good."

"It's about Emilio." She squared off behind the gate, braced her elbows on it, and leaned forward, her chin propped in her hands. "He spoke with me today. You were right, he was spying for Danilenko."

"He confessed?"

"And he apologized. Sincerely, I believe. He said he'd feared I was some selfish American come to dispossess him of the Gardens and ruin his life. He said he soon realized he'd been terribly wrong and had recently taken steps to make amends."

Anatolin was stunned. "How is Silvana handling the confession?"

Julia puckered her lips. "She didn't know before Emilio spoke with me, but he promised to tell her over dinner. We decided it would be best to be honest with her."

Anatolin knew full well who decided it would be best but decided to let the distinction rest. Emilio had kept his nose clean for almost two weeks on his own. If his wife further kept him in line, likely all would be fine.

Julia smiled. "I told him to act like nothing had changed if he ran into Danilenko."

"Good for you. We'll have to think of ways to keep Danilenko from knowing we know."

She grinned up at him. "If my father were here, he'd come up with some outrageously clever scheme. I'm sure you can cook up something equally diabolical."

"I'll get right to work on that."

"I'm sure you will." Something scraped along the wooden gate as she sighed and stood up.

"What's that?" he asked, his gaze traveling to the knot in her shawl and beneath it, where something dark dangled between her breasts.

"The key to the crypt." She held it up. "I've been keeping it close so nobody got any ideas about checking out the family bones before I had a chance to do so myself, which hasn't been a priority. I'm sure my father would never have hidden anything valuable in a such an obvious place."

Anatolin almost choked. "If you were trying to keep the crypt safe from Danilenko, I assure you, not having a key would hardly stop him."

"Oh." She let the key fall. "Right. Would you care to come with me when I take a look tomorrow morning, say around ten?"

"I'd be delighted."

"Terrific!" She put her hand to her mouth to cover a small yawn. "I'd better get back to what brought me out here."

"What might that be?"

"It's a witch thing."

"I see."

"I need to talk to that mandrake over there." She pointed to the stream. "I need his permission to pull him."

"That ought to be quite a sight. May I watch?"

"Why not?" She smiled. "Signora Isabella didn't expressly say I had to be alone."

It was his turn to lean on the gate while she walked back to her spot on the bridge. Then she crouched down, her hand almost touching a flat-leafed plant. A few seconds later, she pulled quickly away and glanced up as if shocked.

"What does he say?" Anatolin asked.

"That he's the granddaddy of mandrakes, if I pull him all the others will move away. Besides, he says, he's very deep, would be a pain to pull up, that there's a smaller one who'd be much easier to pull just ten feet away."

"Are you going to follow his advice?"

She gave a mock frown. "Isabella said these are crafty plants. Maybe I shouldn't trust him."

"Give him a break." Anatolin opened the gate and joined her. "Let's see if the other mandrake is where he says it is."

"It's supposedly on the other side of the stream." She chuckled, turned and crossed the footbridge, shined her flashlight over the sodden ground. "Yep, here it is." She tucked her nightgown between her knees and bent down.

He joined her, leaned over her shoulder. A moment later, she looked up and gave him a smile that wrenched his gut.

"I have his permission to take him."

Her breath warmed Anatolin's Adam's apple. A wispy curl caught on the stubble of his beard. He cleared his throat, stepped back before she again touched his chest. His heart chakra was healing nicely on its own, these days.

"I best leave you to it, then." Wanting desperately to touch the moonbeam that glanced off her hair, he jammed both hands into his pockets, faked a yawn. "See you in the morning."

"Right." She gave him a quick little smile. "In the morning." She turned away, her shoulders drooping with a sigh that belied her cheery tone.

He made himself wait till he was through the gate and across the courtyard before turning to wave a final good night.

Julia was bent low over the smaller mandrake. With a sharp retort rather like some primeval war cry, she plucked the plant from the stream bed and held it up high by its leafy crown. The root dangled in the moonlight—a perfectly formed tiny man.

"What do you think, Andrei, should I name him after Gregor Danilenko?"

"Only if you plan to stick him full of poison-tipped needles."

Her mouth fell open in obvious surprise that he'd think her capable of such an act. "I'm a *strega*, not a Voodoo queen!"

"Indeed you are, sweet Giuliana. Indeed you are. Good night," he said with a wave.

∞

Danilenko's dream had returned, he realized, waking in a sweat. He was shaking from head to foot. His mouth tasted vile.

Again he had fallen asleep at his desk, head on his arms, which were folded over the Giardani papers. He'd lost the dream when his elbow apparently brushed the small bronze tripod off the papers and onto the cold tile floor.

Now it was already the middle of the night, after three o'clock, and there was barely enough time before dawn to accomplish the task he'd set himself. He'd have to hurry, but he felt energized, more hopeful than he had in years. With the dream's return had also come renewed faith in the Giardani heirloom and in its promise of immortality.

Thanks to young Julia's scribblings, he finally knew where the heirloom was.

Where it had to be.

TWENTY-NINE

The old Alfa Danilenko rented while away in Rome purred as he sped through the Calderola. It would blend in with others of similar vintage parked around the base of Montecipriana all week and wouldn't call attention to his foray onto the Giardani property.

Once on the mountain, Danilenko knew how to move undetected, how to disempower any assailant he might meet. He'd chosen his time carefully. After watching the so-called Witches' Brew for days, he was convinced that if he made his advance in its dead hour, when it ebbed to regroup for the dawn, he could better withstand its debilitating effects.

He approached his objective from the steep western slope, where he'd counted fewer campsites the evening before. Just below the meadow, he heard a branch snap. He ducked in the opposite direction, almost stepped over the rim of the hill.

"Who passes there?" a man shouted gruffly.

A bright flashlight blinded Danilenko. He struck out and knocked it away. Throwing himself at the startled man, Danilenko wrestled him to the ground, grasped the man's esophagus to silence any scream. A quick blast of PK, and the fellow was out cold. Danilenko dragged the unconscious body beneath a dense stand of shrubs and continued toward his goal.

Anticipation gripped him. The sky was densely overcast, no moon or stars in sight. The meadow was very dark. He could barely see the large mound that supposedly harbored the Giardani crypt, yet he dared not switch on his flashlight until he was safely inside it.

He stood very still, felt a heightened energy impress itself on his mind. The heirloom was here. There was no mistaking the potency of the psi a holy artifact absorbs. The older the artifact, the more potent its force field, and the Giardani heirloom was clearly of an order of magnitude beyond anything he'd ever experienced, Hitler's baubles notwithstanding.

He crossed in the approximate direction of the crypt, his hands extended as he neared the seemingly dense mass looming against the side of the hill. Thick vines, slimy with predawn dew, tangled in his fingers. He pushed through them, felt nothing but more springy tangles, moved to his left, pushed again. He repeated the viscous probing several times before he felt solid rock, twice more before he rounded a sharp man-made angle and the vines thinned somewhat. Another step to his left, a quick push, and he met cold steel.

The door the Giardani Heiress described in her notes.

His fingers traced the outlines of the winged lions, dropped beneath them toward the right, where he hoped to find the lock. He almost shouted when he felt the depression that had to be the lock's keyhole. Concentrating his full attention upon it, he gave the keyhole a sudden jolt of PK, cracking then dislodging the encrusted rust. A second steady burst rotated the lock.

He shoved against the door, relieved when it opened without the screech of old hinges he'd half expected to hear. His heart was in his throat, his pulse roared in his ears. He closed the door tightly behind him. In a matter of minutes, he would have the object of his desire. He would have immortality—the eternal youth promised him in his dream.

Pulling his flashlight from the tight waistband of his cycler's pants, he switched it on and scanned the interior of the crypt, cringing as his gaze passed over dozens of internments. Obviously, the Giardani hadn't guessed their heirloom would grant eternal life or there wouldn't have been so many of them resting here.

At least fifteen feet wide and twenty-five feet long, the crypt was divided by thick columns, two rows of three with narrow side aisles and a wider aisle between them. There wasn't much room left for walking. Back in the deepest recesses, almost indiscernible in the spiderwebbed gloom, gossamer-draped skeletons were laid out on shallow rock benches. Closer to the center crowded stone sarcophagi, wooden coffins, and cinerary urns—a morbid potpourri of changing funeral fashions.

He glanced down, studied the floor. Clearly, no one had been in the corners for decades, perhaps centuries, but beneath his feet and toward the center of the open space, scuff marks had disturbed the dust coating relatively recently.

Ten years before? Twenty? During World War II? Impossible to tell.

He eased to the center of the crypt, swiping at cobwebs with his flashlight, shining it on the urns. He searched for name plates, for inscriptions, found none. An enigmatic tribe, the Giardani. Tony had been a fine example of this brood, as true to his roots as he'd been to his honor.

The farther Danilenko got from the entryway, the dimmer became the impressions of psi. He would have expected the opposite. He turned and flashed his light on the door, swung the beam from left to right. There was a deep ledge to the right of the door. On it sat a large and seemingly modern vase. Beneath it were a mass of footprints that hadn't had time to dust over. Tony's footprints. Had to be. Danilenko paced over and stood before the ledge. The vase was heavy, its rose garlands deeply cut into amethyst crystal. Tony's favorite color. And Tony's block printing etched on the brass name-plate hung about the vase's neck. ANNA GIARDANI—1896–1982— BELOVED MOTHER.

If Giardani brought his mother home to rest with her ancestors, he definitely brought the heirloom back here with her. Danilenko's confidence swelled. He balanced his light on the ledge, its beam aimed upward to reflect off the vaulted granite above his head. He rubbed his solar plexus, tried to calm himself before reaching for the vase. His extended hand trembled so badly he drew it back. He started to hyperventilate.

Glancing down, he made fists of his hands, took a deep breath, then wiped at the sweat tickling his brow. Nothing helped. He forced himself to call up some tranquil scene.

What came to mind was Tony's backyard garden in far-off California, a serene and restful place, the memory of which even now pulled at the strings of Danilenko's remorse. He replaced it with the vision of Hitler's collection shining on the sordid altar of the Black Mass he'd performed on the way to Marseilles.

That was more like him. Power, not serenity. Lust, not love or loyalty, which had betrayed him long ago. He hardened his will. His trembling ceased. He took up the vase, surprised by the heft of it as he drew it close.

The vase was stoppered by a thick plug topped with a clear crystal ball. Bracing it against his chest, he lifted the stopper. A large scorpion sidled up the rim and tipped over onto the back of the hand that gripped the vase. Danilenko shuddered as its smaller mate toppled back inside. The large scorpion curled its tail to strike.

Danilenko jerked back, flicked it off in time, but dropped the vase, which crashed with a piercing howl to the granite floor, its echo deafening. Furious with the scorpions—with himself—Danilenko crouched beside the broken crystal.

The vase had been so heavy it hadn't shattered. Instead, it split into two sharp halves that glistened dully in the shadows reaching down to the dusty floor. Between the halves, a mound of ash settled as the howl's echo stilled.

Danilenko reached for a twig near the shards, poked it around in the ash, searching but finding nothing but fragments of bone, a gold tooth filling, two. His fingers took a splinter from the twig and he dropped it, realized it wasn't a twig at all but a large unburned fragment of Tony's mother.

Revolting.

Danilenko stood, wrung his hands, brushed at their ashen coating but feared it was a futile gesture. Might he wear Anna Giardani's funereal ash on his fingers till his dying day? Might the splinter of her bone fester and poison him? Make his immortality impossible to bear?

Ridiculous. He had to get a grip.

Immortality. His mind grasped for the thought, steadied. The heirloom, the purpose for this blasted search. Where was it? He held himself still. Felt nothing now.

Nothing!

"Tony!" he shouted uncontrollably. If not with his mother's ashes, where would the sentimental American have hidden a priceless heirloom? The pillar at his right cracked at eye level, pulverized granite trickling to the floor as Danilenko tasted the fury tainting his PK. "You can't stop me from finding it!"

Danilenko blustered deep into the crypt, all calculation, along with caution, flown to the winds. He grabbed an urn, upturned it and watched charred bone and ash sift to the floor, grabbed another and another, found nothing. He pried open a coffin with his hands, gagged at the sickly sweet odor of old death as he rifled through the remains. He threw the lid down and tore off the next.

"*Tony!*" he bellowed, bringing the flashlight down hard on the lid of the next coffin.

As the metal canister hit the lid, so did his PK, spewing an angry cloud of splinters and moldy dust into the air. Ducking from the debris, he dropped the flashlight. It rolled against the base of a pillar and dimmed, throwing the crypt into near darkness.

Danilenko barely noticed.

His rage fed his PK, and with no clear target, he was at its mercy—a superman ripping blindly at the walls with his bare hands while PK stormed through the space around him, crashing, flinging stones, tearing granite tiles from the floor. To his left, a thick slab of wall came hurtling toward him. He threw himself out of its path, but it clipped him and knocked him to the floor. Dazed, he raised his head and stared into the cracked lens of the fading flashlight, only inches from his face.

He propped himself on his elbows, gagged on chalky dust. His hands were covered with his blood. The sight of them against the backdrop of ashen filth he'd created shocked him back to sensibility. If he didn't stop this binge immediately, the rejuvenating energy he'd transferred to himself from Hitler's artifacts would be completely spent and the Giardani crypt would come down around his head. He'd be trapped here. Buried forever.

Fear propelled him to his knees. He grabbed the flashlight, pulled himself to his feet. He had been born with immeasurable psycho-kinetic ability, but what he'd most craved—immeasurable power—had always eluded him. Now it was within his reach. He simply had to keep himself together until he possessed it. He dusted himself off, grabbed the handle on the iron door.

Giving its last gasp, his flashlight caught the glint of metal below the battered ledge on which he'd found Anna Giardani's urn. Metal that hadn't been visible before his outburst. The flashlight useless now, he called up a PK flame.

Blue PK lit the outlines of a small, heavy chest. He reached for its lid. Locked. He blasted it open, caught the glimmer of gold, grabbed for it.

Whatever it was—some kind of belt?—the damn thing packed a magnificent punch. Already he felt its power feeding his own.

"Oh, yeah," he muttered, blindly fingering its linked medallions as the PK haze dispersed. "Tony, you old fool," he added with a grin.

He shoved the dead flashlight back into his pants waistband, opened the door, and stepped out of the crypt.

The predawn mist was receding, the air crisp and clean. He sucked it into his lungs but couldn't dispel the stench of the decimated crypt.

Feeling polluted, still half-crazed despite his triumph, he wrenched the door closed behind him, blasting it involuntarily, realizing what he'd done only as he heard the thick metal scream. But by then he'd reached the shelter of the woods and leapt halfway down the steep ravine, his prize firmly in his grip.

THIRTY

Anatolin jumped out of bed the instant he heard the loud metallic protest. Ten seconds later, he was down in the courtyard, pulling on his boots, blocking the cottage door so Julia could not rush past him. He had no intention of letting her race headlong into danger this time. The sound from the meadow had been ominous, all too suggestive of Danilenko's excessive PK.

Her sweater half pulled down over dark leggings, a bulky electric lamp swinging from a strap on her shoulder, Julia looked disheveled and frightened as she dashed out the door. "May Eve sure has started with a bang." She glanced up the hill, bent to tie her canvas shoes, yanked her sweater down. "That had to be the door of the crypt. It's the only thing metal up there."

"Stay here and let me check it out."

"No way!" She started past him. "Let's go."

He grabbed her arm. "We don't know what we'll find up there."

Gently but firmly, she pulled out of his grip. "If you're coming with me, you'd better hurry." She started walking.

He followed, wondering how in the world he would ever keep her safe when she was so stubborn. "Have you been reckless since birth, or is this a relatively recent behavioral phenomenon?"

She didn't answer, but he knew she'd heard him because he saw her shoulders stiffen.

"When dealing with Danilenko it is unwise to feel invincible."

"I'm not feeling invincible. Far from it." Julia stopped, spun around, her hands on her hips. "Don't ask me how, but I know the danger is already past, the damage is done, and that creep is long gone. You're the telepath. If you'd stop worrying long enough to tune in you might know these things yourself."

The truth of her statement hit Anatolin like a glass of cold water in the face. "Point taken." Stepping up beside her, he lifted one of her hands off her hip and pulled her close to his side. "You're right, of course. Let's go."

They fell into step, climbing swiftly but no longer running. He loved the feel of her small hand in his, the heat of her against his arm, the freshly washed scent of her tousled hair.

"What a dreadful sound," she said, slightly out of breath.

"Like two locomotives meeting on a single track. Tell me, did you have some kind of vision regarding the status of the crypt, or was it more like a vague impression?"

"Neither. It was a hunch, I guess, an intuition—but so strong and clear there could be no mistake."

"Like a voice? Or your friendly silhouette, perhaps?"

"No, *Doctor* Anatolin." She smiled up at him. "A simple intuition."

"Simultaneous with the sound?"

"Actually, yes. Hey!" She gave his hand a sudden tug. "You're trying to distract me."

"Not at all."

He must have been trying unconsciously to distract himself from her magnetism, why he'd never understand. He appreciated how she'd softened his armor, made it possible for him to examine honestly and deeply a few essential truths about his nature, like the cowardly way he'd come to shield the pain of loving purely and profoundly behind his fears for Julia's safety.

Now he recognized true love demanded true courage, and it was past time he muster some. His first step in that direction, strangely enough, was to surrender. To Julia's Goddess, Whose will would inexorably rule the day. To the Giardani Heiress herself, who deserved his full unstinting faith. It wouldn't be easy for him, Scorpio that he was, but nothing worth having was ever easy, or so the wise proverbs said.

They climbed steadily to the rim of the hill, stepped into the meadow.

"Here we are," Julia said with an obvious shudder.

One of the *streghe* guards arrived from the eastern side of the property. Another appeared toward the west, holding his hand to his head, obviously hurt. The man with him half dragged him across the meadow.

"It's Giacomo from Benevento." Julia broke away and ran to the injured man. "What happened?"

"While I was on guard," Giacomo rasped, his voice practically gone, "a big man came up through the steep ravine, jumped me just below the meadow. He knocked me out, though I can't tell you how."

Anatolin knew full well how, and he could sense from her thinly disguised agitation Julia had guessed. Using PK to physically harm others was the vilest use of a psychic gift. The poor *stregone* was obviously badly shaken, his throat and neck very sore. No way he could guess how lucky he was to be talking. How lucky he was to be alive.

"I'm so sorry you're hurt." Julia slid her lamp off her shoulder and onto the grass. Quietly, she examined the lump on the injured man's temple, held her palm gently on his throat, her fingers tracing the darkening bruises.

"I'm okay," the man said.

She smiled but when she spoke her voice sounded strained. "Of course, but you should get some compresses and salve on those bruises right away." She glanced at the other two *streghe*. "I'll be up here a while. Can you please help Giacomo down to the cottage and ask Lucia to assist him and make him comfortable until I return?"

"*Certo*, Giuliana." Giacomo's helper frowned worriedly at the crypt for a moment then tipped his head at Anatolin. The third man took Giacomo's other arm, and the trio started down the hill.

Looking grimly at the crypt, Julia picked up her lamp. "What an awful way to start May Eve. It's liable to be pretty gruesome in there."

She extended her hand. Anatolin took it, smiled his support. Julia led the way to the crypt but came to a stop at the huge iron door. Her dread as she beheld the warped and twisted metal ripped at Anatolin's heart. Though hatred for Danilenko rose up and all but choked him, he forced it away. He must not for a moment forget his first order of business was to assist Julia.

"I can't believe me, sometimes." She let go of him, raised her hands, and pushed them over her brow and through her hair. "I forgot my gloves!"

"You'll be fine without them."

She looked up at him, smiled. "Right." She rubbed her hands together, pulled the lamp around to her front, and flipped on its switch. She used her shoulder to push open the heavy door. Her small grunt became a gasp that echoed through the crypt.

Danilenko had wreaked havoc. Shattered stone and pottery shards littered the floor. Coffins gaped, their contents strewn hither and yon. Three chalky skulls had rolled toward the center of the crypt. Four, if you counted the one Danilenko had obviously half crushed under his boot, judging from the shape of the outline impressed in the dust below its brow.

Danilenko's despicable negative psi still reverberated off the walls. It made Anatolin feel physically weakened, almost ill. "That filthy bastard!"

"Never mind cursing," Julia said, but she must have felt similarly ill, for she swayed back against Anatolin's side, the lamp sliding from her arm.

He picked it up and set it on a ledge. "Danilenko's contempt for the sanctity of death is appalling."

"I guess it doesn't really matter to them," she said with a sigh as she waved her hand around the room. Her shoulders drooped. She glanced down, bent and salvaged a brass nameplate from the debris near the door. "My grandmother," she said with a small sob. She lifted her chin, flinched. "I wonder how many others there were, preserved intact until I came around and stirred things up."

"Don't for a minute feel you're the cause of what happened here. This is evidence the general will stop at nothing to take whatever he wants. For him to lose control to this extent, the object he's looking for must hold tremendous power, could no doubt bring enormous good to the world or wreak untold havoc in the hands of a depraved soul like his."

"Right, and we're no closer to finding it than before."

The energy in the crypt suddenly shifted. A gauzy form materialized. Apprehension raced up Anatolin's spine. "Julia—"

She glanced up, followed the line of his gaze. "It's her, Andrei. My ancestress."

He'd prayed to be shown Julia's mysterious silhouette, focused now into a faded shadow against the dark stone, then a clear female form. Not the ghostly apparition his prior experiences had prepared him to see but something much more like a Divine manifestation. "Beautiful."

"Isn't she?" Julia sounded choked up, her emotions very close to the breaking point. "I sure hope she understands how sorry I am about this mess."

"My dear," Anatolin squeezed her shoulder. "I suspect she understands better than anyone else ever could."

The woman beckoned for Julia to come toward her. Anatolin removed his arm and stayed where he was while Julia walked to the far side of the crypt. The woman reached up and touched her index finger to a crystalline stone that jutted out from the wall.

Julia grabbed the stone and pulled down hard. A loud grinding sound seemed to come from the bowels of the crypt. The solid wall in front of her inched slowly to the left, revealing another vault, deeper and wider than the crypt by twenty feet in all directions.

"The Etruscan tomb," Julia said, awe weighting her words. "I'd not realized it might be a separate structure, or cut this deeply into the mountainside. So everything isn't ruined, after all."

He smiled. "Not even close, it seems. I'll bring the lamp." The woman slowly faded from sight.

Julia hardly seemed to notice. "Hurry!"

He carried the lamp to the threshold of the tomb, held it high, and drew in a sharp breath. Julia whistled softly. The tomb was huge, a marvel of underground architecture consisting of more than one room. Its main vault was round with a substantial central column covered with heavy reliefs. Lining the walls all around were two rows of simply carved benches, interrupted only by three small graceful archways opening to other rooms.

Anatolin glanced down. "From the buildup of dust on the stairs, I'd be surprised if anyone has entered this tomb for centuries."

"Such a conglomeration of burial types. A real hodgepodge."

"Perhaps because the tomb was in use for quite a long time."

Filling the benches and most of the floor were ash urns. Large sculpted stone coffins and terracotta sarcophagi with elaborate lids were clearly visible in the recessed burials on the farthest side, and at the center in front of the pillar, a low cairn of simply mounded stones. He stared at it as one hypnotized.

Julia touched his arm. "Dare we go in?"

Anatolin faced her. "You'll never experience anything else like this again as long as you live."

"Okay, you're right," Julia said, starting resolutely into the tomb.

He descended the steps after her and stayed close by her side as she moved from one ash urn to the next.

"These urns are as charming and whimsical as any I've ever seen, and to think, they might actually represent how my ancestors looked two thousand years ago. I'd sure like to dust a few things off to see them better."

He took off his turtleneck, a dark one that had seen better days, and handed it to her. "I'm sure your ancestress wouldn't want you to wait until the archaeologists get wind of this and cart it all off to a museum."

"I hate to think of strangers down here, even archaeologists, but I suppose it's inevitable." She dusted off an urn, then its neighbor, remarked on the family resemblance, though the sculptures were more like caricatures than portraits. She came to a stop at the second archway. "Can you shine the light in there so we can take a quick look?"

"Certainly."

But a quick look was not to be. Upon glimpsing the room beyond the arch, Julia swept into it and gave a small shout.

"Look! Except for the mural, this room is identical to my little meditation room—without the windows, of course!"

She was right. The tomb's builders had replicated entirely in soft, porous stone a small wood beam-and-stucco room. The room's furnishings were also meticulously and realistically rendered in stone. A few feet from the door sat two straight backed stone chairs, perfect to their upholstered cushions, at the foot of each, a padded footrest. Between them stood a small chest of drawers. Everything faced the far wall, which held a shallow niche done up precisely like Julia's at the cottage, five-pointed star and all, this one ochre.

Julia rested her hand lightly on the nearest stone chair. "I guess Madame Racine was right to call us a conservative bunch. From the looks of this room, I'd say not much changed in our tradition for several millennia. I could sit here now and feel perfectly at home."

Clasping her hands behind her back, Julia walked toward the brightly painted mural that filled a band eighteen inches wide near the room's ceiling. She seemed mesmerized, as if the mural told some fascinating legend.

"What is that?" he asked.

"My family's saga from the time of our departure from our original homeland, through a long sea voyage, to their arrival in this new land." Her voice caught. "The pictographs pretty much match what I've already managed to pull together about our history."

Anatolin was happy for her. This subterranean room was validation of a very concrete sort for the prehistoric roots not only of her family but also of their spiritual tradition, which he was more convinced than ever was an early and undiluted form of what later came to be known as raja yoga. With its emphasis on self-discipline and moral goodness, service to others, conscious command of the life force, and deep interiorized meditation, the Giuliana legacy had all the classic earmarks of that highest of paths for uniting one's soul with Spirit, the union to which Anatolin had all his life aspired. He felt honored to be part of Julia's resurrecting it.

He started toward the door but realized Julia was not finished studying the room. She had become mesmerized once again. Off to his left, she was bent down low, apparently examining a terracotta sarcophagus ensconced in one of the deep chambers carved into the longer walls of the room.

Suddenly, she sat back on her heels, her arms crossed, the knuckles of one hand white against her mouth. Her expression seemed exceedingly sad. "What's wrong, Julia?"

"Nothing's wrong, exactly," she said. "It's just that I finally know."

"Know what?"

"Why my grandmother felt inadequate to take up the Giardani mantle."

Anatolin stepped to Julia's side, clasped his hands behind his back to restrain his instinct to comfort and thus interrupt her. It was painful to watch her suffer, but she desperately needed to learn whatever she could, and it was imperative he allow her free rein to do so. He crouched down beside Julia, close by but careful not to jar her. "And why was that?"

She extended her hand, held it over the sarcophagus lid. It was an elaborate lid on which an almost life-size couple embraced in restful, if not blissful, slumber. The woman was elegantly garbed and bejeweled, the sculpture detailed and very fine, but for a rough, two-inch band of unfinished carving below her waist, where she likely would have worn an ornate kirtle, or belt. The man was handsome, virile, eternally young, every one of his strong features hauntingly rendered with fastidious care.

She took a deep breath. "This woman was my grandmother, Anna, in a prior incarnation. I believe she died young. Without making the Sacred Marriage or bearing an Heiress for the lineage. It seems she chose the wrong consort. A man who was not ready for her or for her legacy but who had to have her, anyway. His uncontrolled lust destroyed them both." She looked away from the sarcophagus, her gaze lost in the past. Her breath came raggedly, her hand trembled, but she kept it extended a few inches above the couple. "That man in this life is Gregor Danilenko."

Anatolin had sensed her insight before she'd shared it, but hearing it spoken aloud shook him badly. He didn't like it but had earlier accepted that Danilenko was karmically linked to the Giardani. It was the only feasible explanation for the extent of the man's obsession.

Julia stood quickly and crossed to the opposite wall, where another sarcophagus was set deep into a matching chamber. Anatolin joined her, his heart beating rapidly, his mouth dry as chalk.

This sarcophagus was even more elaborate than the other. Its lid also depicted a sleeping couple, but instead of being elegantly clothed, this couple seemed to be naked beneath an almost-sheer coverlet embellished with full-blown roses. The woman's only ornamentation was some sort of medallion, mostly obscured by the coverlet, just visible beneath her breasts.

Julia held out her hand and immediately gasped. Her knees gave way. Anatolin caught her around the waist and braced her against his body. She seemed to be struggling to get hold of herself.

Giving him a small smile, she inched away, stood erect. She covered her solar plexus with both hands. "These two were Anna's parents, Andrei." She turned toward him, staring a moment, but through him not at him. Then she closed her eyes. "I'm going back down the hill, now. I think it would be best to clear away the vines outside. Can I ask you to get a crew started on that?"

"Of course." Anatolin tried to read her, but her mind and feelings were guarded as never before.

She frowned. "I wonder if it would be better to contact the local ministry of archaeology or some particular archaeologist?"

"No need to decide, now."

"I guess not, but I sure don't want Danilenko destroying anything more before all of this is documented."

"Your father obviously never found this tomb and therefore couldn't have hidden whatever Danilenko is after down here. Even deranged as he seems to be, Danilenko would sense that." He cleared his throat. "Julia?"

"Hmmm?"

He swallowed hard. "Was there nothing else you wanted to share about this burial?" he asked, pointing to the rose-covered pair.

Tears rushed to her eyes but she held them back. "Anna's parents."

"Yes, so you said."

"Us, Andrei. Long ago, that couple was you and me." Julia squared her shoulders and ducked through the door.

Anatolin lingered behind a moment, his gaze on the lovely face of the woman immortalized on the sarcophagus lid. He hadn't needed Julia to tell him who that woman had once been. The likeness had all her ineffable charm. Nor had he needed her to confirm his own prior incarnation, surprised though he'd been to perceive himself among the Giardani burials. He'd asked her because she'd chosen to avoid the obvious.

It was a wholly uncharacteristic choice, and it worried him.

∞

Andrei caught up with Julia in the crypt. He stopped beside her. Slowly, she surveyed the damage again.

Her gaze came to rest on the badly damaged ledge beside the crypt's exit, above the urn that apparently had held her grandmother's ashes.

"Danilenko took something from there," she said. "Something very sacred. Powerful." The certainty she felt was astounding. "Something worn," she added, a chill passing from head to foot. "By the women buried in this tomb, most likely, in our rituals over many centuries."

"Given the seemingly random damage, I assumed he'd found nothing."

Unable to answer, she just shook her head. Her eyes burned with tears. She moved toward the ledge, her flashlight illuminating a jewelry chest not unlike the larger one in her meditation room.

The chest's lid was shattered. Its contents were gone.

Andrei stepped closer, tipped the chest toward the lamp. Inside, the wood was inscribed with the full-blown rose that Julia now realized signified the Giuliana legacy.

And beneath the rose, three words—*Giuliana's Holy Belt.*

"So," she said, her heartbreak so profound it actually hurt her physically. "I *did* get here too late. Danilenko has won, after all."

BOOK FIVE

RENEWAL

Because of Her they

think friendly thoughts

and accomplish harmonious deeds

calling Her Joy

by name and Aphrodite.

—EMPEDOCLES, FIFTH CENTURY B.C.E.
THE PRESOCRATIC PHILOSOPHERS
G. S. KIRK & J. E. RAVEN, 1957

THIRTY-ONE

Julia sat on the edge of the sanctuary's ceremonial platform. It was time for a break from the final preparations for the May Eve gathering. Until now, she'd kept herself moving full speed, not letting herself dwell on the memory of that gaping chest in the tomb. Giuliana's Holy Belt, gone. In Danilenko's treacherous hands, and no time to win it back before tonight's big event, even if she could somehow conjure up a plan for doing so. But she wouldn't despair. Too much good had come of her return home. It wasn't too late to do more good, yet.

Danilenko could steal every holy thing the Giardani ever used. He could bomb the Gardens with Agent Orange. Whatever. She wouldn't give up. There was still too much left to learn. Andrei had convinced her of all this on the way down the hill, when they decided to keep Danilenko's victory to themselves.

That sweet guy, he'd been so thoughtful today. Under the guise of giving her an update on the clearing of the crypt's overgrowth, he'd sent someone up to check on her at least three times an hour.

She spent most of the morning in a bit of a fog. In addition to the empty chest, the other discoveries in the tomb had given her a lot to think about. They'd also shaken her badly. Coming upon her own entombed former incarnation was the most unsettling thing she'd experienced since coming to Tuscany.

Aside from that shock, though, a lot had come together for her in the tomb. For one thing, she finally understood the affinity she'd felt for Andrei from the first hour she'd known him. In the life she saw this morning, she'd been married to him for at least thirty years. Very happily married, it seemed.

Now it no longer struck her as odd that in only two short months, he already felt like the best friend she'd ever had. And now there was some explanation for her intense erotic attraction to him, as well. Obviously, some of what she experienced as his wife long ago was affecting her still.

Knowing this on an intellectual level didn't solve her dilemma, of course. Her other knowing, far more confusing and much stronger, grew even stronger with every hour that passed. It wasn't just carnal knowing, that much was clear. It wasn't only psychic or intuitive, either, but something more complete. More like cellular knowing, maybe even atomic. Every atom of her being knowing Andrei was the one man for her.

This was a knowing that compelled from within and without, from above and below, was all encompassing. A pure unmitigated motive *spirit* that craved expression in the world, was always present, pervasive but unseen, and most potent when shared. It was Turan, the *spirit* of lovers, of love and of peace, the Aphrodite energy Julia was somehow supposed to carry in the world—the power of Love—both personal and Divine, immense and exacting, almost fearsome in its force.

She'd been somehow warding it off, not welcoming it truly and openly, thus not fully honoring it—and not serving it as effectively as she otherwise might have. The last few weeks flipped through her mind like the cards of a tarot deck, the strange vivid images oddly making total sense. She saw all her mistakes with Andrei, saw how she'd hidden her own fear of intimacy beneath a mask as often as he had, her mask taking the amorphous form of exaggerated respect for his spiritual calling.

How could she hope to carry Aphrodite Turan's spirit in the world if she was faint of heart? How could she uphold the revered title of Giardani Heiress in her new community if she couldn't find the courage to overcome her fear of falling short in the arts of Love?

Back on the purely personal level, how could she so totally *get* Andrei's body language and not act on his unspoken messages of love, confront him and challenge his commitment to her? She simply had to do it, and soon. Resolutely, she put her gardening tools into her day pack, stood and glanced up toward the grotto.

Lucia and Signora Isabella had been puttering up there for the last two hours. Doing what, Julia couldn't imagine. Their preparations in the grotto were meant to be secret, even from the Giardani Heiress. Brushing off the seat of her jeans, she smiled as she realized she was perfectly content to wait and find out what her friends had been up to.

She guessed she really had changed since coming home to the Gardens. Every day now was full of surprises and, most of the time, she didn't mind waiting for them one little bit. Large and small, they delighted her just the same. Not even Danilenko's treachery would keep her down for long.

She just prayed he would stay away until tonight's celebration was over and her newfound extended family had all made it safely back to their homes. She prayed also that the Goddess would keep making clear her next step. She couldn't ask for more than that. Hard though it might be to keep going on faith, she intended to persist. Her pack over her shoulder, she headed down the Etruscan staircase.

Down in the meadow, she was pleased with the tidy new look of the crypt. The weeds and vines had been carted away. The meadow was groomed to perfection, empty now but for herself and her ancestors. The sight of the mangled iron door made her shudder all over again.

Quickly, she pulled a new spool of wide satin ribbon from the front pocket of her day pack and juggled it in her hand as she approached the crypt. She slid her pack to the ground.

She looped the ribbon from the big hinge on the top left side to a peg at the lower right door frame, to the opposite hinge across the bottom of the threshold, and from there to another peg at the top right hand side of the door. Then she closed the X at the top as she had at the bottom. No real deterrent, this, merely a reminder to respect the privacy of the Giardani dead should some wayward celebrant get it in his head to take a look inside.

She stood back, admired the large X, and decided to add a big bow in the middle and call it a day. There was just enough ribbon left. She gave the ribbon ends a clean snip, tucked her scissors inside the empty spool, and set it on the nearby bench while she pulled the ribbon into large, graceful loops. Humming the ritual tune she learned in the sanctuary, she patted her handiwork, stood back, and rested her hands on her hips.

The ribbon reminded Julia of her father's treasure map postcard with its X-marks-the-spot inscription. She took another step backward. She never had figured out the meaning of that third postcard, with its sculpture of Aphrodite ascending from her bath. The photo, well worn after weeks of frequent handling, had lost most of its garish gold leaf. At some point, Julia had decided the gold had probably started off as an X, not a V after all.

What if her father had not meant the gold leaf as some kind of joke? What if he'd meant it very seriously? A very serious, very real clue in the shape of a golden X?

The fragment of Sappho's poetry came immediately to mind: "Leave Crete and come to us, waiting where the grove is pleasantest, by precincts sacred to you . . ."

Near precincts sacred to Aphrodite could mean none other than this meadow neighboring the ancient sanctuary, at the point where the grove or forest was pleasantest. She'd gotten this far in her reasoning several times before this, but there was something changed now, something she couldn't quite put her finger on. She took another step backward.

There was that other message on the card, of course, the one she'd always considered more of an afterthought. "Find the place and take a seat there." Her gaze came to rest on the small stone bench just to the left of the crypt's iron door. She felt an instant chill.

Here was a seat she could take near her ancestors, one she hadn't seen before because the bench had been covered in vines and, unlike the crypt, had been entirely hidden, probably for years.

She walked toward the bench, her heart in her throat. It wasn't just any old stone bench—it was identical to the one her father had built in his Berkeley garden. As a woman, she'd planted violets beneath that bench. As a teen, she'd stashed her house keys in it, down in the same hidden compartment in the hollow leg where, as a ten-year-old tomboy she'd hidden her best cat's-eye marbles to safeguard them from the neighborhood bully.

Julia swallowed hard. She had found another of her father's hiding places. Soon she might find the *real* object Danilenko wanted. She dropped to her knees, leaned forward, barely touched her palms to the granite seat. It gave her a jolt. She pulled back but continued to lean toward the bench. Upon her touch, the four-inch-thick slab of hard stone had started to hum. Using her fingertips only, she brushed it again, lightly.

Whoa! The darn thing kicked her back onto her heels. What on earth could give a stone bench such a high-voltage charge?

Gingerly reaching under the seat, she slowly skimmed her hand an inch or so out from the surface. The trigger that opened the hidden compartment of the bench in Berkeley, a sturdy natural crystal, had protruded at least three inches. Blindly grasping a cool, sharp protrusion, she started to push down, stopped.

She sensed something—a footstep?—behind her.

Her stomach took a dive. Someone was standing directly behind her. She hadn't taken time to consider a single precaution, let alone think up some effective protective subterfuge. She dropped her hands to her knees, stiffened, kept totally still.

How could she have been so careless? If that was Danilenko behind her, any hope of keeping what she'd been about to find would be gone.

"Need some help?"

Andrei. "Whew!" She twisted around and gave him a welcoming smile. "Thank heaven it's you!"

And thank heaven he didn't take the opportunity to give her a well-deserved scolding for being her usual reckless self. His only response was his lopsided smile followed by an almost imperceptible shake of his head.

"Come here, you sneaky Scorpio, and see what I've found." She was weak with relief. "I think we've hit the jackpot, here. Just don't touch the bench, whatever you do. The darn thing's wired, or something."

"Psychic energy." Andrei knelt beside her. He raised his palms toward the bench. "Even I can feel it, and my hands aren't half as receptive as yours. It's psi of the highest order, Julia, so potent and concentrated it's generating enough friction to vibrate this solid rock. No wonder Danilenko went out of his mind and, apparently, he wasn't even close to the right spot."

"Thank heaven for that! My father must have built this bench when he came here the year my grandmother died. Not long after his return, he built an identical one in our backyard. He knew I would recognize this." Julia grasped the crystal again and pushed it down.

The hidden compartment scraped open, its door thumping heavily onto the grass beneath the bench. Another, smaller thump sounded as an indigo velvet pouch slid down and wedged itself into the compartment's opening.

She knew that pouch. For years, it had held her father's favorite tarot deck, the one he used every day when she was very young. Her heart raced. She trembled. Her breath came in gasps. She lowered her head, pressed the heels of her hands to her brow, tried to slow her breathing.

Her mind flooded with childhood memories of her darling father, working hard all his life to take care of her, most of those years by himself. He'd raised her to be the best she could be, pumped her brimful of self-confidence and his own eclectic brand of faith.

Now he'd given her this last precious gift, one he'd probably lost his life to protect. She prayed she wouldn't let him down. If she did, his death would have been in vain.

Andrei put his hand gently on Julia's shoulder. "He loved you well, Julia, and did his best to prepare you to uphold the Giuliana legacy. You won't let him down."

She looked into Andrei's ever-kind eyes and was grateful for his telepathy, grateful for everything about him. Despite her recent decision, this was no time to challenge his commitment. "I sure hope you're able to stay on a while longer, help me keep things going right around this place."

Andrei seemed surprised by her remark. "Certainly!" Or maybe a bit befuddled. "As long as you need me—"

The bench started to rumble. Down in the hidden compartment, the half-exposed pouch glowed as if lit from within. She reached for it. "Got it."

There was a smallish rectangle inside it, wood, she guessed from the feel of it. She angled it free from the cramped opening and set it on the bench. The bench still vibrated fiercely, but the pouch seemed to insulate its contents, which didn't transmit the same force. She opened it and pulled out a small carved box, held it aloft.

With her other hand, she up-ended the pouch. A large tarot card drifted down onto her lap. It was labeled THE EMPRESS. The card's image made perfect sense. A star-crowned woman in a rose-covered gown sat enthroned in a garden by a sacred spring. She held a scepter of magical power. The emblem of Venus/Aphrodite was carved into the base of her throne. On the card's back was another note from Julia's father. The sight of his handwriting brought tears to her eyes.

"Would you like me to read that?" Andrei offered.

"Please," she said, resting the small box on her lap.

He cleared his throat. "'Dearest Lady Bug—If you're reading this, you are probably on your own, but if you found this on your own, you must be in tune. Just stay in tune and you'll learn all there is to know.'"

Julia lost it for a moment and let go a small sob. Andrei cleared his throat again, took a deep breath, and continued reading.

"'All I can tell you about the thing inside this box is that, whatever it is, it was created for only one purpose: to reveal the Divine Mystery at the core of Creation. Thus my mother, who came to fear that Mystery as nothing else, would never so much as lay eyes on it when I retrieved it from Italy. After she died, I brought it back here to wait for you.'"

Andrei fell silent.

"That's it?"

"No, there's more. He says the rest of the family's holy things are hidden around the property, apologizes for that but adds you'll doubtless gather them up in due course. He needed them to mislead an old enemy he suspected might try to destroy you."

"Danilenko." Julia caught Andrei's gaze, gave his hand a tight squeeze. "It's pretty clear the sacred object he stole—the Holy Belt— was probably not the one he believes it is. He'll be furious when he realizes my father tricked him."

Andrei frowned. "We can only hope he doesn't for a very long time."

THIRTY-TWO

The box on Julia's lap was rumbling now, made her feel distinctly odd. She felt overcome by the awe stealing through her, almost tipsy, very glad Andrei knelt close beside her. She opened the box, which was lined in the same velvet as the pouch. All scrunched up inside was a delicate chain made of rosy-hued gold.

"Prehistoric gold," she said, recognizing the genuine antiquity of the object on the indigo velvet. She slipped a blunt pencil from her pack, used it to push the chain gently to the right. The chain's links were very fine. Tiny medallions glinted up at her, their faces a miracle of precision craftsmanship. "And this technique, ages-old and long-lost, is called granulation."

Andrei's smile encouraged her to continue. She worked down through layers of chain and medallions until her pencil came to rest beside a six-inch-wide gold disk literally covered in minute golden granules. The disk had an open star burst at its heart, through which the chain was threaded. She held her breath, hooked the pencil through the disk, and lifted the whole piece from the box, trailing the long chain with its fringe of medallions slowly across her lap.

Andrei's breath was warm on her cheek as he leaned over her shoulder. "Magnificent," he said.

"It really is, isn't it?"

"Be careful. This thing broadcasts the most staggering power I've ever experienced. You're already halfway into a trance."

"Don't worry, Andrei. There's nothing to be afraid of here."

"Wait—" he started in a warning tone.

But she'd already slid the chain over her hands and let the pencil drop away. She held the chain up well above her lap, jiggled it gently, let the disk slide freely. Left to itself, the disk's fragile weight balanced and straightened the chain. It dipped down gracefully at the center, the chain gliding smoothly through the star burst, forming golden rays that extended out into a luminous figure eight.

She lifted the disk high, touched it to her brow.

Blinding light flashed. Vertigo hit hard.

Andrei grabbed her shoulders, blurred out of focus. Was he shouting her name? She couldn't hear him above the roar in her head. The meadow melted into slow-motion soup, started spinning, made a tunnel, slowed. Julia felt lightheaded. Lighthearted, too, like a little kid. She relaxed and went with the flow.

> The tunnel was long. It was cool. The air was soft. The Lady appeared, led Julia to a silvery cave.
>
> "Why, it's like Loutra Tis Aphrodite here!" Only it tasted of lilacs on snow. And the ferns glittered, iridescent. The water, too. And when Julia put her finger to the shiny wall, it went right through. O, well!
>
> The Lady smiled.
>
> There were two pretty chairs across from a star, just like home. The Lady sat in one. Julia sat in the other.
>
> It was hard to focus with the ocean thundering in her ears. The Lady touched Julia's forehead, right in the center. That helped. Everything went still. She looked at the Lady, who nodded. Gave the sweetest smile.
>
> "Andrei says we Giardani are yogis," Julia said. "Are you my guru?"

"In the East they would call me that. You, too, someday, most likely. As in the East, we are a sacred lineage. Look." The Lady touched Julia's forehead again.

In her spiritual eye, Julia saw herself, one priestess among many linking an endless corridor of time.

"Those behind you are your predecessors in the Work, those in front, the ones waiting to come."

"The corridor is the Path to Our Mother."

"Yes, Julia dear, that's right."

"We Giardani have all walked it? Everyone I just saw?"

"In some life or other, we have."

"Okay, we're a lineage, but what makes the Giardani so special?"

The Lady smiled. "It's not that we're special, just that we remember to keep the Tradition, to make the great Effort. We know the Path to Our Mother and can show others the way."

"Using the Gifts?" Julia wrinkled her nose. "All the bells and whistles make me different from everyone else. That can't be good."

The Lady laughed. "It's neither good nor bad. The Gifts are useful. They help you to serve, just as the Teachings do."

Julia loved the Lady's Teachings. She'd keep working hard to get them right. She sighed. "O, but I'm very late."

"You are late, it's true, and we have much to prepare." The Lady smiled again. "Hush, now. Time to meditate."

∞

Anatolin was more than worried. Over an hour had passed, and Julia still grasped the golden disk, her fingers laced through the delicate chain, her trance so deep she couldn't know Anatolin held her other hand, couldn't know he sat by her side on her bed, where he'd gently placed her after carrying her down the mountain.

He hadn't touched her ancient jewel, knew he wasn't prepared to travel where she had gone, knew she didn't need his protection there, or his help. He just had to accept that. And he did, intellectually. It was only his heart that had panicked when he felt her slip away up there in the meadow. It was only his heart that wanted to pull her back now to this reality, where he had some hope of keeping her safe.

Blast his heart. This was only the beginning for her. She was, after all, the Giardani Heiress, a soul destined for spiritual greatness. He'd known that since Cyprus. Why was the reality of it now almost more than he could bear? Why did the inevitable change this event signaled shake him to his roots?

He stood and paced to the edge of the loft, braced his arms on the sturdy banister. He'd come to want Julia's happiness more than he wanted his own. And her happiness, he knew beyond any doubt, depended wholly upon her fulfillment of what she'd been sent here to do. From now on, he would seek his fulfillment in helping Julia achieve hers. There could be no other way for him.

Behind him, he heard her stir.

"Oh, my bedroom," she said softly.

He turned around, impressed by how quickly she'd obviously regained her bearings, another indicator of the deep soul contact her recent meditation afforded her. But beyond that, one glance told him she had changed. Totally and irrevocably. Though still partially entranced, she was sitting up, cross-legged, her heirloom held up to catch the westerly afternoon light through the bedroom window. She was open to him now, he realized. Transparent. He could feel every nuance of her experience, intensely.

"It's all here, Andrei." She looked from her heirloom to him. "The whole Giuliana legacy, magically encoded into this precious gold thing and unlocked, it seems, by some genetic element in my physical cells. I wish my father had simply given this to me in the first place. Doing so might have saved his life."

"A man's first instinct is to protect those he loves."

"I know you're right. I used to get all prickly and resistant when Dad was protective of me, the same way I have with you. I'm sorry about that."

Smiling, Anatolin glanced at the heirloom. "Does this have a name?"

"It's called the Sacred Kestos."

He sensed the name came to her only as she said it, another new phenomenon she apparently took in her stride. "The mythic Aphrodite had a *kestus 'imás*. A halter, of sorts, magically imbued with love, desire, the power to beguile."

"Hmmm." She glanced again from the jewel to him, cocked her head to one side, raised her eyebrows. "I can see how this might be worn as a halter, but it sure wouldn't cover much. It's probably a good thing the Giardani Heiress wears it only for the May Eve ritual. We Giardani made this and we guard it, but it was created solely for the community that gathers on May Eve to honor the old Lover of Mortals." Clearly, she would have shared more but wasn't sure she was free to. She glanced distractedly at her watch. "Only five hours to go and so much left to prepare."

"I thought you *streghe* had finished your preparations."

"The outer preparations are all finished."

The import of her reply took a moment to penetrate Anatolin's confusion—she needed to get back to meditation immediately, felt she hadn't a moment to spare. She would need quiet. He'd see to that. And then there was Danilenko, who might be satisfied for a time with the Holy Belt, but was still a mortal threat.

Anatolin frowned. "I hate to sound a sour note, but perhaps I should take charge of your new treasure until it's time for the ritual. If Danilenko realizes he's wound up with Tony's red herring, he'll kill you for your Sacred Kestos."

"Don't you think he'd kill you just as readily?"

"Certainly he would."

"I think your idea stinks," Julia said.

"Why am I not surprised?"

"Besides, I need the Kestos with me."

He took a step closer. "Then we'll stay together."

"Won't work—"

"If I promise to stay close, more or less, as needed?"

She gave him a scrutinizing look. "Define more or less."

"More if you're alone here. Less if there are others in the house, in which case I could come and go as the situation demanded."

She considered the compromise, winked. "Sounds like a plan."

∞

Julia's meditation room was bright with sunlight streaming through the stained-glass window. Outside her other window, birds sang in the trees, the muted laughter of those working below in the courtyard or the gardens blending in from time to time. Andrei, bless his heart, had wanted to ask folks to keep total silence near the cottage, but that wasn't necessary. She wouldn't notice any sounds at all, before long, planned to go deep right away.

She took her chair, raised her inner gaze, and started silently chanting with her breath, the way the Lady taught her.

The Lady came back from the deep, glanced at Julia, smiled. She pointed to the floor of the cave.

Julia looked down. The floor was moving, real busy, like an ant track hauling spilt sugar. But the crystals were colored, rainbow hued, and they moved in an X on the floor.

A figure eight, really, if you watched real close. So beautiful, those tiny crystals, rounding like that, no end.

"Infinity," the Lady said. "All your lives."

"Every May Eve, past and future, to learn from."

"Yes, dear, that's right."

"Then I've passed all my tests?"

The Lady frowned. "Almost all."

It wasn't right to ask more. Julia would just go deeper, put herself in Mother's hands.

∞

With James steering the Bentley sedately through the Tuscan hills, Madame Racine took advantage of the calm and relaxed into her seat. The last few days had been arduous. She'd earned ten minutes rest.

Only with great effort and more twisting of arms than she liked had Racine managed to secure some scant cooperation from the inner circle. Though their obstinacy might have been most satisfactory under other circumstances, in relation to this situation it appalled her. They never conceded it was time to take steps to block Gregor Danilenko, but at least they agreed to pray for an end to his obdurate suffering, if not an end to the suffering his actions wrought on the targets of his aggression.

Racine's career had been one long juggling act, an artful dance of finding the balance between the exigencies of her service in the world and the strictures of spiritual law. She'd needed constantly to remind herself that when it came to aiding in any crisis, no matter how dire, she could perceive no more than the tip of the iceberg. Only the great ones inspiring and operating through the inner circle could see the whole of any karmic pattern.

She'd try to be satisfied with the inner circle's promise to keep their prayer groups and healing triangles focused on the Calderola. She'd always believed in prayer, the most invincible force in the universe.

With prayer, miracles really did happen. Julia would need one to survive the ordeal ahead.

Racine stared at the large box on the seat beside her. Inside was an exact replica of the gown and veil Julia's great-grandmother wore in the last May Eve celebration. Tony found the fragile originals, beyond repair, in the 1940s. A few months before his death, he sent them to Racine and asked her to have them reproduced. Not an easy task, even in Paris. The original cloth had been spun of finest silk and embroidered with roses in twenty-four-karat-gold thread. Finding enough truly gifted seamstresses to complete the reproduction in time had been difficult, the cost exorbitant. But if the items made from the replicated fabric lasted as long as the previous holy garments had, they would be worth every effort expended.

James opened the window between the front seat and Racine's. "Excuse me, Madame. I thought you might like to note the marked difference in ambience as we come closer to Montecipriana."

"Thank you, *mon ami*," she replied, glancing out the window at the cars lining the road all around the small mountain. People were flocking toward the Gardens. Many whole families could be seen among the crowd, which was animated farther away but grew more solemn, almost processional as it neared its destination.

The window started to close. Racine sat up straight.

"Leave it open, James dear. I need to speak with you, and this is as good a time as any."

James assessed her through the rearview mirror. "Is something wrong, Madame?"

"*Mais, non!*" She smiled reassuringly. "Everything is fine. Just right, in fact. I simply wanted to inform you that the protracted farce of your employment with me will soon be over."

James lifted his eyebrows, exaggerated his pursed lips, and gave her a roguish wink. "What on earth shall the two of us do to make trouble then?"

"Nothing on *earth*, James," Racine answered with a grin. "You may rest assured of that!"

∞

Beautiful beyond words, the deep. Very peaceful. The Lady had gone, and Julia was alone in Mother's embrace.

Joy was real, had a color and a taste and a feel all Its own, called Bliss. It permeated every particle of Julia's being, lifted her afloat, a bubble on a great vast sea.

No cares came here. Memories were soft. Everything was soft, even Julia's form.

"Mother," Julia said, felt a ripple stir the sea, felt Love swell in her heart and release more Joy. "Mother."

Julia sailed on the mantra, drifted to a stop. "Make me wise, Mother, that I might better serve You. Keep me close, that I might never lose You."

A smile wafted over the sea of Bliss, gentle laughter.

Thou and I are never apart, Julia dear. Thou and I are never apart.

THIRTY-THREE

Julia was rested and showered. Since her meditations had deepened, she rarely felt woozy or depleted by her gifts anymore. Tonight, in fact, she felt perfectly centered and balanced, ready for the May Eve gathering. There was nothing left to do but dress, nothing at all left to worry about. Not even Gregor Danilenko. If he showed up tonight, he'd be in the hands of the Goddess, and She wouldn't make mistakes.

"Mother," Julia whispered, rubbing the disk of the Sacred Kestos through the soft chenille of her robe, feeling the chain tickle her slightly as it jangled beneath her slip. Wearing the Kestos, Julia now could move readily to and from the mystic realm of her beloved teacher, and sometimes the outer world seemed like a dream, the inner world her reality. This new, almost seamless dual existence was yet another miraculous gift for which she felt exceedingly grateful.

Back in her meditation room, she looked out the window and up toward the sanctuary, wished her father could be with her this night. She lifted his wedding band off the shelf of the niche and attached its chain through a loop on the Kestos. She patted the pink heart-shaped stone and returned to her bedroom.

"Julia?" Lucia's voice sounded from below. She came up the steps. "Are you ready to dress?"

"Has Andrei gone?"

"Twenty minutes ago, when Celeste and I returned."

"Have the *streghe* finished casting the ritual circle?"

"It is done, Julia."

"Then I'm as ready as I'm likely to be." Her voice must have sounded strained because Lucia gave her a curious look. Julia felt herself flush. "I guess I'm a bit anxious, too."

"Everything will be perfect."

Lucia smiled and crossed to the armoire, where Julia had hung the long white dress she'd worn to the beach on Cyprus. The dress was far from perfect for the occasion, but she hadn't known that until she found the Kestos, and for the present, it was the best she could do.

Lucia opened the armoire door and hung the dress back inside. "No one will ever forget this May Eve." She turned and called back over the balcony. "She's ready. You can bring up the gown."

Julia looked at Lucia. "What gown?"

Madame Racine came up the steps. "The one your father arranged for you to wear tonight." Smiling her most capricious smile, she clapped quickly. "*Vite! Vite!*"

Celeste followed, a large white box in her arms. She placed it on the bed and lifted its lid. Lucia stepped forward and took hold of Julia's robe. The gown shimmered as Celeste lifted it over Julia's head and motioned Lucia to remove the robe.

Julia gasped as the silk settled around her, falling like a whisper against her bare skin. She suddenly realized her slip would interfere with the drape of the Kestos, which needed to find its own locus below her breasts. She removed her arms, tipped the slip's thin straps off her shoulders, and let it slide to the floor before returning her arms to the sleeves.

The gown certainly didn't interfere with the Kestos. Gathered loosely below the gold disk, the gown's classic lines flowed from her shoulders to her ankles in soft folds. Quickly, Lucia slid a pair of white kid ballet slippers onto Julia's feet and wound their satin ribbons round her ankles. Madame Racine stepped forward, holding a filmy veil with embroidery that matched the gown's. She draped it over Julia's head, stood back as Celeste secured it with a crown of spring flowers.

Julia gasped at the sight of her reflection in the mirror on the armoire door. She looked like an image from an ancient urn—or like one of her own recent past-life visions.

∞

The Gardens courtyard was once again serving as the famed *poste del streghione.* It had been full of people when Anatolin crossed back to his office between the barns. Now it was almost empty. Only five elderly *streghe*, two men and three women, remained behind. They would tend the roasts sizzling over the twelve-foot grilles, finish baking the breads and simmering the beans for the communal feast that would close tonight's celebration.

Anatolin would soon finish distributing copies of Danilenko's latest Interpol photo among the guards he'd posted at every approach to the Gardens, though if Danilenko chose to attend the gathering, he would surely find an effective disguise. Julia was not to be alone for an instant. If Anatolin wasn't close, either her friends or an escort of Marco's beefy chums was to accompany her at all times.

Anatolin could only hope the general would decide to hold off his next attack until there were fewer witnesses present to identify him. By then Anatolin might figure out how to stop him for good.

Fifty yards above the courtyard, people lined the path. Up closer to the meadow they stood three deep on either side. After Julia passed between them, they would fall in behind her and follow her up to the sanctuary. Just imagining the spectacle of her leading that procession made Anatolin feel strangely satisfied.

He waved good-bye to the elderly cooks, passed through the gate, and started round the hill to continue passing out photos. He wore a midnight-purple shirt and trousers, the better to blend in with the background. He also wore one of Interpol's small black automatics tucked inside his belt at the back. Useless though any conventional weapon would be against the general's deadly talents, it offered some measure of consolation.

∞

Danilenko had planned to be a continent away by now, but he hadn't been able to leave. The compulsion to see the Giardani woman one last time had been too great. He'd also been dying to see how she'd pull off tonight's event without her Sacred Belt. He had easily passed the sentries in the village of Montecipriana and come into the procession amidst a raucous troupe of Rom dancers he'd hired to escort him as far as the meadow.

The Gypsies were young, none older than their early twenties. They wore vivid, almost psychedelic garb. His disguise, a black velvet cape and matching top hat, fit in well with the flamboyant group, especially after he accepted the ribbon-clad staff and red tambourine offered him by a nubile, dark-haired girl. She danced into the meadow beside him now, her hips undulating to some wine-induced tune only she could hear. She sidled up against him. He bent toward her, slipped his hand up under her midriff, flicked her nipple hard with his thumb as he covered her gasp of surprise with a rough kiss, his heightened vigor feeding on her easy excitability.

A shame he'd had no time for anything more than a tease and needed now to send her away. An irreverent group like hers would seem markedly out of place once the ritual got underway. He handed back her tambourine and staff, put the top hat on her head, and wrapped the cloak around her shoulders. He gave her plump bottom a swat and sent the troupe back to town.

He concealed himself at the edge of the meadow to watch them leave the property then returned to the fringe of the forest. A few minutes later, a stir passed through the crowd.

It was the Giardani Heiress and her company. A group of lively musicians walked up the hill ahead of her, followed by her female attendants of varying ages. Then came the High Priestess herself in the finest of gowns, pure white, of course, embellished with gold.

When she passed him her aura was a glittering cloud. An illusion brought about by the moving torch light? Or was it something more?

She seemed taller tonight. Majestic and eerily familiar.

The music. The torches. The grand procession. It all seemed very familiar.

Passion evoked by the mere sight of Julia Giardani made him acutely aware of every sensation, which addled his thoughts, clouded his reason. He tried to control himself, but it was no use. The longer he watched her the more intractably the desire to be part of her procession took hold of him.

After everyone below him had gone by, he fell in behind them. He carried no torch, so he kept pace with another who lagged back from the rest. Adrenaline raced through his veins. His heart pounded. His eyes stung, not only from the smoke of the torches, but from the fierce emotions assailing him, churning his insides and ringing in his ears.

He shook himself from his sudden daze. The Giardani woman was a force beyond his wildest imaginings. She had obviously found another family heirloom, more potent than the Holy Belt, looped now around his neck beneath his tight black turtleneck. Her heirloom, like his, was obviously hidden somewhere on her person. Enhancing her natural magnetism. Magnifying her powers.

Damn, damn, and *damn!* If he'd waited till now, used Hitler's occult hoard to augment his PK instead of his biological clock, his odds of defeating the fully awakened Giardani Heiress would have been far greater. As it was, he'd made an abysmal mistake. The return of his youth could have cost him everything.

∞

No matter how many times Julia might climb to the sanctuary in the course of her life, she knew she'd never forget this night. Her ritual attendants, Lucia, Celeste and Silvana, carried lidded wicker baskets that held the mysterious Secret Things, but the evening no longer seemed mysterious to Julia. She knew precisely how the ritual would unfold.

When all were gathered above, she would perform the invocation and take her chair on the dais, newly built in the center of the cere-monial platform. One at a time, the *streghe* would kneel in front of her, and the three Wise Crones would ask the ritual question, *Whom do you serve?*

Once the time-honored answer was spoken, *Diana through the Grace of Turan,* Celeste would sprinkle a pinch of gold dust over each person's head, Lucia would anoint each brow. Then Julia would repeat the archaic blessing, clearly patterned after a sacred poem by Sappho, *Shining with gold, you too, Aradia, Queen of the Night, are bound to Aphrodite Turan.* The non-Pagan participants, of whom there seemed to be a surprising number, would receive a similar blessing.

Those who had gifts for the Goddess would add them to the bon-fire built around the altar below the platform, and all would dance to the music of drums, flutes and an antique lyre Signora Isabella brought from Calabria. The music would eventually build to the ritual's finale, when Julia would rekindle the Sacred Flame on the cliff high above while the participants joined hands in a spiral dance.

Finally, united under the Divine Lover for the first time in decades, the community would head back down to feast in the Garden's courtyard. According to the ancient teachings encoded in the Sacred Kestos, these were the simple elements that comprised the Lesser Mysteries.

∞

Anatolin had learned to recognize the latent jealousy and possessiveness Julia's presence in his life had roused. The unfamiliar emotions no longer took him completely by surprise, but they offended
him no less. He'd be glad for the day when he could banish them
forever.

That day was still too far off for comfort. Jealousy had been working on him since the moment he joined the procession. He'd never
seen so many handsome young men assembled in one locale. Not
only Marco and his *streghe* friends but numerous others now
swarmed toward the sanctuary, many movie-star handsome.

One particularly striking fellow with dark, Gypsy features lagged
behind near the end of the procession. There was something about
him Anatolin didn't like, and he was reasonably sure the dislike
didn't spring solely from jealousy. Gradually, he dropped back until
he was a few feet behind, matched the man's pace, and kept a con-
sistent distance between them.

Julia. . . .

He'd missed her ascent of the mountain but prayed he wouldn't
miss a moment of her ritual. Everything she'd learned since he met
her would come to fruition tonight. He regretted his work had kept
him from involvement with her planning, but from what Madame
Racine had shared with him, he knew this May Eve celebration
would be a magnificent accomplishment.

He wanted Julia to know how much he admired and respected all
she'd done. He wanted to witness every discovery yet to come. He
wanted her happy. He wanted her confident, independent as she'd
always been, *and* he wanted her safe.

He wanted her—it was basic as that.

He loved her—would be happy only if he could spend the rest of
his life at her side, protecting and supporting her, doing his best to

help preserve her legacy. He should have taken Rafael's advice and told her as much last week. If he was lucky, there might be some appropriate moment tonight.

Glancing surreptitiously toward the end of the queue, Anatolin adjusted his pace once again as he made his way to the Etruscan staircase. Julia's handpicked Honor Guard stood at the top of the staircase, stopping participants as they entered the sanctuary and exhorting them to cleanse all sorrows and sins in the sacred spring before joining the celebration. Anatolin stepped between the Honor Guards in turn, his gaze straying toward the plateau, which Silvana and the *streghe* had transformed since he'd last seen it.

Torches flared atop tall stakes placed around its perimeter. A bonfire raged near the platform at the front of the ancient *temenos*. Musicians were seated near the back of the ceremonial platform before a veritable wall of roses strung with bright ribbon streamers.

At the center of the platform, a large carved-and-gilded chair stood upon a flower-strewn dais. Julia sat there now.

Someone spoke in a raised voice. Anatolin started. "I'm sorry, were you speaking to me?"

The guard standing to his left rolled his eyes. The one to his right seemed piqued to be required to repeat himself. "Giuliana requests you please relinquish all weapons and intoxicating substances before entering the sanctuary."

"But I'm part of her personal bodyguard!"

"She insisted there would be no exceptions. Absolutely none." The man gave Anatolin a polite but firm smile. "You may pick up anything you leave with us after the ceremony."

Anatolin groaned. Something told him he wouldn't get away with trying to retain his weapon. Quickly, he scanned the crowd. Rafael started toward him, his hands raised at his sides, palms up, in a gesture of futility.

"Sorry, Andrei. Even Interpol got no dispensation. It seems weapons have never been permitted past this point. I heard the mandate from the Giardani Heiress herself. All hostilities must be cast off here lest they contaminate the sacred space."

Anatolin pulled the automatic out of his belt and handed it over. Easy enough to make him relinquish his weapon, but what if some-one—like Danilenko—happened to be a weapon unto himself?

What then, indeed?

THIRTY-FOUR

J ulia stepped down from the dais. She walked to the front of the platform and scanned the faces illuminated by the light of torch and fire. Many she'd come to love, many she'd never even met. All had entered the sanctuary with open hearts, hearts filled with the conscious desire to experience the power of an ageless rite long forgotten by the modern world.

Signora Isabella's large *streghe* family had filed into the sanctuary near the head of the procession and clustered close to the makeshift steps leading onto the platform. Marco and the other young people looked resplendent in their colorful Pagan garb. Directly in front of the dais, Emilio, Maria Sergi, Fiorella Andrade, and old Urbano smiled up from the large group of neighbors Julia had hoped to see here tonight. The rest of the crowd was a blur of faces alight with happy expectation.

To Julia's right stood the three Wise Crones in their dark-blue cloaks. Celeste and Lucia stood to the left. Behind Julia's chair, Silvana quietly attended her basket of Secret Things, her love and support almost tangible. Little Vario looked solemn as he led the goat up onto the dais, where it curled up cozily near Julia's feet. The boy backed away.

Her Honor Guard signaled. Everyone was at last assembled within the sanctuary, around which circled the incense bearers, sealing the energetic shield. Julia lit the incense beside her, watched its smoke curl up into the air. It was time to begin.

∞

Danilenko found a spot on the fringe of the crowd as far from the nearest torch as he could get. From there he watched, deeply shaken and chilled to the bone, as the woman who was the most awesome foe he'd ever known assumed the full mantle and powers of her Divine Benefactress.

This was all so familiar to him. His heart began pounding, crashing in his chest. Blood roared in his ears.

Familiar.

He shook his shoulders to free himself of the sensations, but they held him, anchored him to his spot. The incense had gone to his head. The monotonous music had lulled him into a spontaneous trance the likes of which he hadn't experienced in years.

The web of life had once been the sole source of his sustenance and inspiration. Now it pulsed around and through him once more, rainbow-hued with a gold undercurrent, that same interconnected sea of energy he'd first encountered on the Crimean beach of his childhood. Tonight, though, he was among the amorphous mass, united in an ageless, holy rite. Familiar to him. Yes. Familiar.

His vision blurred. His eyes burned, his memory leaped backward in time. A high place. Long ago. Many lifetimes, many high places. Many rites, but only one pledge. One, undying—an eternal vow—to serve the power of Love forever.

Shame overcame him, for he knew he'd broken his pledge. Betrayed it.

Not once but countless times.

He gazed across the sanctuary. The High Priestess, elevated on her dais, would soon bless him. His craving for her unconditional Love—for her long-spurned healing Grace—all but buckled his knees.

∞

Bracing herself, Julia clasped her hands over the Kestos, her palms absorbing the power passing through its gold disk. She bowed her head as the might of the legacy expanded within her, then she looked up and gazed out over the crowd.

"When our ancestors first consecrated this sanctuary so many centuries ago, they knew terrible forces were abroad in the world, forces which sought to sever the natural close relationships among the Goddesses and Gods of their time. This is why the clans hereabouts pledged to come together in our sanctuary each year in the name of Aphrodite Turan to ensure that Love, the great power She governs, remained eternally honored among our peoples, as it had from the beginning.

"One of our Italian forefathers, the philosopher-sage Empedocles, left us a reminder of the Mysteries once known to all in the Golden Age. About those lost times Empedocles says, *No war-god Ares was worshipped nor the battle cry, nor was Zeus their king nor Kronos nor Poseidon, but Cypris, Aphrodite, was queen.* He also knew the true names and functions of our Lady of the Mysteries and he shares them with us. *She it is who is thought innate even in mortal limbs, because of Her people think friendly thoughts and accomplish harmonious deeds, calling Her Joy by name and Aphrodite.*

"So let Joy stir our hearts, strengthen the harmony among us, and inspire us to do good deeds tonight and always. Let us remember the ultimate purpose of Turan's Mysteries of Love is for each and every one of us to be rededicated to the Divine Lover and Her powers, to their glad renewal in our community, to their rebirth in the world beyond."

Julia took a deep breath, locked her legs firmly, and felt power surge through her.

She raised her hands high above her head and watched as liquid energy, like golden broth, coursed through her inner vision. Raising her voice, she projected it the way Signora Isabella had taught her, singing out the old Giardani invocation.

"The corners are cast, the circle is drawn. Now I, Giuliana, daughter of the Old One, call upon Her to join us in this holy place." She paused, then quickly turned and walked to her chair. Facing the crowd again, she stretched her arms even wider. "Turan, Turana, Venus, Aphrodite—be here now!"

∞

Anatolin watched Julia take her seat and raise her hands to her heart chakra, as if holding there some invisible globe. His daze was so profound it took several seconds to realize she'd actually begun directing energy through her magical Kestos.

She started to pray, softly at first, then more loudly. "O, Great Giver of Life—Lady of the Power that Binds the Universe—Mistress of the Mysteries—hear our prayers! Fill our minds with your Peace which is infinite. Fill our hearts with your Love which is eternal. Part the veil between the worlds and reveal to us Your Holy Presence!"

A moment later, a sea of rose-gold energy flooded the sanctuary, thick like honey, shimmering. Ineffably beautiful. A hum filled the air, turned to soft, joyous laughter that made Anatolin's spirits soar. He felt a peacefulness, a calm surpassing anything he'd ever known. He couldn't have said how long the sanctuary remained perfectly still before one of the cloaked figures stepped forward and threw back the hood of her cloak. Signora Isabella.

"The Lover of Mortals is here—She moves among us!"

∞

The Giardani Goddess did move among them, touching each heart individually, it seemed. Danilenko's breath caught as he realized the effect Her presence was having on those around him. Almost everyone seemed to be experiencing something extraordinary, something numinous.

Many faces in the sanctuary wore bemused expressions. Tears streamed freely down others. He heard small, breathless gasps, saw heads bowed in prayer, knees bent in devotion.

Danilenko gazed around the sanctuary a moment longer, then bowed his own head. He hadn't intended to pray, but he found himself doing so. In the next instant, he was drawn deeply inward.

Internalized, he felt himself lifted as if onto his mother's lap.

∞

In Julia's present state, the meadow was a shining place, pulsing to the flux and flow of the life force, to the hopes and dreams, the pains and fears of the people gathered together in communion. She felt them all, knew them all as her very self.

She knew her Divine Lover better still, knew Her powerful intent to be expressed in the world again, shared in Mysteries like these or otherwise. This night, Turana's own, would bring countless blessings to all and initiation to those ready to accept it, just as May Day's dawn would bring them new birth. Maybe only a few would accept the great Gift this first year, but in years to come, many more would find themselves ready.

Julia, touched profoundly as she was this night, would forever be changed, would herself change many others in

due course. She needed only to keep the Tradition, to channel Love unstintingly, to share always Mother's bountiful
Presence.

∞

The rose-gold color had started to thin by the time Anatolin next
opened his eyes. Julia had dropped her hands to her lap. Slowly she
raised her head. The goat stood up and nudged her knee. People
started to stir. Julia silently lifted her hand and gave Vario a cue.

The boy leapt from the stage, bolted to the center of the open area,
and spun around, his face alight. He raised his arms, gave a cry, and
shouted in a wild, lilting voice. "Let the blessings continue!" He
moved to the head of the line forming at the steps to the platform as
the musicians again began to play.

The sound of the drums, flute and lyre was as timeless as it was
lovely. It strummed through Anatolin's body. The participants filed
past Julia in a steady stream, some three hundred souls, kneeling
before her one at a time, offering their heartfelt love, receiving the
ancestral blessing.

Anatolin's mind raced with anticipation. He felt infused with the
deep, abiding harmony that bound this diverse crowd into a true
community. Early on, he'd realized the tallest of the three cloaked figures was Madame Racine. Like his mother, he'd come to love
Madame very much, especially after she'd spoken so imploringly
about him serving the Alliance in her stead. Earlier today, he'd
decided to take over her job, provided the Alliance accepted his
conditions.

They ought to. The two conditions he'd laid out to Madame
Racine were simple enough. First, working from Paris was out of the
question. He was willing to travel but needed to work from here.
Second, his leadership had to be shared with Julia, which might raise
a few eyebrows among the old-fashioned inner circle, but they had

to understand Julia could never be anything less than full and equal partner in his every endeavor.

Julia. . . .

He glanced at her quickly then lowered his eyes, reverence stealing through him. His heart ached with love and devotion.

He could barely look at her—his shining priestess—his own beloved Giardani Heiress. His heart was wide open at last, any lingering self-restraint blasted to oblivion. His chakra had expanded, enlivened, and he felt uplifted to the point of near drunkenness.

Suddenly, it was his turn to ascend the platform. Dropping to his knees on the cushion at Julia's feet, he heard the age-old question, as he'd heard it asked of those who went before him.

"Whom do you serve?" Signora Isabella's hoarse voice rasped through every fiber of his being.

Madame Racine hadn't coached him as thoroughly as he'd believed. He didn't know how to proceed. When asked the same question, the *streghe* had answered, "Diana," the Christians, "Lord, Jesus Christ," but in truth, Anatolin served neither of those, in particular.

Whom did he serve? Divine Mother—the Great Goddess—Julia's Divine Lover, Turan? All of them, surely, but he felt there was some very specific answer he needed to articulate. He groped for it but his mind had gone practically blank. The only thing that came to him was that he, like Madame Racine, would soon serve as a messenger for the Alliance. He knew only one messenger god.

"Hermes," Anatolin said firmly. "Hermes, by the Grace of Turan."

Signora Isabella stepped quickly toward him. She threw back her head, the hood of her cloak falling away.

She looked more commanding than ever before. "Again, we must ask you, whom do you serve?"

He raised his voice. "*Hermes*, by the Grace of Turan!"

Signora Isabella trilled, a sharp discordant note, sending shivers up Anatolin's spine. "He has come!" she announced, pointing to Anatolin. "Turus, Teramo, Mercurius—Hermes—He who is known as the Messenger comes tonight as the Oldest of the Gods. He has risen! He is among us! Rejoice!"

∞

Julia was stunned. Vario jumped onto the platform with a jubilant shout. "The God has risen. He's risen!" The crowd took up Vario's cry which became a chant that echoed again and again through the sanctuary. The music grew louder, and the *streghe* broke into an intense and sensual dance.

Andrei looked startled. He couldn't have guessed Hermes had evolved from the old vegetation God worshipped as Divine Consort from the beginning of the Giardani tradition. He'd had no way of anticipating what his remark might set in motion, no way of knowing that by naming Hermes, he would invoke the Greater Mysteries.

Until this evening, the Greater Mysteries had been hidden from Julia herself. Only as she climbed to the platform and stared up at the cliff had the Kestos shown her they culminated in a reenactment of the most esoteric and revered aspect of the Giuliana legacy, the Sacred Marriage ceremony.

She stood, felt her veil slip off, saw it float to the dais, but she couldn't worry about that now, or about Silvana hurrying off with her basket of Sacred Things. Everyone in the sanctuary surged toward the ceremonial platform, then once again fell absolutely silent.

"Crown the Chosen One!" someone shouted from the middle of the crowd. "Yes, crown Him!" yelled several others, almost in unison.

Celeste bowed to the community, lifted a flower crown matching Julia's from her wicker basket. Solemnly, she put it on Andrei's head to a resounding cheer. From her basket, Lucia pulled a purple satin cape, which she draped around his shoulders and secured with a tie at his neck. Still on his knees, Andrei looked dismayed as Celeste scattered a whole handful of gold dust over his head, as Lucia anointed not only his brow, but actually undid the top three buttons of his shirt to anoint the center of his chest, as well.

Julia's throat went dry. She lifted her chin, felt the grip of the Goddess again across her shoulders and down her limbs. Whether she and Andrei were prepared or not, this May Eve had become one of those rare occasions when the Giardani consort was chosen by the Old Gods themselves. She swallowed hard. The Sacred Marriage was never to be refused, for it initiated a so-called Seven Year, a time of deep renewal for the whole community.

The *streghe* once again took up their chant, then resumed their dance, the rest of the celebrants joining in. The chant was different now and louder than before. It rang through the sanctuary.

∞

No. Danilenko's heart ceased pounding. It barely beat at all.

No, no, no!

How could the old witch call that upstart, Andrei Ivanovich, by the holy names? How could she give him the hallowed title, Oldest of the Gods? That was Danilenko's and his alone!

Unknowingly, he'd fought his way to the front of the dancing crowd and now stood there exposed. He was panting and dripping with sweat. He felt faint. This wasn't really happening. It was a nightmare, the worst of his life. He stared at Julia Giardani, his dream image clearly in mind.

The cliff, the veil—the lovers' dance. He had to believe in that dream.

Another cloaked figure stepped forward and swept back her hood. He gasped as he recognized Racine's ironic smile. His knees grew weak. She would nail him for sure.

He needed to get back to the dark, but he couldn't move.

∞

Madame Racine's gaze was caught on an exceptionally attractive man who reminded her of someone she'd known long ago. If he hadn't stood completely still in the midst of the wild throng, she probably would not have noticed him, and if he hadn't stared at Julia precisely the way he'd always mooned over the Gypsy seer, Magda, Racine still might not have made the connection.

Gregor Danilenko, large as life, decades too young.

He'd apparently used his ill-gotten psi foolishly, but then, what else might one expect? In Racine's considered opinion, the man was bent on self-destruction. It would doubtless catch up with him soon, but what should she do in the meantime?

She, like everyone who had entered the sacred space, had willingly vowed to cast off all hostilities for the duration of the rites. Moreover, to stop this most blessed of sacraments at this juncture could well be calamitous, not only for Julia and her new community, but for the great plan of the Alliance, as well, and if Racine gave the slightest hint of Danilenko's presence, stop it she would.

On the other hand, if Danilenko harmed Julia—*No!* Racine must not even permit such a thought.

She turned her mind inward for guidance. Her intuition said to do nothing, to let Danilenko merely self-destruct. She tuned in with the inner circle for confirmation, received a resounding yes. Her decision made, she averted her gaze, searched for Emilio Greco, the only other person present who might identify the fraudulent young man for who he was.

Greco was obviously so caught up in the happenings on the platform that he hadn't noticed Danilenko. She sighed with relief, then watched from the corner of her eye until Danilenko turned and hastened back out of sight.

In the next instant, she received absolute validation her choice had been the right one. Before her very eyes, the sanctuary again filled with intensified energy. No one else seemed to notice the luminous forms taking shape against the darkness above the cliff, but Racine saw them clearly. Smiling, each and every one, their hands raised in benediction. Her teachers, humanity's mystic guides, among them her own true guru, who long ago told her there were very special times when the heavens rejoiced and, in the astral realms, even the angels danced.

May Eve had once been one of those times. Now it was once again.

∞

Julia watched spellbound as the crowd gathered at one end of the ceremonial platform and stood swaying, their arms stretched upward, their chant intensifying:

> The God is risen. He's risen!
> The Goddess takes him. She takes him.
> The World rejoices. Rejoices.
> And Peace comes over the land.

They repeated the haunting refrain, still swaying, until the final word turned into one long, sustained hum that rose on the air, then trailed off as the dancers slowly parted to make a path between the stage and the steps leading up the steep face of the cliff.

Julia didn't need to touch the Kestos again to understand what the community expected of her, what her Goddess seemed to demand. Her breath felt shallow, her mind giddy and light, but she knew. The little goat stopped prancing. He rubbed close against her knee then urged her toward Andrei, his horns butting, and not so softly, against her thigh.

Vario rushed toward her, a blazing torch in his hand. "The flame,

Giuliana," he piped urgently. "You and Andrei must light the Sacred
Flame."

Andrei still knelt before her, his aura positively radiant. How
much did he perceive of what was happening to him? She wished
she had his talent for reading minds.

"Don't bother reading my mind, my Lady." He took her hand and
placed it where the oil still glistened on his chest. "Read my heart,
instead."

∞

Anatolin held his breath. Julia still hadn't moved, hadn't said a
word. Would she want him, now? Let him love her tonight and
forever? Catcalls and ribald remarks rose up from the crowd. Lusty
cheers. Relentless clapping to the beat of the music.

Anatolin could barely hear Julia's answer over the din, but he
thought she said, "Andrei, darling."

He suddenly felt such joy he could hardly contain it. "I've been
praying all evening for some quiet, appropriately private moment to
tell you how much I love you, how much I want to be with you as
friend and as lover for the rest of our lives, and look how your
Goddess has answered my prayers!"

∞

"As friend *and* as lover?" Julia asked, Andrei's eyes almost hypno-
tizing her, they shone so brightly.

"One and the same!"

Julia studied his handsome face in the coruscating torch light,
watched the life force spinning unhindered about his heart.
She smiled. So certain he seemed, as if he, too, was suddenly
remembering the many times they'd pledged their lives to each other

like this. So wide was his smile, as if he, too, felt the joy of true soul reunion she felt. It wasn't right, him kneeling at her feet. She dropped to the cushion and leaned her forehead against his. In the next instant, she knew he'd learned everything she knew about what was expected of them both. "Are you sure you really want this?"

"More than I've wanted anything in my life. Are you sure?"

"It's been a *very* long wait."

The catcalls started up again. A few people began a rhythmical clapping. From the center of the crowd came a lusty cheer, then another.

"These celebrants seem restless, Julia. We really should get on with things, so they can return to the courtyard and begin their feast."

She laughed softly, loving it when he joined in, when he put his hand gently around her neck and pulled her close. She brushed her fingertips over his lips but made herself wait to kiss him.

Golden laughter coursed through her mind as Andrei stood, took the torch from Vario, and held out his free hand. Standing, she grasped it and glanced up at the grotto, which the Kestos had shown her was long ago known as the Holy of Holies.

Andrei turned toward the steps leading off the platform, then stopped abruptly as Marco and Niccolò came from the rear with a tall arched arbor like the miniature one Julia found among the holy things. They set the arbor behind the three Wise Crones, who now blocked the way down the stairs.

The third Wise Crone stepped forward, the beekeeper from San Galgano, eldest of the nuns who made the flower crowns and garlands for the ritual. Beside her, Lucia drew a long, delicate chain of fresh violets from her basket and draped it between the beekeeper's outstretched palms while Celeste placed a small jeweler's box in Madame Racine's hand and a pair of golden scissors in Signora Isabella's.

Julia smiled up at Andrei, who raised his eyebrows. "These ancient Fates seemed pleased with us, my love," he said, squeezing her hand.

She was so happy, all she could muster was a nod.

The stately beekeeper spoke. "Raise up your joined hands for all to see!"

Andrei and Julia lifted their clasped hands. The beekeeper wrapped the chain of violets round their wrists three times and tied a loose knot. "They are bound," she said, raising her hands high, then bringing them quickly down. "It is done." The cheer of the crowd was deafening.

Madame Racine stepped forward, snapped open the jeweler's box, and slipped a ring onto Julia's finger, then another onto Andrei's. "They are hereby wed to each other, to this place and its people, and to Our Lady Turan," she said, repeating the ritual gesture. "It is done."

Signora Isabella stepped forward and snipped the knot off the chain. "They are one, yet stand each alone, as must we all in the final reckoning," she said, raising then dropping her hands. "It is done."

The Wise Crones stepped aside. Madame Racine faced the crowd as Signora Isabella pushed Julia and Andrei firmly beneath the arbor.

"Turana be praised!" the beekeeper called out in a clear and steady voice. "Our Lady grants us abundant Grace. This night commences a new Seven Year!"

∞

As spellbound as everyone else, Danilenko stood at the edge of the forest while the Giardani Heiress and her chosen consort crossed the meadow. At the foot of the stairs, Andrei Ivanovich knelt and handed the torch to Julia. Then together, the young people slowly ascended the steps carved into the cliff.

It might have been Danilenko climbing to the grotto but for Andrei Ivanovich naming the Secret God before he'd had the chance. The name had come to Danilenko a full three seconds before his rival said it aloud, a whisper at the very back of his mind.

Danilenko now realized the grotto would be inviolate, that the

Goddess would not allow him near the true Giardani heirloom until the Sacred Marriage rite concluded. He gazed upward. The flaming torch threw long shadows on the jagged cliff face, giving the illusion the two climbing there were indeed the Goddess and God they represented in the Mysteries enacted this night.

Danilenko remembered well what it felt like to be up there—to be the Chosen One. The power of it all. The glory. The wonderment of the crowd reaching you on the incensed air. Not to mention the Giardani Heiress, ever virgin in the true sense of the word. There was a time he might have forsaken his craving to possess the Giardani heirloom and all it would bring him to be up there once more, but that time was long ago, when he'd really been young and had far fewer sins to weigh him down.

Watching the thing from below was too painful to bear. He wouldn't stay to see them rekindle the Sacred Flame, to see his dream go up in that glorious blaze. Too much. That would definitely be too much.

The sanctuary was preternaturally still, all eyes turned to the pair ascending the mountain. Danilenko moved toward the bonfire but couldn't bring himself to consign the Holy Belt to the sacrificial fire. Instead he pushed it into the heap of offerings beside Julia's chair. Let her have the worthless thing.

One lone realization kept him from plummeting into utter dejection. Like all holy artifacts, the heirloom Julia Giardani wore would only grow more mighty in the wake of a rite so powerful as a Sacred Marriage. Best to call up what was left of his psychic shield and find some quiet place to pass the night.

He smiled, anticipation buoying his mood. It wouldn't be hard to wait, seize his real prize tomorrow, when the Witches' Brew ebbed and the sacred aerie atop the cliff released the newlyweds.

THIRTY-FIVE

By the time Anatolin and Julia reached the ledge high on the cliff, the torch had almost burned out, and the grotto was deep in shadows. Julia looked radiant, and rather breathless.

"The Altar of the Greater Mysteries," she said. "If only we could see it."

Anatolin reached over with his unbound hand and gently straightened her flower crown. "*Stephánia*," he said. "The Greeks called these *stephánia*."

"Really?" Julia smiled at him with the same indulgent expression she'd worn that first afternoon on their drive through the Cypriot mountains. "So tell me, what was their name for the Sacred Marriage?"

His heart skipped a beat. "*Hieros Gamos*."

"I knew you'd know that!"

"I hope you still think experts are handy to have around."

"Oh, definitely." She gave him another smile. "But my question is, can they figure out how to light Sacred Flames in wholly unfamiliar places and in near total darkness?"

She looked around, obviously searching for some kind of lamp. He caught the glint of oil in a shallow trough carved into the rock.

"Stand back, my love," he said, using the arm wrapped with hers to scoot her away from edge of the cliff. He heard her breath catch at his words, saw her gaze at him raptly, but he had to keep an eye on the torch, which he'd already tipped down close to the oil.

The oil crackled, then lit. Flames rippled over the trough, jumping high into the dark sky, making a wall of fire that encircled the ledge. The huge lamp was a splendid feat of archaic engineering.

A jubilant cheer rose from below. There was no shortage of light on the ledge anymore. Julia virtually beamed at him. "Guess that pretty much answers my question."

He laughed and pulled her to his side, then returned with her to the rim of the ledge, where the trough was shallow and had already burned itself out. Music drifted up from the ceremonial platform. Signora Isabella stood near the dais, calling the ritual to a close as other *streghe* opened the magical circle. The community again started dancing, their chain winding toward the Etruscan staircase, then gliding down it.

Julia's body felt warm against him as he squeezed the hand bound to his, hugged her closer to his side. Her breath tickled his cheek as she raised her face and gave him yet another sweet smile. Suddenly, the sanctuary below seemed light years away, and Julia and he might have stood on some far distant star for all he cared of the world around him.

He bent his head down and kissed her, lost himself in her softness, in the sweet wet depths of her answering kiss.

∞

Andrei's kisses made Julia's knees go weak. Luckily, he'd noticed and tightened his hold. Eventually, though, she had to try standing up on her own, if for no other reason than to check how close to the edge they stood. She pushed gently away from his embrace and gazed down at the fast-emptying meadow. Then turning toward the grotto, she discovered where Silvana had carried the basket of Sacred Things. It sat beside the grotto's steaming pool, its lid serving as a table for a tray on which sat a plate of fresh fruit, a mammoth carafe of iced water, and a pair of heavy crystal goblets. Beside the basket stood a stack of thick bath sheets. Julia's veil had made it up here, as well, probably in the very same basket. It hung suspended like a curtain between the cliff and the Altar of the Greater Mysteries, which tonight was adorned by a large, satin-covered mattress mounded with crimson rose petals at least three inches deep.

Julia walked around the filmy curtain and stared down at the altar. She shuddered. This was her moment of truth, her own private test of her worthiness to serve the Goddess. Upon that Altar, she would sacrifice the reserve that had kept her all but virgin her entire life. There, she would enter the Sacred Marriage and surrender entirely to the spirit of her very own Aphrodite Turan.

Andrei unwrapped the violet chain from their wrists, looped it around his neck, and stepped behind her. He hugged his arms around her and stared at the rose petals as if transfixed. "How is a man to compose his marriage vows in this temple of sensual delights?"

"Marriage vows?" She thrilled at his joyous tone.

"We're only doing this once in this life, Julia. Even if we didn't have official advance notice of the event, we should still try to do it as perfectly as possible. Surely you agree, my love." He turned her around to face him.

Her eyes misted. "Yes, I *surely* do."

My love—he'd said again. She gazed at him. Would she ever get enough of those two words? Probably not, but with luck, she'd have another whole lifetime to find out. The rose petals were so fragrant she could smell them from ten feet away. Andrei sniffed and pulled her toward them, his touch gentle but electrifying, his profile hauntingly beautiful in the flickering candlelight.

He rubbed his cheek against her temple. "There was a factory I used to visit outside Odessa where they made rose oil. After forgetting about the place for twenty years, last week I dreamed I made love to you there, in a vat filled with Damask-scented petals."

"Must have been a sign." She was trying to keep it light, but was starting into an altogether unfamiliar trance-like state.

"A sign, indeed." He tipped her face up and gave her another kiss, one that practically melted her knees. When he pulled away, she almost sank onto the petals. He took her elbow, held her up as he kissed her palm.

"Mmm." Glancing down, she saw her shoe's ribbon had come unwound. She slipped it off her foot and dipped her bare toes into the velvety crimson mound. "You may be composing your vows, but you're doing just the opposite to me. Maybe you better hurry."

"Oh no, my Lady, my love." He hugged her waist and dropped to his knees, his face burrowing into the folds of her gown. "Not in the least do I intend to hurry. Those vows may well take all night to perfect."

∞

Jest though he might, there could be no restraint for Anatolin. All the unrelieved desire he'd felt for Julia surged through him, filling his veins with passion so fierce he feared he might crush her. Slowly, he pulled her to her knees, kissed her lowered eyelids, the pulse point fluttering beneath her jaw. Her heart was open wide. He could feel her love for him, could see the rose-gold force of it swirling around them, penetrating his every cell.

She started to pray as he carefully guided her gown up over her head then watched it drift like a shimmering cloud to the grotto floor. Her Kestos, which somehow he knew would be worn through the night, glittered richly against her fair, fair skin, its disk aglow just beneath her breasts. "Daughter of Love, you are lovely beyond words," he said with a rasp.

"Darling." She touched the center of his chest, shattering and flooding him with the essence of her love. "Dearest heart."

Every nerve in his body strained as he grappled to regain control. He must not frighten her, must let her show him the way to love her. But his hands, his recalcitrant, hungry hands couldn't wait. As if they had minds of their own, they pulled her close and roved over her flesh, feeling the dips and the mounds of her, tracing the path between her breasts that led to the soft, wet place he yearned to know.

Magnetic as never before, she pulled him toward her, almost drowned him in the delicious, spicy sweetness of her kisses. He broke away from her mouth, kissed the hollow of her throat, leaned her back into the petals. He played his lips over her skin, traced the turn of her hip. He anticipated the taste of her inner thigh, could almost feel his tongue gliding over its smoothness. He wanted all of her, needed to touch and savor her.

She shuddered deeply. Releasing a breathless moan that called to him like a siren's song, she enticed him from his course. She tangled her fingers in his hair, gently but firmly urged him back up to meet her lips. With every particle of his consciousness he explored the mysteries of Julia, his arms wrapping her ever closer beneath him.

He had never been loved as Julia was loving him now, her desire crashing through his senses like an ocean tide, his own reaching out, mingling with hers, rising. He longed to stay with her like this forever but felt her cresting, felt tension passing like a single current through her to him.

"Julia. . . ."

∞

Julia drifted in and out of the lightest of slumbers. Earlier, Andrei had insisted on lighting the dozens of votive candles in the niches encircling the pool. He had wanted to love her in full candlelight.

Now he cradled her close. Waking fully, she listened to his

heartbeat, steady once more, like her own. She would never have believed there could be a man like Andrei, a man who could love with wild abandon yet never lose consciousness of her or the love that possessed her. She rubbed her cheek against the dark, damp hairs on his chest, felt tears of gratitude fill her eyes.

What she and Andrei shared was a miracle, and this was only the beginning. Their earlier loving had been for themselves alone, gifts from the Goddess to quench the fires of their physical desire, but the Kestos had shown Julia much more was required of them.

It seemed only minutes had passed yet she already felt Turana's spirit building within her again, felt her ears ringing as staggering power spread from her core. She felt frightened, realized she needn't be, needed only to go within, let her wiser, priestess self take charge. She cupped her hand around the disk of the Kestos, started silently chanting with her breath, moving toward the dual consciousness she'd come so recently to know.

Andrei stirred. Smiling, Julia watched him awaken, his eyes glittering indigo dark in the candlelight, his lopsided smile wonderful as always. He cleared his throat. "Julia—"

"Hush, Darling." She raised her finger to his lips, stared into the depths of his eyes. "Go within." She turned her body to face his more fully, slipped her arms around his muscled hips, her fingers finding the base of his spine then moving in strange symbols that slowly crept upward in an intricate pattern known only to her soul.

Her own spine vibrated down low with power that inched higher and higher, sending shock waves of joy through her. Her gaze never leaving Andrei's, she opened her whole self to him, pressed the Kestos firmly against his heart and watched his energy quicken, then glow. She knew they would never be the same again, were entering a strange, voluntary death to be born anew, stripped to their fundamental natures, soul flames burning on the Altar of Divine Love.

This was the very essence of true Sacred Marriage, she realized through her daze, a rebirth through Love Herself, Who alone had the power to change fates and grant new life. Her Grace would bring their salvation, their ecstasy and, Goddess willing, their return.

Julia's fingers had made their way up to Andrei's neck. Internalized deeply, he lay perfectly still, his pulse throbbing within her. She covered his cheeks with her palms, her thumbs framed the center of his brow. "Beloved friend," she whispered. "Blessed lover. Husband."

"I am yours forever and forever," he answered, bending his head closer to hers.

Softly, she kissed his spiritual eye. Her breath seemed to cease. Time itself seemed to cease. Bringing Andrei with her, she slipped deeper within than she'd ever been before.

High on the cliff, she and Andrei now danced, a symphony playing through them. Flutes trilled and cymbals crashed, sending them soaring. Drums rolled, reverberating through their joined auras. The music came from them, from their chakras, was their symphony, the song of their undying love. Ascending on the song, their rhythms were one, their unison complete.

Behind them, a vast expanse of vibrant, iridescent color, a curtain of luminous sound, heightened their rapture. Their colors and sounds, their movements, thoughts, and feelings all were a melody playing over and against the curtain's eternal harmony. The curtain was a veil, in truth, one they must reach and rend to know true Oneness.

The veil strained like a great organ reaching crescendo. The sound was deafening, the light blinding, the music pulsing and urgent. It surrounded them, pressed against them everywhere. No boundaries anywhere.

Entwined, they began to spin, creating a spiraling, incandescent, thundering vortex that filled the cliff, surged upward, outward, engulfing their smaller selves in the tide of Grace that passed through them and beyond them, cascading blessings over the world.

A colossal roar ripped through the veil, dissolving and spreading them into the Infinite. They expanded into Love,

Love expanded into them, then the heavens flashed again, and they became three. No time touched them now, no sorrows toned their song. No desires but for endless Bliss.

∞

Anatolin did not want the night to end. He wanted to remain just as they were forever. He hadn't slept, would not sleep, though May Day was almost upon them. Julia's head lay on his shoulder. Her body snuggled against his side and her knee bent across him, her burnished triangle softly pricking his thigh. The golden disk of the Sacred Kestos caught glimmers from the candles still shimmering in the niches. With Julia's soft silk veil for their blanket, they looked almost identical to the pair entombed far below.

Reluctant to move for fear of disturbing Julia's shallow but peaceful doze, Anatolin gazed up at the stars, which he'd loved to observe in Siberia during his exile. How different his life was today from the one he'd lived then, and from the one he'd envisioned himself living before meeting Julia. Knowing her seemed to have transformed everything in his universe but the stars.

The Altar of the Greater Mysteries provided an excellent view of a wide slice of sky. Earlier, he'd watched the Big Dipper sink beyond the dark cliffs to his left. Now Scorpius was near the horizon to his right, and the Summer Triangle, marked by Vega, Altair, and Deneb, sailed high across the indigo vault while Jupiter rose above his head. Not far from Jupiter hung the waning crescent of the moon, whose glare dimmed the stars of the Milky Way.

Anatolin squinted, turning his attention to the corona above the peaks of the cliff. It was less pronounced than it had been only an hour before. The Witches' Brew was starting to withdraw. All too soon, it would abate, ending Julia's temporary respite within the mountain's protective shield, a thought so unnerving he wished he could deny its reality, shut it out entirely.

Up on the cliff face, another votive candle sputtered out, casting the niche in which it sat into darkness. Before she drifted off, Julia gave Anatolin permission to add a prayer niche of their own to those long ago carved in the grotto's wall.

He needed several, there were so many prayers in his heart, but the Giardani Heiress, wielding the weight of her authority, had denied him all but one. He'd have to focus that single prayer very carefully. He would pray, of course, for Julia's continued safety and for the safety of the child conceived at the peak of their union in the Sacred Marriage.

Julia and her unborn daughter, the next Giardani Heiress. Their safety was all that mattered to him now. He glanced down at the tender skin of Julia's shoulder, saw her sigh, as if some dream weighed heavily on her slumber. He gazed at her for the longest time, needing to burn her image not just into his mind but into his soul as well.

Her eyes, when she opened them, were smiling as always. Sleep had added a dusky luster to their golden hues. She reached up and uncurled her hand near his cheek, let fall the crushed petals she'd held as she dozed off. They were warm and moist, their scent enhanced by the heat of her palm.

Happier than he'd ever dreamed he could be, he turned his head and stole a scented kiss from that palm, then pulled her gently onto him again. They merged as naturally and completely as if they'd been born one instead of two.

THIRTY-SIX

ulia folded her veil and put it on top of her gown and Andrei's satin cape, already inside the basket of the Sacred Things. Their flower crowns she placed on their wedding pillows, the chain of violets joining them with a bow. She was too dreamy, too dazzled by the night's events to do anything more right now. The crowns, the tray, the votives, the small vial of rose water they'd added now and then to the pool—everything brought for the Greater Mysteries could stay as it was in the grotto until later today or maybe even tomorrow.

Andrei still lazed in the pool, star-gazing through half-open eyes. Taking advantage of his distraction, she quickly dropped the bath sheet she'd wrapped herself in and pulled on the white leggings obviously packed in the bottom of the basket for her to wear away from the grotto. Her matching cotton-jersey tunic smelled of the crushed rose petals on which she'd laid it earlier.

"So modest you are," Andrei said, his voice husky and dear. His eyes again wore that glazed, wet lover's look.

She averted her gaze. "Not modest, Darling, practical." The Kestos jingled cool against her bare belly as she raised her arms and slipped the tunic over her head. "If we dally getting dressed, we could easily wind up back in those rose petals, and it's time to head down to the house."

"You're absolutely right." He smiled a bit sadly and sighed. "The others will be worried if we take much longer. In fact, I'll be surprised if we make it halfway down without encountering Rafael and Vittorio, probably half the *streghe* in Tuscany."

"Why the *streghe*, for heaven's sake?"

"I'm only joking about that, but I did ask the guards to stay at their posts until you were safely back to the cottage." He pulled himself to his feet and took the bath sheet she offered him. "They're so conscientious they may well have taken me literally and stayed where they were all night."

She bit her lip. "I just hope no one else gets hurt before this is all over." Giacomo's injuries had looked pretty nasty by late morning the day before. He was fortunate to have survived Danilenko's attack.

Andrei pulled on his shirt and slacks, came and draped his arms over her shoulders. "Julia, don't think for an instant you're responsible for Danilenko's sins."

"I dreamed about him in the night. Danilenko, I mean, only I think his name was different."

"What did you dream?"

"That the Goddess Herself wanted him helped, that it was my destiny to do it when the time came, corny as that sounds, part of some special work I was sent back to do." She saw dread flicker across Andrei's face but needed to ignore his inevitable worry just now. She pushed her hands through her hair. "Weird dream."

Stepping back, she bent down and tied the ribbons of her slippers, watched Andrei step into his loafers. She smiled and glanced lovingly around the grotto. So pretty it was, and now so full of memories, both personal and sacred.

Andrei obviously felt the same way. He pulled her into a tight embrace and rubbed his cheek against her hair. "We'll have to spend nights up here, sometimes, to renew our vows."

"You and those vows." He'd said them every way a man could, all night long. Sighing, she gazed up at the stars for a moment. Remembering the lightning flash across Mother's face and the precious little soul it brought them, she gave her belly a tender rub, then pulled away and started toward the stairs. She was brimming over with love, made it only a few feet before she had to turn back and smile. "You will be the world's best father."

Andrei gave her a tender look. "And you its most beautiful mother, my Lady."

"Thank you." Feeling driven to keep moving, she held out her hand.

He reached for it. "I'm suddenly pining for one of your cappuccinos."

"I'll teach you to make them."

"I look forward to that."

They fell silent as they descended the steep cliff and continued to the Etruscan staircase, where Andrei stopped and kissed her again, sending her heart soaring. He kept his arm about her when they started walking again.

She leaned into the shelter of him and listened as her feathered neighbors began to awaken and, one by one, to sing. At the foot of the staircase, she and Andrei stepped into the meadow.

Dawn was not far off. Soon it would lift the darkness and the dewy mist off the sheltered glade.

Julia saw something move near the crypt and came to a stop. "There's someone there," she whispered, her throat cramping closed.

Andrei's grip on her shoulders tightened. The man in the meadow turned toward them. A menacing smirk twisted his face.

"Well, well, the newlyweds, at last," he said, his voice a deep bass rumble, his Eastern European accent barely noticeable. "Andrei Ivanovich," he added with a bow. "How did you find your bridal night?"

"Danilenko!"

Andrei's exclamation shook Julia all the way to her toes.

The muscles in Andrei's neck strained in obvious anger. "I should have recognized him last night," he muttered to Julia.

Danilenko laughed, a harsh strangled sound in the peaceful

meadow. Chills raced up Julia's spine. The hairs on her neck stood on end. At the edge of her vision, she caught sight of Madame Racine arriving with Rafael and Brother Vittorio, saw others stepping forward from the fringes of the forest. She felt more than saw people's consternation.

Looking up at Andrei, she caught his gaze and held it. Though last night's ritual had been important for her legacy's survival, somehow what happened here and now seemed equally so. She stared at Andrei, hoped she could convey just how important.

"Darling, it's time to stop protecting me." She needed his cooperation. "I can't do what I must without your complete support!"

Andrei clamped his jaw tightly, closed his eyes, clearly reining in his anxiety, aligning his will with hers. "Anything, Julia. I'll do anything. I'll be right behind you."

She stepped from under his arm and walked determinedly toward Gregor Danilenko. She wasn't sure what to do next, but she knew only she could oppose his evil and live.

The man had to be stopped. There could be no further destruction at his hands. She couldn't allow it. No *Wanassa* had ever allowed the destruction she inadvertently had.

Long ago.

It all happened long ago, yet Lady's memories were suddenly opened in Julia's mind, fresh as if they had happened only yesterday. She'd been too soft with this one before, had forgotten the Mother's sterner face, spurned the harsh retribution duly apportioned to those who transgressed the Divine Lover's laws.

∞

The Heiress riveted Danilenko with her determined gaze. Foreboding gripped his heart. He hated and feared and adored her, all at once. He should bow in respect, prostrate himself at her feet, though his pride said to spit in her face.

He hardly noticed her consort coming up behind her, bracing her from behind. All he could feel was her masterful psi—sorting him, shifting his memories, his very identity.

"*You* brought me here," he said. "Opened wide every door."

"I did." She flinched, as if only now realizing it.

"To punish me. Torture me. Drive me insane." He hardened his will. "Your time is past and gone, Lady. It's over!"

"Wrong!" Her smile was kind as only a victor's could be. Merciful. Her voice was clear. There was no anger in it, only resolution. "My time has come again, Danaus."

He covered his ears. "Don't call me that!"

Danaus. The murderer. The one judged by the Gods and found guilty, warrior king or no. He had wanted her for his queen. He hadn't raped and killed her, his soldiers had, the incompetent imbeciles! He revolted from the injustice of it all, felt PK ripple up his spine. He loosed it, watched it hit her in sharp, hard bursts.

She merely winced as it doused her etheric web gray. "Oh! You don't like the name Danaus? Okay. Dani, then." Her eyes glowed like liquid amber. "But Dani is a murderer, as well, is he not?"

She impressed images on his mind he'd fought years to forget. The cold winter of '43. His vengeful interrogation, then Hitler's elite seeking him out in Paris, offering the Moon for his help. Too hard to resist.

He laughed. "That Resistance cell was a nest of slugs. The cowards I gave the SS weren't worth the time of day, let alone the directions to Hitler's occult library."

She raised her chin. "Some men reject the path of violence. That does not make them cowards. What about the others, Dani? There were countless others."

She didn't mention her father, though Danilenko was sure she held him responsible. Nor did she say it aloud again—murderer—

but she forced the brand upon him, nonetheless. She passed many lifetimes quickly before his inner vision. He'd murdered in most.

Murder, thievery, treachery—these had long been his stock in trade. "So what!"

"You were a good man once, Dani. The best."

Smiling sadly, she forced another impression upon him. He fought her, turned his mind from it, blasted her again. Metallic fumes licked at his nostrils.

"See it," she ordered shakily, sorting him again against his will, her hands clasped over her navel. "See your true being, your essential goodness!"

∞

Rank PK radiated through the meadow in dark, heavy waves. Racine felt utterly sick, nauseous, and Danilenko had barely begun. She could imagine what it had to be doing to Julia, only an arm's length from the monster. Still, it was hard to stay back. Others had come forward, Julia's *streghe* friends, a few from the village, Silvana, clearly terrified for Julia. Rafael was trying his Interpol best to get people to stay back, but without much success.

Julia's gaze never wavered from Danilenko's face. She leaned toward him. "Long before Danaus lived, you were the Chosen One. The clan adored you. Emulated you. Learned from you. You were their Master of Arts. Their Wise Friend. Their Healer. They depended on you, remember?"

Racine drew in a sharp breath, wished with all her heart Julia had not started to reveal to him this particular life. Danilenko glanced sideways at Racine, obviously recognizing who she'd then been—his *Wanassa*, his Goddess-appointed mate. The damage was done. The karma was ripe, raw, out in the open. So be it. Racine prayed to be shown the right next step.

Danilenko's glance turned venomous. Racine chilled to the bone as he cast his gaze down again, his shoulders sagging. It might have been sorrow he felt, but Racine knew it was rage. When he raised his head, his aura was garish, dark red. He pointed to Racine, snarled at Julia. "She betrayed me!"

Julia shook her head. "I see it all, now. You betrayed yourself, broke your pledge to live always in love and beauty. It was you who left with the warriors when they came to Sacred Mountain—you who sailed north with them to Troy, leaving your people to fend for themselves. That long, bloody siege let the warrior lust loose in you, and that lust spawned every other, set the whole tragic pattern in motion."

Racine felt Julia's compassion, was certain Danilenko was too far gone to feel anything but his own mounting fury. Racine and her companions had unwittingly inched forward, some of the *streghe* just behind them. She felt disgusted by her lack of perception. Julia was the ingenue in all this, Racine supposedly the adept. She needed to see the pattern, find the path to karmic freedom, for herself as well as for Julia.

Racine's heart was practically breaking. Andrei stepped even closer to Julia, tightened his grip on her shoulder. Julia seemed not to notice, so absorbed was she in the sacred drama playing out through her small body. If Andrei could do no more than buffer Julia by grounding the negative psi as it hit her, even that could perhaps save her life.

THIRTY-SEVEN

"Enough past lives, witch!"

Anatolin inwardly cringed from Danilenko's malice but held himself rock solid as more tainted psi rattled Julia like a discordant note through a fine violin then shattered down Anatolin's arm.

Though their faces were ashen, some streaked with sweat or tears, no one in the meadow moved back for safety, as Anatolin might have expected. They'd moved closer, formed a loose circle, Julia's magnetism even now drawing everyone together. He visualized himself absorbing and neutralizing Danilenko's poison, knew that was the best he could do, the best any of them could do, knew also Julia had not felt the worst of it yet.

Danilenko belched another filthy burst of PK.

Reeling from the blow, Julia coughed hoarsely. "Deal with this, Danilenko! Get the lesson!"

"Not a chance!"

"But you do have a chance. That's the Lady's message. Your fate is not sealed. Why do you think we're here today?"

"Huh!" Danilenko snorted. "I'm here for one reason—*only* one."

"Oh, yes," she said, as if remembering some interesting piece of trivia. "Immortality, right?"

Danilenko looked aghast. "The dream—that was your lure!" He stuttered, his spit flying into Julia's face, onto Anatolin's hand. "The dream was your bait for my entrapment!"

For the first time, Julia pulled back, but she didn't cower. "Not *entrapment*, for heaven's sake." She shook her head. "The truth is, I was sent here for you as a special act of mercy. She Who sent me expects me to bring you home, and bring you home I will."

"Home?" Danilenko choked.

Julia kept her gaze steadily on his face, kept her heart chakra open, her focus apparently honed to Danilenko's soul patterns.

"Home?" Danilenko repeated hysterically. "I can *never* go home."

"It's true you've done your very worst, Dani. Misused your intellect, twisted it to justify your sins. Misused your talents to harm and kill others. Abused every sense—let yourself be driven by greed, gluttony, debauchery. I'd rather not name the rest." She sighed. "Turan wants you back anyway."

Anatolin realigned his grip on Julia's shoulder and braced her body with his own. He couldn't see her expressions, but he followed her emotions, precisely. She was afraid, determined. Steadfast in her intent. He checked on the others in the circle. Some sent Julia energy through their upraised hands, others prayed, her high purpose now their own.

Danilenko noticed nothing but Julia. He towered over her, grinned. "I'm damned, pretty girl, and I'll laugh all the way to hell!"

"What a waste." Julia hesitated, obviously wearing down. "That's the pattern, though, the false pride, the intellectual superiority, the arrogance. Holds you back, every time."

Danilenko's eyes blinked fiercely. "Shut up. Just shut up!"

"You are the Lady's own, Dani." She pushed her hair back from her face. The sight of her trembling hands tore at Anatolin's heart. "Renounce your greed, your lust."

"Shut up!" Danilenko howled, PK lashing out in all directions. The air danced with it, casting macabre shadows over the glen, momentarily distorting the faces it passed over.

Not Julia's. Love shone from hers. "Go home to Her, Dani," she exhorted. "Let me help you!"

Danilenko's hands clenched and unclenched at his sides. "Don't speak any more of Her." He cracked his jaw with several loud pops. "And you can't help me—no one can help me. No one!"

Anatolin flinched as Danilenko's despair, a dark vile grief, gushed from his solar plexus. Devastating, but Julia not only held onto her wits, she stayed wholly poised, her empathic pain so intense Anatolin could feel it sapping the last of her strength, blowing huge gaping holes in her aura.

"Dani, Dani!" She shook her head, reaching out to him, trying to penetrate even more profound levels of his polluted mind. "Your spiritual suffering is palpable, your burden of grief and guilt and shame unendurable." She paused for air then psychically pushed him further, probing festered ancient wounds. "You're so strong— the weight of your karma would have broken a lesser soul lifetimes ago. End it now. Cast it off and return to our Mother Divine."

"I can't." Despair rolled off him in waves. "Don't you see I can't? Doesn't *She* see?" He upped his PK, let it rip, knocking Julia to one side. She righted herself, but Danilenko let go another toxic blast.

Anatolin couldn't fathom how she held on. He struggled to deflect the sickening PK. Everyone in the meadow finally fell a step back. Sending Julia everything he had, Anatolin focused, visualized a steady stream of calm psi, energizing her, feeding her depleted system. With relief, he felt her grab the energy like a lifeline as Danilenko's negativity lashed out again and fouled the whole meadow. The newly mowed grass singed brown. The leaves on the nearest trees curled. Anatolin's fear turned his mouth rank.

Somehow, Julia held her own, but Danilenko was building to kill her, and no one could stop him. If only Julia would use her own PK, but she never would in her own defense. If only Anatolin could push her aside, throw himself at Danilenko, inflict what harm he might— anything to bring this to an end.

But he loved her, had to do as he'd agreed. What's more, if he let go, ceased acting as her ground, she wouldn't last another five seconds. He had to keep hold of himself, for her life's sake.

∞

Danilenko laughed at the girl's obvious weakening. "Now," he said with relish, grunting as he lifted his arms. "Now for immortality."

"You won't have it," she whispered, so softly he could hardly hear her.

"You lie!" He bellowed. "I helped make the damned Kestos. I should know what it can give me."

"Now that was an exemplary life. One of beauty, of grace and joy. The kind you could hope to live again, strive toward! Many here today were with you then—your witnesses, Dani, your family."

The images she thrust at him all but broke his will. His memories of that life on Sacred Mountain left him stunned. *Hope.* The word almost crippled him.

The little fool gazed at him. Though her eyes were losing their luster, she'd called up another bright smile. "You're right, you know— the Sacred Kestos *can* grant eternal life."

"Of course it can."

"But it won't for you, now—not on your evil course."

"Bull!" he spat. She was playing with him.

"No. I tell you, The Lady won't permit it." The girl rallied, brought her palms up in front of her chest. Her PK pushed him backward, a strong warning nudge. "Hear me," she implored. "You will never be allowed to steal that which *must* be earned."

Earned? An insipid joke. *Earned.*

"I will have it now!"

His PK gone wild, he brought his hands down on the front of her shirt, ripped it down the middle, baring her breasts. He gasped.

The Kestos glistened against her pale skin. He saw nothing else.

He grasped it, felt pain, searing heat. He couldn't move. The Kestos burned him, but he couldn't release his grip on it. He shook the girl furiously, tried to break away, but the Kestos wouldn't let him go!

Almost smugly, she kept smiling, though feebly. "Give up your lust quickly, or we'll both die. Open your heart, Dani, forgive yourself, choose life."

"Shut up, witch. Shut up and burn!"

His PK blasted Andrei Ivanovich away and smashed him to the ground. It welded Danilenko's hands to the blistering gold chain. He was on fire.

∞

Racine gasped. Danilenko became engulfed in astral flames, and Julia's etheric body had ignited the instant Andrei lost his grip.

Racine clutched Rafael's arm, felt Brother Vittorio brace her by her other elbow. Her breathing was labored. She could hardly keep standing. She remembered now. Long, long ago. Danaus trying to seize power in the clan, trying to impose the male supremacy he'd admired among the Greeks, trying to incite the clan to burn her at the stake for taking a second, more faithful consort during his decades-long absence.

Ever since, she'd sworn no Giardani would ever be burned at the stake, yet it was happening right before her eyes. Nothing anyone could do. Not Andrei—struggling to keep conscious, struggling to his feet against Danilenko's monstrous PK, trying desperately to push through the astral fire to ground Julia again while she still lived.

Racine had never forgiven Danaus. Now Julia would pay the price. But this was not Julia's karma, it was Racine's—perhaps her last—the very piece that kept her from final soul freedom.

Horrified, she stared at Julia's aura. A flaming pillar of blue-white astral fire flickered close, licking not at Julia's fair skin but at the intricate web that sustained and distributed her life force.

∞

"Dani . . ." Julia struggled against exhaustion, fought the despair coming off Danilenko in waves. *Mother!* she cried inwardly. *Don't forsake me, help me, please.* "Cast off your shame, Dani, your guilt. There is nothing left but Turana's Grace. Open your heart and receive it."

"Too late . . ." he half moaned.

"Not too late." Her voice faltered as she caught her reflection in his eyes—ghostly pale, frail and ready to break. She pushed past her fear, needed to touch his heart, but he wouldn't let her. "Till the last sentient moment of life, it is *never* too late. Choose redemption while you can!"

"Go for it, Dani Boy!" Rafael called out. Brother Vittorio said rapid Hail Marys, almost shouted them. Across from Julia, the men's faces streamed with tears. Silvana's, too. Danilenko's was ravaged by pain.

"The Lady smiles at you, Dani, wants to heal you. She loves you so."

Julia felt Mother respond to her prayer, felt a rush of cool Grace pour into her being. Madame Racine, herself once an Heiress, was entitled to help Julia channel it, needed only to acknowledge her debt and release it, end her life though it doubtless would.

Madame seemed resolved, quickly stepped behind Danilenko. Her forgiveness was key to his redemption. Even he seemed to grasp that. Madame caught Julia's gaze, raised her hand to Danilenko's back, covered his heart chakra with her palm.

∞

Danilenko began to retch, then openly to sob. Dawn broke through the mist. With it, a force like a thunderbolt struck inside his head. Lightning flashed, poured blinding light into the meadow.

For an instant, he saw Her face.

The Lady. Beautiful. Compassionate.

His Mother.

∞

Anatolin was back on his feet. None too soon. Julia's etheric body burned fiercely, now, her legs were giving way. Her will alone held her up. He started toward her, heard Vittorio gasp as clear blue-white fire flashed high over Julia's head, then Danilenko's and Madame Racine's.

Madame folded, dying, to the ground, but Julia kept reaching out to Danilenko's soul. "Dani! Say it with me. I choose forgiveness. I choose love."

"I—" Danilenko went lax. "Choose—" His hair turned white, his body obese. "Forgiveness . . ." Finishing in a hoarse whisper, his hands trailing down Julia's sides, he sank backward, half covering Madame's body.

"There, now," Julia consoled Danilenko, her hands reaching down to smooth his hair. She raised her gaze to her spiritual eye, as if entering a deep yogic trance. "It is done."

Almost blinded by tears, Anatolin bolted as her frail body crumpled over the corpses like a rag doll. Rafael got to her before him, searched for Julia's pulse, gave a shake of his head. "Sorry, old buddy," he said. "They're all gone, Julia included."

"Don't even think that, Rafe," Anatolin muttered hoarsely.

He scooped up Julia, clutched her close to his chest, and started headlong toward the cottage, no time to grieve for the loss of their dear Parisienne. The others would have to mop up in the meadow while he took Julia home.

He couldn't look at Julia, now. Any other sight was preferable to the deathly pall on her lovely skin—the satin ribbon of her ballet slipper, for instance, fluttering on the air all the way down the hill.

∞

After the burning, first thing, Julia felt the prayers.

There were prayers all around her, caressing and cushioning her, like bubbles in a foamy bath. Julia blew at them and they scattered, bouncing off and then coming right back, like magnets were in them.

Not Andrei's. His was pink. Stayed close. Was tied to her finger with a thin gold thread. It said *Ever near.* Dearheart. O, deardeardear!

She was weightless, nothing pressed on her anywhere. And she floated. Freely, but for a silky cord attached somewhere, too much work to figure out how.

The prayers were lovely. She delighted in them. Delighted in everything.

The prayers were good for her. Made her feel good. She loved them. Some came from her father's friends. Nice.

Her father.

She saw him. Yes, that was him, down to her left, near the tunnel. She thought herself there. "Can you tell me what's happening here, Dad? Have I really died?"

Her father grinned. "Look who's waiting for you!" He pointed straight ahead, where the light was brightest, and Julia couldn't see a thing. "Catch ya later, Lady Bug," he said, then he disappeared.

The Lady stepped forward, led Julia toward the light. The air was silky soft as always.

Not for long.

The light turned hard. The tunnel sped up. It pulled her

through it, really fast. Got screechy. Julia felt stretched, here then there. All funny and discombobulated.

Then the tunnel straightened out again. *Whew!* Good that was quick.

The Lady held Julia's hand now.

"Am I dead?" Julia asked.

"Shush." *Not important,* the Lady seemed to say.

Julia was fine with that. "Where are we heading?"

"Shush. Just rest for a bit."

"Okay."

She really was kind of tired. That Dani. Wore her out. The burning. But wasn't that ages ago?

The tunnel made a turn before they came to the big light. They went into their cave and sat down. Julia tried to meditate, but Andrei kept tugging at the pink prayer.

More tugging.

She looked at the Lady. "What's he doing, back there? More prayers?"

"It's the sacred word AUM. He's saying it in your ear."

"Why?" The AUM interrupted the astral, made Julia feel kind of hungry.

"He's calling you home, Honey," the Lady said. "He loves you and wants you back."

Julia sighed, couldn't talk anymore. She was all tuckered out, and the physical seemed so far away.

"Soon you'll go back, you know," the Lady said.

"Really?"

The Lady took her hand. "Your work there is not done."

"But I helped Dani, brought him home to Mother, didn't I? Aren't you pleased with me? Isn't She pleased?"

"O, yes." The Lady smiled. "Dani's resting, healing. But he was not the last work you were to do. And your Andrei's prayers are strong. Our Mother has heard them. Think about being a mother, yourself," she added, then disappeared.

Your Andrei. Julia loved the sound of that. . . .

Time had passed, how much, Julia didn't know, but she felt much better. More like herself. More like the mother she soon would be—O joy!

Sweet Giuliana Joy, her daughter-to-come, had decided it was time for them to head back. The question was when Julia would be strong enough. She felt pretty strong, now. Bending her arm up then flexing it like a body builder, she checked it out. No etheric she could see, but would one be visible here anyway?

She stood up and wished herself home. Then the big light was behind her like a hose on full blast. It drummed her forward, through the tunnel, stopped blasting and got real warm and all yellow, like sunshine.

Her father was nowhere in sight. Nobody was here to meet her, but prayers were everywhere, had faces, some she knew and loved. She could hear them.

Bring Julia back, Divine Mother. Lucia's.

Dear Brother Vittorio's. *Mother of God, send our sister home safely.*

Signora Isabella's. *Lady Turan, let Giuliana return to us soon.*

The closer she got, the warmer Julia became. She felt heavier, her thoughts did, too. In fact, thinking herself there didn't work so well here. She had to struggle a bit, but just when she was getting worried, someone reached for her and pulled her on.

Julia focused. Bright scents. Hard air. She'd never heard of such things. She was definitely confused, didn't have a clue how long she'd been healing in the deep.

She was sure glad she'd started back when she had. The Gardens needed her. Her unborn child needed her. Her friends did, too, and she needed them. They were all part of Mother's grand plan.

There was a breeze on the south loggia today, all scented with cit-rus and herbs, just the hint of spicy Damasks in bloom. It was still springtime—she hadn't missed it. She smiled, glanced down toward her lap where Andrei's hand held hers.

Andrei!

He was reading to her from his beautiful Bhagavad Gita. His palm felt callused and rough but his voice was smooth. When he finally looked her way, his dear eyes were kind, as always, and sad—until he realized she was back.

"Julia, my love."

THE GIARDANI

2000 A.D.	Julia returns to Montecipriana
	Reestablishes the Mysteries
1925 A.D.	Anna leaves for America
1498 A.D.	Giuliana instructs Ficino
1345 A.D.	Giuliana battles evil *streghe*
1200 A.D.	Racena travels to Ile de la Cité
	Begins *Giardani Herbal*
900 A.D.	Ana marries Donato
	Donato creates Holy Belt
41 A.D.	Giuliana defies Caesar
390 B.C.E.	Lady restores Sacred Mountain lineage
465 B.C.E.	Dardano attacks Sacred Mountain
	Soldiers rape and kill Lady
650 B.C.E.	Rasenna founds Mysteries academy
950 B.C.E.	Lady founds new Sacred Mountain
	sanctuary in Etruria
1050 B.C.E.	Sea Peoples wreak havoc in Krete
	Ana and Danos lead clan west
1100 B.C.E.	Regional violence threatens Sacred Mountain
	Uli-Ana leads small migration to Lesbos
	Lady tries to establish colony at Knidos
1200 B.C.E.	Danaus, back from Troy, leads small migration
	to Korinthos
1400 B.C.E.	Uli-Ana founds Paphian sanctuary
1600 B.C.E.	Ana founds artisans colony on Kythera
1900 B.C.E.	Lady leads migration across Aegean
	Founds Sacred Mountain on Krete
	Clan Mothers and Fathers create Kestos
2000 B.C.E.	Lady killed resisting invaders
	Uli-Ana resettles clan in Karia
2200 B.C.E.	Ana resists invaders, then marries Daedans
	Clan resettles in Lydia
2800 B.C.E.	Invaders burn home in Ana-dolu, Land of the Mother
	Clan moves near Mt. Ida for ore and obsidian

Lady=Giuliana=Julia   Ana=Anna
Uli-Ana=Rasenna=Racena=Racine

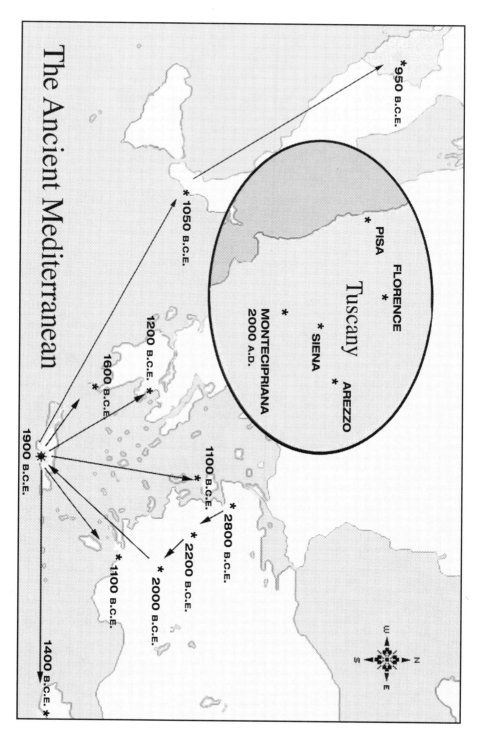

The Ancient Mediterranean

*950 B.C.E.

*1050 B.C.E.

1200 B.C.E.

1600 B.C.E.
*

*1100 B.C.E.

1900 B.C.E.
*

1400 B.C.E.

1100 B.C.E.
*

*2800 B.C.E.

*2000 B.C.E.

*2200 B.C.E.

PISA
*

FLORENCE
*

Tuscany

MONTECIPRIANA
2000 A.D.
*

*SIENA

AREZZO
*

455

AUTHOR'S NOTE

Following his initiation into the ancient Mysteries around 500 B.C.E., the philosopher-sage Empedocles wrote that in the Golden Age of the prepatriarchal era, Aphrodite reigned supreme and symbolized the Love binding and motivating the Universe—the Joy at the heart of Nature. About the same time, an advanced civilization we call the Etruscans flourished in the area of Italy known today as Tuscany. Scholars have not yet learned where the Etruscans originated or how they came to settle in Italy.

The Etruscans said they came from Asia Minor, and certain eastern characteristics in their art and religion seem to support their claim. By the third century B.C.E., they had been thoroughly vanquished, but they left behind in the fertile soil of Tuscany a rich layer of cultural heritage steeped in the mystery and beauty of their enigmatic worldview. Known to them as Turan or Turana, Aphrodite held a prominent place in their religion, for the Etruscans were the most devout and ardent of all ancient lovers.

The spiritual tradition of the Giardani is a fictional amalgam of ancient Greek religion, Goddess spirituality and Raja Yoga. Sacred Mountain, the original seat of the Giardani worship, is based on a recently excavated sanctuary in southern Crete where Aphrodite and her consort, Hermes, apparently evolved from the oldest divinities of the Mediterranean basin and were worshipped continuously from deep prehistory until at least 400 A.D.

The Calderola, Montecipriana and the Gardens are entirely

fictitious, inspired by two all-too-brief journeys through Tuscany and years of voracious research. Madame Racine and her Alliance are imagined from the "Perennial Wisdom" of Western occultism, Julia's Tuscan neighbors and *streghe* friends from various sources, particularly the rich lore of Charles Godfrey Leland.

ABOUT THE AUTHOR

Alexis Masters, lifelong mystic, scholar and yoga practitioner, holds a bachelor of arts in transpersonal psychology from Antioch University, where she also pursued graduate work in comparative religion and feminist theology. A great lover of world travel, her research in ancient religion and Goddess spirituality has taken her to the far reaches of the Mediterranean. She lives with her husband in Northern California, where she is hard at work on her next novel, the sequel to *The Giuliana Legacy*, envisioned as the second volume in a trilogy that chronicles the adventures of the Giardani family and the Goddess they serve.

Alexis is also the founder of *VisionaryFiction.com*, an Internet community forum for readers, authors and publishers of the emerging genre of visionary fiction. Created for all who share a passion for literature with spiritual themes and content, *VisionaryFiction.com* is the place to learn more about what is causing all the buzz in the publishing industry, and to help ensure that the new genre becomes the successful, thriving one needed to meet the demands of today's changing book market. The site contains interactive features for announcing new releases in the genre, for discussing genre standards and issues of craft, and for sharing promotional ideas and community contacts. Visit *VisionaryFiction.com* today, cast your votes for your favorite visionary fiction titles and help shape the future of this exciting publishing trend.

ACKNOWLEDGMENTS

I n the ten years since *The Giuliana Legacy* was conceived, friends too numerous to list have read and contributed generously to the manuscript's clarity and depth. From its ardent earliest readers—Deborah Griffin, Judith Foster and Leah Samul—to those more recent—Bryan Ward, Gail Jarocki, Charlene Brendler and Linda Hubbard—I treasure you and extend my heartfelt thanks to all. Ellen Boneparth, Beth Hedva and Mara Keller have read many versions and remained steadfast supporters throughout. For their unconditional friendship I will be eternally grateful.

With any project of this scope and duration, there must be vision holders—those whose love for the project nourishes and shapes it along with the author's. *The Giuliana Legacy* has been blessed to receive the splendid ministrations of wise woman and freelance editor, Lesley Kellas Payne. The creativity of my gifted children, Kristin and Erik Engstrom, inspired the work at every significant turn. The enduring faith of my spiritual sister, Carol Neff, upheld and sustained the vision in utter defiance of all obstacles, as did the countless sublime meditation services with my extended spiritual family at Paramahansa Yogananda's Self-Realization Fellowship Temple, Richmond.

And then there is Christopher. Husband and partner extraordinaire, Chris Gilmore's soulful caring and quiet courage gave me the strength to endure until Divine Mother's boundless Grace could bring us *The Giuliana Legacy's* newest vision holder—the perfect editor for this book, Lisa Drucker.

Lisa's rarefied sensibilities and unceasing enthusiasm have added more than final polish to the manuscript. I thank heaven for her joyous commitment to this work, for my publisher, Peter Vegso, and for the entire team of consummate professionals at Health Communications, Inc., who have brought *The Giuliana Legacy*, at last, to you.